MATCH ME
IF YOU CAN

Also By Heidi Shertok

Unorthodox Love

MATCH ME IF YOU CAN

HEIDI SHERTOK

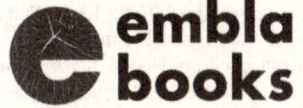

First published in the UK in 2025 by

An imprint of Bonnier Books UK
5th Floor, HYLO, 105 Bunhill Row,
London, EC1Y 8LZ

Copyright © Heidi Shertok, 2025

All rights reserved.
No part of this publication may be reproduced, stored or transmitted in any form or by any means, electronic, mechanical, photocopying or otherwise, without the prior written permission of the publisher.

The right of Heidi Shertok to be identified as Author of this work has been asserted by them in accordance with the Copyright, Designs and
Patents Act, 1988.

This is a work of fiction. Names, places, events and incidents are either the products of the author's imagination or used fictitiously. Any resemblance to actual persons, living or dead, or actual events is purely coincidental.

A CIP catalogue record for this book is available from the British Library.

ISBN: 9781471416323

Also available as an ebook and an audiobook

1

Typeset by IDSUK (Data Connection) Ltd
Printed and bound in Great Britain by Clays Ltd, Elcograf S.p.A.

The authorised representative in the EEA is Bonnier Books UK
(Ireland) Limited.
Registered office address: Floor 3, Block 3, Miesian Plaza,
Dublin 2, D02 Y754, Ireland
compliance@bonnierbooks.ie
www.bonnierbooks.co.uk

For my parents. Thank you for loving me unconditionally–especially during that unfortunate goth stage.

And for the victims of October Seventh. May their memory be for a blessing.

Prologue

I'm halfway through the restaurant when I see him. My brain registers him, bit by bit, like the twisted score of a horror movie slowly rising in volume. Warm brown skin. Sable eyes half-obscured by a baseball cap pulled down low. Fitted tee across a broad chest. Black jeans.

It's been ten years since I last laid eyes on him, but I'd know this man anywhere.

Caleb Kahn.

He's gorgeous. My brain sends out this memo like it's an SOS, some archaic Code Red to alert my baby-making hormones that prime mating material is nearby and to flip my hair and stick my chest out so he notices me among the foliage of the jungle.

Needless to say, I'm horrified.

I've spent the last decade hating this man with a passion, and the idea that any part of me—no matter how small or how fleeting—would find him attractive is deeply unsettling.

I duck behind a pillar and place a hand over my racing heart. It's not that I never expected to see Caleb again. I knew we'd cross paths again eventually, but I naively assumed I would have a little forewarning first. Some time to emotionally prepare myself before coming face to face with my brother's best friend and my honorary childhood babysitter. The one who, despite being only five years older and of no blood relation whatsoever, took it upon himself to help raise me after my father left.

I sneak another peek at Caleb, hoping the first time was a random hallucination, but no such luck. He's still there, sitting at a table for two and drumming his fingers, impatiently waiting for his date to arrive.

My eyes dart around the restaurant, hoping to find another way out without having to walk past him, but it seems my only other option is to try to squeeze through the restroom window.

Calm down, Ashira. So what if he sees you? You have nothing to be ashamed of. After all, Caleb is the one who packed a suitcase and vanished one day out of the blue. Just like my father.

Maybe it would've hurt less if I hadn't loved him so much. Because the truth is that Caleb was the very best part of my childhood. Nearly all my favorite memories involve him. He was the one who taught me outdoorsy things like how to make a campfire and set up a tent, how to attach bait to a fishing pole, and how to jump off a cliff and dive into the shivering cold Hudson River without dying. He showed me how to use a drill, and more importantly, how *not* to. He taught me how to spit like a boss, change a spare tire, and throw a ball.

Basically, he taught me how to be a boy. And I loved every second of it.

I close my eyes and take a deep breath.

My father's abandonment was traumatic, but it was Caleb's disappearance that crushed my soul. Ever since, Caleb has been my daily reminder not to trust people.

"Can I help you?" a waiter asks, gazing down at me curiously. Only then do I realize that I'm hunched low to the ground.

"I'm fine," I say quickly. "Just . . . admiring the view. Nice shoes, by the way."

"Thanks?"

"You're welcome."

Once he leaves, I stand up straight and square my shoulders, determined to march past Caleb like the fearless, capable twenty-three-year-old that I am. Besides, there's a good chance that he won't recognize me anyway. The last time he saw me, I was short with frizzy hair and glasses, and sporting a mouthful of braces—hence his nickname for me, *Tinsel*. I look completely different now.

There's no way he'll realize who I am.

But just as I start walking, a beautiful older woman approaches Caleb's table, her face lighting up when she sees him—and I realize I'm doomed. Utterly, fantastically *doomed*. Because even if Caleb doesn't recognize the adult version of me, his mother certainly will.

Just as I turn on my heel to give that restroom window a try, Dr. Sheva Kahn's gaze meets mine. Her grin widens and she waves me over, and the inevitability of the situation makes me feel slightly ill.

"Ashira!" she calls, in her unique accent that's half Ethiopian, half Israeli. "Come say hi."

And then, in what feels like slow motion, Caleb looks up. His eyes widen and I can practically see the wheels turning in his head as he tries to reckon this random blonde woman with the Ashira he remembers.

Come on, girl. Put one foot in front of the other. You can do this.

And I do, albeit at the speed of someone heading to the guillotine.

Caleb unfolds his legs and stands up. He was always big, but now he seems impossibly tall. At five-foot-eight, I'm not exactly short, but even with my heels on, I find myself looking up at him.

"Ashira?" he says doubtfully. I nod and he adds after a beat, "You look so . . ." He circles his hand in the air as if that one gesture explains everything.

"Yes, I was just thinking that about you," I say, to be on the safe side. Now no matter what he meant by it, we're in the same boat.

"I doubt it," he murmurs under his breath, so quietly that I almost wonder whether I imagined it.

"It's been ages, hasn't it?" I say breezily. As if I haven't thought about him every single day or kept track of the time lost between us. As if I haven't hated and missed him in equal parts.

"Ten years." He dips his head and regards me with serious eyes.

"Gosh, that long?" I put a hand on my hip and shake my head. "We should've caught up sooner."

He gives me a pointed look. "You're not exactly easy to get a hold of."

I suppose he's referring to the fact that I blocked both his phone number and email. Luckily, I've had years to perfect my 'dumb blonde' act and I widen my eyes just enough to seem sincerely puzzled. "Maybe you're doing it wrong?"

"Dialing?"

Amusement dances in his eyes, along with something new, something I've never seen before that causes my pulse to quicken.

"What are you up to nowadays?" Dr. Kahn asks.

"My mother and I started a matchmaking business," I reply, grateful for the distraction from her son's piercing eyes. I've always liked Dr. Kahn. Her good opinion matters to me in a way Caleb's used to.

"Yes, yes, of course," his mother demurs. "You know, now that I think of it, I should hire you to find Caleb someone."

Caleb and I seem equally horrified by the thought.

"That won't be necessary," he says, shooting his mother a glare.

"Are you sure?" Clearly, the Machiavellian within me has come out to play. "Because I have lots of women available. Scores of them, in fact."

His piercing, intelligent eyes land on mine, and I get the distinct impression that he knows exactly what I'm doing. How weird that he can still read me like a book even after all this time. "I'm sure."

"Well, take this in case he changes his mind," I say, handing a business card to Dr. Kahn.

"He won't," Caleb says firmly.

"Blue Moon Basherts," Dr. Kahn reads, holding it far from her face and squinting. I used to be farsighted when I was a kid, so I sympathize.

"My mother came up with the name. She thought it sounded hopeful." I focus all my attention on Dr. Kahn instead of the man beside me who's giving off inferno-levels of heat. "That it would remind people that everyone has a bashert, no matter their background or set of circumstances. Or," I add, shooting a pointed glance at Caleb, "how difficult a person might be."

One of Caleb's eyebrows lifts as if to say, *really?*

"I like that. Your mother is so special." Dr. Kahn lays her hand on my shoulder. "How is she?"

"She's okay," I say, biting my lip. My mother doesn't like advertising the fact that she has heart disease, but people know she's sick with something serious because she's on the community prayer list.

"Good." Dr. Kahn gestures to the table. "Stay and eat with us." She rattles off a directive in Hebrew to Caleb, telling him to bring over a third chair, but I shake my head and take a step back.

"I wish I could," I say, "but I'm meeting with a client soon."

"Ah, okay." Dr. Kahn nods, looking thoughtful. "But what about Sunday night? Are you busy?"

I hesitate, sensing a trap. "N-no?"

"Good." She nods. "Come to our house at seven. Caleb is cooking a delicious anniversary dinner for me and his father."

"Oh, wow, that's so nice." I bob my head several times in a row trying to figure out a good excuse. "Sooo, so nice."

"You must come," she adds, gently squeezing my hand. "I insist."

"That's so wonderful, um . . ."

"Isn't it?" Caleb rests his chin in his palm, all innocent-looking, when *I* know that *he* knows that I'm panicking. "And I have a special pea dish planned."

The urge to stick my tongue at him is almost overpowering. My hatred of peas goes back as far as I can remember, and we spent many nights arguing over them. He'd lecture me about their nutritional importance and in return, I'd flick them at his face.

But if there's one thing that Caleb and I have in common, it's our competitive nature. Both of us would rather die than admit defeat which I suppose explains why he became a Navy SEAL and I turned to matchmaking. Both jobs involve high stakes and trying to stay alive in hostile environments. So if he thinks he can scare me away by talking about peas, then he's got another thing coming.

"Fabulous." I lean toward him and add, "I *adore* peas now. I have them at least once a day. In fact, I'm *salivating* just thinking about them."

"Is that right?" Caleb says, in a tone of voice of someone who doesn't believe a word of what he just heard. "Then you're going to love my cantaloupe and pea salad."

Cantaloupe and peas? I try not to gag. Some food combinations ought to be illegal. "Yum." *Am I scowling? Crap.*

"And Bubby will be happy to see you," he adds.

My smile slips. Caleb's grandmother isn't mean per se, but no one could accuse her of being nice either. "Not as happy as I will be to see her," I reply.

He grins and rocks back on his heels. "I'll just bet."

Dr. Kahn glances back and forth between us like a spectator at a tennis match. "Excellent. We will see you then?"

"Definitely." I smile, narrowing my eyes at Caleb. "I wouldn't miss it for the world."

Something in the air crackles as Caleb bends down and whispers softly in my ear, "Make sure to come hungry."

Caleb Kahn, I realize, has turned into all sorts of trouble. And although the matchmaker in me is already flipping through my mental database for potential matches, the woman in me can't help but wonder just how good a little bit of trouble might feel.

Chapter One

Five Years Later

My grandmother used to say that it was just as easy to fall in love with a rich man as it was with a poor one. My grandfather usually followed that line with one of his own: "Do you know why Jewish husbands die before their wives? Because they want to." And although my mother was a hopeless romantic and worked as a matchmaker, she refused to date anyone herself.

I was a very confused child.

Even now, at the age of twenty-eight, there are still plenty of things about love and life that leave me shaking my head in bewilderment. Such as why men who have perfect aim on the golf course can't manage to keep their pee contained inside a toilet bowl. Or how we women can have rooms full of clothes and still *have nothing to wear*. Or why couples who live together before marriage are statistically more likely to divorce than those who don't. And why do cockroaches exist instead of, say, fairy godmothers with magical wands?

But perhaps the biggest mystery of all is why Caleb Kahn became Orthodox again and bought a house in the community a year ago. For it is a truth universally acknowledged that when a single man moves into the *eruv* and buys a property large enough to raise a tribe of children with room left over to host extended family, *alllll* the mamas come running.

As for my current relationship with Caleb, it's, you know . . . fine. Ellipses and all.

We're not friends or anything, but I've unblocked him from my contact list, so make of that what you will. We've also shared plenty of Shabbos and holiday meals, and the occasional birthday party.

I'm always careful to keep my distance though. I sit as far away from him as possible, and limit our conversations to bland topics like the weather, or how very, *very* busy I am.

But that doesn't mean that I'm not aware of when he walks into a room, or where he is at any given moment in it. The air changes when Caleb is nearby. I can feel it on the goosebumps of my skin, a sort of sixth sense that's uniquely tuned to Caleb.

It's really annoying.

Even more annoying, is that it's hard *not* to look at him. He is objectively beautiful. And despite his advanced age of thirty-three, he's only grown *better*-looking with time. His hairline hasn't receded, his body is in its best shape yet, and the few lines around his eyes only add to his air of intrigue and sex appeal. I know because at least once a week, someone mentions these as a not-so subtle hint that they want to be set up with him.

Just like the young woman currently sitting in my living room, for example. We should be discussing

Yitzchok—the man I set her up with and that she's been dating for the last month. The one she seems to have conveniently forgotten exists since eating Shabbos lunch with Caleb. Sitting across a table from him is, apparently, life changing.

So here we are, talking about Caleb Kahn. As if he's even a viable option. As if he didn't already say no when I mentioned Eidel's name to him a few days ago, the same way he's done with every other woman that I've thrown his way. For a man who claims he wants to get married, he sure has a funny way of going about it.

"Ashira?"

"Sorry." I shake my head and smile at Mrs. Schwartz and her daughter, Eidel. "It's just—can we talk about Yitzchok now? The man you've been dating?" I add, on the off-chance that she's experiencing a sudden case of amnesia.

"In a sec," Eidel replies, batting her hand impatiently. "I'm not done talking about Caleb yet."

OMG. Someone put me out of my misery and kill me.

"Unfortunately," I say, making sure to maintain eye contact because—pro tip—liars never do, "he's still currently unavailable." I say *still* because we had this exact conversation yesterday. Does she think going around in circles will produce a different answer? Because that's not how these things work. "Now, about Yitzchok—"

"But what does 'he's unavailable' mean?" Eidel scowls. "Are you saying he's dating someone?"

Hey, now—that's an idea. Maybe then she'll drop this fantasy.

"It's possible." I bob my head up and down, trying to convince all three of us. The mother and daughter exchange a confused look.

"I mean," I cough, "it isn't impossible. In the realm of what is and isn't possible."

Why can't I just lie like a normal person?

"Did he say he was dating someone or didn't he?" Mrs. Schwartz asks, looking at me like I'm an idiot.

"I don't remember his exact wording." I scratch my neck and tuck my hands under my armpits. If I could go back in time, I'd have put on several more layers of deodorant before this meeting. "But he definitely used the word 'unavailable'."

"That's the only reason he'd be unavailable though, right?" Eidel says, turning to her mother since I've clearly proven myself to be an unreliable narrator.

But Mrs. Schwartz turns to me. "Is it?"

"Is it, indeed?" I tap my chin, pretending this was posed as a philosophical question rather than a literal one and channel my inner Socrates. "Who's to say?"

"What's wrong with her?" Eidel says to her mother, not even bothering to whisper.

Mrs. Schwartz puts up a hand to silence her daughter, then leans toward me. A vein throbs on her forehead, and up until this point, I'd never realized just how intimidating the effects of the cardiovascular system could be.

"*You* are the matchmaker. It's *your job* to say."

My palms become itchy with sweat. Actually, my entire body is turning itchy. If matchmakers could rate clients, I'd give these two a one-star review and then write in the comments section: *will cause spontaneous outbreak of hives. Proceed with caution.*

People like to complain about matchmakers, but no one talks about the grief and hardship we suffer at the hands of our clients. If it isn't one thing they find to complain about, it's another.

"You're absolutely right, Mrs. Schwartz," I say. "And I plan on clarifying with him what he meant. So." I clap my hands and turn to Eidel. "How are things going with Yitzchok?"

"Wait," Eidel says, holding up a finger. "Did you use my name when you spoke to Caleb? Or did you just ask if he was hypothetically interested in going out with someone?"

I take a deep breath and paste on a polite smile, the one that fools everyone except for my best friend Miri. She calls it my sociopath face.

"Yes, I used your name. Eidel Schwartz," I add, in case that was going to be her follow-up question.

"He's probably already dating someone," Mrs. Schwartz says to her daughter.

"Like you're dating Yitzchok," I add pointedly.

"When I had Shabbos lunch with Caleb this past week," Eidel continues, as if both her mother and I hadn't spoken, "I felt this deep connection, and it was unlike anything I experienced before. It was almost like . . ." her eyes turn dreamy, "a preview of love."

A preview of love? What the hell is she talking about?

Clearly Eidel finds something offensive about my facial expression because her own turns into a scowl. "I'm telling you, we had a connection."

Oh child, please. If I had a dollar for every time someone told me they had a connection with Caleb, I'd be drinking piña coladas on a beach right now being fanned with giant leaves by attractive pool men.

"Call him."

I tilt my head at Mrs. Schwartz. Something about her tone of voice seems extra menacing. "Of course," I say. "I'm not sure what time he gets home from work, but I'll call tonight."

But what comes out of her mouth next causes a chill to run down my spine.

"Now."

I blink. "Sorry?"

"Call Caleb *now*."

"You mean . . ." I swallow. "Right now?"

Mrs. Schwartz bares her teeth. Actually shows them to me, like a wolf that's closing in on its dinner. Except a wolf wouldn't have a smudge of lipstick on its canines. It sort of dampens the effect, to be honest.

"Right now," she barks, and I jump a little in my seat.

Another truth universally acknowledged is that the Schwartzs are one of the most powerful families of Brooklyn. They have the money, influence, and connections to satisfy any whim of theirs within the boroughs of NYC, 5 towns, and then some.

Think Vito Corleone. Lady Catherine de Bourgh. Jay Gatsby. The Kennedys, the Rothschilds, the Rockefellers. Then combine them, and *that* would be the Schwartzs.

And in my experience, powerful, influential people don't mind making enemies, especially if said enemy has no leverage. Someone with no money or low ranking in society.

Someone like me.

Despite the fact that I already have eight years of matchmaking experience under my belt, the only reason that Mrs. Schwartz chose to work with me was because she was friends with my mother, who made several matches for their family. I'm good at my job, but I'm still a small fish in a huge matchmaking pond.

I'm hugely lucky to have this opportunity, and all I have to do is not screw it up. Which in theory, doesn't sound hard, but in reality, is turning out to be quite the nightmare. I'd been handling them well enough until now, but today took a massive one-eighty and I still can't understand how we got here.

"Well?" Mrs. Schwartz says, making a flurrying motion with her hand. "What are you waiting for? Call him, already."

I turn to Eidel with a silent plea for help, but she's too busy staring at her mother like she's a genius.

"Yes," Eidel says. "This is a terrific idea."

This is a *terrible* idea.

Mrs. Schwartz nods. "We'll have clarity this way."

I rub my forehead. The woman doesn't want clarity, she wants reassurance; either that Caleb is already dating someone and that his disinterest isn't a personal slight to her daughter, or she wants to be told that not only is he available, but he's practically chomping at the bit to go out with Eidel. Which is simply not the case.

And we all know what happens to the messenger.

"I would call now, but he's at work," I say, wiping my sweaty palms on my skirt.

"So what? He's the CEO of his own company," Mrs. Schwartz says, waving her hands again. "Who's going to fire him if he takes a phone call?"

She makes a fair point. Caleb built his security firm from the ground up, putting his Navy SEAL skills to good use after retiring from the teams three years ago. Now, people from all over the world hire bodyguards from his company to help keep them safe.

"Do it," Eidel urges, taking my phone off the coffee table and handing it to me. I stare at it in horror, as if it's a murder weapon that now has my fingerprints all over it.

Don't do it. There is literally no scenario where this ends well.

But the intensity of the Schwartzs' combined stares is starting to affect my ability to breathe. Each tick of the living room clock sounds like a bomb set to detonate in my ears. I rub a fist over my chest, trying to loosen the knot of tension that's building.

"Let's go." Mrs. Schwartz claps her hands. "Chop-chop."

"I . . ." I lick my dry lips and stand up, gripping the wall to steady me. "Okay. I'll be right back, and let you know what he says."

But Mrs. Schwartz has shockingly good reflexes for a woman of her age. "Oh no, you don't," she says, yanking on my wrist and pulling me back down. "You're going to stay right here where I can watch you."

I can't fault her instincts.

All right, here goes nothing. I take a deep breath and unlock my phone. I lower the volume so they can't hear what he says. *Brilliant.*

"Put it on speaker," Eidel commands.

I sigh, but this might be even better. I'll start off the call by casually mentioning who's listening.

"But don't tell him we're here," Mrs. Schwartz says, reading my mind. Turns out, she's great at that.

I look up from my phone and frown. "Don't you think this is a little unethical?"

Mrs. Schwartz laughs for the first time since we've sat down. "You're funny."

Eidel takes the phone back after I've dialed and sets it on the coffee table. We wait in terse silence as it rings. Maybe he won't pick up. Maybe he'll be in a meeting or getting a haircut or working out at the gym. There's lots of reasons why he might not answer. *Please don't pick up, please don't pick up, please don't—*

"Hello?"

Damnit, he picked up.

Chapter Two

"Tinsel?"

The Schwartzs exchange a confused look. Not for the first time, I wish Caleb had thought to call me something more respectable and intimidating. Switchblade, Black Widow, The Obliterator. The possibilities are endless, really.

"Oh good." I swallow. "You picked up." I pull at the collar of my shirt. Why is it so hot in here?

"I tend to do that when my phone rings."

"Right. Makes sense." I clear my throat. "So, anyway. Remember how I asked if you were interested in going out with Eidel Schwartz?"

"Who?"

"I mentioned her to you on Sunday night." Silence. "At Zevi's house. Remember?"

"No."

What does he mean "no"? I'm going to kill him.

"Eidel Schwartz," I say slowly, and perhaps, a tad aggressively. "I was looking for the ice cream scooper and then you came in to get napkins—"

"Oh, right," he says, like, *now I remember*. "The gold digger. The one you said wasn't the brightest in the IQ department, but could still sniff out a fake Prada from an authentic one."

Shiiiit. A gasp comes from the direction the Schwartzs' side of the room and I squeeze my eyes shut. In all fairness, I'd only said it *after* he said no. I feel like this is an important point. But before I can even figure out how to do damage control, he keeps going, and I'm paralyzed in a state of absolute terror. I'm slowly drowning in quicksand with nothing to grasp onto.

"She's the one who you said was pushy and snobby and that she'd never marry anyone outside the top one percent."

"No, no, no, you silly goose," I squeak. Silly goose? Who even am I? My knee starts to tremble. I bring my hand down on it hard. "That was someone else."

"No, it was definitely her." He chuckles. "I remember because you made a joke about Eidel not being so *eidel*," he adds. Eidel sputters in outrage. As for Mrs. Schwartz, she looks like she's trying to figure out the best place to dispose of my body.

And yes, I did say that about Eidel, but it was more out of wonder than anything else. What are the chances you give your kid a Yiddish name that means gentle and sweet, only for her to turn out to be bold and rude? It's pretty ironic.

But mostly, I said those things as part of a string of rambling nervous consciousness because we were alone in the kitchen and I was trying to find the ice cream scooper as fast as possible without getting sucked into a conversation with him. At least, not the kind where he asks why I avoid talking to him for any length of time. I still haven't figured out how to answer if he does.

"How did you describe the mother again? Wait, let me remember how you worded it—"

My finger reaches toward the screen to end the call, but Mrs. Schwartz smacks my hand away.

"—has the manners of a prison guard and the emotional intelligence of a preschooler."

Silence fills the room.

I am *so* dead.

"I'm about to head into a meeting now," Caleb says, blithely unaware of the trauma he's inflicted. "But it's good to hear your voice." A pause. "Talk soon?"

"Mhm humph." It's the best I can do, considering the circumstances. I hang up and wait for the proverbial shit to hit the fan.

"How could you?" Mrs. Schwartz says in an eerily controlled voice. "What kind of matchmaker says *lashon hara* about her client? Especially to the person she's supposed to be setting her up with, of all people?"

"You want him for yourself, don't you?" Eidel accuses before turning to her mother. "I bet you anything that's what this is about."

My head rears back. "No, I don't! He'd make a terrible husband," I say, imagining him walking out the front door with a suitcase in his hand and carelessly tossing a goodbye letter over his shoulder.

"There you go again!" Mrs. Schwartz exclaims, pointing a condemning finger at me. "You have a real problem, you know that?" She stands up and grabs her purse, then motions for her daughter to follow. "Bringing soulmates together is one of the most beautiful *mitzvahs* in the Torah, but you've turned it into something terrible and ugly." She shakes her head. "You shouldn't be allowed to do this line of work. You've probably ruined more lives than you've helped."

"I'm so sorry," I say, rushing after her. Apologizing doesn't come naturally to everyone, but it's like breathing to me. Probably because my mother was a born and bred Minnesotan, so I grew up seeing her apologize to everyone and everything, including inanimate objects she stubbed her toe on. "I never should've said those things."

"No, you shouldn't have," Mrs. Schwartz replies, yanking her coat off the hanger from the small entryway closet. "Your mother was a good, pious woman. *But you?*" Her eyes glint with disgust. "You must take after your father."

Her words hit like a poisoned arrow straight to my heart.

"I won't allow you to hurt more innocent people." She takes a step forward and I don't even realize I'm moving backwards until my heels hit the wall. "Mark my words, Ashira Wernick—your matchmaking days are over."

Naturally, my panic turns up a notch.

"Sure, that's one option." I swallow. "Or we could sit down, open a bottle of Chardonnay, and talk about life." I give her a hopeful smile, but she doesn't so much as look at me.

"And by the way, Ashira," Eidel says, one foot already out the door, "it's more than just copies of Prada handbags that I can tell are frauds."

I'm struck by the cleverness of her parting line. That kind of riposte would've taken me at least a week to think of. But then she adds, "It's Gucci and Versace too."

"Aaah." I give a weak smile. "It's . . . it's a talent, for sure."

I'm a mess of emotions as I watch them walk away. I'm frustrated at myself for ignoring my intuition and calling Caleb, and I'm ashamed for bad-mouthing the Schwartzs. I'm angry at Mrs. Schwartz for comparing me to my deadbeat father.

Plus, there's the all-consuming, overwhelming panic of her saying she's going to ruin me. Let's not forget that.

I shut the front door then lean against it. It'll be fine, I tell myself. She'll calm down and move on. There's no need to panic. In a week from now, she'll have forgotten all about it. And even if Mrs. Schwartz does try to ruin my reputation, most people have enough common sense to not blindly believe everything she says. Despite her calling me out for speaking *lashon hara*, she's one of the biggest gossips in town.

I flop onto the couch and stare up at the ceiling. If only Blue Moon Basherts was successful enough that I didn't need to worry about being in the Schwartzs' good graces. But with an ever-increasing number of dating apps and the influx of new matchmakers all trying to be the next Aleeza Ben Shalom, it's getting harder and harder to keep the business alive.

My mind drifts to my mother. Most of the time, I try to distract myself from thinking about her. The pain of losing her is still too raw. Maybe it shouldn't be after five years. It's probably not normal to feel like you're experiencing an anaphylactic reaction at the thought of never being able to hug someone again.

She got sick when I was a sophomore in high school and by that time, it was just the two of us in the house. Leah was married and living in Israel, and Zevi was in London attending a prestigious film school.

For the longest time, I begged her to see a doctor, but she had a deep-seated fear of everything medical, and it was only after I found her collapsed on the kitchen floor one day that she got a diagnosis. Heart failure, the doctor said. The left chamber of her heart wasn't pumping enough oxygen and the prognosis was grim.

Overnight, I went from a child to an adult. My mother was no longer able to work or do basic household chores, and I became her caretaker. There were so many days I skipped school because no one else was able to take her to doctor appointments, or because she was especially sick and I worried she wouldn't be able to call for help in an emergency. I attended summer school in order to graduate, and worked as many babysitting jobs as I could to keep us afloat, often bringing the children to my house so I could keep an eye on my mother at the same time. Money was tight, and as my friends left for seminary and college, I was on the phone battling insurance companies to pay for basic life-saving drugs and procedures.

But there were good times, too. My mother and I grew even closer. It was during this time that she began Blue Moon Basherts on account of her inability to work a nine-to-five job. The only silver lining of her illness was that it gave her the opportunity to do what she loved most in the world—bringing soulmates together. Although there was a lot more to the job than simply making introductions. Often it involved coaching someone how to take turns during a conversation, or helping them decide whether to move forward or call it quits. Sometimes it meant counseling couples through challenges. And occasionally it meant being blamed for other people's mistakes. I was her protégé, and I saw it all.

On her worst days, I'd nestle beside her in bed and read out loud to her. And on her good days, we worked on Blue Moon Basherts.

My mother was my best friend. It was her unconditional love that shaped me into the person I am today. And when she died, I discovered that I couldn't grieve the way my siblings did. While Zevi and Leah cried and laughed and told stories about my mother during the seven ritual days following the burial, I sat there numb. I felt nothing. Afterwards, I threw myself into the company we built together. Continuing her work made her feel less unreachable, like she wasn't in some faraway galaxy, but in the house with me, sitting beside me as I matched people. And every time I got a phone call that a couple got engaged, I felt her hug me.

The idea that Mrs. Schwartz could take all of that away is chilling. No, it's more than that—it's *enraging*.

I clench my hands into fists at my sides. I couldn't save my mother, but I'll be damned if I'm going to sit back and let Mrs. Schwartz take away my last thread of connection to her.

Chapter Three

The stress every Friday before sunset is to Orthodox Jews what the zombie apocalypse is to conspiracy theorists. Meaning, *you need to be prepared*. Because once those candles are lit, there are no backsies. If you forget to turn on the crockpot for your cholent, guess what? No cholent for you, buddy. If you neglect to switch off your bedroom light, you better have some sleeping pills lying around to get you through the night. And if you fail to remember to set your oven to Shabbos mode, then cold chicken and knishes are on the menu. In fact, there are so many ways to screw up the preparation of Shabbos that I still have the checklist my mother made taped onto our kitchen cabinet.

But should you make any of the above mistakes on a three-day holiday, then you better hope you've got a nice non-Jewish neighbor who enjoys playing guessing games. Because you're only allowed to have a non-Jew help you provided that you don't ask them directly for what you need. So instead of asking them to turn on a lamp, for example, you'd say, "Do you think it's too dark in here?" At which point, they're supposed to realize to flip the light switch on.

And let's not forget the stress that comes with having to make a three-course meal by sunset.

Anyway. The point is that you should avoid having a serious life crisis on a Friday because your anxiety levels are already sky high. But come Friday morning, I'm already a wreck from having spent much of the night tossing and turning, unable to stop worrying about Mrs. Schwartz.

My phone suddenly rings, and I glance at the time. *What kind of sadist calls at six in the morning?*

Ah. My brother.

"Hello?" I croak.

"Hi, so listen," Zevi says, sounding breathless. "I know it's early, but my plane is boarding and I need to tell you something."

"Umph," I moan, rubbing my eyelids.

"Are you sitting down?"

I bolt upright. Nothing wakes you up faster than someone asking if you're sitting down. I clench the phone. "Who died?"

"Why do you always go straight to that?"

"Someone is missing, then?" I chew on my bottom lip as years' worth of *Dateline* episodes regurgitate in my head. And as we viewers know, the first twenty-four hours are critical.

"No, Ash. No one is dead and no one is missing."

I breathe a sigh of relief. What else could be a legitimate reason to wake someone up at six in the morning? "Does someone need bail money?"

"No offense, but you're not the one I'd call if someone did," he says, which is a fair point. "Now can I tell you or do we have to keep playing Twenty Questions?"

"Sorry, go ahead," I say. In the background I hear the gate attendant making an announcement.

"Okay, so it's not a big deal," he says, "but there's an Instagram post about you that people are talking about."

"About *me*?" I squeal.

"Yeah."

My stomach plummets. For once I was right to panic. "Any chance that this is a good type of post?" I say.

Zevi's sigh lands midway through his chuckle. "I'm sorry, Ash."

"Can you send it to me?"

"Promise not to freak out?"

"I won't freak out."

"Good," he says. "Because it's not a big deal."

Which seems debatable.

"All right, hold on . . . Okay, sent."

A moment later my phone pings. I tap on the message icon and clench my teeth as I wait for it to load. The first thing I notice is that Mrs. Schwartz has tagged me in the post. So, that's cute. She's taken a picture of my company logo and put a large red strikethrough on it, and the words 'RISKY BUSINESS'. Beneath the image is the caption:

> I had the most nightmarish experience with matchmaker Ashira Wernick @bluemoonbasherts. She told ugly, outrageous lies to the man she was supposed to be setting my daughter up with—and even spoke *lashon hara* about me. Have you ever been betrayed

by a matchmaker or had a terrible experience? Drop a comment below. #BlueMoonBashertsBackstabber #UnethicalMatchmaker #LashonHara

My hand flies to my mouth. It's one thing to call me a backstabber, but desecrating my beautiful website design with a warning label?

Below. The. Belt.

I shake my head, trying to wrap my head around the fact that she's being so public in her effort to destroy me. I figured she'd complain about me to her friends or the fish shop guy or the mailman or whoever else she might run into in the coming days. I never would've thought she'd go this far.

"I'm going to take her to *Beis Din*," I declare. One of the Jewish court's areas of expertise is to settle money disputes between Jews. There's no question that the *Beis Din* will see that Mrs. Schwartz calling me out on a public forum is an attempt to ruin me financially.

"I think her husband sits on it," Zevi says.

Of course he does.

"Then I'll go to the one in Chicago," I say.

"Her brother who sits on that one . . . or maybe it's her uncle," Zevi says.

I clutch the side of my head and start to pace. "What am I supposed to do exactly? Just lie back and take it?"

"No, of course not. We'll figure something out." A woman makes another announcement over the loudspeaker, and Zevi must be on the move because the background noise gets louder. "I've got to board now, but stay off social media, okay?"

"Yeah."

"And I'll see you tonight," he says, reminding me that we're eating at Leah's for the Friday night Shabbos meal.

"Okay," I reply. "Have a safe flight."

I stare at my phone after we hang up. My finger hovers over the Instagram app, but Zevi is right—it won't do any good to check social media. I'll just get upset and angry, and I don't even have anyone to take it out on.

I decide to check my inbox instead, and immediately wish I hadn't. I frown as I click onto an email from a client of mine with the subject line: *Apologies*.

Hi Ashira.

This isn't easy for me to write, but I've decided to terminate our contract. You'll hear from my lawyer before the end of next week. I hope you take some time in the coming days to reflect on the damage that speaking lashon hara *can incur, and hopefully through prayer and meditation, find peace.*

I fall against my bed and groan. There's no peace if I have no money to pay my bills. Some of us actually like our electricity and hot water.

Unlike some matchmakers who have day jobs and only get paid after a match is made, my three-month, six-month, and annual contracts are there to provide steady income regardless of my success.

My heart starts to race. I imagine living on the streets in the dead of winter, shivering and hungry. I picture myself clutching an empty tin can while a crowd claps along to a guy's harmonica performance across the street. His talent is mediocre, but no one except me seems to realize it.

And because I have no panhandling skills, I soon wind up dead in an abandoned, dimly lit alley. I finally get my fifteen minutes of fame when *Dateline* does an episode on me titled: *The Matchmaker Meets Her Maker.*

I do my best to resist checking Instagram, but I eventually crack when the notification alert reaches over a hundred.

I'm shocked at how much attention this post is getting. People I've never met before are sharing Mrs. Schwartz's post—people who aren't even Jewish. The more it gets shared, the more traction it gets. I had no idea that there was so much pent-up anger towards matchmakers in the world, but reading through the comment section is definitely changing that.

By noon, the nightmare is in full swing. My phone is blowing up with a flurry of texts and calls from concerned friends, and emails from clients who no longer want to work with me.

Suddenly, anyone who's ever been wronged by a matchmaker—which seems to be just about everyone and their mom—has come out of the woodwork, and within a matter of hours, I'm the ambassador for unethical matchmakers across the globe. My name itself has become a hashtag, positioned between others such as: #*Conniving* #*Untrustworthy* #*Immoral* #*Bluemoonbasherts*

On a conference call with Miri and Sissel, I simultaneously reassure my two best friends that I'm perfectly fine and *completely* unaffected, and uncork a wine bottle and pour myself a tall glass. Between sips and listening to them rant against Mrs. Schwartz, I continue reading posts. I'm torn between righteous indignation and fascination. I've never stopped to think about the other cultures around the world with a rich history of matchmaking before.

Like this woman in India, for example. Her parents paid six thousand dollars up front for an auntie matchmaker who suddenly left her husband and ran away with the client's boyfriend. The post ended with #*Conartist* #*Bluemoonbasherts* #*Manstealer* #*Overpaidmatchmakers* and #*OverpaidPimps*.

I blink. At least no one has called me an #OverpaidPimp.

Then there's the dude in Kenya who's holding a grudge against his *esigani* who gave a false report about his bride's character to his parents. #*Bluemoonbasherts*. A young woman in Beijing said she had been conned by her *Y ue L ao* into marrying an older, poor rural man. #*Bluemoonbasherts*. Then a man from Canada claimed that a widowed Amish matchmaker seduced his son who then left the community and became a Mennonite. #*Bluemoonbasherts* #*Unethical*. Which I find highly suspicious because I don't think the Amish use electricity—much less the internet— like my community on Shabbos.

Within a few hours, I've lost everything. All of my clients have withdrawn from their contracts, probably because they know I don't have the money to hire a lawyer to sue them anyway.

I glance at my watch and feel myself blanch. Shabbos is starting in an hour and a half and I haven't showered or gotten dressed yet. Normally I enjoy the process of getting fancied up for Shabbos, but at the moment, movement doesn't seem like a viable option. My limbs are dead weights, and my brain is a paralyzed mush of despair. So I continue to lie on my bed and gaze up at the ceiling, surrounded by a scattering of used tissues, and feeling very much like part of a Shakespearean tragedy.

Everything I've feared most is coming true, isn't it? My clients are gone, and with Mrs. Schwartz as my enemy, I don't have much hope of recouping my business. Losing it feels just like how I thought it would, like I'm losing my mother all over again.

Mrs. Schwartz wins, I lose. Game over.

Or, you could come back swinging. You could fight back, you could refuse to lie down and take it.

Yeah, in theory. It was so much easier to think that last night before I saw how much damage this woman could cause. I'm like the David to her Goliath, except I don't even have a slingshot.

But then my eyes fall on the framed photo resting on my nightstand. It's one of my favorite memories of my mother and me. She had been feeling good that day so we'd gone out to eat, and someone offered to take our picture when he saw me struggling to get the right selfie angle. The sunshine highlights the backs of our heads like a halo, and we're both beaming at the camera.

I pick up the picture and run my fingers over it, and hear my mother's voice in my head: *The hardest things in life are worth fighting for.* At the time, she'd been referring to my lack of ambition when it came to school, but the principle applies here too.

My sadness lifts and I'm invigorated by my newfound determination. I jump out of bed, energized and feeling fierce, like a Viking woman warrior ready to face battle. I don't know how I'm going to save Blue Moon Basherts, but I will. Because quitting is, to put it simply, not an option.

Chapter Four

But three hours and two glasses of wine later, I find myself reconsidering.

"You know the person that takes your ticket at the movie theater and tears it in half?" I announce at the Shabbos table. "That's going to be me."

The room falls silent, which is really saying something because it's full of people. There's Leah, her husband Isser and my niece and nephew; Zevi and Jack, plus my two closest friends, Miri and Sissel.

And Caleb, whose presence no one had thought to warn me about.

But it's . . . fine. Totally fine.

I tip my head back and drain my glass.

"I think you should set the bar a little higher for yourself, Auntie Ashira," my nine-year-old niece says, her brown eyes shining sympathetically. Golda sets down her five-pound PDR—a Physician's Desk Reference book that was written in the eighties— onto the dining room table. It lands with a thud and disperses a blanket of dust. She bought it with her allowance at a garage sale and has been diagnosing herself and family members with random diseases ever since. Golda has a special place in my heart. She's just so very Anne of Green Gables. Right down to the red hair.

"Yes, but the lower the bar, the more likely I am to excel," I explain.

"Have you had any head injuries lately?" Golda opens the PDR and starts flipping the pages. "You might have a concussion. Unless of course," she adds, pursing her lips, "it's because of your high emotions."

"Eat your chicken, Golda," Leah commands. Golda acquiesces, but closes the book with a heavy, melodramatic sigh.

Zevi tousles Golda's hair. "Auntie Ashira is just being silly. Right, Auntie Ashira?"

"Hmm?" I glance up, belatedly realizing people are waiting for my response. "Sorry, was that my cue to lie?"

Zevi chokes on his drink, and his husband Jack gives him a hard slap on his back.

"Listen, Ash," Miri says to me in a serious tone. "Blue Moon Basherts isn't going anywhere. You're the best matchmaker in the world, and we won't let some evil woman dictate your future."

"And *that* is why you're my best friend," I declare, pointing my fork at Miri.

"But you should still brush up your résumé," Caleb says, peering at me between the flames of the candelabra. "Just to be on the safe side. And again," he adds, before I can even open my mouth, "I'm sorry for causing this mess."

"I'm not saying it's your fault," I sniff. "But I am blaming you."

The corners of his lips twitch. "I'd expect nothing less."

"You could be an airplane!" Four-year-old Mordy says, bouncing up and down in his seat.

"Airplanes are inanimate objects," Sissel explains. Sissel is a chemical engineer and tends to see things through a very black-and-white lens which causes her to unintentionally insult people on a regular basis. But I love her anyway. At least, seventy percent of the time.

"I could be." I tap my chin, pretending to think about Mordy's suggestion. "But only if you were the pilot."

"*Yeaaa!*" Mordy shouts, and knocks over his sister's glass of water.

"Now look what you've done, Ashira." Leah sighs and gets up to grab a pile of napkins.

"*Me?*" I point to my chest. "I'm just sitting here."

"You're getting the children riled up."

I roll my eyes. Leah has a habit of blaming me when she's annoyed. But she's my sister, so I love her anyway—at least, fifty percent of the time.

"Personality changes are common with concussions," Golda flips a page and looks up. "We must be patient with her. Stress interferes with the brain's ability to recover."

"What did I say about diagnosing people, Golda?" Leah scowls as she starts collecting people's plates. "Tell her, Isser."

Isser scratches his head. Their marriage is the kind where Leah tells him to jump and Isser responds, "How high?" She wears the pants and every other item of clothing.

"Golda, please listen to your mother."

"But Tatty—" Golda starts.

"Your father said no, Golda," Leah snaps, taking Miri's plate just as Miri pops a forkful of Yerushalmi Kugel into her mouth. Miri glances down, startled that her plate has disappeared.

"Or I could clean dead women," I muse, pouring myself another glass of Bordeaux. I turn to Zevi. "Remember how Bubbe worked for the *Chevra Kadisha*?" Our paternal grandmother was a sweet, albeit quirky woman, but I suppose you'd have to be to do that sort of job.

Jack blinks. "The *Hevra whowewho?*"

"Bubbe also had a gambling and liquor problem," Zevi replies. "I'm not sure following in her footsteps is the best idea."

"Wait," Jack says, waving his hands. "What is the *Hevra?*"

"It's a society of Observant Jewish women who prepare deceased women for burial," I explain.

Jack tilts his head. "Like a Jewish mortician?"

"Sort of," Zevi says. "But without the embalmment or makeup. It's cleaning the body, then dressing it in special shrouds, interspersed with praying."

"Sweetheart," Jack says to me after a pregnant pause. "I think you should stick to the movie theater."

"Agreed." Miri nods. "Less . . . creepy."

"It's not creepy, *it's holy*," I say. "And dead people don't say things on the phone that could ruin your career." I give Caleb a pointed look, and tear off a large piece of *dabo* that he made—the traditional bread of Ethiopian Jews—and stuff it in my mouth.

"I never said to give up on your dreams, Tinsel. I don't think that at all. But," he pauses, "this could be a long fight and it's smart to have a backup plan until you get your company on its feet again. And," Caleb adds with a barely there smile, "dead people don't do much talking at all."

"Eggshactly," I say, not bothering to wait to respond until I'm done chewing.

"Enjoying the *dabo*?" Caleb says in a mild voice.

"I've had better," I say, then pop another huge piece in my mouth.

Caleb's pillowy lips curve upwards into a grin.

Pillowy lips? Have I gone insane? This is the worst Friday night ever.

I clear my throat and continue, "I was thinking about taxidermy too. It's less holy, of course, but I like animals. I mean, obviously, I prefer them alive," I clarify, waving my hand, with a cautious glance at the children who thankfully aren't listening, "but beggars can't be choosers, right?"

"Maybe you've had enough wine," Miri murmurs and tries to take my glass, but I keep a vise-like grip on it until she surrenders with a sigh.

"Why do all your ideas involve corpses and death?" Sissel wonders aloud.

"They don't," I reply, a little defensively. "There's the movie ticket idea."

"It might as well be," Leah says. "That's where careers go to die."

"Thanks, Leah. Appreciate the sisterly support," I say, then throw another piece of *dabo* in my mouth.

"Ash, honey," Zevi says, "let's slow down on the carbs."

I bite off another piece and stare at him defiantly. Earlier this week, I'd gone in for my annual checkup, and my bloodwork showed that my cholesterol levels were high. Nothing dangerous, but my doctor was a little concerned given my mother's heart disease. He gave me a speech about diet and exercise, and I had every intention of listening, but . . . it turns out that eating vegetables and doing aerobics isn't as much fun as it sounds.

"Don't say that," Miri says, turning to Zevi. "She's way too skinny as it is."

"But her doctor said . . . *oomph*—"

I clamp my hand over my brother's mouth to keep him quiet. That's the last time I tell him anything.

"What did the doctor say?" Caleb gazes between Zevi and me. The concern in his eyes is evident.

"Nothing," I reply. I do however, put the rest of the *dabo* down and stare at it despondently.

He frowns. "It doesn't seem like nothing."

"Why did you tell Zevi what the doctor said and not me?" Leah demands.

"It's not that big of a deal," Jack tells her.

Leah turns to me, accusingly. *"You told him, too?"*

"*Jack*," I hiss. I cannot believe the number of loose tongues at this table.

"I don't understand," Miri says, glancing at Jack. There's no mistaking the anxiety in her voice. "Why can't she have carbs? She's skinny," Miri repeats, as if trying to make sense of a riddle.

"Mrs. Wernick was skinny too," Sissel says to Miri. "But that didn't stop her from dying of heart disease."

The scraping sounds of cutlery against plates come to a pause.

"Well, it's true," Sissel adds defensively.

"It's fine," I say, trying to diffuse the sudden tension. "Everything is fine." The silence grows and with it, my discomfort. "The doctor isn't worried. And I'm going to listen to her advice."

"Good," Caleb says.

"To my health," I say, lifting my wine glass. No one joins me. "The only thing that isn't fine is my business. That's definitely not fine. Could we focus on that for a minute?"

"What's the point of having a business if—" Leah glances at the children who are playing in the living room, "you're not around to run it?"

My heart rate speeds up. Hearing those words out loud causes a chill to run down my spine. *What if I also die before my time?*

"Should we skip dessert and go straight to *bentching*?" Isser suggests, glancing around the table nervously.

"Excellent idea." Zevi jumps to his feet. "I'll pass out the *bentchers*." Zevi opens the door to the buffet cabinet that houses the after-meal prayer books, then shoves one at each of us like a stern schoolteacher.

"Kids," Isser calls and waves them over. "It's *bentching* time."

"*I've got it!*" Jack exclaims, startling us. He points his finger at me. "I've figured out how to save Blue Moon Basherts!"

I perk up. "Really? How?"

"You need the Antichrist."

"Language!" Leah says, and clamps her hands over Mordy's ears.

Jack grew up Catholic, and although I've learned a lot about Christianity from him, I have to admit that this is a new one. "Pardon?"

"You need someone on your side that has just as much power and influence in the community," he explains, eyes lighting up with excitement. "Although technically, that person would be the real savior and Mrs. Schwartz would be the false one."

"Is anyone else following this?" I ask, glancing around the table.

"What I'm saying is that you need to make the biggest match of the year, if not decade," Jack says, his face growing more and more animated and he waves his hands. "You need a big celebrity. If you were able to make the match of the century—something big like Prince Harry's second wife—"

I bring my hands down on the table with such violent force that the candlesticks wobble. "He broke up with Meghan?" I gasp.

"No, no," he says, with a dismissive wave of his hand. "It's just an example. Although," he adds, like he can't help himself, "it would be nice to see Harry reunited with his family, wouldn't it? Imagine the sheer joy and *simcha*." He pronounces the last word as 'sim-kah' instead of the phlegm-in-the-back-of-your-throat sound.

"You're so cute." Zevi kisses his cheek.

"No PDA," Leah barks. My sister is such a prude that sometimes I wonder how she ever managed to get pregnant.

But would Jack's idea actually work? My mind flashes back to my childhood when my father used to tuck me into bed and tell me fairytale stories, usually some variant of a young, beautiful woman cursed by a jealous, postmenopausal woman. But the ending was always the same—the young couple fell in love and lived happily ever after. Because no matter what the problem was, whether it be dragons or overbearing stepmothers or jealous witches that weren't invited to a party celebrating the birth of a royal baby, love was the answer.

Every. Single. Time.

Could this really be the answer this time, too? Could finding a celebrity their happily ever after be the solution?

"That's *brilliant*, Jack," Miri says, eyes round with excitement. "We need to find someone that everyone admires, rich and famous, and good-looking, of course. Somebody that has that elusive *something*, but that no one has been able to find a spouse for yet."

A light bulb goes off in my head, and by the looks of it, in the others' as well. One by one, everyone at the table turns to stare at Caleb. And when he realizes what's happening, he shakes his head. "No. Absolutely not."

I'm quiet, unsure how to feel. On one hand, he could be the answer to my prayers, but on the other . . . *it's Caleb*. The man that I'm determined to keep my distance from.

"Don't be a dick," Sissel says to him.

"Language," Leah sighs, rubbing her temples.

"Please, Caleb," Miri pleads, holding her hands together, prayer-style. "You tick all the boxes. Everyone in the community respects you, you sit on the boards of all the major institutions—"

"Not all of them," he interrupts, looking unsettled.

"But the most important ones," she says, and he looks away, unable to argue with that. "And ever since that article came out, you've been famous," Miri adds, referring to the feature in *New York City's Culture* magazine, "25 Most Eligible Bachelors in NYC".

"C-level famous, but still," Sissel adds. "And even I, as an asexual, realize that you've got that elusive . . ." She pauses and makes a sound from the back of her throat and claws her hand at the air, like a Bengal tiger that took a few swigs of vodka before going onstage.

Caleb opens his mouth and then shuts it.

"That's it," Leah declares, standing up. "Mordy, Golda. Time for bed."

My mind continues to churn. Could this really be enough to repair my damaged reputation? It's possible. Especially if the magazine does a follow-up feature on his engagement and Caleb is quoted as saying what a phenomenal matchmaker I am.

Caleb opens his mouth a second time, and we all lean forward as if to hear his answer better, only to watch him close it again. He looks pained and uncomfortable, and I realize with sinking clarity that this isn't fair to him. He's not my favorite person by a long shot, but this is my debt to pay, not his. And while he did start the avalanche of my demise, I was the one who spoke badly about Mrs. Schwartz and her daughter in the first place. I was wrong to do it, and I alone should be the one to fix it.

Besides, I'm used to taking care of myself. I got a head start on adulthood at fifteen while everyone around else carried on with life as normal. I'm more than familiar with being thrown into bad situations and figuring things out on my own. This isn't new ground to me; I've done this before and I can do it again.

I'll be fine.

If there's one thing life has taught me, it's that one way or another, people always leave. First it was my dad, then Caleb, then my mother. The only person it has ever been safe to rely on is me.

"Fine." Caleb gazes at me. "I'll do it."

I'm momentarily caught off guard and I shake my head. "No, don't worry about it. I've got this."

His gaze flickers for a moment, then he reaches for the bottle of Scotch. I chew on my bottom lip. I don't love how it feels to be someone's reason to drink, especially when that person usually sticks to one glass of wine, at the most. So when he takes a third shot, I decide to intervene.

"Really, Caleb," I say, alarmed. "Forget it. I don't need you or anyone else to be some kind of sacrificial lamb. I'm a strong, independent woman, perfectly capable of figuring this out—"

"It's not a big deal," he interrupts. Determination sets in his eyes, as though he knows he's about to enter the battlefield and may never return.

"I don't need you to play the hero," I say, shaking my head. "I can save myself."

"I know you can." Something flickers in his eyes. An emotion I couldn't even begin to name. "But why should you have to?"

We stare at each other for a long moment until I grow uncomfortable and look away. I realize that everyone at the table has been watching our exchange like we're a Superbowl game with only seconds left on the clock.

"Do you—" I start. I rub my neck, wondering why this is so hard. "I mean, do you even want to get married anytime soon?"

From what I know, he hasn't dated since moving into the *eruv,* and it's definitely not from a lack of offers. What I do know, thanks to Zevi, is that Caleb isn't a virgin. He's had his share of girlfriends over the years, although they never seem to stick around for any significant length of time.

He hesitates. "Sure."

"Did you see that? He hesitated," Sissel whispers.

Caleb frowns. "No, I didn't."

"You did," Isser says, and Miri nods. Zevi is, of course, too immersed in *bentching* to comment.

"Look, I hate to break it to you, sweetheart," Sissel says to Caleb. "But you're not getting any younger. Nobody wants their dad to shuffle in with a walker and an oxygen tank to watch them perform at their Chanukah play."

"I think I have a few more years before that happens," he says dryly.

"You're *thirty-three*," Sissel says in a daunting tone. "Almost thirty-four."

"Which is young." He gives her his most intimidating scowl. It's the one that usually puts the fear of G-d in everyone—except of course, for the people who know him best.

Sissel leans forward. "What other lies do you tell yourself?"

"Really, it's fine," I cut in before anyone gets murdered. "I've got plenty of options."

"Yeah, yeah, we know." Sissel nods, waving a dismissive hand. "Movie tickets and dead people."

"No." I narrow my eyes at her. "I can find a Caleb-equivalent. I'm sure he isn't the *only* sought-after bachelor in this town."

Silence.

"I can't think of anyone else," Miri says.

Zevi furrows his brows. "There was the hot, rich Persian guy but he got engaged recently."

"We could try to break them up," Sissel suggests.

"Caleb was literally featured as a top bachelor in a popular mainstream magazine," Miri adds.

"He was also in the top five," Jack points out, then turns to Caleb. "Right?"

Caleb shrugs. "I don't remember. The whole thing was dumb."

"Then why did you do it?" Isser asks.

"It was good publicity for my company." The fabric of his white button-down shirt bunches as he crosses his arms and I find myself momentarily transfixed by his biceps. *It's the wine*, I tell myself. "If I had to do it all over again," he continues, "I wouldn't. It wasn't worth what came with it."

"You mean the women, don't you?" I try not to laugh, but it's hard. Zevi once mentioned in passing that Caleb had gotten more than one stalker following the magazine issue's release.

"I'm glad you find me being in danger amusing," Caleb murmurs, standing up to help clear the table.

"It's just—" I laugh. "You're a big guy. And a SEAL—"

"Nothing in the military prepares you for being chased by a group of thirty women, trying to tear your clothes off," he says primly, carrying a tray of potato kugel into the kitchen. I bend over in laughter and clutch my stomach as I visualize the scene.

Ten minutes later, the table is cleared, the after-meal prayers said, and everyone has started piling out.

"Read to me, Auntie Ashira!" Mordy shouts, running out of his bedroom and dragging me by my hand.

"Okay, okay." I laugh and kiss his cheek. "You guys go ahead," I say, with a wave to Zevi and the others. "This could take a while."

"We'll wait," Zevi says. Since driving is forbidden on Shabbos—all twenty-five hours of it—walking is the only option.

"Zevi, please. I walk around at night all the time by myself."

His eyebrows slam together. "I wish you hadn't told me that."

I laugh again, and Mordy tugs on my hand. "Goodnight!" I call, and hurry into the hall before anyone can protest.

I cuddle with Mordy in bed and after twenty minutes of reading him every construction truck book imaginable, his eyelids finally close and his breathing turns slow and even. My smile briefly falters as I think of how much my mother would have loved seeing Mordy and Golda grow up. I shove the thought into the dusty attic of my brain along with the rest of my messy emotions.

I head towards the kitchen to say goodbye to Leah and Isser. But then I see a shadow of a man standing near the hearth, and I shriek in surprise.

"Caleb," I say, putting a hand over my heart. "What are you doing here?"

"Waiting for you."

"For me?" My heart skips a beat and I swallow. "Why?"

"Because," he says, handing me my coat, "you and I are overdue for a talk."

Chapter Five

The night air is crisp and the barren trees provide little protection from the wind. The city that never sleeps is as awake as ever, and a cacophony of noises accompany us as we walk: the sounds of traffic, dogs barking, the occasional wail of a baby. And one bearded man in particular, with questionable hygiene, in the middle of a rather heated debate with himself.

I sneak a glance at Caleb, noting the seriousness in his face. It feels bizarre to walk beside him, just the two of us. I'm sure anyone passing by assumes we're a regular couple out for a late-night stroll instead of . . . well, whatever it is that we are. Not friends, but not enemies either. More than acquaintances though.

I frown. Caleb has yet to speak, but I'm certainly not going to be the one to break the silence. He said he wanted to talk, so why isn't he? He's either psyching himself up to tell me he'll agree to the matchmaking scheme but with a million conditions, or he's trying to figure out a graceful way to bow out.

I almost wish that Jack hadn't thought of this idea in the first place. I'm teetering on the precipice of sanity as it is, and this new development is pushing me precariously close to the edge.

The traffic light turns red and we come to a stop. Caleb gazes down at me through his ridiculously long eyelashes. He doesn't say anything and as the seconds tick by, my hands get clammier. Still, I'm determined not to be the one to break the silence.

A pigeon pecks at some garbage on the sidewalk behind Caleb, and it's killing me not to point it out. The silence isn't normal. And why does he keep looking at me?

"What?" I yelp, buckling under the pressure. "What is it? What did you want to talk about?"

"Us," he says simply, as if anything about that word is simple.

"Us?" The pronoun feels entirely too personal, too intimate. Not at all appropriate.

The light changes and Caleb gestures for me to resume walking.

"If we're going to work together—if you're going to be my matchmaker—we need to clear the air first."

"Uhmph," I reply. Which about sums up my feelings on the topic.

"I've been picking up on some hostile vibes," he says, "starting about fifteen years ago."

"Have you tried burning sage? That might do the trick."

"Jews don't burn sage. Only brisket and kugels."

I almost smile. "Yes, I hear that, but," I wave in his direction, "I feel like you need all the help you can get."

"Reading the antagonism loud and clear, Tinsel," he sighs. "But I still don't know why."

Okay, clearly, one of us is quite stupid. And so far, all signs are pointing at him.

"Beautiful time of year, don't you think?" I say, sticking my hands into my coat's pockets. "Not too cold, not too warm."

"I'm starting to wonder if you missed your calling as a meteorologist based on how often you bring up the weather."

Laughter slips out of me, and I quickly try to cover it up with a cough.

"It feels like there's a huge wall between us, Tinsel," he says in a quiet voice, "and you're doing everything you can to keep it there. And for the life of me, I can't figure out what I've done wrong." He pauses and I feel the heaviness of his gaze. "So I'm going to need you to spell it out for me."

Any idiot with half a brain would know why I'm mad, and Caleb is as far from an idiot as it gets. How dare he pretend to be one? That's my brand.

He stops on the sidewalk to face me. "Why are you mad?"

"I'm not." The words fly out of my mouth automatically.

He gives me a look. "I think we both know that's a lie."

"Do we?"

"Want me to walk you back through a timeline of evidence to help jog your memory?"

"I'd rather you offer me a bribe instead."

He gives me a faintly amused but mostly exasperated gaze. Even as a kid, I used humor as a shield. Joking was my armor against things that made me uncomfortable or sad. Nothing could be so terrible as long as I found a way to laugh about it. Even if it was usually in my own head.

"Ashira—" he begins, but I cut him off.

"I take Zelle, Venmo, PayPal, Apple Cash—"

"How is it possible to have the appearance of a grown adult and yet be stuck in a child's state of mind?"

I gaze at him innocently. "I'm just trying to help." But the truth is that I can't let him in. I can't allow myself to be vulnerable with the man who crushed my spirit all those years ago. I refuse.

"You know what?" he says, continuing to walk. "I'm just about crazy enough to offer you money if you promise to stop joking and take this conversation seriously for two minutes."

The problem, I realize, is that I *want* to let him in. I miss Caleb. I miss our friendship. And it terrifies me.

"It doesn't have to be money, per se," I reply. "I'm not that mercenary. It could be a designer handbag of my choosing. Or a cute pair of boots."

"You don't say," he drawls.

"Oh, but I do." I nod. "Just the other day, I found the most adorable secondhand pair of Louboutins on eBay, and in surprisingly *fantastic* condition—"

"If I had to choose," he cuts in, "I'd rather talk about the weather."

"They're knee-length and shiny, black patent leather. Now, they are stilettos, which do of course require attention to detail as to where you're stepping. If you're not vigilant, you can find yourself stuck in sidewalk cracks or sinking into grass, so you have to really know what you're doing in order to—"

"Tinsel," he exhales slowly. "You and I were close once. Remember?"

I can't bring myself to respond, but at least I refrain from yapping on about the boots. Baby steps.

He glances at me. "I made sure you did your homework and ate your vegetables."

"Still traumatized from that."

"—I made sure to keep you safe—"

"—No one asked you to—"

"—You were like a little sister to me—"

"—I'll have to take your word for it—"

"—I would've taken a bullet for you—"

"You dying would've been an easier pill to swallow than disappearing out of nowhere," I say hotly, my repressed emotions rising to the surface. My mouth drops open, shocked by the words that flew out. Caleb looks equally stunned.

Yet now that I've started, I seem unable to stop. "You disappeared overnight, you abandoned me—"

His head rears back as if I had slapped him. "It wasn't like that—"

"*It was exactly like that.*"

"I wrote you a letter—"

"Oh, yes." I laugh and pick up the pace. "The letter that explained your abandonment. How kind of you. It made you *slightly* better than my father."

"You don't mean that," he says horrified, stopping on the sidewalk.

"Of course I mean it," I reply hotly. "Did it not occur to you that you left just like my father had?"

He sucks in a sharp breath. "I didn't leave remotely like that jackass did—"

"*Yes, you did!*" I'm so revved up that I don't realize my voice is raised until I notice people staring.

"Then you obviously have amnesia," he retorts, also raising his voice, "so let me remind you of a few facts."

"My memory is fine, thank you."

He looks like he's debating a few options, none of which end well for me. "Fact number one," he says in a low, even-tempered voice, "every time I tried calling that first year, you refused to come to the phone."

"You weren't calling to speak to me, you were calling for Zevi," I say, reliving the hurt. I resume walking, and so does he. "I was an afterthought. A chore. Your personal charity project that you could do to pat yourself on the back."

"Why would you think that? You've never been any of those things to me," he says, eyes flashing at me in anger. "Never."

"Never?"

"Never," he repeats. "Not even when you started a fire in my parents' kitchen and I took the blame for it."

"Well, that was kind of your fault," I feel the need to point out. "Who leaves a seven-year-old in a kitchen with the stovetop on?"

"I had to pee, and I expressly told you not to touch anything."

"And you thought I'd listen?" I make a *psshh* sound and shake my head.

"You were never any of those things. Not even when you called Aviva and told her I had a crush on her," Caleb continues.

"You're welcome, by the way. It worked out for you, didn't it?" Aviva was his first official girlfriend, and he brought her to the house on several occasions. I always felt a smug sort of pride knowing that I played a role in bringing them together. A born matchmaker, my mother had called me.

"Why did you guys break up, anyway?" I ask.

"It was so long ago." He shrugs. "I can't remember."

"I wish you had talked with me first. I've saved a lot of couples from splitting up."

"I have no doubt that you're excellent at your job now, Tinsel, but since you were twelve at the time—"

"Convenient excuse," I sniff.

"It is, isn't it? Fact number two," he continues brusquely, "I wrote to you. Both email and paper mail. I even included stickers," he adds. "Do you think it was easy to leave the barracks when you're in pain from all the physical ass-kicking to then drive around until you find a store that sells bunny stickers? Do you know how rare bunny stickers are?"

I pause. I hadn't known that there were stickers in his letters because I threw them in the trash without opening them. My heart softens. And bunny stickers, no less. I did have a thing for collecting those.

And yet, I've held on to this resentment for almost two decades. I'm not ready to forgive his abandonment that easily.

"Not even around Easter?"

"Fine, yes, one month out of the year, Tinsel. Good point." He casts me a disparaging glance.

"I'm just saying, you could've bought in bulk."

He mutters something under his breath that sounds suspiciously like "Un-fucking-believable."

"Or you could've bought dog stickers," I remark. "I liked those too." But his glower prompts me to put up my hands and mumble, "Sorry, sorry. And thank you."

"You're welcome." He gives a stiff nod. "Fact number three, I came to see you on my first visit home, and what did you do?"

"I think it's supposed to be cloudy tomorrow," I say, desperately trying to change the subject.

"You opened your bedroom door and tried to beat me with an iron hanger. I still have a scar in fact."

I look at him horrified. "You do?"

He starts unzipping his jacket. "I'll show you."

"No, don't!" I glance around, panicked. "I believe you. Just . . . Please keep your clothes on. And I'm sorry about that. I really am."

He gives a brief nod of acknowledgement, then continues. "Fact number four, it was Zevi's idea not to tell you ahead of time. He said you'd be sad and try to change my mind, and that you'd get over it faster as long as I sent you stickers and candy."

"Wait—" I pause on the sidewalk and shake my head. "It was Zevi's idea?"

He nods. "Ask him if you don't believe me."

The wall I built slowly starts to chip. I'm beginning to realize that my perception of the past is misconstrued where Caleb is concerned. Maybe I had been reliving the pain of my father's abandonment and taking it out on Caleb. I was seven years old when he left and never sorted out my emotions. My mother was too much of a wreck herself and was just trying to survive on a day-to-day basis, and Leah and Zevi were in no shape to help me.

The only advice I got came from my paternal grandmother. Someone quite odd and definitely not all there. "You know my trick?" she said to me after she found me crying in my room one day. "I take all the bad feelings, pack them in a suitcase, and store them in the attic!"

"What attic?" I said confused.

"This one," she said, tapping the side of her head. "And then you lock it up—" she mimed it as she spoke—"And throw away the key," she finished, pretending to fling a key over her shoulder. Then she spread her hands wide and trilled, *"Taaaah daaaah!"*

I know now that this wasn't the healthiest advice. But I took it anyway, and discovered that life was easier when you lived on autopilot. Existing without feeling helped me survive the hardest years of my life. Now, at twenty-eight years old, I find myself unwilling to open that attic door. I'm not a fan of pain.

"You actually sent me candy?" I say, clearing my throat.

"A green Laffy Taffy with every letter."

"My favorite." I smile sadly. "Such a waste."

He turns to me abruptly. "Didn't you get my letters?"

"Uhm. Yes." I nod. "But also . . . no?"

"Explain the 'no' part."

"I threw them out without opening them." His eyes narrow and I rush to add, "But if I could go back in time, I definitely would. Actually," I joke, tilting my head, "it probably wouldn't have helped anyway since I hadn't evolved yet to accept bribes."

He mutters something unintelligible under his breath and I bite back a smile.

"And you should've known better than to listen to Zevi," I say, sidestepping a questionable substance on the sidewalk. "He avoids confrontations like they're a life-threatening disease. This is the guy who was going to *marry a woman* just to avoid telling my mother that he's gay."

Caleb chuckles. "Yeah, that was dumb of me."

We walk in silence for a while, both lost in our thoughts. I hadn't realized how much he cared. I didn't know that in my effort to protect my heart, I hurt his. And if I were to be completely honest, I wasn't being fair to him. He had just turned eighteen and was just a kid himself, trying to live his truth. My resentment slowly melts away and it feels surprisingly good too. I feel lighter somehow.

But.

Forgiving someone is very different to trusting them, I remind myself. And even though I understand the past in a new light, there's no taking back the fact that he still left. He still signed up for a lifestyle where he'd be absent from my life, aside for a few weeks a year. He still left the Orthodox way of life. It's hard to trust someone who one day picks up and becomes a different person.

Who's to say that he wouldn't do it again? Who's to say that he wouldn't have a midlife crisis and abandon his wife and kids to chase some childhood dream of becoming a rockstar? After all, the biggest predictor of the future is the past.

"Looking back," Caleb says, breaking into my thoughts, "I think I was afraid that I'd take one look at your sad face and crumble."

I blow out a long breath. "I'm sorry, Caleb. I shouldn't have given you such a hard time. And," I add, swallowing against a sudden lump in my throat, "you're not like my father."

He looks equal parts hopeful and suspicious. "Do you mean that?"

I nod. Mostly, anyway. "And you don't have to buy me the boots."

He laughs and shakes his head as we continue walking. "I'll get them anyway."

"Well, luckily for you," I say, with a teasing smile, "I do accept peace offerings."

"That is lucky." His eyes dance with humor. "So," he pauses and casts me a glance, "are we good?"

"We're good." I smile. I can talk about other things besides the weather with him now. I just need to remember to keep my heart at a safe distance, that's all. That way, if he disappears again and moves across the country, or even the world, it won't be a catastrophe. It'll just be a bummer. Like that twinge of irritation when you realize you left something important at home, but know that it's not the biggest deal.

"Good." I nod. "So now that we've got that out of the way," I say. "Tell me what you're looking for in a wife."

"Right. The thing is," he pauses and runs his hand through his thick hair, "there's one more catch."

Chapter Six

I groan. I *knew* it. "What?"

He puts his hands in his pockets and stares into the distance. "It's no secret that you're an attractive woman."

I'm so caught off guard that I almost walk into a streetlight. What the— I tilt my head and stare at him. *Is he hitting on me?*

"If you weren't Orthodox, you'd probably be on some runway in Paris. Or on a magazine cover."

OMG. He's definitely hitting on me. I almost laugh at the ridiculousness of it. Except it's not funny because now I have to say no, and now it's going to be even more awkward to be his matchmaker.

And then suddenly, out of nowhere, and *without my consent*, my mind generates a series of images. Caleb pinning me in place with his eyes. Caleb gently placing his lips over mine. Caleb's tongue slipping into my mouth and—

I shudder.

From disgust. Yes, definitely from disgust.

"So when I tell you that your diet and lifestyle concern me," Caleb continues, completely oblivious to where my mind had been, "it has nothing to do with how you look, but everything to do with your health.

Because being gorgeous on the outside doesn't mean you can't still wind up getting sick. Like your mom," he adds quietly.

I blink. I know I heard the word gorgeous, but it was sandwiched in the most confusing way. I shake my head. "What?"

"I'm not saying that your mom got sick because of her lifestyle, I don't want you to think that. All I'm saying is it couldn't hurt to do everything possible to live cleanly."

I shake my head again. There's so much to unpack here. He thinks I'm gorgeous and that I have an unhealthy lifestyle, and that my mom might've died because she was the same way?

And what does living cleanly mean, anyway? I suppose it's too much to hope that he's referring to hygiene.

"So, I thought we could make a deal," he says.

I glance at him wearily. "What kind of deal?"

"I'll hire you as my matchmaker, as long as you take on some healthier habits."

My eyebrows shoot up. I don't like the sound of that *at all*. "Like what?"

"We'll start slow—"

There's that pronoun again. "What do you mean *we*?"

"I'll be your support buddy and health coach." He catches the look on my face and adds, "Stop panicking, Tinsel. It's not that bad. I do this all the time, you know."

"Oh really? How many other matchmakers have you tried to blackmail?"

"This isn't blackmail."

"Well, it's something," I mutter.

"I volunteer for an organization that helps rehabilitate wounded veterans," he says. "If they can do it, you can do it."

"That is such a false comparison, and an insult to soldiers everywhere," I say, to which he laughs.

"It's a fair trade. I'll hire you as my matchmaker and in return, you'll get health lessons. As a matter of fact," he says, eyes lighting up, "there's a marathon coming up in five months that I was planning on doing. It's to help raise money for heart disease research in women."

For a moment, I'm speechless. "Is that because of . . ."

"Your mother," he finishes with a nod. "Zevi was supposed to run it with me, but he dropped out of training. Too busy working on getting his latest project off the ground. I think it's some kind of reality dating show."

I nod. Reality dating shows are all the rage nowadays, and Zevi tends to skip the gym when he's making a pilot to pitch to all the major networks.

"Why don't you join me instead?"

My head abruptly swings in his direction. "Pardon?"

"The time frame isn't ideal," he continues, unaware of my growing dread. "Training should ideally start six months in advance for a beginner. But you're not one to back down from a challenge, right?"

"Only because no one's challenged me to run twenty-six miles before," I say. The very idea of it makes me feel ill. "I definitely don't mind turning this challenge down."

"I get it." He nods.

Whew. "I'm so glad—"

"Just like I don't mind saying no to a bunch of blind dates."

I gaze at him in horror. *Uuugh*. This man. And just when he was starting to get on my good side, too.

"That isn't—you—" I'm so upset that I can't get out a full sentence.

"I just thought of a way to make this even more interesting."

"No, no." I shake my head. "It's plenty interesting enough as it is."

"We could have our own race, and see who accomplishes their goal first If I get engaged before the five months are up, I win, and you win if you run the marathon before I'm engaged. It's basically a win either way for you," he adds.

He's evil. He knows I can't walk away from something that has the word *win* attached.

So," he smiles, resting his shoe on one of the front steps, "do we have a deal?"

I cross my arms. All frustrations aside, this might be exactly what I need to get my health back on track. There have been times when I forced myself to exercise and eat things like walnuts and berries instead of donuts and chocolate milk, but I've never stayed consistent.

"The problem is me," I finally say. "I'm not disciplined."

He nods. "I'll help you."

"I can be stubborn."

"So can I." His dark brown eyes glint with challenge, reminding me how competitive we both were as children. I was a shockingly good ping-pong player despite the height discrepancy, and there were times when both Zevi and Caleb refused to quit playing until they beat me.

If there was ever a game worth playing, it's this one.

"Okay, Kahn." I nod. "Deal."

In the non-Orthodox world, we'd probably shake hands at this point, but touching the opposite sex isn't allowed in our community. Except for immediate family members and grandparents, you're not even supposed to give someone a high-five. You can't even touch your fiancé until the glass is broken under the wedding canopy. Being *shomer negiah* is so ingrained in my purview that I rarely stop to think about it.

But standing here with Caleb, under the cover of a beautiful night sky, I imagine slipping my hand into his and feeling the heat of his touch. I wonder how much pressure he would apply. He seems like the type who'd give a strong handshake, firm and confident.

Gaaagghh. What was in the wine tonight?

"Okay, then." I clear my throat. "Now tell me what you're looking for in a wife."

He shakes his head. "It's late, and," he dips his chin at my house, "you're home."

"Oh no, you don't." I shake my head. "You don't get to avoid this part of the conversation."

"It's late," he repeats.

"Are you going to turn into a pumpkin at the stroke of midnight?"

"—It's dark—"

"—So what?"

"—I have to get up early to go to shul—"

I point my finger at him. "You're coming inside and you're going to answer my questions, and I will tell you when you can go. Otherwise, the deal is off," I call over my shoulder as I climb the front steps.

"Ashira," he says, hurrying after me. "Stop. This is a terrible idea." I ignore him as I unlock the door. He rants about how inappropriate this is, how unnecessary, and *yichud* this and *yichud* that. He's awfully jumpy about being in a house alone with the opposite gender considering the fact that he wasn't *shomer* at all for fifteen years. Maybe even longer. I'm pretty sure I caught him holding Aviva's hand once or twice.

"I'll leave the door ajar, okay?" I say. "Or would you prefer it all the way open? You seem nervous."

"I'm not nervous. I'm concerned for your reputation," he says, crossing his arms. "Don't you think inviting a man into your house late at night where anyone can see would be the nail in your coffin?"

He's right, of course. And if I hadn't had a few glasses of wine tonight and if I didn't feel like he was trying to get out of our deal, I probably wouldn't be doing this.

"Can I take your coat?" I offer.

"No, I'm good."

I shrug off mine, feeling slightly self-conscious as he watches. The fabric of this dress is clingier than what most would consider *tznius*, but it's cute and hey, at least it covers my elbows and knees.

"Do you have any potato chips?" Caleb says abruptly, turning in the direction of the kitchen.

Potato chips? Is he having some kind of early midlife crisis?

He opens the cupboard and frowns. "Did you move the junk food?"

"Yes, two decades ago." I pull open a different cabinet and gesture inside. "I've got a whole array of flavors. Help yourself."

"Thanks."

I sit at the kitchen table and watch as he selects salt and vinegar, and digs in. This is so wrong. The man sees junk food like other people view arsenic.

Understandably, I'm concerned.

Is it because he's alone in the house with me? Or because I'm making him answer a few questions about what he's looking for in a wife? Because this is the easy part. The blind dates are what sucks. It's like getting a root canal, but at least then you're given laughing gas to help ease the pain. With blind dates, you take so much time getting ready and putting your best self out there, only to either be disappointed by your date or have them reject you. Unless, of course, it's a match. Even then it usually collapses by the second or third date.

And dating for marriage comes with high stakes. Everything is *forever.* Like, is this the person I want to wake up with *forever*? Is this the person that I want to *forever* parent my children with? And most importantly, is this the person that I'll want to have sex with *forever*?

All of which is hard to determine when there's no touching of any kind allowed. Until you're officially married, at which point, you immediately go from your first kiss to your first time together—once the wedding is over, that is. Depending on who you talk to, it's either incredibly romantic or incredibly awkward.

And unless you're more modern, it's frowned upon to take too long to decide; the longer you're together, the more likely you are to find things to fight about. Plus, the temptation to touch each other gets harder the longer you're around the person.

So, I get where he's coming from. But still . . .

"Aren't you concerned about the amount of chemicals in there?" I say, pointing to the bag.

"I'm trying very hard not to think about it."

"Caleb, stop, you're better than this," I say, moving to pull the bag away, but his reflexes are quick and he slides it out of my reach. I frown and watch him take another big handful. "Why are you doing this?"

"I'm not allowed to eat chips?"

"It's a sign of a mental breakdown, and I'm afraid it's because of me."

He leans back in the chair and crosses his arms. "I wouldn't call eating chips a sign of a mental breakdown."

"It is for you." I watch him pop another few into his mouth, and I add in a warning voice, "Don't make me tell you how many calories are in one serving."

"One hundred and forty. And I don't care."

"You seem a little . . ." I stop and chew on my lower lip, wondering how to word it. "Don't you want to get married?" I ask for the second time tonight. Because something isn't adding up here.

"Of course." A flash of emotion skitters across his eyes as he lifts them to meet mine.

And then without permission—it's *always* without permission—my mind takes me back to a night five years earlier when Caleb's mom had invited me to her and her husband's twenty-fifth wedding anniversary. I didn't want to go, but I also couldn't *not* go after I saw the challenge in Caleb's eyes.

After dinner, I volunteered to do the dishes and Caleb joined me. I reminded myself to keep my distance, that he was nothing but trouble, but before long, we fell into our old rhythm of teasing and chatting.

Although it was different, too. Our eyes caught here and there, lingered an extra beat. There was something in the air.

Everyone else had left by that point, and Caleb's parents sat on the couch drinking champagne and going through old photo albums.

"I think your parents have the best marriage I've ever seen," I said, passing him a wet plate.

"Yeah." He stood beside me at the sink, his hip against the counter. "I think it helped they were friends first."

I nodded. I'd heard the story of how they met countless times. Caleb's mother had been one of the thousands of Jewish Ethiopian children rescued in a daring mission called Operation Moses carried out by the Mossad. She'd met her future husband, Dr. Yishai Kahn, in Israel at the age of twenty when he had taken a gap year and she had been a guest speaker at an event commemorating the operation. They had a common interest in medicine and ended up becoming friends. By the time she was offered a scholarship at the Albert Einstein College of Medicine and he'd been accepted into NYU's Grossman School of Medicine, they were already married and somewhat Orthodox, *and* raising six-year-old Caleb.

And the rest, as they say, is history.

"I agree," I said, pumping more soap onto the sponge. "It's nice to have that strong foundation to start off with."

"Although," he said, after a pause. "It can be tricky too."

I turned to look at him. "What do you mean?"

"If you cross that line and it doesn't work out, it's impossible to go back."

"True." I handed him a glass. "Sad, but true."

"What would you do?"

I tilted my head. A few strands of hair came loose from my ponytail and fell across my face, and I used the back of my sudsy hand to swipe the hair back. "What do you mean?"

"I mean," he said slowly, leaning closer and dabbing some leftover suds off my face with the dish towel, "what would you do if you developed an attraction to a friend?"

Chapter Seven

My body understood what was happening before I did. My pulse fluttered. My stomach fluttered. A minute later my brain caught on, and then it fluttered too. Then my eyes dropped to Caleb's lips. I couldn't help imagining how it would feel to have them pressed against my own. More shockingly, I realized that I wanted to.

"I—" I swallowed, suddenly confused by my body's reaction to having Caleb this close. Was I having a hypersexual crisis? Was that even a thing?

"I don't know," I murmured, as my cheeks burned with heat.

His eyes pooled with intensity. My back was pressed against the sink and he put a hand on either side of me, effectively trapping me. My breathing quickened with excitement. Then he tilted his head and whispered in my ear, "When you figure it out, let me know."

But my hormones had already figured it out and were busy shouting step-by-step instructions. *Find the nearest room with a lock. Tear off his shirt Tarzan-style. Dance naked to Meghan Trainor's 'All About That Bass'.*

Such a good song.

But then the Judge Judy in my head banged her gavel and barked, "*Unless you suddenly changed your mind about marriage, maintain a minimum of fifty feet from his Royal Hotness at all times."*

Had I changed my decision to never get married? No, I definitely hadn't. I'd long since decided heartbreak wasn't worth the risk, not now and not ever. I'd seen how my father's abandonment destroyed our once happy home. I spent countless nights in bed, unable to fall asleep, worried that I'd wake up and discover that my mother had vanished too. I remember watching Zevi pretend to be sick so he wouldn't have to go to shul on Shabbos and sit alone in the men's section. I saw how matchmakers treated Leah differently because she came from a broken home—it was another reason why my mother wanted to become a matchmaker. She wanted to help level the playing field for those with extenuating circumstances.

And if the fairytales my father read to me were true, that love was always the answer, then what did that say about my father? Had he lied all those times he said he loved me? Or was love not always the answer?

I didn't know. But I knew that the girl who was abandoned by her father grew into the woman who didn't trust men to stick around.

Which meant no nude dancing to 'All About That Bass'.

Caleb drew back and searched my face. He'd always been perceptive and all the more so when it came to me. I don't know what he saw in my eyes, but he cleared his throat and stepped back.

And that was that.

The rustling of the chip bag snaps me back to the present.

I watch him chow down like there's no tomorrow and it makes me feel guilty by association. "Do you want some Vitamin C with that?" I ask, getting up. "I think I have orange juice in the fridge."

"Orange juice is nothing but glorified soda."

"I guess I won't offer you a Coke then." I fill up a glass of water and hand it to him. "Gotta keep hydrated in this weather," I joke, gesturing to the window where the wind howls against the pane.

"Are we back to discussing the weather?"

I shake my head and smile.

My mind drifts to the years that have passed since the night of that anniversary dinner. I know he asked Zevi about me over the years. But I was back to being annoyed with him, and couldn't help but wonder if he saw that night as some cheap opportunity to mess around with a virgin. I didn't trust him, and I was grateful that I had the sense not to listen to my hormones and lunge myself at him the way I wanted to. But I think about that night more often than I'd like. And sometimes I find myself wondering if he does too.

I clear my throat. Time to put on my matchmaker hat. "I'll try to keep this process as pain-free as possible."

"Considerate of you."

I smile. "So," I say, "what are you looking for in a woman?"

He reaches for more chips. "I don't know."

I give him a long, hard stare. If he thinks he's going to get away without answering this question, he should think again. "You must have a general idea."

"Not really."

"Nothing at all?"

"Well," he taps his fingers against the tabletop, "I'd prefer someone who doesn't hate football."

I look at him funny, wondering if that's supposed to be a dig at me. I hate football. It's stupid and violent and shortens the players' lifespans. Not to mention the fans whose blood pressure spikes when their team loses. "O-*kay*." I paste on a bright smile. "Anything else?"

"I don't want to be dragged around malls." I force my eyes not to circle upwards. As a pre-teen, I used to beg Caleb to take my friends and me to the mall. He hated every minute of it. "And," he adds, pointing at me, "I don't want to have to fight with her about eating vegetables."

Message received.

"Let me see if I have this straight—you want someone who enjoys football, hates shopping, and loves vegetables. Is that right?"

He nods. "That about sums it up."

"So, basically," I say, "you want to marry yourself."

He chokes on a potato chip as he starts to laugh.

"Look, Caleb. Those are all great. Obviously." *Even though they seem suspiciously the exact opposite of me.* "But what about more substantial things?"

"I prefer women with darker skin and hair," he says, his eyes traveling to my light-skinned face and blonde hair. "The shorter the better."

Well, that felt personal.

"When I said substantial, Caleb, I wasn't referring to skin or hair color, or the length of her legs," I bristle.

"I didn't realize I'd be judged on what I was looking for."

I gaze at his neck and picture squeezing it. Is he trying to irritate me? Because it very much feels like he is. "What about her personality? Or *Hashkafa?*"

I've seen plenty of divorces happen because of philosophical differences and how best to observe the Torah and commandments, especially once couples start raising their children.

"I'd like her to be accepting and non-judgmental."

I nod. Finally, we're getting somewhere.

"Do you care about race?" I ask and he shakes his head. "Do you care if she comes from a broken home? Or what about *yichus?*"

"Good *yichus* would be nice," he says. "It would definitely help my kids out."

I nod. In Judaism, if the mom isn't Jewish, then the kids aren't. But having good *yichus*—coming from a long line of respectable family and Torah scholars that you can trace back all the way to the old country—brings a whole new status.

"I'm assuming that you don't want someone from a broken home then," I say lightly, careful to keep my voice absent of emotion. Even someone with good *yichus* can't overcome the stain of being a product of divorce.

It isn't fair, but few things in life are.

You'd never know it now, but at one point, my family was considered prestigious. We had money and decent *yichus*, not to mention a peaceful home filled with light and laughter. At least, that's how it seemed in my innocent and childlike mind.

"Really, it's not that important," he says, holding my gaze. If I didn't know any better, I think he was trying to reassure me not to take offense. "I'd rather have someone that I can connect with."

"Don't worry," I say firmly. "I'll find you someone who can be all that and comes from good *yichus*."

He stands up and puts the potato chips away. "Do you think someone like that would be interested in dating someone like me?" he asks, with his back to me.

"Yes. Are you kidding?" I say, taken aback by the question. "How can you even ask that?" Needing something to do, I stand up and start to sweep the crumbs that had fallen onto the floor.

"It's not as though I come from good *yichus*."

Well... He does have a point. People of well-respected lineage usually marry into similarly prestigious families.

"Your family is lovely," I say firmly. "Who cares if your dad is from an irreligious family from the Bronx, or that your mother grew up in poverty in Ethiopia and then Ramat Beit Shemesh?" I say, waving my hands. "She's freaking *amazing*, and your dad is a total sweetheart." Needing something to do with my hands, I take his spoon to the sink and run it under soapy water. "Seriously now. How many people can say that their mother is the director of neurology at Mount Sinai Hospital? Or that their father is an electrophysiologist at NYU?"

"I appreciate what you're doing here, Tinsel, but that's not what counts as good *yichus*."

"Good *yichus* can kiss my ass," I say, pointing my finger at him. "Your family is awesome, full stop."

But no matter what I think, conventional standards within the greater community might disagree. Caleb's paternal side consists of agnostic Jews and his maternal side is made up of Ethiopian-Israelis. He isn't exactly what people think of when *yichus* comes to mind.

The fact that he moved from Israel to America at seven was another huge adjustment. Kids laughed when he read certain Hebrew letters with the "T" sound rather than the "S", or pronounced words with "Oh" instead of the Ashkenazi "Oi."

Caleb nods, then gazes into the distance, lost in thought. "It's funny, but in some ways, despite all of our success," he says, "I'm still that scared little boy from Israel with the dark-skinned mom."

"All of which are things to be proud of," I say, scowling. I put the broom away and use a rag to scrub at a food stain on the counter. I'm getting pissed off, but I'm not sure at who. All I know is that humans make things so much more complicated than they have to be.

"Agreed. But it doesn't change the fact that I felt different growing up, or that at times I still—" He stops abruptly and rubs the back of his neck.

"You still feel different?" I say, after a pregnant pause.

"Of course," he says so quietly that's almost hard to make out. "But it's more than that too. It's this feeling of not belonging. Not fully," he adds with a shake of his head.

"I'm sorry, Caleb." They're empty words that accomplish nothing, yet I feel compelled to say them anyway.

He waves his hand. "Don't apologize. Your family never questioned the validity of our Judaism or made us feel anything other than loved and accepted. And there were many others too, of course," he adds. "But," he shrugs and smiles grimly, "it's the negative messages that we hear loudest."

I nod. Why is it that most people can be kind and loving, yet the ones who aren't carry the greater impact? It's as if our brains are wired to believe whatever validates our biggest fears rather than what boosts our confidence.

He stands up and does a questionably fake yawn. "Anyway, I better get going. But I think you've got a pretty good idea of what I'm looking for."

I try not to show my disappointment. Just when I get a glimpse into the real Caleb, vulnerabilities and all, he runs away.

"Sure. It's a start anyway." I glance at his perfect body as I follow him out of the kitchen. "I hope your body survives the chemical warfare you gave it."

He chuckles and runs his hand down his face. "I can't believe I did that."

"You are a very naughty man," I say. He quirks an eyebrow at me over his shoulder and I blush. How did that come off as dirty when it sounded perfectly innocent in my head?

"Stop overthinking, Wernick," he says, zipping up his coat. "I know what you meant."

The rush of relief I feel is admittedly, pathetic.

"Have a good night," he says, opening the door.

"Caleb—" I stop him, and when he turns around, I have no idea what I meant to say. I only know that I enjoyed his company tonight, and it made me realize how much I regret letting our friendship go for so many years. "I just wanted to say that I'm glad you're back."

He gazes at me, confused. "In Brooklyn?"

"Yes. No." I shake my head. "I mean, yes, that too, but also, here." I gesture in the space between us. "With me."

A slow smiles spreads across his face. "There's nowhere else I'd rather be," he says softly.

And somehow, that small, little statement lights a path straight to my heart.

Chapter Eight

It's Sunday morning, and my dream is interrupted by pounding on my door. I groan and drag a hand down my face. I'm getting too old for this.

"Coming, I'm coming," I croak, my voice still slightly hoarse. I unlock the door and open it to find my longtime neighbor on the stoop. "Shouldn't you still be sleeping?" I say by way of greeting.

"Someone's got a bad case of bedhead." Bernice chuckles as she steps inside. "A little mousse and a comb can go a long way, you know."

"Yes, well." I rub the aching spot on my forehead that always coincides with my neighbor's arrival. "I was sleeping until two seconds ago when someone started hammering on my door."

"That's why you should give me a key," she replies. "Then I wouldn't have to wake you up."

Not in this lifetime.

I take in Bernice's appearance —somewhat-brushed gray hair, face devoid of makeup, the flowered housecoat with food stains.

"You're in flats?" I say, my hand flying to my mouth. On her feet are a very sensible pair of sneakers and frankly, I feel traumatized by the sight of them.

"What do you expect?" she says defensively. "I'm almost a hundred years old."

"Don't give me that." I close the door behind her, and put my hands on my hips. "You're the youngest, hippest seventy-eight-year-old I've ever met."

"Not anymore, I'm not."

"I've had it," I say, reopening the door. "Go back home and change into something more appropriate. The next time I see you, you better be wearing sequins and red lipstick."

"This is the new Bernice," she says, lifting her chin. "She embraces her age and being natural. She doesn't need to cover herself with makeup or dress like a Vegas showgirl."

"But it's who you are—in here," I argue, pounding my chest. "It's what makes you light up inside."

"This is my new identity, so you better start embracing it."

I sigh. I still can't get used to her new appearance. Up until her husband's death eight months ago, she loved getting dolled up every day. She'd even have a face full of makeup just to take out the garbage. At four-foot-ten, she claimed her four-inch wedge heels were less about fashion and more about functionality, but I knew better. She went regularly to the salon to dye her roots platinum blonde. Every first of the month, she got a mani-pedi to swap her fake nails for a new dazzling color and print.

And though her black leather miniskirts and shiny go-go boots might've seemed at odds with the reading glasses around her neck or the brown age spots on her hands, she *worked it*.

She used to work out too. She did everything from Pilates, to yoga, to tai chi and whatever else people who enjoy pain do.

But then her husband died, and her zest for life went with him. She rarely leaves her house anymore—except to come to my place, which she's been doing increasingly often. She only wears floral housecoats and her gray hair is showing. It's like she scoured the internet for a senior citizen costume.

But seeing her now in a pair of flats—that's a whole never level of despair.

"And stop obsessing about me," she adds, walking into the kitchen. "You've got your own problems. You gotta get moving if you want kids. Your clock is already halfway broken."

"Even a broken clock is right twice a day," I quip.

She makes a face as she shuffles to the refrigerator. "Not in this instance, it isn't."

"I don't want children," I remind her. Not really. Sure, once in a while, I think it would be nice, but I always manage to talk myself out of it. When my mother was still alive, I went out with some men to make her happy. I never told her that I'd long ago decided that I would never get married. I didn't want her dying thinking I'd be alone.

"Make yourself at home," I say, watching Bernice raid my refrigerator.

"I had four children by the time I was your age," she adds.

A fact she likes to remind me of often.

"Coffee?" I ask, pressing the power button of my Keurig, last year's joint Chanukah present from Miri and Sissel.

"Now we're talkin'." She pulls out a half-eaten pizza bagel from yesterday's lunch and takes a bite, crumbs falling out the corners of her mouth. I come over with the broom and start sweeping, then follow it up by taking my handheld vacuum and shoving it inside the toaster.

"Why are you always cleaning?"

Because I'm always anxious. Whenever I feel unsettled or irritated, I clean. And I don't just clean. I clean like the royal family is coming to stay and I have thirty minutes until their arrival. I get on my hands and knees and scrub every inch of the floor, peek under every cranny, and polish the silver.

It started when my mother became too sick to take care of household chores. I discovered that cleaning was an escape, a way to tune out the stress and focus only on the job at hand. And although I couldn't control the mess of losing my mother, I could control how clean the house was.

It wasn't everything, but it was something.

"It's calming," I say.

"It isn't normal," Bernice remarks between bites of her pizza bagel. "Never in my seventy-eight years in this world have I seen someone vacuum inside a toaster."

"Watch it, you're next," I say, waving the vacuum at her as crumbs fall from her mouth.

Bernice isn't ready to date, but that hasn't stopped me from searching anyway. It isn't that I don't respect her feelings or understand her need to mourn. It's more that I don't see the harm in looking.

Also, there's a serious shortage of elderly Jewish men—especially good quality ones. I wonder if I could import a guy from another country, like those mail-order brides. I wonder if it'd be the worth the time and money. Are relationships with language barriers better or worse?

"What are you thinking about?" Bernice says, cutting into my thoughts.

"How to get you a new husband," I reply.

"Worry about finding yourself a husband. What do you wanna watch tonight?" Bernice asks, slowly getting up.

"What are the choices?" I say, returning the handheld vacuum to its charger.

"*Golden Girls* reruns or *Golden Girls* reruns."

I see the rest of my life so clearly it's frightening: Bernice and me, night after night staying home and watching the same old TV shows while my friends get married and have families of their own. It never bothered me before; in fact, I used to look forward to being Auntie Ashira to everyone's kids. I don't know where this sudden hollow feeling is coming from, but I'm thinking it's Bernice.

I could still change my mind, of course. It's not too late to get married and have babies of my own. But whenever I think about it, my throat starts to close and I get sweaty with panic. There are too many loose variables that come with marriage and children. Too many things I can't control.

Yet, I still envision it at times. I imagine growing a baby inside of me and holding it for the first time. I picture holding their tiny hand and kissing a soft cheek. I imagine rocking it in my arms and singing bedtime prayers.

"You got any toilet paper I could borrow?" Before I have a chance to respond, she's disappeared around the corner.

I shake my head and pour some creamer into the mug. In the wake of her husband's death, I've not only become her early-morning companion, but also her preferred place to shop. Which isn't ideal, but I'm willing to tolerate it if it makes her life easier.

"I thought we talked about this."

Her head suddenly peeks out from the sliding door of the hallway closet, causing me to jump.

"Sorry," I say, putting a hand over my racing heart. "What did we already talk about?"

"How sensitive my *tushie* is. You know the kind of havoc this will wreak on my fissures?" She tosses the toilet paper carelessly back onto the shelf, but it hits at the wrong angle and falls to the floor, unrolling as it goes.

"My Saul had a lot of faults, but at least the man knew the difference between Charmin Ultra and Quilted Northern. He cared about the tears in my anu—"

"Yup, okay," I interrupt, massaging my throbbing temples. "I'll be more considerate next time." I pick up the roll of toilet paper and re-ravel it as best as I can. "Saul was a good man."

"Meh. He was all right," she grumbles, heading back to the kitchen. "He had his faults like everyone else.

Sometimes people turn their dead loved ones into angels, but I promised Saul on his deathbed that I'd never do that. That I'd remember everything that was wrong with him."

"I'm sure that gave him comfort," I say, turning around so she doesn't catch me struggling not to laugh.

"When you love someone, really love someone, you gotta love their imperfections too. It's the things that you overcome as a couple that cause your love to grow, you know? So I told Saul that I'd remember him exactly as he was, faults and all."

I turn around. "That's really beautiful, Bernice."

She takes a deep breath and swipes at her eyes as she sits down at the table. I silently push a tissue box toward her, then add cream and sugar to her coffee.

I give her a sad smile. "You must miss him a lot."

"Mostly I miss not having anyone to yell at," she laughs and swipes at her cheeks.

"Oh, come on." I grin and carefully put the mug in front of her. "You yell at me all the time."

"I know." She shrugs. "But it just isn't the same."

I laugh and prepare her usual breakfast: an Ego waffle with lots of butter and maple syrup, then finish it off with a dollop of whipped cream. "Here you go, mademoiselle."

"Mmm, look at that masterpiece," she says, diving in. "You spoil me, you know that?"

"I know. So," I say, joining her at the table and taking a sip of my coffee. Aaah. *Chemical Heaven*. "What are your plans for today?"

"I was debating whether or not to take a shower."

"I vote yes."

"I was thinking of scrolling through Amazon."

"Fun. Looking for anything specific?"

"One of those toilets that come on wheels. Commodes, I think they're called."

"*Bernice.*"

"What?" She picks up her mug. "I'm not allowed to celebrate the coming days? The closer I come to end of life, the sooner I can be with Saul again."

My breath catches, and I swallow. *This*, right here, is the cruel side effect of love. Yet another reminder why I can't let myself open my heart to someone. I've been where Bernice is at. Well, not the searching for wheelie toilets on Amazon. But I've been paralyzed by grief.

"When my mother died," I say, "people told me that time heals all pain."

"Yeah, I know. I'm pretty sure I was one of them." Bernice shakes her head. "Sorry about that. Now I know it's a big fat lie."

"It is, isn't it?" I nod. "Honestly, some days I think it gets worse with time."

Bernice shakes her head. "Don't quit your day job, kid. Grief counseling doesn't suit you."

I laugh. "You're right, I suck at this."

"Eh, it's okay. You make a great cup of coffee."

"Thanks, Bernice."

"You think we need therapy?" she says.

I cringe. Nothing sounds worse than baring your soul to some stranger only to hear them tell you that you've got issues. "I don't."

She nods. "Yeah, I don't either. Therapy is for people who don't know that they're crazy yet. I already know we are, so what's the point?"

"Thanks, Bernice."

"And we don't need to talk to heal from our pain. That's what bourbon is for," she replies.

I snort a laugh. "You know what you need?" I say, getting up to wash her plate.

"A nap."

"A man," I say, waving the sponge at her.

"Not this again," she groans.

"I'm not saying that this person would replace what you had with Saul," I say, pumping soap onto the sponge. "But I really think it might help heal you."

"If that's the case, why aren't you dating?"

"It's different. My grief is for my mom." And for my dad. Not that I'd say that. There's something especially embarrassing about grieving for someone who clearly didn't love you back. And yet, I can't seem to help it.

"So what?" she says. "It might still help you."

"I will eventually," I lie, just to get her off my case. "But we're focusing on you right now, and you need to get back out there, girl. Take the bull by the horns. Get back on the saddle."

"You're mixing up metaphors," she says, handing me her empty mug. "And don't talk to me like I'm some woman who just broke up with her boyfriend," she says, crossing her arms. "I'm a *widow*. I was married to Saul for fifty-eight years."

I shut off the faucet and turn to her. A wave of shame washes over me as I realize how insensitive I've been. "I'm sorry, Bernice. I'll drop it."

"Good."

"Do you want a hug?"

"Do I look like a hug-me-Elmo doll to you—*ach!*" she squeals as I put my arms around her. "And if I do ever decide one day to go on a date, I'm dragging you with me," she adds.

"That's fine."

"And you're going to have your own man there too. It'll be a double-date."

"That's not fine," I say quickly and step back.

"I'm not interested anyway." She glances around the kitchen. "I could sell my house and move in here," she says, looking around. "It might be a squeeze to move in all my furniture, but it'll be fun. We'll keep each other company and you'll do all the cooking."

OMFG.

"And if I want sex," she adds, "I'll call your hot brother."

I don't know whether I'm more bothered by the idea of her moving in with me or her fantasizing about my brother.

"Still gay, Bernice."

She makes a face. "Still?"

"Yup." I massage my pounding temples. Living with this woman would be the death of me—or her. I could definitely see the makings for a murder-suicide.

She makes a harrumph sound. "Well, anyway. I was thinking just the other day how we'd make excellent roommates. It'd be us two old maids, kind of like *The Golden Girls*—"

"Okay, I'll do it. I'll go on a date," I say quickly. I'd walk over hot coals at this point if it helped her find someone else to move in with.

Her eyebrows rise with surprise. "Oh?" The disappointment in her voice shows that she was just messing around with me. That's her modus operandi when she's bored.

I nod. "A hundred percent."

"But this isn't for a while, if ever." She has a sudden twinkle in her eye as she adds, "and my guy better be hotter than yours."

"That goes without saying. Are we sooo excited?" I tease, gently bumping my hip against hers. "Should we get our hair and nails done and wear matching sparkly outfits?"

"You're being ridiculous. And anyway," she sniffs, "not everyone is meant to wear sequin jumpsuits."

"No," I say, tapping my chin. "I suppose not."

But my imagination goes there anyway; Bernice and I, all dolled up and wearing matching outfits and go-go boots, drinking champagne in a Porsche convertible—well, not in this weather. A stretch limo, then.

I smile as I picture introducing Bernice to her second *bashert*. There's a lot of mixed opinions in Judaism regarding soulmates, but everyone seems to agree that you can have more than one in the same lifetime. Some sages say you can have up to seven, and some say that there are two different levels of soulmates. While others believe that because there's freedom to choose, it's possible to spend your entire life without marrying your soulmate.

Imagine having *seven* possible *basherts*, and still somehow managing to screw it up.

And despite the lack of romance in my own life, I still get a thrill when I foster it for others. There's no better feeling than helping two halves of the same soul come together, and I'm buzzing now at the knowledge that there's a man out there just waiting to be introduced to Bernice. I guess you could say I live vicariously.

"You got any Desitin?"

Geez, talk about a buzzkill.

"No," I say, "isn't that for diaper rash?"

"I got diaper rash, all right. My *tushie* is as sore as an eight-day-old's penis." I cringe and she adds, "Get it? Because of the *bris*. You know how the foreskin gets—"

"*Aaaggh!* I'll go to the store now and get you some." I shoot up from my chair and make a beeline for the door. Her chortle of laughter follows me as I grab my coat and purse.

Whoever her second soulmate is, I sure hope he has a sick sense of humor.

Chapter Nine

The next ten days go from bad to worse to *OMFG, you've got to be kidding me*. Not only does Caleb show up at my house every morning at five freaking am for a run that leaves me dripping in sweat, but the matchmaking is one dead end after another. I finally get a client by introducing myself to a new woman at shul, only to find out that I have no one to set her up with because my matchmaking colleagues—women that I've worked with for *years*—will no longer talk to me. Matchmakers that I thought of as friends are suddenly ignoring my calls and texts, and others have literally crossed the street when they saw me coming. A few had the grace to apologize and explain that they've got kids to feed and a mortgage to pay. While no one was explicitly threatened, no one had to be. No one wants to risk having a Schwartz as an enemy.

In this industry, exchanging names and information is *everything*. I've gone from being, if not at the top of the matchmaking game, at least somewhere in the middle, to a lowly bottom feeder. My chances of saving Blue Moon Basherts become slimmer with each passing day.

Which is why so much is riding on tonight. Not only have I signed up for a speed dating event to recruit men for my database—and I'm taking Sissel with me to double our chances—but it's also the first blind date that I've set up for Caleb. It feels almost too serendipitous to be true. Miri's new roommate, Nayma Berliner, seems to have it all—looks, intellect, and charm. She's Sephardi and follows Persian Jewish traditions, is petite with sultry dark eyes and olive skin, and a law school student. But the best part is that she's been in love with Caleb from the moment she caught a glimpse of him at her cousin's bar mitzvah twenty years ago. She once paid her cousin thirty-five dollars to pass on a love letter she wrote, although she thinks he trashed the letter because she never heard back.

"How do I look?" Nayma asks, stepping back from the phone so I can see the full effect. But walking and FaceTiming in heels is trickier than it sounds and I catch myself moments before tripping over a crack in the sidewalk.

"Stunning," I reply. "That's a 'love at first sight' kind of dress."

"Right?" Miri says, circling Nayma with the critical gaze of a true fashionista. "Few people can wear this shade of red, but it looks amazing against your eyes and hair."

Sissel peers at the screen over my shoulder. "Are those zippers functional?"

"No," Nayma laughs. "They're just part of the design."

Sissel shakes her head in disapproval. "If I designed clothes, there would be pockets and zippers and no scratchy fabric. And no tags. I *loathe* the tags," she adds in an ominous tone.

"They're the worst," I say, patting her arm. I'm a little nervous about taking Sissel with me because ... well, she's Sissel. She has no filter and can come off as rude. But Miri couldn't come, and hopefully Sissel will be better than nothing. I've made her promise not to insult anyone tonight, but we'll see how long that lasts.

"I've got to run to finish my hair and makeup," Nayma says, blowing a kiss. "Thanks again for arranging this, Ashira."

"My pleasure." I smile. "Have fun and good luck tonight!"

"Who needs luck when you look this good?" Miri says.

"Poor Caleb might have a heart attack when he sees her," I add.

"Why?" Sissel says, taking my phone and gazing at the screen. "Has he never seen a hooker before?"

"*Sissel*," I breathe, horrified, and she looks at me, like, *what?*

"Sorry, sorry, calm down," she says, moving her hands in an up-and-down motion. "I meant a high-class one. It's a compliment," she adds when she sees my face.

"You're done," I hiss.

"Uh, thanks?" Nayma says, not looking all that flattered. "I've never been told that before."

"Is this your first time in a slutty dress?"

"O-*kay* then," I say, grabbing my phone back. "We're going to hang up now. Have fun and I expect a full report by the end of the night."

"Do you think it's slutty?" I overhear Nayma ask Miri as I hang up.

"Sissel," I say. "What did we talk about not doing earlier?"

"Not insulting the people at the singles' event."

"Well, yes, that's true. But could you also try not to insult anyone in general? Anywhere at any time?"

"That's a big ask."

"It really isn't."

"I'm like a parking meter, Ashira. I can only do a few hours at a time."

I sigh. "Let's aim for four, then."

"Fine. I'll try," she says, glancing my way. "But only because I pity you and what's become of your sad, pathetic life."

"How do I start the meter? Is there a button I can press?"

"It starts when I'm ready. Also, you look weird," she adds.

I glare up at the sky where I image G-d is smirking down at me. "First of all, Sissel," I say, "my life isn't sad. I'm just having a small bump in the road."

"More like a catastrophic collision."

"And second of all," I continue, "I have to wear a disguise so the organizer of the event doesn't recognize me."

"Yeah, but between you and me, that wig makes you look like Miss Muffet."

"That's fine."

"It's not a compliment," she adds.

"New rule," I say sharply. "You can't insult me either."

"But—"

"No."

"Can't I even—"

"*No.*"

"You really challenge our friendship sometimes, you know," she says as we turn a corner.

I pat her arm. "I believe in you."

We pass a new bodega that I haven't seen before. In case the small rectangular-shaped *mezuzah* affixed to the doorpost didn't give away that the owner was Jewish, then the name of the store would: *Bubbe's Bagels.* As with many strictly kosher establishments, there's a list of certifications on the glass front door to reassure Orthodox Jewish customers that they needn't worry that some items inside aren't kosher.

"It smells good," Sissel says, pausing on the sidewalk to peer inside.

"Want to go in?"

She glances at her watch. "Okay, but we've only got eight minutes."

"Noted," I reply and open the door. It's smaller than I had expected with a large glass display case swallowing up much of the space. Inside the case there are all kinds of bagels, along with other classic Ashkenazi fillings like lox, smoked salmon, and liver. The menu on the wall is written in colorful chalk, including foods like matzah ball soup, knishes, and kugels.

"Hi there," says a guy with a yarmulke on his head. He's got a white apron on with a nametag pinned on it that says Bruce. "How can I help you?"

"Do you have any garlic and onion bagels?" Sissel asks.

"No way," I say, catching her by the arm. "You can't have bad breath at a speed dating event."

"I'm not going to eat them now. Besides, you know I'm not actually interested in dating any of them." She turns to Bruce and says casually, "I'm asexual."

I rub my temples. I really hope she keeps that information to herself tonight.

But Bruce surprises me by saying, "Cool. What's that like? And how many of these bad boys do you want?" he asks, holding a bagel with tongs.

"Two," she replies. "And it's awesome not being attracted to anyone. It must be such a time-sucker. I'd much rather be with my friends than rubbing against someone else's genitalia."

"I'm going to wait outside," I say weakly.

Bruce meets my eyes and laughs, and it suddenly occurs to me that he's cute. I glance at his ring finger to see if he's married, even though you can't always tell because some Orthodox men don't wear wedding bands. "Any filling or did you want it plain?" he says, turning back to Sissel.

"Plain," she replies. "And that's it for me, thanks."

"All right," Bruce says, tapping the screen. "Want a receipt?"

"No thanks." She holds her Apple Watch near the scanner.

Bruce turns to me. "Anything for you?"

"I'm fine, thanks. By the way," I smile and lean my arm on the counter, "do you happen to be single?"

"Don't worry, she's not hitting on you," Sissel says as two pink circles appear on Bruce's cheeks. She grabs the small paper bag and tucks it under her arm. "She's a ruined matchmaker who needs to recruit people for her database."

"*Sissel.*"

"What?"

Bruce gazes between us, a polite, but slightly disturbed smile on his face.

"I'm not ruined," I explain. "I've just had a small setback. A tiny one." I throw Sissel a warning glance to stop her from contradicting me. "Anyway," I say, turning back to Bruce. "If you're interested, I can—"

"I appreciate the offer, but . . ." He shakes his head. "I don't do matchmakers. I mean, I don't *use* matchmakers." He blushes all over again and chuckles. "Sorry. You know what I mean."

"I know what you mean."

"Let's go, Ashira," Sissel says, opening the shop door. "I don't want to be late. My cortisol levels are already going through the roof."

"Here," I say to Bruce, sliding my business card across the counter. "In case you change your mind."

"Sorry." He shakes his head. "I won't." He takes a rag and wipes the counter down. "Do you want the card back?"

"No, keep it," I say, walking backwards. "You never know."

"Watch out," Sissel cries just as the back of my legs crash into a chair. I grimace in pain and clutch my leg.

"Don't worry, I'm okay," I call out to no one in particular. Bruce gives me a sympathetic look as I limp toward the door.

The door shuts and Sissel grins. "That was funny."

"It could've been worse," I say, in an attempt to self-soothe.

"I don't know about that."

I shrug. "You win some, you lose some."

"You lost all of yours."

"*Sissel!*"

"Sorry, sorry."

"I don't think I'll be going back there anytime soon," I say as we approach a traffic light.

"Well. I'll let you know when I've had my bagels," she replies as if their quality might be worth a return visit.

I pat her arm. "You do that."

* * *

The restaurant hosting the singles event has the perfect romantic atmosphere. The tall, plush velvet banquettes and round tables give the illusion of privacy, while the single red roses and flickering tea lights on each table lend a certain warmth to the air. Tickets for the event were forty-five dollars, and in return, participants get hors d'oeuvres, two drinks, and if they're lucky, the phone numbers of the people they matched with.

From gazing around the room, there seem to be an equal number of men and women, ranging in age from twenty to mid-thirties. Some are obviously anxious from the way they're biting their nails or how they're stooped over like they're trying to make themselves invisible. Conversely, there are the alpha males that are easy to spot because they spread their arms and legs to take up as much space as possible, or the boss women who stare at you coolly, without blinking or smiling.

I've hosted plenty of singles events in the last eight years, so I know what to expect. They're always exhausting because there's so much planning that goes into them. By the time they're over, I need at least a few days to recover.

The woman running it tonight has always been a little lukewarm toward me. She was one of the first to ignore my messages after the Schwartz fallout, so even though I'm in a disguise and using an alias, I'm still nervous that she'll figure out who I am.

She claps to get everyone's attention, and then explains what to expect. Every woman is assigned to her own table and card, and the men will rotate between them at ten-minute intervals. By the end of the night, participants hand in the cards with checkmarks next to who they liked, and if both people put down a check, then it's a match, and they're provided with each other's phone numbers.

For better or worse, I'm seated next to Sissel's table. She keeps giving me the side-eye and doing weird hand gestures to get my attention as the woman talks. I pretend not to know her and scooch a little further away.

Finally the event begins, and I straighten in my chair as the first man approaches. He's handsome and you can tell he knows it too. He's got a certain look in his eyes that screams confidence and a swagger to match.

And great taste in shoes.

"Love the cowboy boots," I say as he takes a seat. I touch the business cards in the pocket of my sweater to double-check that they're still there.

"'Course you do. I could tell the moment I laid eyes on you that you're a woman of high standards." He winks.

"I don't know about that." I smile. "I think my standards are pretty low. As long as there's no obvious food stains or holes, I'll wear it. Unless I haven't done the laundry in which case, I'll probably put on something with food stains." I take out a card and lay it on my lap. *Should I slide give it to him now or wait until the ten minutes are up?*

"Baby girl, no. A woman like yourself deserves to be in designer fashion and displayed on a pedestal."

My eyebrows lift at being called *baby girl,* but maybe it's a Southern thing? And what's with the *displayed on a pedestal* part? Do I look like a doll? "A throne, yes, but pedestal?" I shake my head. "That sounds too much like giving up my power."

"You don't need power, darlin'. What you need is a man to take care of you so that you can stay home and raise the kids."

I sit on my hands so I don't accidentally slap him. After all, there are plenty of women—and men—who thrive in the stay-at-home parent role. But this guy is setting my teeth on edge.

"What if I want to work outside the home?" I don't know why I feel the need to test him, but there's something about him that just doesn't sit right with me.

"You wouldn't need to if you had me."

"But what if I *wanted* to?"

He heaves a sigh that comes from the sole of his boots. "Careful now," he says, shaking his finger. "You're starting to sound like one of them liberated women with hairy armpits who doesn't appreciate a man's guidance."

I'm desperate for business, but not this desperate.

"You know," I say, leaning forward. "I think you might benefit from taking a deconstruction class of toxic masculinity—"

"Good Lawd," he cries, slapping the table. "Is there any woman out there that hasn't lost her damn mind? I'm sick and tired of this crap.

"How's about I just chop off my testicles and serve them up on a tray, baby girl? You'd like that, wouldn't you?"

I wrinkle my nose. "Actually, I'd prefer you sign up for the class."

"That's not going to happen, sweet thang."

I tilt my head and study him. "Are you some kind of method actor? Because you're very good if you are."

"What role would I be playing?" he says, looking bewildered.

I shrug and lift my hands. "A chauvinist pig?"

He pushes his chair back and stands up. "I think we're done here."

"It was nice meeting you. And remember what I said about those classes," I call out as he walks away. He gives a backwards swipe in the air which I take to mean that he probably won't, but hey, at least I tried. Sissel gives me a smug look as if to say *at least I haven't scared mine away.*

I write 'NO' next to the cowboy's name. Seven more minutes left. I wonder if I set a record for the shortest date ever. Oh well. You can't win them all.

Maybe the second guy will be the charm.

Chapter Ten

When the bell rings, everyone switches. The next man sits down and introduces himself as Mordechai. He's not the most attractive man in the room, but hopefully his personality will be more pleasant than my last guy.

"So, Mordechai," I smile. "Tell me what you're looking for in a wife."

"I'm not too picky," he says with an easy smile. "All I need is someone nice and loving. But I can't handle a jealous woman, and there are a lot of them out there. I couldn't go anywhere with my ex-wife without her accusing me of checking everyone out."

His eyes dip down to my chest and linger for a solid three seconds. I scribble an X next to Mordechai's name.

"And I want someone who will support me for who I am," Mordechai continues, oblivious to my X mark. "I don't want anyone trying to change me. Why is that so hard for people?" His eyes drop back to my chest, and I glance down too just to make sure there isn't a big stain.

"Do you think your ex-wife had a point?" I say, dipping my head down to get him to look at me. "Do you think you have, say, wandering eyes?"

"No. She was paranoid."

"Are you sure?"

"Of course, I'm sure." He crosses his arms and scowls.

Apparently, bringing so many business cards might have been overly optimistic.

"Are you the jealous type?" he asks. "Because it seems like you might be."

"No," I say firmly. "But I do notice when someone's eyes drift to places other than a woman's face." I give him a meaningful look.

He rolls his eyes. "You sound just like my ex-wife."

"I never met her, but I'm betting she had a point."

"Great," he replies and stands up. "Maybe she's your *bashert*."

I snort. "Well, between the two of you, I know who I'd pick."

I watch him leave. Unfortunately, he heads straight to the organizer and although I can't hear what he's saying, I can definitely guess based on his wild hand gestures in my direction.

Uh-oh.

"What on earth are you saying to these men?" Sissel asks as the bell rings.

"Nothing," I say, all innocent.

"Yeah, right," she scoffs. "Looks like I should've given *you* a speech."

"It's not my fault I'm getting jerks," I grumble. Am I being extra testy tonight, or are the pickings really that slim?

"Do your best not to insult the next one," Sissel adds in a lofty tone of voice. "It might be hard, but I believe in you."

"Shuddup," I mutter, biting back my smile.

The next guy is small and sweet and brings out my nurturing instincts. We discuss his hay fever, his allergies to penicillin and sulfa drugs, and whether the Mayo Clinic website or WebMD is better for self-diagnosis. At the two-minute mark, I mention that I'm a matchmaker and surreptitiously hand him my business card when no one is looking. His face slightly falls, but he takes the card and promises to be in touch. My first win!

The next man spends the entire ten minutes describing the first stage of his childhood after I ask where he's from, but I still slide him a card because A) he might just be overly chatty because he's nervous or B) learning to pause and pose questions to your date is something that I've successfully coached people on before. If that doesn't work, there are women out there who are hard of hearing. As every matchmaker worth her salt knows, sometimes you've got to think outside the box, or even within spitting distance of it.

"Hi, I'm Lior," says the next one. "You look familiar," he pauses and squints at my nametag, "Sissel Miri."

"Yeah, I get that a lot." I clear my throat and touch my gold locket that holds a picture of my mother inside. "I think I just have one of those faces."

He doesn't seem convinced. "Have we dated?"

"No," I say, trying not to be offended that I'd be that forgettable. "Anyway," I nod, glancing at the timer, "tell me about yourself."

"Okay, sure." He nods and smiles. "I'm a third-year medical student."

I smile. All right, now we're talking. "What area of medicine do you want to go into?"

"Hopefully dermatology, but it's very competitive, so we'll see."

"Why dermatology?"

"It's convenient for family life. You don't get paged a lot, and I plan on being as hands-on as possible helping my wife with our babies in the middle of the night."

"That's sweet." A doctor who's committed to helping his wife. If I can sign this guy on as a client, it'll be a huge win. He might even have other doctor friends he could recommend me to.

"And the money is good, especially if I want to partner with a plastic surgeon. Insurance has been detrimental to private practices—" He stop and snaps his fingers. "Wait—were you one of those contestants on that reality TV show? The ones where they take unattractive people and give them a bunch of cosmetic surgeries and then viewers vote who had the biggest transformation? My ex-girlfriend made me watch it with her."

I make a sound that's somewhere between a gasp and a squeak.

"You look kind of plasticky," he adds as if I was too dumb to catch his meaning the first time around. Maybe it's my disguise? Although I don't think my wig and glasses and heavy eyeliner make me look "plasticky".

"Not in a bad way," he says, taking in the look of horror on my face. "Although you might want to use less filler in your lips."

"Can I get a refill?" I call to the bartender, holding up my empty glass. Unfortunately, the bartender is busy chatting up the waitress. And for the record, my lips are one hundred percent natural, but because I don't believe in shaming women who do use filler, I don't correct him. Because it's about the sisterhood, dammit.

"Hey, wait a minute." His eyes suddenly light up and I get bad juju in my gut. "You're that matchmaker, aren't you? The one that Mrs. Schwartz hates."

"What? No," I say a little too quickly, eyes darting around anxiously in case anyone heard him. "And lower your voice please."

"You looked better as a blonde, in my opinion," he says.

Buddy, I don't remember asking.

He leans forward. "Did you really insult Mrs. Schwartz to her face?"

"Can you *please* lower your voice—"

"I'm not judging," he says, putting up his hands. "If anything, I admire you. I'd never have the guts to do it knowing how easily she can ruin anyone she wants to with one small snap of her fingers."

"That's not— S-she didn't ruin me," I sputter, crossing my arms. "I'm fine," I add firmly. "Everything is fine."

We gaze at each other in silence. Based off the look on his face, he isn't buying it. And sadly, neither am I.

"I'm considering taxidermy," I say, folding my arms. "As a backup plan."

He blinks. "Taxidermy?"

"I loved stuffed animals as a kid. It's kind of similar," I muse. "In a way."

"Uh . . . ah." He clears his throat and glances around the room. "Sorry, I just have to . . ." He stands up.

I wait for him to finish his thought, but he's in such a hurry to leave that he doesn't seem to realize he left me hanging.

Perhaps I should've kept the taxidermy part to myself. Oh well. Easy come, easy go.

By the end of the night, Sissel and I have handed out five cards, which isn't a huge number, but it's still five more than at the start of this event. And that's a win to me.

* * *

Back at home, I curl up on the couch with a thriller as I wait for an update on Nayma and Caleb's date. Just as the main character discovers the bloody corpse of homicide victim number seven, my phone rings.

"Nayma?" I say, glancing at the time. It's barely nine o'clock—this is either an incredibly good sign, like she's calling from a bathroom stall to rave about him, or an incredibly bad one, as in she's already back at home because the date was just that bad.

And really, how bad could a date be with two hot Jews and amazing Chinese food?

"Hiiiii," I trill, already imagining the speech I'll make at the Shabbos party leading up to their wedding. Not that anyone expects me to say something, but I think it's only appropriate for the matchmaker and childhood friend to give a little speech since—

"I didn't like him."

I close the novel and sit up straight. What? Had I misheard her? I must have. "Sorry, what did you say?"

"I didn't like him." Nayma heaves a long, dramatic sigh. "He's *very* different one-on-one than he is in a group setting."

"I mean, to be fair," I say, scratching my head, "everyone is. At least, a little?" I add when she doesn't say anything.

"This was more than a little, Ashira," she says. "Whenever I've seen him at shul or some other community event, he talks with people. As in, he responds back. He seems to understand the general concept of having a conversation and what it entails. But tonight he barely spoke two words. He basically said hello and goodbye."

"That—no." I shake my head. "That doesn't sound like Caleb. Are you sure you were sitting with the right guy?"

"Yes, Ashira." She says my name like a teenage daughter says *Mother*. "I know what Caleb looks like. Maybe your friend was right," she adds gloomily. "Maybe he thought I looked like a hooker."

I sigh. "He wouldn't think that, and you looked lovely."

"Then why wouldn't he give me a chance?" Her voice carries a plaintive tone. "The moment we locked eyes, I could *feel* him closing up."

"Maybe he had a bad day at work?"

"Or maybe he just doesn't like me." She makes a small whining sound. "I mean, he's still gorgeous and

I'm in awe of him, but there was no spark, no connection, you know?"

"It'd be hard to make a connection with anyone if they didn't talk," I say, quietly thinking. Caleb can be quiet and he's been mistaken for being snobby before, but barely scraping two words together? That doesn't sound like him at all. "Maybe he was nervous?"

"I don't think so," she says. "He didn't seem nervous. He seemed bored. The only time he asked me anything was to see if I wanted dessert."

I shut my eyes. I'm going to kill him.

"I'm so sorry," I say. "Do you want me to talk to him and see if I can—"

"No," she interrupts. "We've already agreed it wouldn't work out."

"Really?" The traditional protocol is for the couple to tell the matchmaker their thoughts rather than each other. "How did that happen?"

"At the end of the date, he said it was nice meeting me, but that he didn't think we were a match. It was literally the only sentence he spoke the entire night."

"I'm so sorry, Nayma," I say flabbergasted. "I totally thought you guys would hit it off."

"I know. I did too," she replies sadly. "Oh well. At least I've got four other backup husbands."

"You do?"

"Logan Lerman, Eyal Booker, Bar Brimer, and Noah Schnapp. In that order," she adds.

"Noah Schnapp from *Stranger Things*?" I laugh. "Isn't he a little young for you?"

"He's twenty. That's plenty old."

"Okay," I say, amused. "So, all your backup husbands are celebrities. And they probably have private security to keep them safe from overzealous Jewish matchmakers like me."

"Probably. But that's fine because I'm going to take a break for a little while and focus on my schoolwork."

And another one bites the dust. "Law school must be incredibly demanding."

"Yes, but I'm also trying to make it as a novelist. I'm writing a mystery about Bigfoot."

"A mystery about Bigfoot," I repeat. "Huh."

"It's very good."

"Right, yes," I say, although not entirely convincingly. "Is there romance in it?" I ask.

"Initially, yes, but then it results in a murder-suicide."

"Wow." I pause and scratch my head. "So, it's a science fiction thriller?"

"I'd market it as commercial historical fiction, actually."

"Aah okay," I reply, confused. "Well, anyway, let me know if you want to start dating again. And good luck with your book."

"Thanks. Have a good night!"

I hang up, then swiftly dial Caleb's number. I will be *cool, calm, and compassionate.* I will treat him with the dignity and respect he deserves, just as if he were any other client of mine. And no matter what he says or how he says it, I will absolutely not, in any shape or form, lose my temper.

Chapter Eleven

"Hey." Caleb's smooth, relaxed voice comes across the line. "What's up?"

"Oooh, nothing much. Just calling to see how your date went."

"It was fine."

"Oh?" I say, in a neutral voice, although my head is screaming WTF. "Fine, huh?"

"Yep."

Silence. At the thirty-second mark, I say, "Are you still there?"

"Yeah."

"Look," I sigh, feeling my neck muscles twitch. "I'm going to need more feedback from you than one word that's more neutral than Switzerland itself."

"She didn't do it for me."

I stand up and start to pace. "Were you not attracted to her?"

"It wasn't that."

"Was it her personality?"

"Maybe," he says after a slight pause.

Maybe? "Was she too . . ." I trail off, hoping he'll fill in the blank. Unfortunately, he doesn't. "Perfect?"

"She talked a lot."

I roll my eyes. "Could that have been because you didn't talk enough?"

"I spoke," he says, though not with much conviction.

"Really? What about?"

A pause. "The lack of spice in the soup."

I bite down on my inner cheek. "Anything else?"

"I asked if she liked the steak. And at one point, we discussed carbonated beverages."

I rub the pinch in my forehead. "Caleb, did you think she was dressed inappropriately?"

"No." A pause. "Why? Was she?"

I lift my hand in the air, then let it drop at my side. It's as if he wasn't even *there*. "What was wrong then? Physically, she everything you asked for, and she's brilliant, too."

"There was nothing wrong with her, I just . . . wasn't feeling it."

I tilt my head back and rub my eyes. I know he's withholding information from me but it's not as though I can wave a magic wand and get him to confess whatever the problem is.

I frown as a thought occurs to me—he wouldn't intentionally sabotage the date, would he?

"Can you do me a favor next time," I say, "and force yourself to talk, even if you aren't feeling it?"

His sigh carries the oppression of every put-upon man in the history of mankind. "I'll try."

"That would be amazing." Look at me, being all patient with a client struggling to do the bare minimum of what's required of him.

I flick on my bedroom light and start to wrap up the conversation. "Okay, I'll head back to the drawing board and we'll be in touch."

"How was your speed dating event?"

I pause. "You knew about that?"

"When will you learn, Tinsel, that I know everything?"

Zevi. It's always Zevi. Telling him anything is like taking out a billboard in Times Square.

"How was it?" he repeats.

I flop onto my bed and close my eyes. "Traumatic."

"That bad?"

"Yes. And stop smiling."

"How do you know I'm smiling?"

"I can hear it in your voice."

"Sorry." He clears his throat. "How's this?"

I grin. "Much better."

"Any eligible guys?" he asks.

"Aren't you more curious to know if there were eligible women?"

A pause. "Sure. Of course."

"I wish I could tell you, but we got there too late to mingle so I didn't have time to speak to any of them."

"And the men?"

I groan. "No, don't make me talk about it. It's too soon."

"That bad, huh?" he says, the grin creeping back into his voice.

"Let's just say that I'm going to need a lot of time—and chocolate—before I can open up about it."

He chuckles.

I shake my head. "Anyway, don't worry. I'm going to find you someone who will Blow. Your. Mind."

I hear him exhale. "No rush."

Easy for him to say. He's not the one trying to save a business and running precariously low on cash. Soon I'll have no choice but to get a real nine-to-five job, unless I decide to stop eating and using electricity and water. I wonder how awkward it would be on the scale of awkwardness if I were to ask Bruce for a job at the new bodega. I'm thinking around nine point eight.

As if Caleb can read my worried mind, he says, "Do you need money, Tinsel? Because I can—"

"Stop right there, Daddy Warbucks," I say, cutting him off. "I'd sooner sell my organs than accept charity."

"A bribe then."

I laugh and flip onto my stomach. "As if I'd buy that now. I'd know it was charity in disguise."

"I worry about you," he says quietly.

I pause, taken aback by the admission. I can hear the concern in his voice and if I'm completely honest, I'm touched that he cares, and that I take up space in his head. Zevi worries about me, as does Leah in her own way, but they have to. They're family. Whereas Caleb isn't and yet . . . I don't know. It's confusing what he is to me.

"That's sweet, but you don't need to." I wait a beat and when there's no response, I joke, "I have at least two jars of peanut butter in my pantry which could keep me alive for another few weeks, easy."

"Hilarious," he says dryly.

I smile. "In all seriousness, I'm good. Really," I add because I can tell he doesn't believe me. And I've got Zevi for backup. "But thank you," I add.

"Don't thank me. I haven't done anything."

"You're right," I tease. "I take it back."

He chuffs a laugh, and for a few moments, neither one of says anything. There's something nice and comfortable about the silence. But then a loud yawn escapes me.

"Go get some rest. sleeping beauty," he says. "I'm giving you the morning off tomorrow to give your body time to recover from all its hard work."

"Thank G-d," I breathe. I love my recovery days, as Caleb calls them. Although, in a surprising way, I have come to enjoy our runs. Somewhat, at least. "Goodnight, Caleb."

"Goodnight, Tinsel."

* * *

The chiming of the doorbell wakes me up the following morning. I sleepily make my way to the door only to discover no one is there. But then I look down and see several bags of groceries on my doorstep. There's a handwritten note stapled to one of the handles of the bag.

This is for my peace of mind
—C
P.S. Three cans of beans should add another few months to your life. ;)

I feel a small amount of self-indignation at the gift, but another part of me, the one that is touched by the time and effort that went into this, wins out. I snort with laughter as I reread his note, then bring the groceries inside. Naturally, everything is healthy and requires washing or chopping. After I unpack it all, I send Caleb a text:

> No Cocoa Pebbles?

His reply comes a few minutes later:

> Is there a child in your house?

I laugh.

> Only the one currently writing.

He replies with a crazy face emoji.

I chew on my lip and stare at my screen, unsure what to write next. I type out *thank you*, but then I delete it because what if he makes a habit of this? What if I start to expect grocery bags on my doorstep every Monday morning only for them abruptly stop coming once he gets married? Or what if he takes it upon himself to buy all of my groceries from now on, and before I know it,

I'm a kept woman? *What if I start to like being a kept woman?*

After a few more minutes of typing and deleting, I finally write *thank you* and attach a smiley face, then slide the phone across the counter before I try to undo it. But then it dings with an incoming text and I lunge for it.

> *That's what took ten minutes of bubbles dancing on the screen? I was expecting a brilliant piece of literature or at the very least, a short sonnet.*

My lips spread into a wide grin.

> *The bigger question is why were you staring at the screen*

> *Casanova is leading a team meeting. He's been yelling for fifteen minutes straight now though it's unclear about what.*

I laugh, picturing the scene. Casanova, whose real name no one knows except Caleb, is an Arab Israeli and former IDF special-ops whose unit worked in counter-terrorism. Now he's the chief of security for the synagogues and temples in the borough, as well as Caleb's second-in-command. And although he has the striking good looks of a Hollywood legend, he's definitely no charmer. Even the rabbi is scared of him and that's really saying something since everyone is scared of the rabbi. And unlike our judicial system, Casanova presumes everyone is guilty until proven innocent, especially when someone he doesn't know attempts to walk into our synagogue.

I respond with a laughing emoji and set my phone aside. It's time to brainstorm ideas on how to recruit more singles to add to my database. It has to be something different, something big and fun that will attract people—particularly ones who have no connection to the Schwartzs. I grab a notebook and pen and wait for inspiration to strike. And wait. And then wait some more.

Eventually my phone pings with an invitation to a Chanukah party. Then it hits me—a singles Chanukah mixer! How fun would that be?! What better way to meet your soulmate than bonding over a bloody battle that resulted in regaining our temple in Jerusalem? #GoodTimes #SorryNotSorryGreeks

The only question now is, where to do it? I need a venue that is classy, but also free. Which narrows my options down considerably. In fact, it narrows them down to a big fat zero.

Unless . . .

Chapter Twelve

I glance around the crowded room and smile in gratitude. The Chanukah party is underway, and thanks to my hard work and amazing networking skills, I found the perfect venue.

"Thank you everyone for coming tonight," I say, raising my voice over the chatter. "We have lots of fun activities planned. But before we get this party started, I want to give a special shoutout to our generous host, Caleb Kahn, who practically *begged* me to use his house for tonight's event." I clap and grin at Caleb, who rolls his eyes good-naturedly at me. While it's true that he said "Hell no" and "Over my dead body" the first ten times I asked, somewhere between the twentieth and thirtieth time, he caved in and said, "Fine. But you owe me."

I knew he'd come around.

Once the applause dies down, I add, "Caleb is going to light the menorah now, and then tell the story of Chanukah. And after that, we can get this *par-tay* started." I add a *woo hoo* and wave my hands like a dorky parent chaperone at a school dance. Caleb must agree because he pauses lighting the menorah to glance at me with a pained expression.

I can hardly believe how many people showed up. It was a brilliant move on my part to have Caleb host the party because every eligible female between the ages of eighteen and eighty signed up. When word got around about the number of women going, the men swiftly joined too. And because the main floor and finished basement are about 4,000 square feet combined, there's plenty of space for people to move about comfortably.

". . . *leh-hahd-lik nayr cha-noo-kah*," Caleb sings in his beautiful melodic voice, standing before the giant eight-branched candelabra in front of his living room window for all the world to see. The miracle of how a single jar of oil lasted for eight nights following the Greeks' destruction of the Temple, never fails to inspire me. It's a reminder that light will always outshine the darkness. And placing the menorah in front of a window is a signal and prompt to be proud to be Jewish, especially in times of hardship.

After Caleb lights three candles—because it is the third night of Chanukah—the fifty or so people in the room sing and clap to *Hanerot Halalu*. Based on how the singles are dressed, there's a mix of observance among the group. Some of the men are wearing yarmulkes on their heads, and a few women are too. Some are dressed so modestly that everything from their collar bones to their ankles is covered, while others are wearing plunging necklines and miniskirts. There are two men near me sporting beards and long, curly sideburns, but instead of wearing the traditional Hasidic garb, they're in T-shirts and jeans. Hasidic hipsters.

I'm always taken aback when other people are surprised that Orthodox people are quite varied. The media tends to box us all together in one way, when in fact, there's a huge range of observance and traditions within the Orthodox community.

Caleb commands the room, describing how Antiochus IV had banned Jews from practicing Judaism, killing those who disobeyed, and plundered the Holy Temple in Jerusalem. I smile, watching how everyone hangs on to his every word.

I glance across the hallway to the dining room where servers are putting the finishing touches to the buffet table.

"Sissel," I whisper-yell, bending backwards to see her. Unlike me, she isn't trapped in a crowd of people. "Can you make sure that they have pink applesauce for the latkes?"

She gestures to the menorah. "Did you forget that women aren't allowed to work when the candles are lit?"

Ugh. There are times during the year when Jewish women are forbidden to work as a "reward" for being better than men. Well, not better exactly, just holier. Unlike men who have historically fallen prey to idol worship and other scams, Jewish women have remained steadfast in our belief system and therefore, get credit for our continued existence.

So, yeah. Basically better.

"It's not work, it's just asking a simple question," I say.

"*Shhh*." She puts a finger over her lips. "Can't you see that I'm trying to listen to the story?"

"You already know the story."

"Yeah, but I'm having fun watching that woman in the green dress eye Caleb like he's a lollipop she wants to lick."

"*Sissel.*"

"Okay, okay. I'm going," she mutters.

I continue running through my mental checklist when I notice Zevi and Jack huddled in a corner of the room, each wearing a garish holiday sweater. Zevi's has dreidels on it with the words *they see me rolling,* and Jack's sweater has a winking Santa saying, *I got ho's in different area codes.*

Everybody's interest is captured by Caleb's powerful storytelling—something that doesn't often happen when there's a crowd of Jews who have yet to be fed. But then it's not every day that Caleb speaks. He talks with the easy confidence of someone who not only belongs, but has *arrived.* You'd never guess by watching him that he still sometimes feels insecure.

I find myself smiling at him. I can't help but marvel at how the once-bullied kid grew up to be one of the most respected and sought-after men in the community. People go to him for advice on everything, from *halachic* questions to where to buy the best bourbon to settling financial disputes. Even things he has absolutely zero expertise in, like medical stuff. It's kind of hilarious.

I startle as Sissel taps my arm, and turn to her expectedly. "Don't freak out, but the caterer left early and none of the servers can get a hold of her. They think she sampled the hard cider a little too much. Also, the third and fourth batches of *sufganiyot* never came."

I shake my head. "What?"

"And there are no sugar cookies either. The baker has the flu."

When I tried calling the caterer I used to work with for events, it went straight to voicemail which wasn't sketchy at first—until I noticed she had blocked me on social media. And that is how I ended up with a catering company with a 2.4 Yelp review average.

Thank you, Mrs. Schwartz.

"Also did you ask for the latkes to be charred?" Sissel asks, tilting her head. "Or did you just hire an idiot?"

"*Charred?*" I put my hand over my chest and try to breathe. This is a disaster.

"I told you not to freak out," she says.

"I'm not freaking out," I bark, which causes a few heads to swivel.

"Oh, and one of the servers just left because she found out her uncle died. And then another server left to offer emotional support."

I press my fingers to my forehead. *Stay calm. Breathe.* It could be worse. At least we have plenty of liquor.

"And the caterer thinks they swiped some of the liquor on their way out," she adds.

I clench my jaw, and try not to think violent thoughts. After all, I remind myself, the poor girl's uncle just died. And maybe she was very close to him. Maybe he was like a father to her. Maybe he even raised her—

"And guess what?" Sissel says, lowering her voice when someone shushes her. "The pink-haired guy said that she doesn't even have an uncle." She snorts. "What do you think of that?"

"I think I'm going to kill her," I say firmly, and push my way through the crowd, determined to get my liquor back.

"Ashira, wait!"

I'm almost at the front door when I turn to the sound of Miri's distressed voice. She looks stunning in a hot-pink dress that perfectly complements the auburn in her hair and brings out the natural rosiness in her cheeks.

"My cousin needs to talk to you," she says, pointing to a man hovering in the hallway. I can only see his profile, but he looks to be mid-thirties, average height, and good-looking in a clean-cut way. "He's having a relationship crisis and needs your advice—"

"Can you tell him that I have to do something first? I'll just be a minute."

Miri stops me, grabbing my arm, and hisses, "He's *crying*."

I glance at the front door longingly. "Are you sure it isn't allergies?" I whisper, but it's too late because she's already maneuvering me toward him.

"Here she is," Miri says in a falsely brightly voice. "And don't worry, Lieber, you're in good hands. The best," she adds reassuringly.

Seeing the pain in his eyes, I can tell that this man is suffering a lot more than I am. I force myself to let my anger at the servers go. "Hi," I say gently, "I'm Ashira."

"I'm Lieber," he sniffs. "Sorry to drag you away from everything," he says, and makes a vague hand gesture.

"No worries, I could use a break anyway. Miri can take over. Right, Miri?" I say, knowing she's memorized the schedule as much as I have.

"Absolutely." She nods, but I can detect the panic in her eyes. She's not big on leadership type roles.

"You'll do great." I glance around, trying to think of the best place to talk to him. Both the main level and the basement are set up for the party, which leaves upstairs as the only option. I chew on my bottom lip and wonder how bad it would be to use Caleb's study, given that it's attached to his bedroom. (I might have given myself a quick tour of his house while he was at work and I was setting up, but it was strictly for professional reasons. And I have to say, his underwear drawer is way more organized than mine.) His study does at least have a desk and a couch which is a lot more professional than any of the other bedrooms. Or bathrooms, for that matter.

"There's an office upstairs we can use," I say, moving aside the rope at the bottom of the stairs with the '*do not enter*' sign attached.

I lead him down the long hallway and twist open the bedroom door. Caleb's master suite is my version of heaven. The room is bright and airy, and has his-and-hers closets that are each the size of my living room. The 'her' closet is completely empty, including the built-in cabinet drawers which I felt was incumbent upon me to check—as both the party planner and matchmaker.

His bathroom has a large shower and an even bigger jacuzzi, and his king-sized bed has the most comfortable mattress that I've ever laid on (I might have accidentally fallen on it during my tour) and his bedding carries the scent of his soap. (I also might have accidentally sniffed his shampoo.) The huge TV screen facing the bed is perfect for all-night Netflix binges. If I had a bedroom like this, I'd never leave.

I usher Lieber into the office and after a moment's hesitation, close the door. I don't want anyone to get the wrong idea, but Lieber might feel weird having a large bed in his peripheral vision. He sits on the couch and I hesitate briefly before deciding to join him on it. There's enough space between us that it isn't weird, and it feels more natural to sit closer to someone than behind a desk when they're sniffling with tears.

"Here," I say, handing him a box of tissues from a side table. He mumbles his thanks and pulls out a few. "Whenever you're ready, you can tell me what's going on and I'll do my best to help."

"My wife and I have been separated for a few months now, but I was hoping we could reconcile. She wants to move forward with the divorce, but I want to get back together. I tell her it's best for the kids for us to stay together, but the truth is," he pauses and draws a shuddering breath, "that I never stopped loving her."

Oy. I nod and stay quiet while he takes a minute.

"I just found out today that she's seeing someone. And not only that," he adds, fresh tears forming at the corners of his eyes, "but she's been seeing him behind my back for a while now."

"Oooh." I wince. "I'm sorry."

"Yeah." He laughs without humor. "It turns out he's the boys' swim teacher."

I suck in a sharp breath. "Aren't there rules against that sort of thing?"

"Cheating on your spouse or dating your kids' swim teacher?"

"Both?"

"I used to think it was sweet the way she always wanted to take the kids to the swimming lessons. He wears Speedos. And he looks good in them too," he adds.

"That is impressive," I allow. "But—physical attraction isn't enough for a relationship to survive on," I say.

"He's also young and smart. And charming. And he has no back hair."

"Uhm, again, that's not key to a successful relationship. And I'm sure you're every bit as smart and charming," I say, going with the assumption that he might be when he isn't having a nervous breakdown.

"He's British too," Lieber adds gloomily.

Oh, he's screwed. Few women can resist the pull of a British accent coupled with physical attraction. "I'm so sorry."

"Do you think there's any chance that I can win her back?"

"Lieber," I say gently, "do you really want her back? After the way she's treated you?"

"Yes. And anyway, it's my own fault," he sniffs, reaching for another tissue. "She said if I hadn't worked such late nights, then she wouldn't have felt the need to get attention elsewhere."

"That's so not cool." I shake my head. "And that doesn't give her a pass to cheat and then blame you for it."

"She said she couldn't help it. That there wasn't even a choice to make." He gazes at me imploringly. "Do you think that's true?"

I sigh. "I think maybe it's her truth." He hangs his head and I say after a moment, "Lieber, what advice would you give your daughter if she were in your shoes?"

"I only have sons."

"Your son, then."

He shrugs. "To follow his heart, I guess."

Wow. I rub my eyelids. This man really does need my help. "Doesn't your son deserve a wife that wants to be with him? That chooses to be with him?"

He sighs and rests his forehead in the palm of his hand. "Yes, I know. And you're right. But have you ever loved someone so much that you can't handle the thought of not being with them? That it's hard to breathe without them?"

"Yes," I say softly. "My mom." I find myself briefly thinking about my father.

"Oh—I'm sorry," he says, looking guilt-stricken.

"It's fine. Losing someone you love is hard. And usually, we don't have any control over it."

A fresh set of tears run down his cheeks. "So, you're saying I have no hope?"

Bernice was right. Grief counseling really isn't my forte. "No," I say carefully. "I just think you should challenge what your hopes are."

He looks at me. "Huh?"

"You hope your sons will be in mutually loving relationships, but you can want that for yourself too. And it sounds to me, like that person isn't your wife."

"But she might be," he argues. "We could go to marriage counseling. It doesn't mean that we can't figure this out and grow stronger as a couple."

"A hundred percent." I nod. "But," I add gently, "she has to want that too. Does she?"

He looks away and is quiet for a long minute. "No. She doesn't." He swallows. "She said that for the first time in her life she's happy."

"Oh, Lieber," I sigh, feeling a pit in my stomach.

"But I want *her*." He hunches his head on his lap and starts to softly cry again.

My own eyes well up. I grab a tissue, then kneel down in front of him on the floor. I don't touch him, but I allow him to see me, to know that he isn't alone.

"Lieber," I say, after a minute. "Do you only love one of your sons?"

He looks taken aback. "No, of course not." He sniffles.

"So your heart can love more than one person."

"It isn't the same," he says, growing irritated.

"I know it's not." I nod. "But you are capable of loving someone new. But not now," I add. "I think you need time to grieve and to learn to love yourself."

He blows his nose into his tissue. "This was not the advice I wanted to hear."

"But it might be the advice you needed to hear?" I say with a hopeful smile.

He shakes his head and gives me a small smile. "Miri is right. You are the best."

"Awww, thank you." I laugh. "And honestly, you're going to be—"

Without warning, the door opens, and when I look up, there's a figure standing there with a stunned look on his face.

Caleb.

Chapter Thirteen

"Hi, Caleb." I gulp. "Fancy meeting you here."

Caleb takes in the scene before him: Lieber crying on the couch and me on my knees attempting to soothe him. After a pause, he says, "Am I interrupting something?"

Lieber stands up and swipes at the remnants of his tears. "No, we were just finishing up. Thank you so much," he says, turning to me.

"Of course. Miri can give you my number," I say, getting to my feet too. "Feel free to call me anytime."

"Thanks." He nods. Caleb steps back and the three of us make our way out of the office and head to Caleb's bedroom door, trying very hard to pretend that this isn't weird.

I'm about to follow Lieber out through the doorway when Caleb steps in front of me, blocking my exit. "Stairs are down the hall, to the left," he tells Lieber. Then he closes the door and leans against it, crossing his arms.

I gaze at him nervously. He doesn't look like he's in a festive holiday mood. In fact, he seems quite unhappy.

"Is this about me using your office without permission?" I ask.

"No. It's about you bringing a man into my bedroom without permission."

"Oh." I swallow. "Well, technically, it was your office, so . . ."

"Which is technically attached to my bedroom."

"Such a great room by the way," I say with enthusiasm, gesturing a wide arc with my hand. "Ten out of ten."

"Glad you like it." He lifts his chin in the direction of the bed. "Sit."

I scratch my neck. "I don't think that's particularly appropriate given that it's you know, a bed, and we're alone in a closed room and—"

"*Sit.*"

"I suppose I could rest for a minute, sure, why not?"

I kick off my heels and sit cross-legged on the bed while Caleb begins to pace and deliver a long lecture on everything he's had to suffer, starting with hosting this party.

"But it's a big mitzvah," I interject. "And you're *so* great at mitzvahs," I add, unabashedly trying to butter him up, but he ignores me and keeps going.

"Twenty minutes ago, I had to physically break up a fight between two drunk guys trying to beat each other with wooden cue sticks."

I consider that. "But on the plus side, good cardio?"

He throws me a death glare. "Then I had to calm Zevi down after he got worked up because he thought Jack was flirting with someone."

Knowing Jack, he probably was. Although to be fair, I've caught my brother-in-law flirting with inanimate objects on more than one occasion. Once it was a naked bronze sculpture and he'd had a bit too much to drink.

"Then a woman threw herself at me," he continues, waving his hands as he paces. "And then *cried* when I finally pried her off."

"Poor thing," I say.

He stops pacing to glare and point his finger at me. "*I'm* the poor thing."

I try not to laugh, but his outraged expression coupled with his deep voice saying that he's the poor thing proves too much for me and I burst into giggles.

"Glad you find this amusing," he says, crossing his arms.

And so help me, I do. I know I shouldn't, but the more I try to stop, the more I laugh. My unprofessionalism continues to grow in leaps and bounds.

"I—" I clutch my stomach as I laugh—"I'm sorry—"

"You don't look sorry," Caleb says, sinking down on the end of the bed.

My stomach flutters at seeing him on the bed—with me on it, no less—that it only increases my nervous laughter.

"Sorry," I manage to eke out between snorts. I take a pillow to use as a sound buffer, but he grabs it from me. I try to swipe it back, but he's too fast, and I end up swatting the air instead.

"Reel it in, Tinsel. I know you're capable of having a mature conversation."

"Normally," I agree, pushing back some flyaway hair. "But apparently not tonight."

There's a loud crashing sound from downstairs. I cringe.

"I should go and see what happened," Caleb says, shifting his head to gaze at his bedroom door. "But I don't want to."

"I really am sorry, Caleb." I chew on my bottom lip. "I didn't realize it would be this rowdy. Or that I wouldn't even be around to help because I'd have to give emergency therapy to Miri's cousin."

"It's okay." He rubs his forehead. "You did the right thing. It's why we love you," he sighs.

"Who's 'we'?" I tease, flopping down onto my side to face him. "Because I only see one person here."

"You know what I mean."

I laugh and wag my finger at him. "Admit it. You *loooove* me."

"*We*—your friends—love you."

"Uh-uh." I shake my head and grin. "*You* love me. Say it again, but with proper grammar this time."

He rolls his eyes. "I tolerate you, Wernick."

"Oh, you *tolerate me*?" I say, deepening my voice to imitate his. "I think it's a bit more than that." I shouldn't be doing this. I shouldn't be in Caleb's bedroom and on his bed. And I definitely shouldn't be toying with him like this. But I'm having too much fun to stop. Even if it does feel a bit like playing with fire.

I should head back to the party.

And I will. In a minute.

"Repeat after me." I clear my throat and put my hand over my heart. "I, Caleb Hersch Kahn, pledge allegiance to Ashira from this day forth. I admit that she's a mad genius, brilliant in every way, and declare my undying loyalty forever and ever."

He tries to hide his smile behind his hand, but I can see it in the crinkles around his eyes. Knowing that I'm the one that put it there makes me feel inordinately proud.

"You *loooove* me," I singsong. "I know it and you know it."

"I know that I'm a lot happier in here with you than I am out there," he says, dipping his chin in the direction of the door.

"Same," I say, and he turns to me with a raised eyebrow.

"Really?" he says doubtfully.

"Are you kidding?" I gesture around the bedroom. "This is the best room ever. If I lived here, I'd never want to leave. I'd order room service and happily work from this bed forever. You've got this movie theatre screen TV—hey," I say, gazing around. "Where do you keep the remote anyway?"

He points to the nightstand and I open the drawer. The remote lies on top of some papers and as I reach for it, my eyes catch my name on one of them.

"What's this?" I say, pulling it out.

"Nothing," he says quickly. He tries to grab it, but I jump off the bed and race to the bathroom and lock the door.

"Ashira," he says from the other side, "this is a huge invasion of my privacy."

"I know. And I'm so sorry." I unfold it all the way. It's a printout of one of our text conversations, the one where I thanked him for getting me groceries. My eyebrows furrow. Why would he print this out and then hide it in his drawer? And why is he so embarrassed about it?

I slowly unlock the door and open it. Caleb is leaning against the wall with his arms crossed and a scowl on his face. I stare at him for a moment and he stares back, the air thick with tension.

"Uh, Caleb?" I say, and hold up the paper. "Why did you print this out?"

He shakes his head. "I don't want to talk about it."

"But—but—" I stutter.

"Let's go back to the party. I think Miri needs you."

"Yeah, but wait," I say to his turned back, and rush to block his exit. "I don't understand—"

"I like reading it, all right?" He puts his hands on his hips and gives me a death glare.

"This?" I say doubtfully, holding up the paper, just to confirm.

"It was a nice conversation," he says defensively.

"This?" I say again, glancing down at it to see if I missed something.

"Yes, *this*." He grabs it from me and folds it up again, then puts it in his back pocket. "Can we go back to the party now?"

"Uhm, well . . ." I tilt my head and study him. I don't understand what was so special about our conversation, but the fact that he printed it out and likes to read it makes my heart swell with warmth. "Did you print it so you could read it on Shabbos?"

He neither confirms nor denies it.

"What if I want to keep it?" I ask, mostly as a social experiment.

"You don't deserve it."

I bite back a smile. "But I want it."

He shakes his head and wags his finger at me. "Don't do the cute thing. I'm too mad at you right now."

"I do a cute thing?" My eyes light up. "What is it?"

"Stop it."

"Talking?"

"The talking, the big blue eyes, the way you move, the everything," he says, waving at me.

My heart skips a beat.

"Don't do the silent cute thing either," he warns. "I'm not in the mood."

I have a silent cute thing too? Butterflies dance in my stomach.

"No smiling either," he adds.

"Is there anything I can do?" I ask innocently.

"No."

I lift my hand. "Can I just say one tiny thing?"

He heaves a sigh. "What?"

"I think it's sweet," I say earnestly. "And I'm glad you have it, and that you like to read it."

We gaze at each other for a long moment and my pulse starts to quicken. A charge buzzes in the air and my heart hammers against my ribs. I don't know what this silent energy between us is, but it's impossible to turn away. I'm stuck, paralyzed by the pull in his eyes.

I always knew they were a dark brown, but I've never noticed the slightly darker ring around them before. They're mesmerizing, like two shiny onyx gems glimmering against a dark sky. For the first time in my life, I understand why they say eyes are the windows to the soul. His are like endless tunnels that if I gazed at long enough, I might uncover his secrets. His innermost desires. His heart.

I don't know if he moved closer or if it was me, but suddenly the distance between us has shrunk. My mouth goes dry.

"Ashira," Caleb murmurs.

The heat in the room turns up, and his half-lidded gaze drops to my lips. I swallow, suddenly terrified. Because the fact that I want him to kiss me right now with a desire bordering on desperation is absolutely horrifying.

Yet sexy too, a devil on my shoulder whispers.

But then my conscious rears its ugly head. *This is Caleb! The man who dropped both Judaism and you overnight. Do you really think he wouldn't do it again? He's the definition of unstable. And what about Blue Moon Basherts? Is it worth ruining your one chance to save it for a kiss?*

The devil on my shoulder shrugs. *Maybe? Try it and see?*

But then I think of my mother and the company we built together—her very legacy. And I take a step back.

"I think someone's calling me."

He lifts an eyebrow, but doesn't say anything.

"I have to go," I add, ducking under his arm.

"Chicken," he says softly.

He's right, of course. I am a chicken. And the worst kind, too. The kind that runs away and digs its face in the sand rather than confront reality. As much as I try to help other people heal their hearts, I'm unable to heal my own.

Because I'm scared. I'm so fucking scared that I don't even want to go to therapy. I don't want to heal. The pain is what protects me. It's the reminder not to trust anyone, to not allow myself to be in a position where I might get hurt again. Life isn't predictable and people certainly aren't. I'd much rather play it safe and continue nursing a broken heart than have to start from scratch.

I'm an imposter. No matter how easily I dispense wisdom and guidance, and how much I promote love and marriage from the moment I wake up until the moment I go to bed, I can't follow my own advice.

I hurry out of the room without a backwards glance.

Chapter Fourteen

The following morning finds me jogging to Bruce's bodega. Caleb texted this morning that he couldn't join me for today's run, so I went solo. I've been putting in a good faith effort to eat healthier and work out. I've discovered exercise helps turn my anxiety down a few notches. Although I'm still unable to stop thinking about the disaster that was yesterday's Chanukah party. The whole thing was a catastrophe of the highest order. Caleb was in a terrible mood the rest of the night, standing in a dark corner and glowering at anyone who so much as dared to glance his way. I tried to stay behind after everyone left to help him clean up, but he kicked me out along with the others.

Which I get. First, I discovered the printout. Secondly, I ran away when he was seconds away from kissing me.

I can't believe I almost kissed him. I almost kissed Caleb Kahn.

I put a hand over my pounding heart. This is bad. As in, really, seriously, life-changingly bad.

Okay, let's not panic. So what if there is an attraction between us? It's just a small, harmless crush. And it makes sense. We have a childhood bond and we're already integrated into each other's families. There's no denying that he has a soft spot for me.

My mind starts to wander into dangerous territory. Could I be with Caleb? He's a decent man, after all. I can't imagine him being anything other than a devoted husband and father. He's dependable and honest. The type of person who would show up on time to pick his kids up from school. The kind who'd never forget his kids' birthdays or wedding anniversary. I smile, picturing him running to the grocery store late at night to satisfy his pregnant wife's cravings.

Caleb is the archetypical hero of every story. A rare breed of human that would immediately put aside his own needs to care for others. He would literally take his shirt off and give it to someone he saw shivering on the side of the road. That's simply who he is.

I slow my pace to a brisk walk.

If I'm honest—truly, honest—none of it matters, anyway. Because even though Caleb might be all that and a side of chips, I'd never be able to marry him. How could I live with myself knowing I threw away my one shot at saving my mother's legacy?

No. *Absolutely not.* I couldn't do that to her.

Besides, marriage is best reserved for people without trust issues. I'd always be looking over my shoulder, waiting for the other shoe to drop.

Some people aren't meant to have it all. *I'm not meant to have it all.* And there's not much point in longing for a husband and children when that type of happiness is reserved for people who aren't like me.

People who aren't broken and still haunted from the ghosts of their pasts.

At least I can help facilitate it for other people. And though that may not be *everything*, it's still more than nothing.

Speaking of which, I managed to get ten people to sign up to my newsletter which the Internet stresses is important for continued growth, and two more made appointments to meet with me one-on-one. Which is huge! Both belong to Reform temples so thankfully they run in a different crowd to Mrs. Schwartz.

I arrive at the bodega, rosy-cheeked and out of breath. There's a small line ahead of me and I wait patiently near the end of the counter. "Good morning, Bruce," I say cheerily. "How are you?"

He looks up from sifting coffee beans and smiles. "I'm good, *Baruch Hashem*. Still windy out there?"

"How'd you guess?" I laugh, pushing strands of hair out of my face.

He taps the side of his head. "I'm clever like that. One coffee and a cream cheese and lox bagel to go?"

"You got it." It's Bernice's favorite, and her face lights up every time I give it to her. Since discovering the bodega three weeks ago, I've gotten into the habit of stopping by on my bi-weekly journey to collect Bernice's dry-cleaning, and not just because the coffee is fantastic. I'm determined to get Bruce to join my database because he's a total catch. Who doesn't want a hot single guy who knows his way around a kitchen? Which immediately makes me think of Caleb.

This is getting ridiculous. He's taking up way too much of my mental real estate.

Focus, girl.

"Do you have plans for Friday night dinner this week?" I say to Bruce, all casual, peering into the glass display case.

"Yeah, but nothing too exciting," he says, leaning back. "Just eating with my family."

I nod, trying to play it cool and not overly eager. "If you want, you could come to my sister's house. She makes a mean chicken and matzah ball soup. You'll love it." That wasn't too desperate sounding, was it?

"I assume she's also single based on your enthusiasm?"

"Hah!" I say, feeling smug. "She's married."

"Then you must be planning on having single women there."

I try not to look guilty because dammit, that had been my plan.

"I won't be able to make it. Sorry," he adds, not looking sorry at all.

"But you just said you don't have any exciting plans this week."

He fiddles with the coffee machine. "Yes, but they're still plans. It's rude to cancel."

"But it's your family, they'll understand. I bet they'd be happy to hear that you're spending Shabbos with new friends," I add. Perhaps I'm laying it on a bit too thick at this point.

"Listen," he says, turning toward me. "I know what you're up to and I'm not taking the bait."

"I have no idea what you're talking about," I say, gazing at him as innocently as one can when lying. "I just happen to think you'd have a great time if you came. Providing you removed the stick out of your *tuchus* first."

"Okay, one," he says, pulling out the container of whipped cream from the fridge. "Our friendship has not yet reached the stage where we can comfortably talk about objects up our *tuchuses*."

"Agree to disagree."

"And two," he continues, "despite what you said, I'm sure there would just happen to be a single woman or two at this Shabbos meal who you think would be perfect for me."

I picture my two closest friends—asexual Sissel, and Miri, whose specifications are so precise that it's as likely to find this person as a needle in a haystack. "There might be two women there," I allow, "but neither of them would work for you."

"Is this some reverse psychology trick?"

"I don't know." I tilt my head and smile. "Is it working?"

"No." He laughs. "But I give you credit for trying."

"*Please.*" I put my hands together and give him puppy eyes. "Let me help you."

"I don't want help, thank you very much. Aren't there other people you can harass?"

"I'm not harassing you," I say, arching an eyebrow. "And this is a tough business, for your information. It relies heavily on word-of-mouth referrals, and lately the only mouth talking about me is Mrs. Schwartz's. And as you know, the speed dating event didn't work out," I say diplomatically, choosing not to point fingers at anyone. *Ahem, me.* "Plus the Chanukah singles mixer last night was a complete disaster."

"What happened?" Bruce looks up from running a spoon under water.

"Broken cue sticks. Battery and assault. A bookshelf crashed when someone tried to climb it."

Bruce blinks. "Why would someone try to climb it?"

"There might've been more alcohol than food," I say, scratching my head. "Or at least, edible food," I add, thinking of the burnt latkes. "Turns out that's a bad idea."

He laughs.

"So, you'll come for Friday night dinner?" I ask, batting my eyelashes.

"No." He frowns. "Look, Ashira. I'm happy being single."

"Nobody's happy being single," I say, like a good matchmaker would.

"Aren't you happy and single?"

I open my mouth and then shut it. Am I happy being single? I think it helps that my two closest friends are. But I'm sure one day Miri will find her needle in the haystack. Zevi and Jack want children and have mentioned the possibility of using a surrogate or adopting. Sissel eventually wants to move to San Diego for the weather. Which leaves Bernice and me watching reruns of 1980s' sitcoms.

"This isn't about me," I say.

"Hey, if I throw in a free muffin will you stop pestering me?"

"I do love a good bribe." I gaze at the muffins in baskets on display. "But it depends on the flavor."

"Naturally."

"A blueberry one will get you one week," I say, tapping my chin.

"And the chocolate chip?"

"Two weeks."

His eyes light up. "What about the flaxseed?"

"I'd consider that an act of vengeance."

"What—why?"

"Are you kidding? Nobody likes flaxseed."

"I like flaxseed," he says. "I've loved it since I was a kid."

I give him a sympathetic look. "Some would call that child abuse."

He rolls his eyes and using a pair of tongs, holds up a chocolate chip muffin. "You can have this if I get *three weeks*."

"Two weeks."

"Two and a half."

"Sold!" I smile and roll my eyes.

The door opens, and a young woman with bouncy brown curls walks inside. She has a huge smile accompanied by a pair of adorable dimples. "Oooh, she's attractive, don't you think?" I whisper to Bruce. Maybe I could set these two up!

"That's my niece."

"What? Really?" I gaze at him suspiciously. "Are you sure?" Given that women start having children at an early age and continue until their bodies are no longer fertile, it isn't uncommon in our circles to have an uncle or aunt of similar age to their niece or nephew, but I have to make sure he isn't bluffing just to avoid an awkward matchmaking situation. Which has become my specialty in recent days.

"What are you inferring about my sister-in-law?"

"Nothing," I say quickly, putting up my hands. "I don't even know the woman."

"Hi, Uncle Bruce," the young woman says, approaching the counter. "How are you?"

Bruce turns to me with a smirk. "Did you catch the 'uncle' part of that sentence?"

"You got lucky this time," I say, and he laughs.

"Don't even think about trying to matchmake me with my customers," he says, handing me my coffee. "I'll start losing business."

"Or gain more," I suggest, holding my phone up to the scanner.

"Did I miss something?" the young woman says.

"This is Ashira," Bruce says. "She's a very persistent matchmaker."

"Nice to meet you." She gives me a warm smile. "I'm Rivka."

"Nice to meet you too." I give her my most charming, non-desperate smile. "You don't happen to be single, do you?"

"She's twenty-one," Bruce says. "And I'm not letting her date until she's at least thirty-five."

"Actually," Rivka laughs, "I just told Abba last night that I wanted to start dating, and he said it was about time."

"My brother is an idiot," Bruce informs me.

"Twenty-one isn't that young," I say. After all, I have friends who got married within months of graduating high school.

"She's still too young to rent a car," he says. "You want to know why car companies have that rule? Because the prefrontal cortex isn't fully formed until twenty-five. They're still kids trying to figure out who they are and what they want out of life." He shakes his head. "They can't possibly know who would make a good life partner at that age."

"That might be true for some people," I concede. "But it isn't for everyone. Lots of people get married young and are still happily married decades later. My great-great grandmother got married at sixteen. I'm told they were very happy together."

He cringes. "That's horrible."

"Actually, the horrible part was that my great-great grandfather had been nine years older. I guess it was common back then."

Bruce waves his hand. "You're done."

"Is he always this cranky?" I stage whisper to Rivka.

She smiles and shakes her head. "No, he's usually pure sunshine."

"What can I say? You bring out the worst in me," Bruce says with a small, nearly imperceptible grin.

"See?" I beam at him. "That's proof that we've reached the highest level of friendship."

Bruce snorts as he slides a muffin into a small paper bag. He loves me, I know it.

"Has anyone ever told you that you're unreasonably stubborn?" he says, handing me the bag.

"Maybe." I smile. "But my brain tends to filter those types of comments out."

Bruce chuckles and shakes his head. "See you later, Ashira."

"Thanks for the muffin. See you next week!"

"Two and a half weeks!" he shouts as I slip through the door.

I turn around and call back, "Sorry—matchmaker math!"

He pretends to throw a rag at me and I laugh. Rivka calls out her own goodbye and we step outside together.

"Hey, before you go," I say, and reach into my coat pocket, "take my card. I'd love to meet with you. I've got time all this week."

"Okay, great." She nods and smiles. "We'll be in touch."

"Just don't tell you-know-who," I add, dipping my head in the direction of the shop door. She laughs. "Don't worry. He'll be on a need-to-know basis."

"Like when you're a week away from your wedding," I joke.

"Exactly."

In an ideal world, I wouldn't try to set up a couple with a twelve-year age gap, but I have bills to pay and Rivka seems like the sweetest gir—er, woman. I give myself a mental smack. Besides, everyone knows that women mature way faster than men, so in a sense, Rivka and Caleb should be about the same age at this point, maturity-wise. She's also his type physically.

Rivka might very well be the answer to my prayers.

Chapter Fifteen

I met with Rivka and her parents two days later, and the three of them were absolutely delightful. Rivka works at a Jewish women's modest clothing store, and in her spare time, she volunteers at the children's ward in NYU Hospital, reading and playing with patients. She isn't a fan of football, but I told her to save that piece of information until the marriage contract is signed. The good news is that the family read the magazine article featuring Caleb when it first came out, and all three of them unilaterally decided that age is just a number when someone like Caleb Kahn comes along.

All I need to do now is to get a yes from Caleb. Which is proving a lot easier said than done. I don't know what's going on in that head of his, but I'm starting to get mad. Yesterday, he texted that he'd have to miss tomorrow's run due to an early meeting, but I don't buy it. Over the last sixteen hours, I have left him two voicemails and several texts. I swear, if he isn't lying dead in a ditch somewhere, I'm going to kill him.

I just have to find him first.

Fortunately, he and Zevi share their locations with each other, so Zevi was able to be my secret spy informant. Unfortunately, he's at Johnnie's, a small and unassuming boxing club in the Bronx that's supposedly trained some of the best boxers in the history of the sport. I've only ventured there once before when Zevi was interested in joining a couple of years ago, and lasted all of five minutes. There was just too much testosterone and tension and blood and spit.

But, as I head toward the subway station, I reason what's a little body fluid when you're a matchmaker on a mission?

Twenty minutes later, I'm pushing open the glass door, causing the attached bell to jangle. "Hello," I say, approaching the decrepit old white man behind the desk. "You must be Johnnie." I only remember this because Zevi had mentioned that the son of the original Johnnie is also named Johnnie, as well as his son and grandson. So the odds are definitely in my favor.

Johnnie, however, doesn't even glance up. Two hearing aids peek out between tufts of white hair and I consider reaching over the desk to try to adjust the volume since they're obviously not working, but on the flip side, he could get a heart attack from the shock. Better not to.

"HI!" I shout, which probably isn't much better, but he seems used to it, and calmly blinks. "CAN I GO TO THE RING?" I wait for him to respond or wheeze or something, but nada. If his chest wasn't moving, I'd doubt he was alive. "HAVE A GREAT DAY!"

I open the door that leads down a hallway and wrinkle my nose. The scent of testosterone, sweat, and bad attitude fills the air. Boxers are a unique breed of people, in my opinion. They're disciplined, hard-working, competitive, and probably missing some crucial part of the brain. Why else would someone intentionally put themselves in a position to get pummeled? It makes no sense.

"Hey, sweetheart," a guy in his forties says, holding a gym bag over his shoulder. "Who you looking for?"

"Caleb Kahn."

"He's in the ring. Second door on the left."

"Thanks."

"You be careful now," he calls over his shoulder. "That man's been spoiling for a fight."

I pause. On second thought, maybe I should visit him some other time.

Come on, Ashira. Don't be a baby. He's not going to hurt you.

I open the door and take in the scene. It's like a caveman convention where men across all demographics gather to showcase their grunting noises. Everyone is sweating and panting as they lift barbells or jump rope or run on treadmills, and they all have really hairy armpits. There isn't a woman in sight, and it makes me wonder whether this is some exclusive boys club that requires a certain percentage of testosterone to join.

The ring is in the center of the room and I gingerly make my way over, careful to avoid getting hit by one of the many punching bags hanging from the ceiling. Glancing up, I notice that Caleb and his sparring partner are shirtless. Which is . . . not a big deal. There's absolutely no reason for my heart to be galloping right now. After all, I've seen Caleb's naked chest a thousand times before, back in those lazy summer days when we'd hang out at the Kahns' backyard pool. From the age of five until I reached thirteen, I'd seen Caleb in swim trunks more times than I could count.

It might be slightly awkward, but he's left me no choice. What else am I supposed to do? I don't have the luxury to sit patiently and wait for him to call me back. I'll just keep my eyes on his face and get him to commit to a date as quickly as possible. I can be in and out of here in thirty seconds, as long as he cooperates.

I step over someone's gym bag and approach the ring. "Hi, Caleb!" I call out.

He turns around in surprise. "W-what are you— *Oomph*," he says, right as his partner's fist connects with his face. My hands fly to my own face and I wince. That looked really painful. But he gets his vengeance a moment later by landing an uppercut to his opponent's jaw, and that's when my eyes accidentally drift to his chest and stomach.

I have to remind myself to breathe. *Holy mother of—*

"What are you doing here?" Caleb spits out his mouth guard and spares me a quick glance.

"Uhm." I swallow, guiltily turning away. His body is simply . . . I mean, I can't even . . .

"Ashira?" he prompts, ducking out of the way of his opponent's glove.

"Sorry," I say, my eyes straying back to his chest, feeling like the worst sort of pervert. But I'm struggling to understand why Caleb wears shirts. If I were a man and had his chest, I'd walk everywhere topless. And I do mean *everywhere*. Business meetings, running errands, going to shul.

My eyes dip lower and I suddenly realize that it's not just his chest that's awesome. It's his butt and legs too.

"Are you okay?" Caleb asks, dancing on his feet while keeping his eyes on his opponent.

Am I okay? No, I'm not okay! I was already having wet dreams about this man, and that was before I saw him in all his topless glory. Now that I've seen the magnificence that is Caleb's body, I can never unsee it. I always knew Caleb had an amazing body in the same abstract way I know that the Scottish Highlands are beautiful from watching *Outlander*, but it's completely different seeing it in person.

"I didn't know you had tattoos." The words slip out of my mouth like an HR nightmare, causing me to blush bright red because now he knows that I'm a peeping Tom.

"You never asked," Caleb grunts, blocking a hit.

Secretly, I've always thought men with tattoos are sexy even though it goes against the Torah. I don't know why it's so hot; maybe I've been programmed to think that inked guys are tougher, or at least, have a rough exterior, but their insides are soft and sweet, and just waiting for a good woman to come along and nurture them. At least, that's how they come across in books and television.

I wish he'd stay still for two seconds so I could read the passage inked on his skin. I can make out a trident, an American flag, the Star of David. And is that a skeletal frog?

"Is there a backstory for the creepy frog?" I ask, but he must not hear me because he doesn't answer.

I give up all pretense of being a good person and lean in for a closer look. His chest is like a bronze sculpture come to life, all muscles and ridges and flawless golden-brown skin. *So many muscles.* I sigh.

"Tinsel."

I blink. Caleb caught me staring again. I swear, someone ought to lock me up, I'm a hazard to myself.

"Sorry, yes." I clear my throat and avert my eyes. "You haven't been returning my calls."

"I've been busy," he says, then swiftly delivers a punch to the guy's stomach. *Ouch.*

"Yeah, I see." I wince. "This is such a violent hobby," I say, tensing up as the two of them dance around each other. "Wouldn't you rather play chess or crochet?" I peek at them between my fingers, not wanting to see what happens next, yet also wanting to admire Caleb's body. It's hard to say which part of my brain will win out.

His sparring partner laughs and Caleb seizes the opportunity to pummel him. I turn around because *oy*.

"I'll call you later," Caleb calls out to me. "I can't talk right now."

Yeah, as if I'm going to fall for that. "I'll be fast," I say. "So, I found a girl that I think you're really going to like—"

Caleb mutters something under his breath that I can't make out. Except for the F-word. That one came out crystal clear. Maybe he was talking to the guy in the ring.

"She's in her twenties—" I say. #MatchmakerMath

"Too young," Caleb cuts in.

Imagine how he'd react if he knew just how young Rivka actually was. *Best not to go there.* "She's super sweet," I continue, ignoring him. "And your type, physically. You know, the complete opposite of me," I add, and then immediately want to shoot myself. *Why did I say that? WHY?!*

Apparently, I'm not the only one shocked by my comment because I hear an *oomph* from Caleb. He was probably caught off guard, and the other guy took advantage of that moment and punched him.

"Anyway," I say quickly, trying not to think about the violence happening behind me, "does Saturday night work? Seven o'clock? I can make all the arrangements. All you have to do is show up. And talk," I add.

"How—" a pause, the floor reverberates with thumping, "considerate—of you," he says, though he doesn't sound all that grateful.

I jolt as I hear a body crash down onto the mat. My heart jumps into my throat as I picture Caleb bloody and unconscious. I spin around, preparing to see him hurt. Instead, Caleb stands above the man wiping his brow. I exhale with relief, but then immediately feel bad for the guy. He's someone's son after all.

"I'm so sorry," I say, leaning on the ropes. Someone ought to apologize and I doubt Caleb plans to. "Can I get you anything? Water or . . ." I trail off as I see blood trickle down his nose. "A doctor?"

The man ignores me and spits out his mouth guard. "I hope you shit whatever crawled up your ass," he says to Caleb.

Oh dear.

"Sorry, man," Caleb says, holding out his hand. "I didn't mean to—" Before Caleb can finish his sentence, the guy grabs Caleb's hand and forces him to the ground where he lands several punches to Caleb's face.

"Stop that!" I exclaim, ducking under the rope, just as the man hits Caleb square in the eye. "You're hurting him!"

"Yeah, that's the point—" the man starts to say, but is cut off when Caleb's foot kicks him down. Unfortunately, he isn't the only one that falls.

"What are you doing in here?" Caleb looms over me, looking furious. "You could get hurt."

"*You're* one to talk," I say, gesturing wildly. "This is not okay. This is an awful, stupid sport and you're leaving right now." In my peripheral vision, I sense the other guy coming to his feet, and I quickly stand up and step between them. "Don't even think about," I warn the bloody nosed man and hold up my hand, "or I swear to G-d, you won't live long enough to regret it. I've got mafia connections," I add, because why not?

The man stares at me for a beat, and my body tenses up, unsure of his reaction.

"Kahn, tell your crazy bimbo bitch to step aside."

Caleb goes still. "What did you just call her?"

"I called her a crazy-ass bimbo bitch."

Technically, the 'ass' part is new, but details. "You can run your dirty mouth all you want," I say calmly, "but we're not going to take the bait."

"But we will take an apology," Caleb says in a tight voice.

The guy laughs. "You're not going to get one."

"That's okay," I say quickly, glancing between the two. "No apology needed. But let's pause today's session because emotions are running high and—"

"Bitch, I'm going to fuck you up," he says and lifts his hand. Just as I process that I'm about to get hit, Caleb punches the guy so hard that he collapses like a deck of cards.

I blink. I think Caleb just saved me from getting a black eye. I turn to him and say, "Thank you."

"You're welcome," Caleb replies, keeping his eyes on the man. Based on his scowl, I get the impression that he'd like to punch the guy a lot more.

"Is he going to be okay?" I ask, as the guy groans and rubs his face.

"I hope not," Caleb replies, tearing off his gloves.

The man's left eye is starting to swell. Even though he meant to hurt me earlier, I can't help but feel concern for him now. "Maybe I should go grab him some ice."

"Why? He was about to take a swing at you," he adds, as if I didn't already know that.

"Yes, but—"

"No '*buts*'," Caleb cuts me off. "There's never a good excuse for laying a hand on a woman, Ashira."

I nod. He's right, of course.

"And you," he says, ducking under the rope and holding it up for me, "are leaving."

"But we didn't finish talking yet," I say, thinking of Rivka.

"I completely agree."

"You do?"

He nods, but there's a scary glint in his eyes. And I get the feeling that whatever it is he wants to talk about, it isn't his love life.

Chapter Sixteen

"... irresponsible ... could've gotten seriously hurt ... concussions are not a joke, Ashira ..."

He is in a mood. It's been a full ten minutes since we've gotten into his car and he's still ranting and raving about how I shouldn't have gotten inside the ring, and how lucky I am that I didn't wind up paralyzed.

I decide to cut him off at the twelve-minute mark with the question that I've wondered for fifteen years. "Why did you stop being Orthodox?"

He glances at me, clearly caught off guard, and his chest rises and falls as he draws a long breath. "I suppose you want the long version?"

"I'll settle for both."

He smirks and shakes his head. "The short version is that I wanted to give back to the country that took my mother in as a citizen, and it was nearly impossible to be Orthodox in that setting."

"Okay." I nod. "And the long version?"

"Is a lot more complicated." He sighs. "You know I had a hard time in school being a Jew of Color."

"Yes."

"And that definitely laid some of the groundwork for wanting to explore a different world. I wanted to feel that sense of belonging."

I gaze at his strong, chiseled profile. "And did it?"

"Yes and no. On one hand, there's a tight brotherhood when it comes to your team members and in the SEAL community. But on the other hand, I was still the only Jew. I was still . . . 'other'."

"What's that like?" Growing up in Brooklyn, surrounded by people who look like me, I don't know how that feels. My mother used to describe her childhood in Minnesota, saying how Jews stood out like sore thumbs, how her brother had pennies thrown at him in public school, how she'd been cursed at walking beside her family outside the synagogue, and so forth. But I never experienced that.

"Being 'other'?" he says, to which I nod. "It's like walking into a room and having all eyes turn on you, judging your every move. Your every action is dissected through the lens of what you look like rather than the content of your character. And ultimately no matter how hard you try, you'll never be *enough* for either the Black community or the Jewish one."

My heart breaks. It's almost incomprehensible to me. How could one of the most—no, *the* most decent person never feel enough?

I blink. When did I realize that Caleb is the most decent person I know?

"I haven't walked in your shoes, so I know it's easy of me to say this." I pause. "But maybe the acceptance and the sense of belonging that you need, that we all need, isn't necessarily found in one community or the other, but in the handful of people who love you best."

"Yeah." He smiles. "You're right."

"I'm always right."

"No, that would be me."

I laugh and accidentally snort. "Anyway. Would you like to know more about Rivka?"

"Who?"

"Rivka Stareshefsky. Your date for Saturday night."

"Jesus," he says, punching the defroster button. "Not this again. I told you I'm not interested in dating a child."

"Anyone over eighteen is a legal adult," I protest.

"Anyone under thirty is a child to me."

"That seems extreme." I cross my arms. "I'm the matchmaker here. Where's your trust?"

"Non-existent. Speaking of which, how's your diet and exercising coming along?" he says.

"A lot better than your dating life. Some of us take our commitments seriously." Much of it has to do with the fact that he rings my doorbell five days a week to help train me for the marathon. He also texts every other day asking what I had for breakfast, or how much sleep had I gotten, and sends the most boring articles relating to health. I tend to read those at bedtime since they put me to sleep.

He smirks a little and rubs his jaw. "I guess that's fair."

Does he hate dating so much? Or is it really because of the age gap? For all he knows, she could be twenty-eight or twenty-nine. I don't understand why he's being so difficult.

Then an image of the night we were in his bedroom flashes across my mind. The way his eyes pierced into mine, and how the space between us shrunk into almost nothingness.

But then I think of my mother and the company we built together. The matches we made, the happiness we brought to so many people. The countless hours of coaching and therapy. Blue Moon Basherts is my mother's legacy and I'm not going to throw that down the drain because I have a little chemistry between my VIP client.

I clear my throat. "Caleb, you're my only hope. Without you, I lose my mother's business."

"No pressure or anything," he mutters under his breath.

"It's okay, I understand." I heave a dramatic sigh and lean on the center console. I inhale his scent of shampoo and bodywash. "I'm used to men letting me down. My father, as you know, abandoned me as a child."

"Stop it," he says, glancing at me. "I know what you're doing."

"My mother is dead," I continue, "and I'm all alone in the world."

He shakes his head. "Not falling for it."

"I'm a sad, poor orphan girl," I say as he breaks at a red light. He turns to me and I gaze into his eyes, channeling sad, poor orphan girl energy.

"You're a thorn in my side is what you are."

"Yes, I understand." I emit a pretty little sigh and blink my eyelashes at him. Maybe this is the cute thing?

"Stop looking at me like that," he groans, turning away.

Yup. Definitely the cute thing.

"Like what?" I say innocently.

"Like a cute, poor orphan girl."

"Oh." I nod. "I'm sorry." The light turns green and Caleb lets out a long breath. "You can drop me off anywhere around here," I say.

"Here?" He glances at me. "Why?"

"This is as good a place as any to practice being homeless. I need to know what to expect, after all."

"Tinsel, I swear . . ." He pinches the bridge of his nose, trying not to laugh.

"I hope you'll come and visit me sometime. Provided, of course, that I find a cardboard box large enough to entertain."

He snorts a laugh, and then exhales a long, resigned sigh. "Okay, okay. I'll go on the date." He glances at me. "Happy now?"

"Hey, you're the one who signed up to do this in the first place, remember?"

"I know," he mutters, switching lanes. "It's my own doing. I can't help myself. When you look at me with those big blue eyes of yours, I turn into a raging idiot."

Something like sunshine fills my body, and a giant, goofy grin spreads across my face. The idea that I have the capacity to turn Caleb Kahn—one the most powerful, not to mention, *desired* men in Brooklyn—into a "raging idiot" seems utterly ridiculous. And yet, the evidence is there. I start to tally it up like a prosecutor convincing a jury. First, he agreed to this matchmaking scheme. Then he woke up early one Sunday morning to drop off groceries for me. He gave me a key to his house to set up the Chanukah mixer and he's yet to ask for it back. The email printout of our conversation that he keeps in his nightstand. The "cute" thing. And he did once call me gorgeous.

But he also said I was like a little sister to him.

I think back to the night of the Chanukah party when we were in his bedroom again. He didn't look at me like I was a little sister to him then. He looked at me like I was a woman. Like I was a woman and he was a man, and that he wanted nothing more in that moment than to consume me.

I shiver.

"Are you cold?" he says, and promptly raises the heat.

"No," I squeal, and feel my face turn red. *Something is seriously wrong with me.*

I stare straight ahead as he drives. People tend to see what they want to see. After eight years of matchmaking and counseling couples, there's no doubt in my mind about that. So the real question is, do I want Caleb to desire me?

I blush. The answer is resoundingly—though shamefully—*yes*.

Let's suppose for a moment that he does desire me—is that why he's dragging his feet when it comes to going on dates? But if he did like me, wouldn't he have said something by now? I'm so confused. I wish I could just give him a truth serum and ask him.

I wish my mother was here. She'd know what to do. And thinking of her brings me back to the present and the stakes that are involved. No man is worth losing my mother's legacy.

I give myself a mental slap and clear my throat. I am Caleb's matchmaker, his dating handler, and nothing more. Speaking of which. "Give me your phone," I say, holding out my hand.

"What for?"

"I need to put the date in your calendar."

He sighs and removes his phone from his coat pocket. I try to take it, but he moves it out of my reach. "Hold on," he says, glancing at me. "I have to do face recognition."

"That's dangerous to do when you're driving. Just tell me the code."

"No," he says tightly, keeping a firm grip on his phone. Why is he acting so weird?

"Do you actually think I'm going to steal from you?" I ask, slightly horrified.

"Of course not." His eyebrows pinch together. "Besides, I *want* you to take my money."

I roll my eyes. "Your phone, sir."

"Patience. I'll do it at the next red light."

"You literally just merged onto the interstate," I point out.

"Do you want music or radio?"

"Neither, I want your phone."

"Why are you so stubborn?"

"I could ask the same of you. Now hand it over."

"*If* I give you my phone," he says slowly, staring straight ahead, "and tell you the code, you have to promise me not to talk about it."

"The code?" I ask, confused.

He nods. "Promise me you won't ask questions."

I glance at him, somewhat concerned. Could he have had a concussion from all those hits? Because I can't for the life of me understand why a row of numbers would be something I'd have to promise not to talk about.

"You have my word."

"Okay." He hands the phone to me, then takes a deep breath as if to compose himself.

"Ready whenever you are," I say.

He nods. "Okay."

"Okay."

After another long pause, I say, "Caleb—"

"060295."

My heart skips a beat. I turn to look at him, but he stares straight ahead, stone-faced. I swallow and gaze at the phone in my hands, my eyes going blurry.

"Don't read into it," he says, breaking the silence. "It was just the first thing that popped into my head."

I nod, not trusting myself to speak. I clear my throat, then press the sequence of numbers that happens to coincide with my birthday. I go to his calendar app and type in the information for his date.

We drive the rest of the way in silence. When he pulls up in front of my house, I unbuckle the seatbelt and open the door. "Caleb?"

"Hmm?"

"This sad, poor orphan girl doesn't feel so alone anymore."

"She was never alone, Tinsel. She always had me."

For the briefest of moments, I wonder if I'm wrong about Caleb. Maybe he wouldn't be the type to abandon his family. Maybe, just maybe, he'd be the type to stick around and raise his kids and be a good husband. Maybe taking a chance would be worth it for someone like him.

But my father was sweet, and look how that turned out. No, I remind myself, he's too much like my father for comfort. They were both nurturing and kind, and then they both left out of the blue one day. The only difference is that Caleb returned and my father never did.

And even if Caleb wouldn't do what my father did, I still need him and the publicity that comes with making the match of the century. Maybe in a different time or place . . .

Clinging on to the company that was my mother's dream is my number one priority. Because as long as I keep doing what I do, she lives on, and so does her legacy.

* * *

The next two weeks fly by in a series of highs and lows, with the ratio of lows being five to one. I signed two new clients thanks to Miri's recommendations, but then both backed out, my boiler broke, followed by my pride because I had to borrow money from Zevi to fix it, and then he gave me a loan to cover my cost of living until I get back on my feet, and now I feel like a total #AdultFail.

The only positive has been that I'm able to run three miles now without wanting to curl into a ball and cry. At least there's that.

But the lowest of the low was when—

No. I'm not going to go there. Absolutely not. Instead, I'm going to relax and enjoy the scent of these obscenely expensive hair products and—

"I'm just SO MAD!" I yell, my eyes flying open. I bang my hands on the armrests of the chair in Miri's salon. "That woman is a monster."

Miri frowns down at me. From this angle, I can see directly up her nostrils. They're clean, thankfully. It's ten o'clock at night and I'm in her basement apartment, which she's converted part of into a hair salon, all because she wanted to try out a new haircut and needed a dummy dumb enough to let her.

"And I'd take her to the *Beis Din*, but she owns that too!" I continue. I pull at the collar of the smock. "This is choking me."

"It isn't choking you, look—there's three fingers' worth of space here—"

"She even chases me in my dreams. There's no escaping her. She's *everywhere*," I hiss. "Like G-d—but evil."

"She does seem slightly obsessed with you," Miri says, gently pushing me back down so my head is in the sink, then turns on the faucet.

How does Mrs. Schwartz even find time in the day to come up with new inventive ways to ruin me? Is she really that bored? Can't she get a normal hobby?

"Adding my name to the community prayer list and telling people to pray for me because 'I have an invisible illness of the tongue' is so . . . so . . ." I shake my head, words failing me.

I grab Miri's wrists and tug until she's at eye-level with me as she yelps in protest. "Be honest—doesn't that sound like some kind of STD to you?"

"No, it sounds like a made-up disease that no one will believe," she says, removing my hand from her arm. "Now close your eyes and relax. Let me wash the shampoo out."

I close my eyes and try to let the warm water soothe me, but my thoughts are racing. Even old wounds from childhood are opening back up. Specifically, a sleepover I wasn't invited to back in seventh grade. Apparently, I'm still not over that.

I open my eyes. "Do you know what it's like to have a classmate from elementary school—who has since moved to Australia and either doesn't care about the time difference or can't do math—call you in the middle of the night to make sure you, and I quote, *'hadn't died before she could apologize for not inviting you to her birthday sleepover'*?"

Miri shakes her head and laughs. "That's awful."

"And then I couldn't go back to sleep for the rest of the night because the child in me was really hurt."

"I'm so . . . sorry," Miri chokes out between her laughter. "I don't know why Dini didn't invite you."

I gasp and twist my neck to look up at her. "How did you know it was Dini?" I point my finger at her. "Were you there?"

"Um, yes?" she says, no longer laughing. "But she made everyone promise not to tell you about it. So, that was considerate of her . . . in a way?" she adds when she sees my darkening expression.

"Whose side are you on?" I say, feeling my maturity level rapidly decreasing.

"Yours, of course." She pats my shoulder. "Did she say why she thought you were dying though?"

"Remember Rachel? The quiet girl that always wore her hair in braids?" She nods. "She told Dini that she'd heard I had *oral cancer.*"

Miri grimaces and reaches for a towel from the cabinet. "Oh my gosh."

"And now I'm hurt that Rachel didn't call me! I thought we were friends. I know we lost touch and everything, but she couldn't bother picking up the phone to say goodbye?" I shake my head. "I'm not expecting her to make funeral arrangements or start a fundraiser to help cover my medical bills or anything, but at the very least, I'd expect a phone call or text or—"

"Sweetie." Miri pauses combing my hair and gazes at me through the mirror. "I think we're getting a little carried away here."

"Instead, she calls Dini of all people!"

Miri nods. "I can see why that's hurtful."

"And the few clients I do have are all, *maybe you should focus on your health right now.* And now I think I might actually be sick. What if she cursed me?" I put my hand under the cape and clutch my heart which is beating unnaturally fast. "Do you see the mind games that Mrs. Schwartz is playing?" I get a small thrill every time I call her that.

"Do you want some chamomile tea?" Miri asks, putting down the comb. "I'll make you a cup," she says before I have time to respond.

"I don't like tea," I protest.

"Think of it as medicine."

"I hate medicine. And you know what else happened yesterday?" I call after her. "Golda came home from school and asked my sister why her class is praying for Auntie Ashira. Because the only explanation the teacher provided was that I was '*going through a rough time.*' Yeah, I wonder why!" I yell.

"Hurry up," Miri mutters to the hot water machine.

"You know, I used to be against murder," I say, crossing my arms. "But lately, I've been reconsidering my stance."

"Let's try to take some deep breaths," Miri says, then demonstrates it for me.

"Is this your way of saying you won't be my alibi?"

"That too."

I tap my foot restlessly. "Do you think if I sent Mrs. Schwartz flowers and an apology note she'd move on?"

"Maybe?" Miri tears open a tea packet. "I don't know. But I suppose it couldn't hurt."

"Yeah, or maybe," I say, "I should add her name to the *Tehillim* list and make up some brain disease. Or better yet, hire an assassin."

"Let's put those ideas on hold for the moment," she says, bringing me a Styrofoam cup with steam rising from it. "Careful, it's hot."

"Do you think anyone would miss her if she disappeared?" I ask.

Miri points to the cup. "Try the tea, Ash."

I stare down at the murky liquid with the tea bag inside. "Must I?"

"Yes," she replies firmly. "You definitely must."

I murmur the Hebrew blessing and take a sip. It's both hot and revolting. I gag.

"Oh, it can't be that bad," Miri protests.

"And yet, it is."

Miri shakes her head and takes the cup from me. "Speaking of your questionable taste, how's your arrangement with Caleb going? Has he been making sure you keep up your end of the bargain?"

"Yes. He's on his Israel trip and still managing to get disturbing products masquerading as food delivered to my door."

She laughs. "What, like spinach?"

"*Yes!* And arugula. *Alfalfa sprouts*. Half these things do not look meant for human consumption. Cow feed, yes? But people?" I shake my head. "I can't decide if this is just some elaborate prank on his part."

She laughs as she sprays product onto my wet hair. "Have you tried any of it?"

I purse my lips. "I've stared at it."

"I don't think that counts."

I think about Caleb as Miri blow dries my hair. It feels like ages since I last saw him. He left two weeks ago to go on a men's trip to Israel, where he and other prominent members of the community are volunteering their time and money to support families who've lost loved ones since the war.

I've been trying not to read too much into the fact that Caleb's phone's passcode is my birthday, but at the same time, I can't *not* read into it. He could've used Zevi's birthday or his parents' anniversary or made up some random combination, but he didn't. Instead, he chose the date that I came into this world. And he was obviously embarrassed by it too.

It feels significant. But it doesn't necessarily mean that it *is*, or at least, not in any meaningful way. It might be a sentimental thing because of how close we were as kids. How much he enjoyed being in that older male-figure role. There's no way to know what goes on in someone else's mind. Half the time, I struggle understanding my own.

"When does Caleb come back?" Miri says, shutting off the hair blow dryer.

"Tomorrow."

"Are you excited to see him again?"

I narrow my eyes at her. "Why would you ask me that?"

"I don't know," she says innocently. "It just popped into my head."

"Well pop it back out," I command. "I'm a little nervous to tell you the truth," I add after a moment. "I found him his next date, but I'm worried he's going to mess it up."

Right before he left for his trip, he'd taken Rivka out on a date, and the following morning she called me up and told me that she couldn't stand him, and that being rich and handsome didn't give him the right to talk nonstop. Apparently, he walked her through the entire timeline of his existence, starting from his mother's pregnancy right up until the moment he picked her up at her house. And he never once paused to ask her anything about herself.

"How do you know it's Caleb's fault?" Miri says. "Maybe the women are exaggerating or upset because he wasn't as into them as they would've liked."

"Caleb claimed they were both exaggerating, but . . ." I lift my hands and then drop them. "There's no way to know who's telling the truth. I wasn't there. I wish I could hire a spy," I add wistfully.

"Why hire someone when you can do the job yourself?" Miri winks and plugs in the curling iron.

I tilt my head. "Are you saying what I think you're saying?"

"It's the only way to know for sure. And this way," she adds, "if it is his fault, then you can see exactly what he needs help with and coach him on how to improve."

I close my eyes and groan. "I really hate it when you're right."

"Cheer up." She smiles. "I can lend you the perfect disguise."

Chapter Seventeen

There's an expression in my community that says bringing two soulmates together is more miraculous than the parting of the Red Sea. While I like a challenge as much as the next person, I don't see why it has to be this hard. I know that on the scale of things that need to be fixed in this world, meeting your soulmate is low on the totem pole, but it's still messed up.

You know what else is messed up? People. They may not realize they are, but I do. For one thing, they lie all the time. They say all they want in a spouse is a kind, salt-of-the-earth, good person, but it's a lie. In the eight years I've been in this business, this is what they're really after:

What Men Want in a Wife (in order of importance)

1. Gorgeous.
2. Isn't crazy.
3. Cooks like their mom.

What Women Want in a Husband (in order of importance)

1. Money/status.

2. Isn't a jerk.
3. At least two inches taller than they claim to be.

And if uniting two soulmates is considered a bigger miracle than the parting of the Red Sea, then in Caleb's case, it's like trying to part the Red Sea without G-d's help. Not only without G-d's help, but while Caleb stands there saying that it's never going to part because the science says so, and you might as well just give up already, over and over again, until you lose your mind and take a rock and either smash it over his head or your own.

Which is probably how tonight will end.

As a general rule, I don't like to deceive people. It's rude and it's a sin. But there are always exceptions that need to be made, and Caleb Kahn—bless his soul—is one big helluva exception. Which is why I refuse to feel guilty about spying on his date tonight. It's in both our interests to see how he handles himself, and to observe whether there's chemistry between them. That way, if he tries to tell me it didn't work, I can try to figure out why he thinks that. I'll be able to see and hear the big picture.

"Are you ready to order?"

I glance up from the trifold menu and into the smiling face of a waitress. "I already did, thanks." *Why aren't they here yet?* It's ten minutes past the reservation time—I know because I'm the one that made it. He was so moody about the whole thing that I half-expected him to tell me to go on the date myself, then report back. Which, in all honesty, would probably work better.

But then, it is a Saturday night and the traffic is awful.

"I can take that from you then," the waitress says, starting to pluck the menu out of my hands.

"*No,*" I nearly yell, my fingers tightening around the leather. *Does she not recognize a shield when she sees one?* "No, thank you," I say, trying to appear calm and soften my voice. "I like looking at it. In case I want to order more," I improvise. "And could you please tell the other wait staff that as well so they don't try to take it from me?"

She stares at me for a moment, like she's thinking about arguing but decides against it in case I'm one of those weirdos that leave generous tips, as opposed to one of those weirdos who is just a weirdo. "Yeah, sure."

Sadly, for both of us, the appetizers here are more expensive than my usual weekly food budget. I've ordered a soup that apparently *Chef* recommends, as though we're buddies and he knows what I like. I also made sure to say I'm vegan because protein doesn't come cheap.

A few minutes later, I hear a woman's flirty laugh, and I immediately know that they've arrived.

I quickly use the camera on my phone to check my disguise is still in place. I have to admit that I like it. Wearing a midnight black wig makes me feel like a sexy siren. A mysterious vixen. And with the cat-eye glasses and red lipstick, I look like a hotter-than-hot librarian.

Zevi thought the brown contact lenses and the faint lines of facial hair I drew above my lip was unnecessary (regarding the former) and frightening (regarding the latter). Admittedly, it does lessen the sexy vibe, but the smallest details can make the best disguise. And aside from the facial hair, I think I might do this look more often.

I take a quick peek. They're sitting too far away for me to hear anything, but that's fine. Mainly I'm here to make sure that Caleb keeps his promise and stays for an hour *minimum*. Since his longest date on record has been half of that, and because there's a severe lack of trust between us, I feel the need to watch him. Like a hawk.

I had bumped into Netanya Li a few weeks ago at shul. She and I used to babysit for the same family as teenagers, and our hours overlapped enough that we became friends. Our paths separated when she went to college and last I heard, she was working for NASA as a rocket scientist—literally—but I had no idea that she never married.

As I stood in shul that day, getting hissed at for talking too loudly, I knew beyond a shadow of a doubt that *finally*, I had met Caleb's *bashert*.

Which isn't to say that he still couldn't mess this up. I've seen plenty of couples self-sabotage before their eventual reunion and then marriage.

Netanya Li, like Caleb, is also multiracial and the product of immigrants. Her mother's side of the family has lived in Mexico for as far back as they can remember. They might even have been part of the Jews that settled there in the 1500s after being expelled from Spain.

Her father's side of the family are descendants of the Jews of Kaifeng, a small subset of Jews that go all the way back to the Song Dynasty.

Netanya, like Caleb, knows the struggle of being different. She understands the pain that comes from not fitting into a box, and the emotional exhaustion from answering the same questions over and over again—was she adopted? Did she convert? Did her parents convert? Both of which are questions that Judaism says you aren't supposed to ask. Could she see as well with slanted eyes? Had she ever eaten someone's dog?

She once told me that even the well-meaning people don't realize how hurtful their comments can be. Every time she hears, "You're so lucky. Multiracial people are the most beautiful," is a subtle reminder that she's different. "Not that being different is a bad thing," she once said to me. "But it can be lonely."

Netanya's laughter cuts into my thoughts, and I sneak a glance at them. They look good together, like they belong with each other. Anyone passing would probably assume that they were any other elite New York City couple.

She laughs again, louder than the first time. Whatever it is Caleb is saying, she's loving it.

I wish I was sitting closer so I could hear what they're talking about. But so far, it sounds promising, and they seem to be taking turns.

"Here you are, Chef's apple and butternut squash soup," says a new waiter, carefully placing the bowl before me.

"Thank you. By the way, would it be possible to switch to that table over there?" I point toward Caleb and Netanya. "The one that's two tables away from that couple."

He glances behind him and frowns. "Unfortunately, tonight we're expecting a large crowd, so I'm afraid that won't be possib—very well, then," he says when he sees me slide two twenty-dollar bills toward him. "Follow me."

That money was supposed to be for my taxi ride home because I don't like using the subway at night—train pervs get handsy after twilight, or should I say *more* handsy. But maybe the facial hair will keep them at a safe distance, though I wouldn't bet on it.

With the menu acting as my face shield, I follow the waiter to the new table.

"Excuse me," Caleb says, flagging down the waiter. And then I freeze because Caleb, I slowly come to realize, is looking straight at me.

But in the next moment, he looks away, and I let out a breath. He says something to the waiter, but my heart is beating much too fast for comfort and I slide into a seat, with my back parallel to Caleb's. I set my menu up just in case one of them suddenly gets up to use the restroom. You can never be too careful.

". . . your poor parents," I overhear Netanya say with a small giggle. "What happened when they found out it was you?"

"Can I get you anything else?" the waiter says, interrupting my eavesdropping. "Some wine, perhaps?"

"No, thank you."

"A salad?"

"I'm fine. Thanks."

"Bread?"

"Please leave."

He sighs the sigh of someone used to dealing with difficult customers, nods once, and leaves. *Finally.*

But it's too late, I missed the story, and now they're in the process of ordering the most expensive items on the menu. A steak for Caleb and lamb chops for Netanya. They're also getting a bottle of wine to share.

"And you own a security company?" Netanya says, after the waiter leaves.

"Yes."

"What's that like?"

"It's fine," he replies, sort of brusquely. I take a sip of my soup and cough from the unexpected spiciness. Water glugs down my throat as I desperately try to put out the fire.

"That's nice," she says, after a pause. When he doesn't add to that, she clears her throat and says, "So . . . what do you do when you're not working, like for fun. Do you have any hobbies?"

He nods. "I have movie nights with my mother."

What? No, he doesn't. Dr. Kahn might watch a documentary here and there, but she forces Caleb's dad to watch them with her, not Caleb.

Netanya laughs, then abruptly stops. "Oh—you're serious. Oh."

"Not all the time, of course," he says, and I can hear her audible breath of relief. "Just three to four times a week."

"Oh, wow. Okay. That's . . . nice."

I close my eyes and force myself not to leap over the table and throttle him. Is he trying to test her? Because so far, I'm the only one rising to the bait.

"I like reality dating shows, even though I know they're not that real," she says with a small laugh. "What kinds of movies do you like to watch?"

"Holocaust ones," he says, and I facepalm. *Who does that? Who even says the word Holocaust on a first date?*

"So . . ." Netanya is clearly struggling with her next words, "you watch Holocaust movies with your mother three to four times a week?"

"Yes."

OMFG. I lift my hand and drop it. If that doesn't make a woman want to go home with you, nothing will.

"Wow. I had no idea there were that many of them," she responds, sounding bleak.

"We rewatch our favorites, of course," he says, in case Netanya held any lingering doubts that he was normal. So, that's great.

"Of course," she says, after a beat.

"It's important to make time for your mother as an adult."

"Right." A long moment passes. "I talk to my mom once a week."

"That's it? I FaceTime mine every morning," Caleb remarks. "She helps me pick out my outfits."

Right, that's it. The only way this man will ever get married is if he meets his bride for the first time under the wedding canopy. Clearly, there are a lot more issues here than simply learning how to take turns talking.

Unless he's intentionally sabotaging this date. But why would he? I drum my fingers on the table and bite my lip. Could it be because of me? Because of that time we almost, maybe, might have kissed? He was very specific that he wanted someone who was the opposite of me physically.

It's all so confusing.

"Oh, thank G-d, the wine is here."

Good luck with that, sister. I doubt there's enough wine in the world to improve this date.

Wait— I tilt my head. *What was that about reptiles?* I wish I was sitting in the other chair so I could at least see Caleb's face. Maybe he thinks he's being funny?

The waiter approaches with their food and I use the distraction to switch seats. This is much better. Now I can see their profiles at least.

"You want to know how I am with reptiles?" she says, then gulps down her wine.

"Specifically, snakes," he says, and I cough as my water goes down the wrong way. Caleb glances at me for a moment, and then turns back and glances again. I pretend there's something on the floor that I need, and duck my head under the table while simultaneously trying to stop coughing.

"What an interesting question," Netanya says, refilling her wine glass. "I'm not much a fan. Why do you ask?"

"I'm thinking of getting a cobra. And naming it Bubbles."

My head hits the side of the table as I resurface and I moan in pain. Caleb lifts an eyebrow at me and I frown in return. Does he— does he know it's me? How could he possibly have recognized me in this genius disguise?

"As in . . . a real one?"

Caleb nods. "King cobra are eighteen feet. Can you imagine?"

"No," she says, pouring herself a third glass. "I really can't."

"I found a company in Florida who will bring him straight to my door."

This isn't true, it can't be. Caleb likes animals, but an eighteen-foot cobra isn't a real animal. If it doesn't have fur, then it should be in its own category of species called *scary as hell.*

"What do you think of our matchmaker?" Caleb says suddenly, swirling his wine glass.

Yup, he knows it's me. Not only does he know it's me, but he's going to show me that he knows it's me. I lean back and cross my arms. This should be fun.

"Ashira?" she repeats, slightly surprised. "Oh, I love her. Why?" she asks when he doesn't respond. "Don't you?"

"She's okay," he says after a pause. A very lengthy pause. "But do you ever wonder if she has control issues?"

I give a mental shrug. That's fine. He can have his fun. I'll wait it out until he gets tired of playing.

"Control issues?" Netanya purses her rosy lips. "I don't know about that."

"I bet she wishes she could be on our date right now, for example," Caleb says, "and feeding us lines."

It'd be going a lot better if I did. That much is for sure.

Netanya shakes her head and laughs. "She's only ever been great with me."

I smile. *Hah! Thank you, Netanya.*

"But I guess she can be a bit pushy," she adds. My mouth drops open. *What is she talking about?* I'm not pushy!

Caleb nods. "It's impossible to say no to her."

Is it my fault that I happen to know better than everyone else? And plenty of people say no to me all the time! Most of the time, in fact. That's how I ended up in this position in the first place.

"But she means well," Netanya says, taking a bite of food.

Gee, thanks.

"It's kind of you to give her the benefit of the doubt," he says. "I'm not sure I would."

Okay, that's it. I take out my phone and start to type him a text.

> *I AM NOT CONTROLLING!!!! OR PUSHY!!! And what were you thinking, talking about Holocaust movies with your mom and 18 ft pet cobras??!!! Are you INSANE?*

"Sorry," he says to Netanya, pulling his phone out from his pocket. "I have to make sure this isn't a work emergency."

I watch the corners of his lips twitch as he reads my message.

"Everything okay?" Netanya asks.

"Yeah, sorry," he says, glancing up at her. "It's just a text from the crazy lady who sometimes stalks me."

I hang my head. Great, Caleb. Just . . . great.

"You have a stalker?"

He finishes swallowing before replying, "Yes, but she's mostly harmless. I'd block her number, but I don't want her to lash out."

"What does the 'mostly' part mean?"

"I found her in my bedroom a few weeks ago."

It was his office, I nearly shout.

Netanya gasps, and I've decided I've had enough. I throw my napkin on the table and stand up, then jerk my head to signal for him to follow me.

It's time for this "controlling" matchmaker to inform the hottest bachelor of Brooklyn that he is a complete and utter *dating disaster.*

Chapter Eighteen

Caleb saunters into the darkened hallway a minute later. I open the restroom door and gesture for him to go inside. "Want to tell me why you're spying on my date?" he says, all casual innocence as he leans his back against the wall.

"Isn't it obvious? Look at you," I say, spreading my arms, only to knock my hand against the hand dryer. I wince and tuck it under my armpit. "You're the hottest of hot messes."

He props the back of his shoe against the wall and tilts his head. "This coming from the woman with red lipstick and facial hair."

I put my hands on my hips to restrain myself from strangling him. "Tell me the truth—are you intentionally sabotaging these dates?"

"No," he says, but I remain unconvinced.

"No? So you're saying that you actually have Holocaust Mommy-and-Me playdates and have plans to get an eighteen-foot cobra?"

He crosses his arms. "Do you cross-examine all of your clients?"

"Just the most difficult ones."

He shakes his head wordlessly.

My mind flashes back to the night of the Chanukah party when we almost kissed, the printout of our conversation, and the way he looked at me the other week when he said I'd never been alone. The password to his phone coinciding with my birthday. And then I understand all too easily why.

No.

No, no, no.

I'm overthinking everything. It is something of a talent of mine. And sure, Caleb is kind and supportive, but that's what friends do. In fact, he's gone above and beyond what many friends do. He shows up at my house most mornings and runs with me in cold, bitter weather. He delivers groceries so I no longer have to shop for food. He even noticed my tennis shoes were starting to get worn, and the very next day he casually handed me a pair of top-of-the-line sneakers. Statistically speaking, there are probably tons of platonic friends who made out, or at least wanted to at some point in their friendship. Call it science, call it curiosity, I don't know. Maybe people get bored and figure it's a good way to kill time.

Ever since the anniversary dinner five years earlier, when that spark between us first ignited, there's been a pull lingering behind our interactions. A very small, very tiny pull. So miniscule that it's not even worth thinking about.

Then again, maybe I'm the only one who had an itch.

"Because you've said you want to get married and have a family," I continue, then clear my throat. He nods. "Unlike me," I add, glancing away. "I'm never going to marry anyone."

He studies me for a long moment. "You think that now, but maybe one day—"

"*Noooo.*" My blood turns to ice knowing the direction of his thoughts. That I might have a change of heart one day and make a different choice. That life without marriage and children might be too lonely to bear. That maybe I'd overcome my fears of abandonment and determine that love is worth the risk in the end. That love is always the answer.

"Can I ask you a question?" he says, taking a step closer.

My heart starts to pound. All I can think is, *I'm not ready for this* because once he puts it out there, there's no going back.

The worst part is, I'm not sure that I'd want it to.

"Why are your eyes brown?"

"Huh?" I blink.

"Your eyes. I know I've been out of town for the last two weeks, but I'm pretty sure they were blue when I left," he says, since I must appear confused. Which I am. How did we go from discussing love and marriage to my eye color?

"I—" I shake my head, clearing my thoughts. My heart slowly returns to its normal pace. "These are contacts." His eyebrows lift, clearly impressed. "Yeah, I know," I say, feeling smug. "I am that good."

He tries to frown, but it comes out as a twitchy smile. "You're definitely something."

I feel a thousand times lighter now that the danger has passed. "You probably want to hire me now to work for you as a super spy or something," I tease.

"If only that was an actual job title."

"I'd make a great spy. Admit it."

"The thing about spies, especially 'super spies'," he says, making quotation marks with his fingers, "is that they have to be able to blend into a crowd. They have to be forgettable."

"Easy." I nod. "I can totally do that."

He shakes his head. "Nothing about you is forgettable, Tinsel."

I lean against the wall, suddenly dizzy.

"Also," he adds, stepping back to open the bathroom door, "red lipstick and facial hair are a conspicuous combination."

And then he's gone. I'm left all weak-kneed and shaky, and he's completely unaffected. What if I had thrown myself at him and he had to pry me off, like that woman at the Chanukah party he told me about?

I splash some cold water on my face, remove the contacts, and wipe off my mustache and lipstick. There's no point in going back to the table, so I decide to flag down the first waiter I see to pay for my meal and leave, but as I open the bathroom door, I see Caleb walking toward me.

"She left," he says, looking bewildered.

My mouth opens in surprise. "Netanya?"

He nods, and hands me a napkin with scribbled writing:

Sorry, I don't think we're a match. Best of luck!

I lean against the wall and groan. There goes another one. Although this time, I have to accept some of the blame. If Caleb hadn't been gone from the table for so long, she might not have left. Who am I kidding? Even if she had stayed the whole time, it's not like she was going to want a second date.

I glance at Caleb to see how he's handling the news. He looks lost in thought. Could he be having a change of heart now that he was stood up? Is he one of those men who loves a good chase? I wish I could crawl inside his brain.

"Are you okay?" I ask gently.

"It's just . . ." He shakes his head and sighs. "I hate eating alone in public spaces."

I give him an odd look. What is he up to? "You could have them pack it up for you."

"It's a waste of plastic."

"You could fix yourself dinner at home."

"And waste a good rib-eye?" He tsks.

"Caleb," I say, trying not to laugh, "would you like me to join you for dinner?"

He strokes his thumb against his bottom lip. "I suppose that could work."

"The sacrifices I make for you," I tease as we head back to his table.

"I'll reward you with a rib-eye."

"I don't want a steak, I want a hot dog."

"I doubt there's a children's menu."

"Shut up."

He laughs and when the waiter comes over, I order a chicken wellington with mushrooms. Halfway through the meal, it occurs to me that there's a strong possibility that

Caleb has dating anxiety or commitment issues because he's back to being himself again. And when he's himself, he's completely delightful. A total catch.

At first glance, you'd never guess that someone like him could have dating anxiety, but the more I think about it, the more sense it makes. Why else would he still be single at thirty-three?

Something else falls into place, too. Hypothetically, if you wanted to get married and have a family, but had overwhelming dating anxiety, then it makes sense that you might convince yourself that you're in love with the female friend that you've known forever who doesn't want to get married. How much more convenient would that be than having to put yourself out there and make a fool of yourself?

And a fool, he did.

"Bubbles," I scoff, shaking my head. "If someone gets a snake—which I'm against because they belong in the wild to slither happy and free—but *if* someone does, the very least they could do is give them a respectable name."

He glances at me, amused. "Such as?"

"Danger. Killer." I shrug, and add, "Fang."

"What about Dolly?"

"No."

"Princess?"

"So wrong."

"Fluffy? Giggles?"

My mind drifts to thinking about wild animals and how sad it is when they're kept in cages in a zoo or circus. They need to roam and kill each other, the way G-d intended. Anytime someone is made to be in an unnatural environment, including humans, they're on edge—or worse, depressed. Many animals need to be in their natural habitats in order to thrive.

Humans are like animals in many ways. Some flourish around friends in busy places and some are happiest alone at home for long periods of time.

I study Caleb. Perhaps fancy restaurants aren't his happy place. And how can he show off his best self when he isn't comfortable to begin with?

My thoughts are interrupted when our waiter returns with our dessert—a red velvet mini cake for me, and a non-dairy lemon cheesecake mousse for him—and as I close my eyes and savor the heavenly flavors, an idea comes to me.

Chapter Nineteen

"Caleb," I say, my eyes flying open. He glances away as if he's embarrassed to be caught staring at me. "Where are you happiest?"

"In the boxing ring."

I grimace. Maybe I didn't phrase the question right. "Is there an activity that relaxes you?"

"My morning run. Lifting weights." His lips wrap around the spoon and for some reason, I can't look away.

"So, uh, physical things?"

"Mmm hmm." His tongue licks at a corner of his mouth where a dab of mousse landed. "Want some?" he offers, holding his spoon out.

"I . . ." My cheeks heat up. *Aaarrgghh—stop it with the blushing! It's not like he offered to put the dessert on interesting parts of your body and then lick it off.*

"Do you feel okay?" Caleb asks. "You look flushed."

"I'm fine," I say brusquely. I try to focus on what I'd been saying. "Is there anything besides punishing your body that brings you joy?"

"I can think of a few things," he says in a husky voice, then swirls his tongue against the spoon. The things he's doing to that spoon is obscene. Borderline illegal.

"Do you mind?" I say.

"What?"

"I'm trying to have a conversation, and meanwhile you're . . ." I stop and make hand gestures at him.

"Eating?"

I cross my arms. "I've never seen anyone eat like that before."

He flashes a crooked smile. "Are you blushing, Tinsel?"

Okay, I've had enough. I push my red velvet cake at him and then steal his mousse. I don't even like lemon-flavored desserts, but I can't continue to let him distract me.

"I wanted that," he says, gazing at the spoonful of mousse in my hand.

"The cake is delicious," I say. "Try it." I tentatively take a lick of the dessert, expecting to hate it, but an explosion of flavors burst on my tongue causing it to tingle.

"Ohch my gawd," I moan. "It tashes shooo good!"

Caleb's eyes skitter across my face, and he clears his throat. "Yes. I know."

"Wow." I didn't know that food could make your tongue tickle. Is there such a thing as a mouthgasm? Because I think I just had one. "How's the cake?" I ask.

"Not as good as the mousse."

"I completely agree." I take another huge spoonful. "Anyway," I say, returning back to the topic at hand. "Besides the gym, where else makes you happy?"

He finishes chewing and wipes his mouth with his napkin. "Work."

Work. I shake my head. What is wrong with this man? I was hoping he'd say relaxing after work with a drink or hiking in a forest or something. It makes me scared to ask what his other favorite places are.

But I suppose work could do. It's definitely a step up from the boxing ring, that's for sure.

"So, Caleb," I say, and he puts down his spoon and gazes at me expectedly. "I don't know if you know this, but as a matchmaker, I also provide coaching lessons to my . . . special clients."

"I see."

"And you are very, very special."

The corners of his eyes twinkle with amusement. He lifts up his glass of water and murmurs, "Do you think so?"

"Oh, I know so. Which is why," I continue, "I think it would be a good idea to do a practice dating session at your work. You could pretend that I'm your date and give me a grand tour, and then give me some tips on self-defense, for example, how to kill someone like you with my bare hands. And if at any point you have an impulse to start talking about Kristallnacht or getting a pet tarantula, I'll coach you through it."

"I can't teach you to take down someone who's twice your size and a trained fighter. It's not possible. And," he adds, before I have time to protest, "there's no concept of *shomer* in a self-defense class."

"First of all," I say, holding up a finger. "Just because I may not be able to make you unconscious, doesn't mean that there aren't tons of women out there who could."

"Sure," he acknowledges with a slight shoulder dip. "As long as they're around six-foot-three, somewhere around the two-hundred-and-thirty-pound mark, and a trained fighter," he adds. "Under those circumstances, I completely agree."

"Yeah," I say, leaning forward. "And they're out there too. Lurking in the dark, waiting for the right moment to strike big, arrogant men."

"I guess I'll be sleeping with the light on tonight," he says, looking relaxed and confident, and not at all like someone who understands the meaning of fear.

"You're so annoying," I say, causing him to laugh.

"I can't believe Zevi never taught you self-defense," he says, shaking his head.

"When would he have had time to? He was in London and when he came home, he was working nonstop on his film production company."

"Didn't he come home to visit?"

"The first year he did, but then he ran out of money." I shake my head. "Back then, he barely had enough money to eat."

"I didn't realize," he says after a pregnant pause.

"He wouldn't have told you." I shrug. "He tried not to tell me either, but as you know, I can be *pushy* when I want to be, so I harassed him until he confessed. He didn't want me to worry, just like I didn't want him to worry about how hard it was for me to take care of our mom." I blink. Whoa. Where did that come from?

A shadow crosses his eyes. "When did your mom get sick?"

I think back to the day when I found her collapsed on the kitchen floor. It was the scariest moment of my life, coming home from school to discover my mother's unconscious body. I drag my finger down my cold glass of water. "I was fifteen."

"Where was Leah?"

"Married and living in Israel."

He slowly shakes his head. "Then, who took care of your mom?"

"I did."

"But—" He looks perplexed. "You were a kid. You must've had help. A home nurse or something?"

I snort. "Do I look rich and famous to you?"

"But you were a kid," he repeats. There's a wrinkle between his brows that wasn't there a moment ago. I glance down at my plate. I hate seeing the pity in his eyes.

"I grew up fast," I say, twisting my napkin. "It wasn't easy, but I was lucky in a way," I add. "I packed a lifetime of amazing memories in those seven years with her. Some people can't stand their mothers," I add, thinking of Sissel's relationship with her mom. "Mine was my best friend. I like to think she still is—once in a while I talk to her," I hear myself confess. "I know she's dead," I add quickly. "I'm not one of those people that thinks Elvis Presley is still alive hiding out on some island somewhere. It just makes me feel better to think that she's nearby, and that she can hear me even though I can't hear her.

"You probably think I'm pathetic," I say, thinking aloud. *OMFG. I'm a train veering off the tracks. Someone put a gag in my mouth and save me.*

"Hey," he says softly, and waits for me to look at him. "I think you're the strongest person I know." I start to scoff, but he cuts me off. "You are. You singlehandedly bore the burden of taking care of your mom. You were a child and you had no one. And," he takes a deep breath, as though he's trying to contain himself, "I'm sorry I wasn't there for you."

Aaaaah. Don't you dare cry. Remember what Bubbe said: Keep the feelings in the attic. Rein it in, girl.

"It's fine," I say, forcing a cheery smile. "You were protecting our country with your super-secret spy skills."

"Do you ever—" he abruptly stops.

"What? Do I ever what?"

"Think about your father? As in, hunting him down and killing him?"

I snort and some water goes up my nose. I cough and reach for my napkin. "Sometimes," I confess. "But I've mostly made peace with the fact that he's a dickwad. Did you know that he wrote my mom a letter about a decade after he left?"

He shakes his head. "No. I didn't know that."

"Yeah." I swallow. "It was short and not so sweet. Something to the effect that he had gotten to the point where it was leaving us or killing himself."

"No," he breathes.

I nod. "My mom was all, *'we can't judge and bearing grudges is pointless'*." I shrug. "I disagree. I think bearing grudges is motivational. Like, me living my best life is the best kind of revenge on my dad. And Mrs. Schwartz," I add.

"Hmm."

I glance at him. "What?"

"Nothing."

"It isn't nothing. You made a *hmm* sound for a reason."

"No, I mean—" He breaks off and shakes his head. "I see your point, and I agree that it is the best kind of revenge."

"But?"

"But living your life in order to prove something to someone else might not be a recipe for happiness."

I swallow, caught off guard by my emotions.

"How are we doing?" our waiter says, appearing at the table. *We're almost crying, thanks for asking.* "Can I get you anything?"

Caleb glances at me, and I point to my mousse and say, "I'll order one of these to go."

"Very good. And anything for you, sir?"

"Just the check. Thanks."

"I'll be back with that in a moment," the waiter says, then glides away.

I clear my throat, eager to change the subject. "Anyway, what's the point of self-defense if I can only take on someone my own size?"

Luckily Caleb doesn't insist we finish our last topic. "The point of self-defense is to give you enough time to escape a bad situation, no matter the size of the person you're fighting. But *killing* someone twice your size with your bare hands isn't realistic. And as a general life rule, it's better to escape someone than to kill them. But," he adds, "as far as teaching you, there's still the issue of *shomer*."

"Can you teach it without touching?" I ask. "Do you have diagrams you could use instead, or mannequins?"

"Diagrams or mannequins," he repeats under his breath, looking appalled.

I shrug. "A YouTube short?"

"That is not how this works, Ashira." My eyebrows lift at him *Ashira-ing* me. "You need hand-to-hand practice with someone in order to build the muscle memory necessary—"

"Forget it," I interrupt, waving my hand. "It's too complicated. Let's just have you give me a tour of the building, and then we can have a picnic in your office where we can roleplay."

Unfortunately, Caleb is suddenly invested in the idea. "Every woman should know self-defense."

"Agreed. Just like every man should know to limit the number of times he mentions his mother on a date."

He flashes a grin. "I'll try to remember that."

"Good."

"You know what, Gunnilda can teach you."

"Gunnilda?"

He nods. "She's one of our top operators. She was part of *Jegertroppen*, Norway's female armed special forces."

I think about that. "So, could she kill you with her bare hands?"

"Definitely."

I grin, glad to know there's at least one woman who can physically intimidate a seasoned warrior like Caleb. "Is she huge then?" I ask.

"She's not small."

"Is she nice?" I ask uneasily. I'm not exactly someone with a high threshold for pain.

"She isn't not nice, exactly."

"What does that mean?" I'm not sure I like the picture he's painting of her.

"She's a little rough around the edges, that's all."

This is not going to end well for me, I can feel it in my gut. No one named Gunnilda is going to be concerned about my pain tolerance. "Maybe we should take a pottery class together instead."

"I thought you wanted me to be in my element."

"That was before I was worried about my physical safety."

"You'll be fine. Gunnilda knows what she's doing."

Stop worrying, Ashira. Just do whatever it takes to save the company. I picture my mother's face, and it strengthens my resolve.

On our drive back home, I broach the subject of Netanya Li. I still can't quite figure out what he's looking for when I set him up with women who tick all the boxes.

"What did you think of Netanya? Putting aside how it all went down, did you like her?"

"She was all right."

Not exactly the enthusiasm I was hoping to hear, but maybe it's his anxiety talking. It's probably trying to convince him of all the reasons it's safer to say no than take a leap of faith. "Would you have wanted a second date, in theory?"

"Not really."

"It's scary." I nod. "But I think that if we give you some tools for your toolbox, and a tranquilizer or two, you might be surprised how painless dating can be. Especially once you meet someone you really like."

He doesn't respond. A sudden wave of guilt washes over me. Am I selfish for doing this, for using him to save my business? Even if that's true, isn't it still good for him to put himself out there? How else is he going to find the love of his life?

Strong and steadfast. Consistent. Those are the things he needs from me right now, though he may not know it. I have to stay focused on the goal, and not get caught up about his feelings.

The traffic light turns red and he brakes to a stop. Light illuminates the bottom half of his face and I notice the subtle frown on his lips.

"I'm sorry," I blurt, lowering my face into the palms of my hands. "You don't have to do this."

"You have nothing to apologize for," he says, turning to me in surprise. "I want to help you—"

"And yourself?" I cut in, my voice hopeful.

"And myself," he says wearily. "And there's nothing wrong with the women, not at all. But something's missing."

"What?"

He shrugs and stares ahead. "I have no desire to stay up and talk to them all night. I don't think about them when I'm not with them, or count down the moments to when I can see them next. I can't picture waking up with them every morning. I can't see them being the mother of my children. I don't feel the fire," he murmurs, turning to me. "The heat. That at all consuming need to trace my lips down every inch of their body and press their curves against mine."

My mouth drops open.

"Although," he says casually, pushing on the gas as the light turns green, "I have to admit, Netanya Li was pretty hot."

Welp. That was a bucket of cold water on my fire.

"So . . . do you want me to try to set up another date with her?" I say, feeling confused.

"No." He shakes his head. "Were you not listening to a word I said?"

"Uh, I was," I reply. "But there were a lot of conflicting messages."

He exhales the long, exhausted breath of someone who's nearing the end of their patience. "My point is, that despite the fact that Netanya Li is gorgeous and has a great personality, I still have no desire to be with her. None."

"So basically," I say with furrowed brows, "you're looking for an elusive connection that can't be described on paper."

"Exactly."

Great. This should be a piece of cake.

Speaking of which. He pulls up in front of my house, and I hand him the box with the lemon cheesecake mousse inside. I unbuckle my seatbelt and say, "I had you buy this for you."

The curve of his smile makes me feel slightly giddy. "Thank you, Tinsel. No one's ever had me buy myself a present before."

I laugh. "See you in the morning."

"Get a good night's sleep. Tomorrow is our tempo run. I've mapped a route for intervals and hill repeats."

I groan as I open the door. "You're evil."

"Come on." He laughs. "You know you love it."

What I do love is spending one-on-one time with him. Not that I can admit it. Even as our friendship grows, I know that it can't last. Once he's married, there won't be any more morning runs or deep conversations or food deliveries appearing on my doorstep. His time and focus will be for his wife and new family. Exactly as it should be.

I feel a sharp pang of sadness.

A car honks, and I realize there's a line of vehicles behind us.

"Don't wait for me to get in," I say. "I've got my key in my purse."

He nods.

Am I surprised at the angry symphony of honks as I walk to my door and let myself in? Not even a little bit. Wild horses couldn't come between Caleb and a mission to protect someone he cares about.

I give Caleb an exasperated wave as I close the door, and smile as he drives off. He won't be my close friend forever, but that's all the more reason to appreciate him while he is.

Chapter Twenty

It's a Tuesday which means dropping off Bernice's dry-cleaning, and visiting my buddy Bruce on the way back. It's been several weeks since our little "break", and I can tell I'm growing on him.

I open the bodega's shop door and wait in line for my turn.

"Oh good," he says with a straight face, "it's you again."

"Hello dearest Bruce, it's so good to see you."

"I'm sure," he murmurs, and starts preparing a lox and cream cheese bagel. Bruce has gotten into the habit of giving me free food with my coffee, and like a stray cat, I keep coming back for more. "How's your love life?"

"Our agreement is that I give you free food as long as you don't harass me."

"Really?" I drum my fingers on the counter. "I don't recall agreeing to that. By the way," I say, "I need a favor."

"Something more than free lunch twice a week?"

"Yup." I nod, and he sighs. "So, you know my neighbor, Bernice? The one whose dry-cleaning stuff I pick up and drop off?"

"Mmhm," he murmurs, pressing buttons on the coffeemaker.

"Well, I think I know a guy that she might like, but she's made it very clear that she won't go on a date unless I go with her. And I have to bring my own date too. But it wouldn't be real," I quickly add. "The date, that is. So . . . can you do it?"

"*Me?*" He looks slightly appalled by the idea. Not even slightly, actually. Just straight-up appalled.

"Calm down, it's just a one-time fake date for my neighbor's sake."

"Why are you asking *me?*"

I shrug and try to look innocent. "Why wouldn't I ask you?" Maybe I'm trying to draw him out of his shell, slowly and cautiously, as one would with an injured squirrel. If I wanted an injured squirrel to join my database, that is.

"Is this a setup?" he asks, narrowing his eyes as he hands me my coffee. "Am I going to get there and find out that I'm Bernice's date?"

I laugh. "No, definitely not. Although," I add, still laughing, "she'd love that."

"I'll think about it." He puts the food in a small paper bag.

"Thanks." I make a show of bringing out some pennies and nickels and throwing them into the tip jar. "Don't spend it all at once."

He shakes his head and smiles. "Get outta here already."

"We'll be in touch. *Byeee*," I call and wiggle my fingers.

But instead of going home like normal, I make a small detour.

* * *

Looming in front of me is an old brick mansion that has been converted into a Jewish funeral home. This was where Bubbe, my paternal grandmother volunteered in the seventies and eighties, before her back gave out. For many years, she was a member of the *Chevra Kadisha*, the Jewish burial society that perform *taharas*—cleaning and dressing the deceased in plain white shrouds before the bodies are placed inside their caskets.

It's not your average kid's playground, but it was like a second home to me.

For years after my father left us, my grandmother helped pick up the slack by babysitting me so my mom could work and take college classes at night. The transition from being a normal, middle-class family to being poor and labeled as 'broken' isn't something that goes away. Those feelings of shame and grief become part of you, as if someone has taken a hot iron and branded them on your soul.

The funeral home was my escape—the place I looked forward to going to when Bubbe did her *taharas* in the basement along with two other women. The only part I never ventured to was the bottom level where the bodies were kept.

The owners of the funeral home, Lenny and Betty, lived on the third floor, and always made me feel welcome.

Lenny was often in and out, depending on how many funerals he had to run that day, but Betty was a homebody. Though they didn't keep kosher, Betty made sure to keep some snacks certified by the OU—Orthodox Union—for me. She taught me how to play Gin Rummy, Slapjack, and War. When she had friends visit, we'd play Mahjong, and while they sipped on their fruity cocktails, she gave me Manischewitz grape juice in a plastic cup. I always suspected the cocktails tasted better.

A fierce wind snaps me out of my reverie as I climb the front steps. The door is locked, and I ring the doorbell. I remember how Bubbe had once panicked because she couldn't find the key to the freezer where the bodies were kept, and explained that bad guys like to steal corpses. I chuckle about it now, but it was a bit much for eight-year-old me to take in.

But that was Bubbe for you, eccentric to the core.

"Can I help you?" a woman's voice rings out.

I swivel my head to the camera with the intercom attached. "Hi, I'm an old friend of Mr. Horowitz's, and I was hoping to chat with him for a few minutes."

"Is he expecting you?"

"No, but I'm—"

"Name?"

"Ashira Wernick."

"Hold on. You want elevator music?"

"Uhm." I blink. "I'm not really a fan, to be honest."

"What do you like then?"

"Uh . . . I like most pop."

"Who are your favorite artists?"

I cross my arms and wonder if this is some kind of entrance quiz? "I love Lady Gaga and Bruno Mars. Coldplay. Madonna. The Beatles—"

"What are you, a hundred years old?" the woman says, not sounding all that impressed.

"Twenty-eight, but I've got an old soul." I don't bother to explain that these were the artists whose music my mom and I listened to together on her sickbed. Some of them were vomited to as well, but I try not to think about that.

"Do you like Aidan Bissett?"

"Sorry, I don't know who that is," I say as a gust of wind slams against my face. I tighten the scarf around my neck and wonder where I went wrong. Why am I discussing musicians outside on one of the coldest days of the year? "Could you let me in?" I ask. "It's freezing out here."

"What's your name again?"

"Ashira Wernick," I say, between jump up and down. Gotta keep the blood flowing.

"Hold on, please. And you said no to elevator music?"

"Correct," I say through clenched teeth. I swear, this woman is worse than a phone and internet bot.

After a few minutes that feels more like twenty, a young woman opens the door. She can't be a day over eighteen, sporting pink hair, black lipstick, and too many piercings to count. Her shirt says, *Embrace the rage*.

"I can't believe you don't know who Aidan Bissett is," she huffs. "He's the best new musician around."

She's embracing the rage, all right.

"Is Mr. Horowitz around?" I ask, not wanting to get sucked into another music debate. I step inside, but I keep my coat on. The heating in this house is as bad as I remember.

"Maybe." She gazes at me suspiciously. "How do you know him?"

"We go way back. He and his wife used to watch me when my grandmother did *taharas*." My eyes land on Betty's picture hanging in the parlor, and I go closer and run my fingers across the frame, feeling a lump form against my throat. I remember hearing about Betty's death a while back, but I couldn't go to the funeral because my mother was too sick to be left alone. I sent flowers and a note, but I wish I had done more.

"I'm her granddaughter," the woman says, dipping her head toward the picture.

"Ooh." I turn around and gaze at her in surprise. "I had no idea."

"Yeah." She studies the photo of the Betty, with the conservative gray bob and pearl necklace, before turning back to me. "We don't really look alike."

A burst of laughter escapes me, and I cover my mouth because, well, dead people.

"I'm so sorry for your loss," I say, clearing my throat. "I have a lot of great memories of her."

"I didn't know her very well," the woman—girl, really—says. "She had dementia for like, a decade."

"Oh my gosh. I had no idea." I was thirteen when Bubbe died, and I hadn't seen either Betty or Lenny since. "What's your name?"

"Sadie."

She doesn't look like a Sadie. I guess I was expecting her to say something along the lines of 'Viper' or 'Spike'.

"Nice to meet you, Sadie. How is your grandfather these days?"

"Why are you here?" she says, leveling cool eyes at me.

I guess we're leaning into the rage again.

"I'm a matchmaker," I say. "I have a neighbor who's recently widowed and the first man I thought of was Lenny."

Mostly because of Lenny's off-brand humor. He never had a shortage of dead people jokes, although he made sure Betty wasn't within hearing distance beforehand; she thought it her wifely duty to smack his upper arm every so often just to keep him in line.

And also, there aren't that many eligible older men. There's a fair amount that I wouldn't set up with my worst enemy, and some widowers or divorcees that enjoy being single for the first time in decades and have no desire to remarry.

"I doubt he'll be interested," she says after a long moment. "He's got a girlfriend he met online and he's obsessed with her."

"Oh, never mind then." I shake my head. "I don't want to suggest it if he's already involved with someone."

"I think it's worth a try," she surprises me by saying. "Honestly, I wouldn't be shocked if his girlfriend turned out to be a man writing from a Nigerian prison."

I grimace. "Especially if he starts wiring money overseas."

Her face turns slightly green at the thought. "Wait here," she says. "I'll see if he's interested in coming down."

Some five minutes later, I turn to the sound of footsteps approaching. Behind Sadie is an older version of the man I remember, thinner and stooped over, but otherwise in seemingly good health. His thick white mustache fans across the breadth of his lips and his smile stretches from ear to ear.

He comes to a stop in front of me, and I think we're both amused to find that I'm the taller of us two now. "Ashira Wernick, is that really you?"

"It's me, all right." I grin. "How are you, Lenny?"

"Can't complain. Still putting the '*fun*' in funeral," he chuckles. "Say, do you know what funeral homes have in common with pet supply stores?"

"No," I laugh. "What?"

"Cat litter and no cats!"

Sadie rolls her eyes. "That one needs some work, Zayde." She turns to me and explains, "The cat litter balances out the smell of . . ."

"Rotting corpses!" His raucous laughter is contagious and inappropriate, and I can't stop myself from joining in.

"I got another one," he says, slowly sitting down on one of the armchairs flanking the fireplace.

"Oh my gawd," Sadie says in a flat voice.

"Why can't you cremate a clown?"

"I don't know," I say, sitting down on the couch. "Why?"

"Because they burn *funny*!"

"Hilarious," Sadie says, as Lenny and I dissolve into another round of giggles.

"Wait, I got another one. Whaddya call—"

"Zayde," the girl cuts in. "Did you know that Ashira is a matchmaker?"

"A matchmaker?" He turns to me, looking surprised. "What happened? Did you not get accepted into college?"

I shake my head and laugh. "I didn't apply to any."

"Eh, don't worry about it," he says, with a wave. "You're not missing much."

"How would you know, Zayde? You never went to college."

"So?" He shrugs. "I've never eaten pork, but I'm not missing that either."

"I've eaten pork," she replies, "and trust me, you're missing out."

"That reminds me of a new joke about Hell I heard recently. You ready for this, it's a good one—"

"Ashira," Sadie quickly interrupts. "Tell us about your very single, very attractive neighbor."

"Uh, right, yes." I sit up straight and smile. "So, I have a lovely next-door neighbor whose husband died earlier this year. She has a great personality," I say, even if it is a bit of stretch. "She's seventy-eight and in amazing shape. And sharp as a tack."

Lenny takes it all in, looking a little uncertain. "I don't know, Ashira. The last time I went out on a date was around the time of the Civil Rights Act."

"That is a really long time," I say, nodding. "I can see why that would be daunting. But if it makes you feel better, Bernice hasn't been on a date in about that long too."

"Bernice, did you say?" He tilts his head and narrows his eyes.

I nod and wonder if he knows her. "She's about this tall," I say, and gesture to my shoulder. "Unless she's not in her heels, and then she's about half a foot shorter. She loves sequins and leather. Pretty quirky—"

He barks a laugh. "You're trying to set me up with Bernice Rubin? Or whatever the hell her last name is now?"

I exchange a glance with the granddaughter as the uneasy feeling doubles in size. "Yes?"

"And you said she has a *good personality*!" he scoffs. "That's the lie of the century."

Hopes deflates out of me like a sad, old balloon. "Sure, she can be a bit much, but she's a good person. She shows up for people. When my mom was sick, she helped me in a lot of ways." I cross my arms. "How do you know her?"

"I dated her in high school."

"No!" My jaw drops. "I don't believe it."

"Believe it, all right. We went from lovers to enemies overnight."

"I didn't know you had a girlfriend before Bubbe," the granddaughter says.

"*Girlfriends*," Lenny corrects with an arched eyebrow. "But Bernice was my first love."

"Wow," I whisper, shaking my head. Goosebumps are on my arms. "You have to admit that this sounds a lot like fate."

"It sounds like a worse fate than having a colonoscopy without anesthesia," he replies.

"Ewww, Zayde. The visual," Sadie groans.

"What happened between you two?" I ask. "How did it end so badly?"

"I'll tell you how—I caught her *shtupping* Ernie Schlossinger! On my birthday, no less!" he exclaims.

I watch the emotion play across his face and I'm struck by the intensity and the length of time that he's held onto his hurt. In my eight years of matchmaking, I've reunited old flames before, but never had a case quite like this.

In the early days of my career, I once saw my mother patiently counsel a couple who had come to her for marital guidance. I remember the hours of shouting, accusations, and the periods of tense silence. I don't recall what the result was, but I remember asking my mother why bother spending all that effort when the couple clearly hated each other's guts.

"Because' Ashiraleh," she had said with a smile, "sometimes love is like a flame. As long as there's still a spark, you can rekindle the fire."

Looking at Lenny now, all fired up and red in the face, I wonder if that's true. Could Lenny, deep down, want a second chance with Bernice? It's possible, isn't it?

"And one more thing," Lenny says, getting up from his seat. "You tell that woman that I've got a special casket with her name on it, and I'll make sure it takes a shortcut to *Hell*."

On second thought, maybe my mother had no idea what she was talking about. She did tend to see love through rose-tinted glasses. Sometimes I wonder whether she reasoned away any warning signs of her own marriage.

"It was nice seeing you again, Lenny." I smile and stand up. "I don't think I've ever properly thanked you for opening your home up to me. This funeral home holds some of my best childhood memories."

"Said no child ever," the granddaughter murmurs.

"Eh." He shrugs, a small grin tugging at his lips. "You were a good kid. And unlike your neighbor," he adds, "you are always welcome to come here and visit."

They walk me to the door, and as I step outside into the cold, Lenny calls out, "Don't be strange!"

I laugh, suddenly recalling the familiar dialogue we used to have when my grandmother would come get me. And luckily, I still remember my line. "You mean, don't be a stranger."

He winks. "That too."

I smile. Despite the frigid temperature, a warm glow travels throughout my body. Although the matchmaking expedition didn't work out, I'm still happy I came.

But do I plan on delivering Lenny's message to Bernice? Hell no.

Chapter Twenty-One

The following day finds me riding buckled and blindfolded in an unmarked white van on my way to Caleb's workplace. I was considering having Caleb's next date take place at work—that being his most natural element—but not if this is the only mode of transport.

"This all seems a bit excessive," I say to the driver, the legendary Casanova himself. "Don't you think?"

"No."

"What exactly is the point of blindfolding me?"

"I tell you how many times already, this compound is secret location."

"And you think some bad guy will discover I've been there and then do what exactly? Torture me to find out where it's located?"

"Yes."

"I doubt it," I say. "And honestly, it's a little hurtful that you don't trust me not to buckle under pressure." *I would so buckle under pressure.* "It must be hard not to trust anyone."

"Who said anyone?" he replies. "Just you I not trust."

"Again, hurtful."

"I trust Caleb." I hear the tick-tick of the signal and I grab onto the door handle as the car takes a sharp turn. "And Allah."

"In that order?" I joke.

"You make me want to put mouth gag on you."

I laugh and roll my eyes, though it's a wasted effort since he can't see. The car jerks to a stop and I nearly fly through the dashboard. Casanova's driving style is in perfect sync with his personality—abrupt and aggressive.

"So, what is it about Caleb that makes you trust him?" I ask, mostly to distract him from his road rage. He's spent the whole journey shouting how everyone is an idiot, that this guy drives too slow, that idiot too fast, and that other one must be on meth. *Did I not see how he cut right in front of us?* At which point I had to remind him that some jerk blindfolded me.

He found that hilarious.

"Tell me about you and Caleb. Why do you trust him so much?" I try again. I know they met a long time ago at one of the annual training events between the U.S. Navy SEALs and the Israeli IDF's equivalent Shayetet 13, but I have no idea how they formed such a close bond.

"Listen, little civilian," he says. "People in special forces, no matter what country we serve, we are the same people. Same personality traits. Same stubbornness, same high intensity, same ego. Always out to prove who is fittest and smartest. But during an operation, there is no *I*, there is only *we*."

I have to admit, that sounds exactly like Caleb. He's competitive and stubborn, but when it comes down to it, he always puts other people's needs above his own.

"Many years ago, we were in Croatia, teaching their commandos skills because they idiots over there and know nothing."

Yep. There's that ego he was just talking about.

"One night, we get free tickets to go to the Serbia-Croatia world cup qualifier." He stops and sighs. "We could smell the players' armpits, that's how close our seats were."

I wrinkle my nose. "Gross."

"Yes, it was wonderful," he says. "But then some psycho started shooting at people. And you know what Caleb did? He covered me with his body to save my life. He didn't have to, but he did."

"Wow," I say softly. I imagine the scene. The chaos and the fear that they must've felt. It's one thing to train for a battle, but quite another to live it—especially when it wasn't a battle, but a football match.

"But, neither of you got hurt, right?"

"Not me, but Caleb, yes. That Yehudi took three bullets for *me*—a Sunni Muslim. And in that moment, he became more than just my friend. He became my brother," he says in a thick voice.

"That's really beautiful," I say, even though the thought of Caleb getting shot makes me feel ill. It makes me wonder what else he's been through as a soldier, or how many other injuries he's sustained. There's an entire fifteen-year period of his life that I don't know much about. I feel unexpectedly choked up.

That is, until Casanova starts to lecture.

"You civilians," Casanova continues, "can never understand what it's like to be feet in boots."

I blink. "Feet in boots?"

"Boots in feet?" he tries. "Boots on floor?"

"Ooooh." I laugh. "Boots on the ground."

"Yes, yes, whatever," he says in an impatient voice. "You live in different world. You cannot understand what it's like."

I've noticed the way Caleb always changes the subject when someone broaches the topic of his service. He seems to act as if the fifteen years he spent in the military was a bad vacation he never wants to remember. Now though I wonder if it had more to do with the audience. Maybe Casanova has a point, maybe I can't understand what it's like. But I'd still listen. And I'm surprised to realize that I *want* to. I would want to hear about Caleb's time in the military, and more about Caleb in general.

For matchmaking purposes. Strictly professional.

"Does he talk about that stuff with you?" I ask.

"Sometimes."

At least he has someone he can talk to. And hopefully, he'd be able to share those things with his wife, whoever she ends up being.

Casanova turns on the radio, signaling that our heart-to-heart has come to a close.

When we arrive at the property, which Casanova informs me spans two-hundred-acres, he finally removes my blindfold. I blink against the blinding sunlight.

"Whoa," I say, gazing around. This place is beyond huge. "Is that the main office?" I ask, pointing to a wide, three-story glass-fronted building straight ahead.

"Yes. *Yalla*," he says in Arabic, and motions for me to follow him inside.

A prominent *mezuzah* in a beautiful wood casing adorns the top right side of the front doorpost and I smile as I reach up to touch it, then kiss my fingers.

"Why you do this?" Casanova asks, mimicking how I kissed my fingers. "Caleb doesn't."

"Some Jews have different customs," I explain, as he holds the door open for me and I walk inside. "Some touch it, without kissing the hand, and some don't touch it at all."

He nods, glancing back over his shoulder at the *mezuzah*. "The Torah words inside—it protects your people, yes?"

"Sort of," I reply. "But more than anything, it's a reminder to Jews that G-d is the only one who can protect us."

"And these," he smirks, pointing to the metal detectors and the somewhat bored-looking workers attending them. "Go on, then," he adds, motioning with his hand.

"Seriously? You're going to scan me?"

"And your purse."

"And my purse," I mutter under my breath.

"Don't worry," he says. "For you, I do it myself."

"Great."

He holds out his hand expectedly and I pass my purse to him with an exaggerated eye roll. At a nearby table, he unzips the purse and turns it upside down. I watch the contents fall out, some crashing to the ground as he gives it several vicious shakes.

He makes a show of putting on gloves and examining every item, like he's never seen a packet of Tic Tacs or a tampon in his life.

"You mind?" he asks, already inserting a piece of my gum inside his mouth. "*Ech.*" He makes a face and spit it out. "Why you buy tropical? They have no mint?"

"I'm sorry," I say. "I'll make sure to keep your taste in mind the next time I go shopping."

Using a tweezers, he lifts up a tissue with red splotches. "This your blood? Or someone else's?"

"It was my nail polish," I say, and wiggle my fingers to show him the red color on my nails. "I forgot to throw it out."

He gazes at my nails and then back at me suspiciously.

"Does he do this to everyone?" I call out to the other guys.

"Only the people he likes," one of them responds, which causes the others to laugh.

"Are you done yet?" I cross my arms and frown at Casanova.

"Wow. Wow, wow." He gives me the side-eye over the crumbled receipt in his hand. "Lots of toilet paper. Expensive kind too."

"Only the best for my neighbor," I say tightly.

By the time we're in the elevator, I'm convinced the ambience of this place is not conducive to romance. High blood pressure, yes. But love? Definitely not.

When the elevator doors open on the fourth-floor, Caleb is there, waiting to greet me with a smile. It feels like ages since I last saw him when in fact it had only been some thirty odd hours. We skipped our run this morning since it was a recovery day.

"Hey, you." He's in a fitted olive green henley that hugs his muscular body, and I imagine how his skin would feel beneath my fingers.

"You good?" Caleb asks, tilting his head. I was caught staring like a total pervert. OMG, I'm no better than that speed dating Mordechai. Heat crawls up my neck and face, and straight up to my brain.

Be a professional, FFS. I clear my throat. "Never better," I say with a bright smile.

"She didn't like my driving," Casanova reports.

"Or being blindfolded," I add. "Although now I can cross off being abducted on my bucket list."

Caleb narrows his eyes at Casanova. "That was not necessary. Don't do that again."

"Okay, okay." He lifts his palms in surrender. "What about mouth gag? Yes or no?"

"Go," Caleb commands, pointing to the elevator.

Once the elevator doors close with Casanova inside, Caleb dips his head. "C'mon. Let me show you my office."

His office is more spacious than I had expected. Aside from the desk and two chairs facing it, there's a punching bag in one corner and a bench press and weights. There's even a small kitchenette, complete with a mini refrigerator and coffee station.

"You look nice."

"Oh—thanks." I smile, inordinately pleased. I'm in a light-blue knit sweater set that matches my eyes. "I'm on a fake date, after all."

He smiles. "Want something to drink?" he asks as the door clicks shut behind us.

"Gin on the rocks."

"Sorry, I'm fresh out of that. How about some green tea instead?"

I shudder. "No thanks."

He sits down on the chair in front of his desk. "Matcha?"

"I don't even know what that is."

"It's a type of tea. It's very good for you."

"Okay, here's tip number one—don't offer any weird beverages on the date. You know what you need?" I snap my fingers. "A chilled bottle of champagne in an ice bucket. On a tray. With scattered rose petals."

He looks confused. "Huh?"

"Too much?" I nod. "Yeah, that's more of a proposal thing. Do a nice Chardonnay instead. Also," I add, glancing around the room. "I'm going to have to make some minor tweaks here and there."

His eyebrows lift. "Like what?"

"Like bring in a velvet loveseat."

"Absolutely not."

"You only have office furniture," I point out.

"Because this is an office."

"And then there's the lighting issue," I continue, pretending not to have heard him. "We'll need scented candles and tea lights." I smile as I picture it. "Doesn't that sound romantic?"

"No, it sounds like a firefighter's worst nightmare."

I suck on my bottom lip and consider his point. "It should be fine—as long as no one trips."

Caleb looks like he's about to argue when there's a knock on the door, and he goes to open it. "Hi, come on in," he says to an extremely tall woman with a broad, athletic frame and a long blonde braid steps into the room. She looks like an Icelandic goddess or a Viking warrioress, fresh off the ship and ready to battle the natives.

Definitely over six feet, I decide. And definitely not in my weight class.

Please don't let this be Gunnilda.

"Ashira, meet Gunnilda," Caleb says. "Gunnilda, this is Ashira."

I put on a brave face as we shake hands. Her deadly grip and unflinching eye contact do not put me at ease. *Why isn't she blinking?*

"Hello," she says. Every inch of this woman is terrifying—her thick neck and wide shoulders, muscles bunching and clenching everywhere I look. She cracks her knuckles and adds, "I'm looking forward to our lesson."

Sweat forms on my temples. I glance at Caleb. Doesn't he realize how sadistic she sounds? But he seems completely indifferent. And most disturbing of all is that she doesn't smile. Not even a little. Not even a smidge. What kind of person doesn't smile?

A psychopath, that's who.

I turn to Caleb and say accusingly, "I thought I'm here to help you practice dating."

"I thought we could do both," he says.

Gunnilda grins and wiggles her eyebrows at me.

"I'm sorry," I shake my head. "But I'm not comfortable with a female instructor."

Caleb's eyebrows reach his forehead. "Excuse me?"

"I don't feel comfortable touching a woman."

Gunnilda shrugs and starts heading to the door. "I'll get Casanova."

"*No!*" I yelp. "Sorry," I say, wiping a bead of sweat off my forehead. "I just . . ." I turn to Caleb. "I'd rather you teach me."

"Uh—" He scratches his head. Clears his throat. "Even though there will be . . ."

"Touching. I know."

Gunnilda watches us with interest, like we're her new favorite sitcom and all she needs is a comfy chair and a bucket of popcorn.

"But, out of curiosity . . ." I trail off and actually think about what this might entail. "What kind of touching?" I'm pretty sure it involves a fair amount of crotch-kicking based on Hollywood action movies. "Like, will it be . . . *interesting?*"

Gunnilda grins and then turns to watch Caleb for his reaction. I get the distinct feeling that she can't wait to entertain everyone with this story as soon as she leaves.

Caleb looks very uncomfortable. In fact, I don't remember ever seeing him look so awkward before. "I guess that depends on what you find interesting," Caleb says, scratching the back of his neck.

"A groin kick?"

"You won't be doing that," he says quickly.

"Too bad." Gunnilda smirks. "I'd like to see it."

Caleb has apparently had enough of her company because he opens his office door and says, "Thanks for coming by, Gunnilda. I'll let you know if we need you."

She gives me a small disturbing smile and then she's gone. The door clicks shut and the room feels smaller without her here.

"So," he says, leaning against his desk, "where were we?"

"Wondering how life led me to this point. Because I'm pretty sure I suggested we take a pottery class instead."

"You did. And then I nixed it. But," he pauses, "are you sure you want to do this?"

No. Yes. I close my eyes and think. This isn't casual touching so it's not really breaking any *shomer negiah* laws—it's for life-saving purposes. It's basically the same thing as going to a male gynecologist.

In fact, it could be argued that touching in this way is a *mitzvah*. G-d therefore, totally approves.

And if I have to shimmy out of my tight skirt and do this in my leggings, so be it. It's still way more modest than having a pelvic exam.

"Yes," I say. And then I whip off my skirt.

Chapter Twenty-Two

"Um, all right," Caleb says, staring at the ceiling. "You can tell me to stop at any point if you feel uncomf—"

"Do you feel uncomfortable?" I ask.

"Nope," he says, still gazing up at the ceiling.

"Because you're not looking at me," I add.

"Did you want me to?"

"Well, not in a creepy way," I say quickly. "But basic eye contact would be nice."

He tears his gaze away from the ceiling and looks at me, oh so slowly.

"Good." I nod. "Now just don't look at my legs."

"Don't look at mine either," he says, and I laugh.

"Do we need a safe word?"

He blinks. "A safe word?"

"Or a safe gesture?" I shrug. "That way, if you start to tap out, you can give me the signal and I'll release you. And then no one has to die."

"I'm not too worried, Tinsel." The corners of his lips twist into a crooked smile as he pulls off his henley, leaving his white undershirt on. My mouth goes dry as I see how it clings to his broad shoulders and chest. "Take off your shoes."

"I knew you had a foot fetish," I say, unzipping my ankle boots. "You are so the type."

He points a finger at me. "I do *not* have a foot fetish. And no flirting in my classroom."

I laugh again. It feels so good to live in the moment and have fun, instead of worrying about my dwindling bank account, and whether I'll be able to save my mother's business, all while wondering what Mrs. Schwartz will do to me next. Aside from the social media post, she's scared away prospective clients by intimidating other matchmakers from networking with me. In a business that relies heavily on word-of-mouth, upsetting the wrong person can mean the end of your career.

Being here with Caleb is exactly what I need to decompress. Out of the hustle and bustle of the city, it's easy to pretend that it's just the two of us in another dimension, far away from the real world.

Caleb's undershirt bunches and flexes as he moves furniture out of the way. I lean against the wall and admire the scenery.

Finally, he puts his hands on his hips and looks at me. "Ready?"

"Bring it," I say confidently. But when he takes a step toward me, I squeal, "Wait—maybe . . . we should shake hands first."

Caleb's eyebrow lifts. "Shake hands?"

I nod. "It'll be less awkward that way—us touching for the first time."

"We've touched before," he says, but he's scrunching his face in that way people do when they're not certain of something.

"When?"

"I don't know. When we were kids." He shrugs. "I'm pretty sure you crashed into me on rollerblades more than once."

"But that was *years ago*. Decades. We were *children*."

"I still have the scars."

"Really?" I seem to have given him a lot of scars. My eyes rove over his body curiously. "Where?"

"You want to play Show and Tell?"

I cover my embarrassment by laughing hysterically into my hands and collapsing onto the floor. "Sorry," I gasp, between peals of laughter, "I think I'm nervous."

"It's natural to be nervous your first time," he says in a husky voice.

"*Stop that*," I squeal, clutching my stomach.

"Stop what?" he says, trying to look all innocent. But then he snorts a laugh.

"Come on." He holds his hand out to me. "Let me help you up."

My laughter dies down as I gaze at his hand. *You can do this. You can touch a man.* "Okay."

"Whenever you're ready," he adds as the seconds tick by.

"I think I'm more than just nervous," I say quietly. "I think I'm scared."

"Of me?"

"No." I shake my head. Caleb has never made me feel scared, quite the opposite in fact. So, what is my problem? Am I worried that G-d will be mad at me? Disappointed? Maybe a mixture of the two? Although if I'm perfectly honestly, I've long suspected that G-d set the bar so low for me that it's practically non-existent.

Is it about Caleb, then? Am I nervous that touching him will lead to something that might spin out of control? Will us doing a simple self-defense class cause a tornado-like effect that tosses everything stable into the air, and leaves only devastation in its wake? Is that it?

"Honestly," I say, blinking up at him. "I don't even know."

"Hey," he murmurs, and a flash of tenderness crosses his eyes. "It's just me, okay?"

I nod. And though I don't say it out loud, I wonder if that's the problem. This isn't about touching any man, it's about touching *this one*.

"I've got you," he says, wrapping his hand around mine. The warmth of his skin feels like getting hugged by the sun. He pulls me to my feet and wraps me in the warmest, safest embrace I think I've ever had. I close my eyes and lay my head against his chest, inhaling a combination of men's body wash and fabric softener.

"See," I say, with my cheek on his shoulder, "I told you there was nothing to be scared of."

The rumbling vibration of his laughter relaxes me further. I sniff his shirt like a bloodhound tracking a scent. "I love how you smell. What laundry detergent do you use?"

His brown eyes flicker down at me with amusement. "Whichever one happens to be closest to my hand."

I take a fistful of his shirt and breathe deeply. "Mmm. Spring Breeze with hints of lavender."

"I swear, Tinsel," he sighs, tucking my head under his chin, "you get weirder by the day."

The door suddenly opens and we jump apart like guilty teenagers. Casanova faces us with disapproving eyes, and waves his hand in the space between Caleb and me. "What this is? A new type of self-defense?"

"Uh, no. W-we were just warming up," I say, turning beet red. I grab my skirt and put it back on. For some inexplicable reason, touching Caleb feels like less of a sin than being caught in leggings by Casanova.

"Is there something I can help you with?" Caleb says to Casanova, his voice containing the merest hint of impatience.

"No. I here to help you. I think you maybe forget about Jewish laws *yichud* and *shomer negiah*."

Caleb scowls at him. "The door wasn't locked, so we're good."

"What about *shomer negiah*?" Casanova leans against the desk and crosses his arms. "Because I saw *negiaaaah*."

"I saw you break your Ramadan fast before sunset on three separate occasions. *With liquor.*"

"Exactly." Casanova nods. "What kind of friend does that? You should've stopped me, like I do for you now."

"What did I miss?" Gunnilda says, coming into the room with a bag of pretzels.

"Very immoral touch," Casanova replies as he takes a few pretzels from Gunnilda. "Not for your innocent ears."

"It was a hug," Caleb says, exasperated. "And what the hell are you two doing in my office anyway?"

Gunnilda shrugs. "I was bored."

Caleb silently points to the door in response. Gunnilda sighs and leaves.

"You too," Caleb says to Casanova.

"You need me."

"I don't."

"But—"

"*Out.*"

Casanova gives one last disapproving look before leaving, and Caleb calls out, "Shut the door!"

"So bossy," Casanova mutters, then shuts the door with a loud bang.

Now that we're alone again, an awkward silence stretches between us.

"Should we dive into the lesson then?" Caleb says.

I'd rather go back to hugging, but there's no way to say that without making things weird.

I nod. "I'm ready."

* * *

On second thought, nobody is ready to face suffocation. It's against human nature. I don't know what I was thinking. I can't believe people pay money to practice this. Just listening to Caleb describe what he's going to do and how I should respond is making me wonder if being attacked in real time might be less painful.

"I think we should talk about this," I say, backing away.

"We've done nothing but talk about this for twenty minutes."

"Can't I be the bad guy instead?"

He places his hands on his hips. He's clearly trying to rein in his frustration. "And what," he says slowly, enunciating each word, "would be the point in that?"

"To deepen your empathy," I say after a moment. "To understand how it feels to be a vulnerable woman."

"I already have plenty of empathy for vulnerable women," he says, closing in on me. "That's why we're doing this."

My back hits the wall and I swallow. Caleb is going to make his move any minute and my hands fly instinctively to my throat. "Didn't you once say I have a fragile neck?"

"A fragile neck?" He lifts an eyebrow. "I don't even know what that means."

"Me neither," I say, edging to the right. Unfortunately, he moves to the left. "But I feel like I have one."

"Interesting." His arm shoots out and he plants his hand on the wall, landing with a soft thump inches away from my face. His entire body is like a portable concrete house that's closing in on me and I gasp.

"Breathe, Tinsel. It's just me."

I'm being ridiculous, I know. But knowing doesn't make any of this any less scary. There's something about being trapped that sends me into an absolute panic. Maybe it does for most people. All I know is that it's hard to think. "I thought self-defense was going to be more like karate," I whimper. "If I had known there was going to be choking and being pinned—"

"I'm not going to choke you. I'm going to hold you tightly."

"Around my neck!"

"Breathe."

Even without checking a mirror, I know that my eyes are huge and wild, like a terrified animal's.

"Wouldn't you rather practice here with me than out in the street with an attacker?"

"I'm not sure." I gulp. "Which one would end faster?"

"Wrong answer," he replies, gently fanning his thumbs near my collar bone. I instinctively put my hands on Caleb's chest to stop him from coming any closer. But he pries my hands off his chest and says calmly, "I'm going to trap you soon and it will feel scary—" He pauses as I let out a small whimper. "But do your best not to panic because if you do you will lose your gross motor skills, your hearing, and you get tunnel vision."

"I think I had a head start on all three of those."

"On the count of three. One, two—"

"Wait—what's my safe word?"

"There is no safe word."

I gulp. "That sounds really unsafe."

"The point of this exercise is to work through your anxiety and do the steps we've talked about. Panicking in the classroom is good. Although," he adds thoughtfully, "you're the first student I've had who's panicked before we started."

"I have claustrophobia," I say defensively.

"That is unfortunate." He nods. "And three."

In one quick move, Caleb turns me around and has his bicep curled around my neck. He isn't applying the kind of pressure that deprives me of oxygen, but the vise-like grip has me bucking and yanking at his arm.

"Safe word, safe word!" I shriek.

His grip loosens, but he doesn't let go. His other hand is now snaked around my waist which makes me feel double-trapped.

"Stay calm," he says in a gentle, measured voice.

"Fuck calm!"

"Close your eyes and relax your muscles," he murmurs. "What you're doing now is a natural instinct, but you're wasting precious energy and it's not effective. Take deep breaths through your nose. Remember that you're okay, you can breathe, that you're with a friend you trust."

"*Ex-friend*," I grunt and buckle against him.

"Tinsel, honey, *relax*."

I'm so caught off-guard by him calling me honey that I actually stop moving.

"Good girl," he hums. "Now close your eyes and take a minute to center yourself. Deep breaths, in through your nose and then slowly exhale through your mouth."

I manage to force myself to cooperate and shockingly—it works. I'm relaxed enough now that I no longer consider biting him.

"That's it," he says. "Do you remember what I said to do in this situation?"

I concentrate and think back. "Duck my chin to create space."

"Excellent. And that will do what?"

"Give me room to breathe."

"Good. Try it."

I dip my chin and use the front of my head to butt against his arm.

"There you go," Caleb grins and releases me. "See that? You're a natural."

"At panicking maybe."

"You did great. You survived."

"Which is easy when someone isn't actually choking you."

"You got to start somewhere." He pulls two water bottles out from his mini fridge and tosses one to me. "The mind is the most powerful tool in your arsenal. When you learn how to rein in fear and discomfort, everything else becomes easy."

"If you say so."

"Okay." He claps. "Let's run through that again, but this time add the kick."

"The one that's aimed at your testicles?"

"Yes, but remember, you don't actually kick my testicles," he says, a small wrinkle appearing between his brows. "Just like I didn't actually choke you. You kick my thigh instead."

I nod. "I'll try my best, but I can't make you any promises."

"Right, I forgot," he sighs. "Be right back."
"Why?"
"I'm getting a groin pillow."
"What happened to our trust?" I call out to him.
"It's your aim I don't trust," he yells back.
Which, I suppose, is a fair point.

Chapter Twenty-Three

I turn over onto my side and blink at the time on my phone. It's a little past two in the morning. I smile as I think about yesterday and how much fun I had with Caleb, not just with the self-defense part of it, but afterwards too when I coached him through a few different dating scenarios. We have a lot of fun together, and if he were a girl, he'd probably be one of my best friends.

Sadly, I have to go for my morning run solo today. Caleb left for the airport shortly after our self-defense class to meet with a politician client in Washington. I scroll through the selfies I made him take at the end of our class and laugh at some of the faces he made.

I startle at the sound of something crashing to the floor coming from the opposite side of the house. I freeze, blood pounding in my ears.

More rustling movement. *Someone is in my house.* And all I can think is, *Caleb didn't prepare me for this situation.*

Adrenaline courses through me as I throw back the covers and glance around the room in search of a weapon. There's a lamp, a chair, a desk, and pencil.

Think, Ashira, think.

What kind of idiot doesn't keep a pair of nunchucks in her bedroom? Or at the very least, a butcher knife.

I could call 911, but I'd probably be dead by the time the police showed up anyway, this being Brooklyn and all.

Which is why I grab my phone and call the *shomrim*, the organization made of Orthodox Jewish men on call 24/7, to help anyone who has an emergency. They exist in every major Jewish community around the world, and the best part about them is that show up fast.

"Shomrim, what's your emergency?"

"Someone has broken into my house," I whisper.

"What's your address?"

I rattle off my address and stay on the phone with the dispatcher, peeking through my blinds to look out for my saviors. Barely five minutes later, a car screeches to a stop in front of my house, and two people race out.

With my heart hammering in my chest, I run to let them in. The two bearded men in yarmulkes and *tzitzits* tell me to wait by the door so that I can run out if I need to.

I huddle against the wall. My body shakes. How did someone break inside in the first place? Did I forget to lock my door?

A piercing scream cuts through the air. It's a woman.

The bad guy is a woman?

"Get out of my house before I call the cops!" a familiar voice yells. Bernice.

A mixture of relief and irritation flood through my body in equal amounts. I don't know how she managed to break in, but I suspect it involved snooping through my drawers and finding a spare key.

"I'm so sorry," I call to the men, running to the kitchen. "I didn't realize that it was—" Whatever I'm about to say disappears as I slowly process the fact that there seems to have been a volcanic explosion in my pantry. Shelves lie on the floor, broken bottles of wine and vinegar are scattered about the kitchen, colored shards of glass glinting from the morning sun. A bag of sugar spilled out, along with a bag of flour. A can of tuna fish rolls to a stop near my feet.

I bend down and pick up the can and place it on the counter. Then I look at my small, elderly neighbor in dirty sweats, trying to figure out what's going on in that head of hers.

"I'm sorry, Ashira," she says, flustered. "I-I couldn't sleep. I wanted to bake chocolate chip scones for breakfast, but I didn't have all of the ingredients, so I came here instead. But then I slipped on the stepstool and crashed into a shelf, and then it broke—"

"It's okay. Are you hurt?" I ask, taking her hands and examining her. She has scrapes on her arms and there are already a few nasty bruises forming.

"I've got a first aid kit," offers one of the men.

"Thanks." I nod. "That'd be great." I help her sit down, then grab her a glass of water as the man tends to her cuts. Bernice's face doesn't have its usual color. "Are you okay?" I ask, tilting my head. "Like, really okay?"

She barks a humorless laugh. "Am I okay? Look at me, I'm a mess." She rubs her eyelids. "I don't know what I was thinking."

"It's fine."

"No, it isn't." She shakes her head. "The more time passes without my Saul, the more I miss him. Time doesn't heal wounds—it makes it *worse*."

"Grief isn't linear, Bernice. And everyone falls apart at the one-year *yahrzeit*," I say, as I realize it's been nearly a year since Saul passed away. "It's like an unwritten rule."

"That's over two months away."

"You're getting a head start, like the overachiever you are." I pat her shoulder. "Now drink up." I turn to the men. "Can I get you guys anything? Coffee or water or," I glance out the window at the rising sun, "cereal and milk?"

They shake their heads and laugh.

"Coffee?" I ask, feeling like I have to offer them something for coming out here for nothing. "I have some pastries too. Sit down and I'll put some things on the table," I say, tapping into the Jewish woman gene that compels you to feed anyone who enters your house. These men must recognize that they're not going to get away without eating something because they join Bernice at the table.

I step over various debris and turn on the coffee maker, then do my best to assemble a semi-normal breakfast for the kind volunteers.

"I'm sorry, Ashira," Bernice says. "What a mess I've made."

I wave my hand. "It needed a remodel, anyway."

"Except you're not handy. And you have no money," she reminds me.

"Okay, no. Well, fine," I huff and roll my eyes. "Not at the moment, but my business is going to take off soon."

"The sad part is that she truly believes it," Bernice says to the men.

"Of course I do." I open the refrigerator and take out the milk. "You can accomplish anything if you work hard and don't give up on your dreams."

"Not always," one of the men says. "I did everything I could to become an NBA player. I played for hours, every single day after school. I joined clubs. I trained for it since I was the age of twelve. And I was *good*. Really good."

"It's true," his friend says.

"But by my thirty-seventh birthday, I gave up. I accepted the fact that I'd always be five-foot-six."

I clap a hand over my mouth, trying to contain my loud burst of laughter.

"And five-foot-six," he continues, ignoring my reaction, "is still too short to be in the NBA. No matter how good I am."

"Oy vey," Bernice says, shaking her head. "The delusion of your generation would be impressive if it wasn't so very sad." Luckily, the men seem to find that hilarious.

"By the way," the other guy says to me, as I bring plates and napkins to the table, "if you want, I know a handyman who volunteers for *chaverim*. He could fix this for you, free of charge."

"Oh." I swallow, suddenly uncomfortable. "I don't think I could accept charity."

"Don't think of it like that." He shakes his head. "Think of it as a group of people who like doing *mitzvahs*. Otherwise, they wouldn't volunteer. And it sounds to me like you could use a bit of help," he adds gently.

"We're interested," Bernice declares as I bring a plate of pastries to the table.

"Ignore her," I say firmly.

"You got a pen and paper?" the guy asks, ignoring me instead.

"I got it." Bernice sticks her hand down her shirt and removes a notepad from her bra, then whips out a pen from her other cup. Both men blush and look anywhere other than at the small woman at the table with them. "It's a *bissel* warm, but luckily it's a cold day." She chuckles and slides the items across the table to the man.

"Bernice!"

"What? It's good storage space."

I briefly close my eyes and rub the lids. "Don't worry," I call to the guy, and open my drunk drawer. "I have something less gross you can write on."

The man looks relieved when I shove an old receipt and pen at him. "Thank you."

"Your generation is so squeamish," Bernice comments, tucking the pen and pad of paper back inside her bra.

"I don't think this is a generational issue," I say to her.

"Here's his number. His name is Shaya Rissman." The man hands me the receipt and adds, "Just between you and me, if you gave him work, it'd be doing him a favor. He could use the distraction. His fiancée broke up with him a month ago and he's been taking it hard."

"Oh no. That's awful." But potentially wonderful for me. "Poor thing."

The second guy nods. "He's been a wreck."

"Are you sure that doing backbreaking labor for free is going to help?" I say doubtfully.

"Shaya is happiest when he's helping others," the first man replies. "Trust me."

I flip through my mental Rolodex of available women, wondering who I could set him up with. Rivka? Netanya?

"Well, you've come to the right woman," Bernice says, putting a cookie on her plate. "Ashira is always looking for more men to add to her collection."

"Okay, wait," I say, laughing nervously, glancing at the men, "that sounds really bad out of context—"

"First there was the speed dating, then Bruce, and then of course, Caleb. Every day, it's someone new. Who are you going to pick tomorrow?" she says, turning to me. "My dry-cleaning guy?"

"Don't be absurd," I mutter, "he's married." I turn to the men and open my mouth to explain when their cell phones emit an alarm in unison. Their eyes scan their phones with silent, solemn expressions. Within seconds, they're on their feet and racing out the door.

"Thanks again!" I call after them. I tell myself not to worry that their last impression of me will be that I "collect men" but it's one of those things that's easier said than done.

I head back to the kitchen. It's time Bernice and I had the conversation that's been percolating in my head these last two weeks. I've got a feeling that it will evoke some strong emotions, but there's only so much that this particular matchmaker is willing to put up with.

"Bernice," I say, sitting down across from her. "Does the name Lenny Horowitz mean anything to you?"

Her head jerks up and she gazes at me with suspicion. "Maybe."

"Okay." I grab a plate and put a small croissant on it. "Want one?" I offer, and she shakes her head.

"Why'd you bring him up?"

"Who?" I say, unable to resist driving her a little crazy.

"*Lenny!*" She waves her hands impatiently. "The man you just mentioned."

"Oh, right." I nod. "I ran into him a few weeks ago. He says hi, by the way."

"He did?" She tilts her head and gazes at me doubtfully. "Lenny Horowitz?"

"The very one," I say. "I mentioned your name and his face lit up." In anger, but no need to mention that. I take a bite and finish chewing before adding, "He said you were his first love."

Her face morphs from suspicion and doubt to a blushing woman talking about her crush. "What a sap," she says, hiding her smile beneath her napkin. She clears her throat. "What else did he say?"

"That he caught you *shtupping* Ernie Schlossinger on his birthday."

Bernice sighs and puts down the napkin. "Don't tell me he's still mad about that, all these decades later."

"Can I ask you something, Bernice?"

"Is it about what I'm leaving to you in my will?"

I decide to ignore that. "Why did you cheat on Lenny?"

"Why does anyone cheat?" She shrugs. "I was an immature idiot. I had had a crush on Ernie since junior high, even though he ignored me at every opportunity. But by twelfth grade, I'd grown some curves and learned how to do my hair and makeup. And guess what happened?"

"Ernie finally noticed you."

"No, but Lenny did. And he was so funny and oh, did we laugh together." She smiles to herself. "And the truth is that I loved Lenny, I truly did. But I couldn't manage to get rid of the idea that Ernie was the one I was destined to be with."

"The guy who ignored you for years?"

"He once asked to borrow a pencil," she says. "We made eye contact. It was intense."

"The eye contact?"

"Stop interrupting me, already. I'm trying to tell you what happened."

"Sorry, sorry," I murmur, hiding my smile behind the rim of my mug.

"Anyway. He and Lenny had some friends in common, and pretty soon, we all started hanging out together. And I admit, I might've crossed the line a few times."

"What do you mean?"

"I flirted with him, you know, the way girls and boys do."

"Sure," I say, even though I don't actually know. I never had male classmates or played with boys, except for Caleb, but flirting had never crossed our minds. Although recently . . .

"I suggested we go skinny dipping," she continues, "just the two of us, this one time—"

"I don't think that's flirting, Bernice," I cut in. "I think that's outright propositioning."

She scowls. "Didn't I tell you not to interrupt me?"

"Sorry." I mentally roll my eyes. "Do continue."

"And he brushed me off every time. Until he got drunk at Lenny's birthday party. I was wearing a cute little polka dot minidress and we were sitting next to each other on the couch, and his fingers skimmed the edge of my dress, near the top of my thigh—"

"Lah lah lah, I can't hear you," I say loudly, and plug my fingers in my ears.

"You're such a prude." Bernice bats her hand. "Anyway, one thing led to another, and Lenny came to find me when it was time to cut the cake. That's when he discovered us on his parents' bed, with me sucking—"

"*Aagghh!* STOP."

"Lenny had a similar reaction." She nods. "But angrier."

"Yeah," I say, shaking my head. No wonder he had such a hostile reaction when I brought up her name. "That's like the worst birthday ever."

"I'm not going to defend myself," she says. "I was young and stupid."

"And selfish," I murmur under my breath.

"Yes, thank you, Ashira," she says in a clearly sarcastic voice. "But I learned my lesson. And anyway," she shrugs, "it all ended up for the best. I met my Saul, and Lenny met his . . ."

"Betty."

Bernice nods. "Was she with him when you ran into him?"

"No, she passed away. But I knew her well when I was a child. I knew both of them, in fact."

Bernice gazes at me in askance. "What are you talking about?

"My dad's mom volunteered for the *Chevra Kadisha* and I'd go with her. While she was doing her thing in the basement, Betty, and sometimes Lenny, would babysit me."

"Huh." She shakes her head. "Small world." She stands up to bring her plate to the sink, but I intervene in case she steps on something and trips. "What was she like?" Bernice asks, sitting back down.

"Betty?" She nods. "She was wonderful. Nice to everyone. She didn't leave the house much, but she had a lot of friends. They'd come over and play card games. Those women could talk for hours." I smile, remembering it all. "And she kept a special container of kosher snacks just for me."

An unreadable expression flitters across Bernice's eyes, but it was too fleeting to decipher. "She sounds nice. I'm glad for him."

"But," I add, "he seems pretty lonely now."

"Don't get any ideas about setting me up with him," she says, shaking her head. "I'm probably the last person on earth he'd want to date."

And I can't help but notice her phrasing, and that she didn't say she wasn't interested, only that she was sure *he* wouldn't be. And although he claims that to be true, I'm not convinced that it is.

In fact, I think Lenny never got over Bernice, and I think Lenny is exactly what Bernice needs to get back on her feet—*and* back in her heels.

Chapter Twenty-Four

If someone had told me years ago that a day would come when I'd be so desperate to fill my database that I'd pimp my friends at the *keilim mikveh*, I'd never have believed it. And yet . . . here we are.

I glance around and shiver. The small room has minimal heating, probably just enough to keep the pipes from freezing. There's a counter along one side of the wall where people put their packages and things, and beside it is a large, heavy lid that covers the *mikveh* water. When I once explained to the non-Jewish woman that lives next door to the *mikveh* what people did inside here, how Orthodox Jews purify any and all non-disposable utensils that come into contact with their food, she looked at me aghast and asked why.

"In case they've been in contact with any unkosher food. And to purify it."

If you have to use your friends as man-bait, Fridays—*erev Shabbos*—are the best days to do it. Nearly every Jewish woman I've ever known has sent their young adult son on an emergency trip to the *mikveh* on a Friday to *toivel* last-minute hostess gifts or new serving trays or utensils.

"Stop that! I don't want to wear lipstick!" Sissel says, batting my hands away. "Especially not red lipstick. Not with these freckles."

Sissel is a little sensitive about her coloring. She says she has brown hair with red highlights, but her hair is actually the color of orange peels.

"Can you at least take your hair out of its ponytail?" I say. "Maybe have it curl provocatively over one breast like a Regency romance novel?"

Sissel turns to Miri who's posing like a mannequin. "Did you hear what she just said to me?"

"Shhh," Miri replies in a husky voice, like a smoker's. "I'm getting into character."

I give her a thumbs-up. I know I've been asking a lot of my friends lately, but I've got four women in my database, thanks to Caleb's bad behavior. I desperately need to recruit more men. Since Miri and Sissel are attractive single women themselves, I might as well give them the opportunity to participate in this mitzvah. And who knows—maybe Miri might meet her *bashert* this way. How's that for a great meet-cute?

"And why *here* of all places?" Sissel continues, gesturing around the small room. "Don't you think the men's gym is smarter?"

"I thought about that," I say, "but just because men work out doesn't mean they're kind people, whereas guys who *toivel keilim* are both strong and nice."

Sissel stares at me. "You've lost your freaking mind."

"You have to admit, it's a workout, schlepping all these pots and pans and dishes or whatever. And the guys who do it so their mothers don't have to—"

"Or their wives," Sissel mutters.

"Well, yeah, there'll be some married men, too, but maybe they'll have a single brother or friend," I say.

"And the point is that these guys are good, kind men with great biceps."

"Although not everything requires biceps," Miri says, back in her regular voice. "Like a package of silverware, for example."

"You. Get back into character," I tell her.

"What are we even supposed to say to these men?" Sissel asks.

"It's a fair question," I say, nodding. "You could ask them what the blessing is and then slip into the conversation that there's this great matchmaker you work with, and then real casually, hand them my card."

Sissel gives me a once-over and shakes her head. "Don't you think it would work better if you weren't dressed in disguise like a punk rocker? You could just be honest and give them your card yourself."

"No." I shake my head. "I need you to rave about me in case they've heard the rumors that I've gone insane."

"You have gone insane."

"I think I hear someone coming," Miri says.

"Quick! Be sexy!" I whisper, then scooch back to avoid getting hit by the swinging of the door. Two women come inside with shopping bags and towels and they pause, surprised to find three women in the room standing around, doing nothing.

One is in a headkerchief and the other is in a wig that's obviously a wig, signifying that they're both married. Otherwise, I'd try to recruit them too.

"Are you in the middle of something or can we go ahead?" the older woman asks us, dumping her bag on the counter beside the lid of the mikvah.

"No, we're uh, we're waiting for our stuff," I say. "Uber," I add.

She lifts her eyebrows, but turns her attention back to the young woman and takes the towels from her. "Start unboxing and look everything over to make sure that there are no stickers attached. I'll get this ready," she murmurs, laying out the towels on the other side of the lid. "Where is the mesh bag? We need it so we don't lose our stuff in the water—"

"Here you go," Sissel says, holding out the long red bag to her. "I was using the handle like it was a fidget spinner. It's really calming for my social anxiety."

I lay my hand over my forehead and close my eyes. Perhaps I should've left Sissel at home.

The two women then spend what feel like an eternity dipping dishes, silverware, pots, pans, and anything that would come into contact with food into the small pool that contains rainwater. The younger woman must be a recent bride because she's brought enough brand-new stuff to outfit an entire kitchen. Either that or she's got a major shopping addiction.

The door opens suddenly and a young, muscular man steps one foot inside holding a huge box. "Oh sorry," he says with a polite smile. "I'll come back later."

"No!" The word rips from my throat at a decibel best described as "desperate." They're almost done," I say, then turn to them. "Right?"

"But you're after us," the older woman says. "He might as well come back later."

"Will do," Hot Guy says, and disappears out the door. It all happens so fast that when I look out the window, he's already reversing in his car. And I can't even memorize the license because half of it is covered in snow.

Miri gazes at me sadly and even Sissel looks disappointed. By the time the two women leave, our spirits are low.

"I'm cold." Sissel sighs. "And hungry."

I take off my sweater and give it to her, then search for the bag of pretzels in my purse. I always keep food on me in case I'm out with Golda or Mordy and one of them gets hungry and needs to eat immediately or else they get hangry.

"I don't like the big pretzels," Sissel says. "Do you have the small kind?"

"Do I look like Mary Poppins to you?" I say, gesturing to my small purse.

"How's my hair?" Miri asks, patting it.

"Perfect." I glance out the window where a car is just pulling up. Unfortunately, it's not the car that Hot Guy was driving, and the elderly man that eventually gets out isn't the type I'd expect to see here. He's not only very old and frail-looking, but is bent over and has a severe limp. And it's *icy* out here.

"Maybe he has a grandson," Miri says, trying to be optimistic.

"Or a picnic basket full of deli sandwiches," Sissel adds.

I laugh. "I'll be right back," I say, opening the door. "I'm going to see if he wants help. Hopefully he won't be too macho to accept."

"See if he has snacks!" Sissel calls out.

An icy wind brushes against my cheeks, making me wish I hadn't forgotten to put moisturizer on earlier today. "Hi." I give a warm, friendly smile to the man as he approaches. "Would you like me to *toivel* that for you?" I say, pointing to the shopping bag in his hand.

"What?"

I repeat my question, louder this time, and he nods. "What a nice service. Thank you," he says, handing me the bag.

I don't bother correcting him because it probably helps his pride to assume that this is some new feature that the mikveh provides. I glance at him over my shoulder to ensure that he got back into his car safely, then heave a sigh of relief once he's inside.

"I'm thirsty. Did he have any drinks on him?" Sissel says when I return inside.

"Girl, you are something else." I put down the shopping bag and unzip my purse to get a juice box. "There you go," I say, tossing it to her. "Would you like a coloring book and crayons with that?"

She nods. "Yeah, that sounds good."

"I was kidding," I laugh, removing the mikvah lid. "My purse isn't big enough to hold all of that anyway."

"What you call kidding, I call teasing," Sissel says, crunching loudly on the pretzels.

There are only two metal serving spoons in the bag, so it doesn't take me long to *toivel* them. When I return the items to the man through the car window, he tells me to wait, and then extracts a few dollars bills and holds them out to me.

"Don't worry about it," I say, waving my hand. "The mikveh pays me well."

"Give it to charity," he says, so I nod and pocket the money.

Back inside, Miri says she has to pee and Sissel says she does too. I'm starting to feel like a severely underpaid babysitter. "There isn't a bathroom here," I say.

"I know, but there's a gas station across the street," Sissel says.

"Okay, fine. But be quick in case the Hot Guy comes back or someone else turns up."

"We will," Miri calls over her shoulder.

"And hold onto each other," I shout. "Don't rush, it's icy!"

I take out my phone and scroll through my emails. I'm still getting invitations to be a guest on podcasts and a few shows, but definitely not as many as I used to. But I'm not worried. Soon enough, I'll find Caleb his perfect match, and in a year's time, this will all be like a distant bad dream.

And then, to my great surprise, Hot Guy walks in. "Is now a bad time?" he asks, pausing again at the door.

I shake my head no, scared to speak in case he recognizes me. I frantically text the group chat to tell Miri and Sissel to come back ASAP and then try to think of a way to stall him without talking. I lean against the counter and smile at him, reminding myself of Ariel from *The Little Mermaid* after Ursula had stolen her voice. Except Ariel hadn't been wearing a bright blue wig and goth makeup and fake tattoos on her neck.

He hums to himself as he takes off his coat and rolls up his sleeves. The man clearly works out based on the bunching of his shirt's fabric when he moves. "This water is freezing," he says conversationally, marking himself as an out-of-towner. Very few born and bred New Yorkers are this chatty with strangers. "I keep hoping it'll warm up because my fiancée has me coming in here every other day," he adds, chuckling to himself.

I deflate like a balloon, but he doesn't notice.

"The things you do for love though, right?"

"I guess," I mutter, disappointed.

I startle as Miri races in, panting and out of breath. "Hi there," she purrs, putting her hand up against the doorpost and sticking her hips out. I appreciate her effort, but instead of sexy, she looks like someone who would greatly benefit from physical therapy.

"This man is the best fiancé, schlepping out here all the time," I add, hinting to Miri that he's already taken.

"Oh." Her shoulders drop and she frowns. "How nice."

"I'd do anything for her," he grins, drying his hands on the small towel he brought. "I never knew happiness like this until I met her."

My heart fills with warmth seeing how in love he is. Despite everything, I find myself grinning back. "That's beautiful," I say.

"Yeah. Amazing," Miri adds glumly, slumping against the wall.

"Thank you, have a great day," he says on his way out.

Miri and I gaze at each other with silent disappointment. "Maybe this wasn't the best idea," I confess after a minute.

"Probably not," she agrees. "But it was worth a try."

Sissel bursts through the door, waving a shopping bag with the gas station logo. "Guess what?" she says, all excited. "*I bought a coloring book!*"

Chapter Twenty-Five

Exactly one week later, I'm unpacking my small overnight bag in one of the spare bedrooms in Caleb's house. Tonight's Shabbos meal is in honor of Caleb's grandmother's ninety-third birthday, but due to the expected ten to twelve inches of snow coming, his parents, grandmother, Zevi and Jack, Miri, Sissel, and I, are all sleeping over until Shabbos ends on Saturday night.

I finish my makeup and spritz on a little perfume, slip on my heels, and then voila! I close the door behind me and start to go downstairs when I notice Caleb coming down the hall. I pause on the step. My heart rate quickens, but that's only because he startled me and nothing remotely to do with the fact that he looks stunning in a new gray suit. Or maybe it's less about the suit and more about the way he wears it? I feel like this topic requires more analysis than I have time to give it.

He's fastening his watch when he sees me. His lips curve up into the smallest hint of a smile and I blush at the realization that he caught me staring.

To be fair, it's been over a week since I've seen him. He only came back from his trip to Washington this morning, and when I got here half an hour ago, Jack had let me in saying Caleb was in the shower. He definitely smells nice from where I'm standing. Although I also thought he smelled good when he was sweaty and had me in a headlock, so maybe I'm not the best judge.

Even though we haven't seen each other, we've been texting here and there. Just little stupid things like funny memes and cat videos, and him holding me accountable to working out and eating better. I've always liked to dance, so I started including that in my daily routine, and if Bernice happens to be over, I make her join me. That woman can shake her *tuchus* like nobody's business.

"Hey."

"Hello you!" I grin a little too enthusiastically to disguise the fact that I feel intensely awkward. After all, the last time we'd been in the same room, we were sweaty and had our hands all over each other. And now we're supposed to go back to not touching? Even though I know he gives the best hugs in the world? What kind of cruel and unusual punishment is that?

"I didn't know you were here," he says, stuffing his hands into his pant pockets.

"Jack let me in. You were in the shower." *Don't you dare picture him in the shower! And stop blushing!!! Aaarrgghh.*

"Ah." He clears his throat.

"It's a great shower," I add because the silence is killing me. As is the fact that I'm still not touching him. "I gave myself a tour of it once." *Shut up, shut up, shut up.*

"I . . ." He shakes his head and laughs. "I'm not surprised."

"Yeah." I swallow and grip the banister as a ridiculous thought crosses my mind. It's the kind that should not be shared under any circumstances, not even under threat of death, because it is strange and bizarre and only the weirdest type of person would think it. So, I will keep it to myself and no one will be the wiser.

"What's got you so quiet?" Caleb says, moving closer to the top of the stairs.

His close proximity makes me feel slightly off-balance, which given that we're standing at the top of a long staircase, is not a good thing. And because I've never been great at multitasking, the thought slips out. "Do you think being un-*shomer* is like double jeopardy?"

His eyebrows lift in twin peaks of confusion. "What?"

I should've let myself fall and break my neck.

"I'm not following," he adds, tilting his head at me.

I clear my throat and straighten my shoulders. If I act confident, everything will be okay. "Double jeopardy is when the constitution protects a citizen's right from being tried for the same crime twice."

"Right." He looks at me strangely, so I don't think he's falling for the pseudo-confidence. "But what does that have to do with being un-*shomer*?"

Sissel appears in the hallway, causing my nervousness to ratch up a notch. This is just what I need. "E-excellent question," I stammer.

"What are you guys talking about?" she says, sidling up to us.

"Nothing," I reply at the exact same time that Caleb says, "The American judicial system."

"But I heard the word *shomer*." Sissel wiggles her eyebrows and gazes between us, and I close my eyes in despair.

"Who said what about being *shomer*?" Zevi jogs down the hall from the other direction.

"These two—" Sissel waves her hand between Caleb and me "—were whispering about it."

OMFG. Shoot me now.

"We were not whispering," I say quickly. How did this turn on me so fast?

Zevi's eyes narrow in suspicion. "You and Caleb were whispering about being *shomer*?"

Sissel nods. "Yes."

"No!" I scowl at her.

Caleb darts me a look that says, *Don't worry, I'll cover for you. Even though I have no idea what I'm covering for.* "We were talking about double jeopardy."

"*Double Jeopardy*?" Dr. Kahn peeks her head out of an open bedroom which I can only assume means that she heard our entire conversation and probably knows that I was imagining her son naked in the shower. So that's great.

"That was an excellent movie. Did you see it?" She gazes at her son expectantly.

Caleb shakes his head. "I don't think so."

Sissel scrunches her face. "But what does that have to do with being *shomer*?"

Everyone turns to me, and I sigh in defeat. Keeping my eyes on the huge chandelier that runs adjacent to the sweeping staircase, I say, "I was just wondering whether—in theory—if someone had already been un-*shomer* with someone, if touching the same person again would be considered another sin. Or would you get a pass?"

Sissel breaks the silence that follows with, "I'm going to need a lot more details before I can answer that."

Zevi glances at me, displeased. "Is there something I should know?"

"No," I laugh nervously, touching my throat. "It's just a question I have. In case a client asks me."

"There's no concept of double jeopardy in the Torah," Caleb says, his face giving nothing away. "So should a client ask, the answer would be that it's still breaking Jewish law, whether or not it's the same person."

"Good. Wonderful." I feel my face turn a bright tomato red. "Knowledge is power."

"But," Caleb continues thoughtfully, rubbing his thumb across his bottom lip, "if it was me in that situation, and I really liked a woman—if say, I wanted to marry her . . ." He pauses and shrugs. "I'd probably follow her lead."

There are somersaults in my stomach. I keep my eyes on the banister and say, "Even though it's a sin?"

"That's what Yom Kippur is for," he replies, and everyone laughs. Personally, that's my least favorite Jewish holiday, but I bet Caleb and the other health nuts love the idea of a twenty-five hour fast.

I glance up and see that Caleb is studying me. I swallow and turn away. My question was for non-sexual touching, like a platonic hug, but I guess I hadn't made that clear.

Was that Caleb's way of sending me a message? Or was he just answering my question without any underlying subtext? And is there a store that sells human muzzles?

"I think it's time to light candles," I announce, then hurry down the stairs. But as soon as I reach the bottom, I wish I hadn't because I make eye contact with Caleb's grandmother who's perched on a bench in the front hall.

"Well, well. Look at what the cat dragged in."

"Hello, Mrs. Kahn." I paste on a bright smile. "It's so nice to see you." The ninety-three-year-old puts my nerves on edge like nothing else. She lives in an assisted living home on Ocean Parkway, but often stays at Caleb's parents' for Shabbos. "Happy Birthday! How are you doing?"

"A lot better than you. You look like a Prom Queen reject," she says, pointing one long leopard-print painted nail at my pink dress. "I heard your business is in the toilet and your life is falling apart."

"Bubby," Caleb warns, coming down the stairs. My relief is instant.

"What?" she says, the picture of innocence. "It's not like she doesn't know."

"It's okay." I smile and try to shrug it off. "Every business has its ups and downs."

"Yeah, but what business turns their home into a brothel?"

I blink. "What?"

Mrs. Kahn nods. "I heard you expanded your business into prostitution, and that you give a Friday night discount as long as the customers pay ahead of time, so it's not breaking Shabbos. And don't say 'what'," she adds. "It makes you sound stupid. And trust me, child, you don't need people referring to you as the dumb matchmaker *and* a whore."

My jaw drops, and I find myself unable to form words. Caleb seems equally stunned.

#Schwartzstrikesagain. #Rightonschedule #Getthewomanarealjob

"Code Friday25," she continues blithely. "Oh, my friend Eugene wants me to ask you if you give group discounts."

Someone makes a strangling gasping sound and I realize that it's me.

"You're running a brothel?" Sissel says, gazing at me with what looks like a new level of respect. I glance up and see not only Sissel on the staircase, but also my brother and both of Caleb's parents. "No wonder you were asking about being *un-shomer*."

Perfect. Just . . . perfect.

"What—" Caleb shakes his head. "Go back to the beginning, Bubby. Who told you this?"

"You know my friend Marna—she's the one with the gorgeous granddaughter who's in medical school—remember? The one who said she was interested in meeting you, but you blew her off? That one?"

"Would that be the one that's still in her twenties and an atheist?" he says in a pleasant voice. "Or did those things change since you last brought her up a month ago?"

"You'll never get married if you keep this ridiculously high bar of yours—"

"I'm sorry," I cut in, arranging my hands in a timeout signal. "Could we go back to the part where Marna told you I was running a brothel?"

"Can you believe this girl?" Mrs. Kahn says to Caleb. "She can't handle not being the center of attention for two seconds."

I hadn't realized I was grinding my teeth until Caleb whispers in my ear to relax.

"Bubby," he says sternly. "What did Marna say about Ashira?"

She sighs, clearly put out from having to stay on task. "Marna said that someone saw a man follow you into your house late one Friday night and that he was there for about half an hour, and then he left—"

"*What?*" I shake my head. "That is absolutely the biggest lie I've ever heard. Never in my life have I invited a man into my house late on a Friday night—"

"Or," Caleb cuts in, giving me a pointed look, "did you once insist on a man coming into your house late at night so you could interrogate him on what he was looking for in a wife? Even though he was concerned that this situation might be misinterpreted if someone were to see it?"

"Oh." Well, shit. My shoulders slump and I frown. "Yeah, that might've happened. But it was only once," I add, steeling my voice. "And whoever saw us has—"

"Us?" Miri says. I whip around and see that Miri and Jack have joined us too. "Do you mean . . ." She trails off and waves her finger between Caleb and me.

I nod. "It was that night we ate at Leah's house and Caleb stayed behind to walk me home."

"Is that all he did?" Zevi says. He narrows his eyes at Caleb, as though he's considering trying out some boxing moves on him.

"*Zevi.*" Caleb puts his hands on his hips. "Come on. You've got to be kidding me."

"I knew it," his grandmother says. "I had a feeling this was going to happen. You've gone and gotten the wench pregnant, haven't you?" she says to Caleb, gesturing at me.

Everyone's eyes swivel to my stomach, including mine.

"Now I'm not saying that you need to get rid of it," Mrs. Kahn continues with a sigh. "But I will say that I'm too old to help raise anybody's child at this point in my life." She turns to Caleb and adds, "Had you chosen the atheist doctor instead, well . . ." She lifts the palm that isn't grasping her cane. "Who knows? But it's too late now, isn't it?"

"All right, Ma," Caleb's father says after his wife whispers something to him. He comes down the stairs and hooks his arm around his mother's. "Time for a nap."

"I don't need a nap, I just woke up from one," she grumbles. "Why is everybody always trying to get me to nap anyway?"

"I'll bring you a nice hot cocoa—"

"That stuff always puts me to sleep!"

"A drop of Benadryl," Caleb's mother whispers to our questioning faces. "It's harmless."

"I was in the middle of an important conversation in case you hadn't noticed," Mrs. Kahn says to her son.

"How about I'll bring you one of those romance books you love with the naked men on the cover," Caleb's father says.

A long pause follows. "Get me the one with the sexy pirate. He's got an eye patch and an earring in his *pupik*."

He winces. "Yes, Mother."

"Ash," Zevi says, after they left. His eyes peer into mine. "I'm going to ask you this once and I want the truth—did Caleb take advantage of you?"

"Don't be ridiculous!" I start to sweat. If my own brother doesn't believe me, then who will? "I'm not even his type," I add in exasperation.

"What are you talking about? You're exactly his type." Zevi waves his finger accusingly at Caleb. "Every girlfriend he's ever had looks just like you."

Caleb's jaw drops, and he gazes at his friend in shock.

"No . . ." I shake my head. "That can't be true. He told me he's attracted to the opposite of—"

"Are we in counting time?" Caleb cuts in sharply. The eighteen-minute period before sunset is the most stressful of all because it's your last chance to do any last-minute fixes, while also needing to keep an eye on the clock because if you go over time, then you've lost your chance to light candles.

Jack, the Catholic in the room, nods. "You have three minutes left."

"Thanks for not telling us earlier," Sissel exclaims, running past him.

"It's not my job to babysit grown women," Jack shouts back.

It doesn't take long for Caleb to convince Zevi that the very idea of the two of us together is utterly ridiculous, and I feel slightly miffed that Zevi and the others agree so rapidly. It isn't *that* preposterous! Especially if it's true that Caleb's girlfriends looked like me—but then why did he tell me that he's attracted to the opposite? Did the brunettes reject him? I highly doubt that.

Meanwhile, everyone else mistakes my quiet for depression over the gossip about me being exchanged in the senior citizen cafeteria on Ocean Parkway. Which although is sad, doesn't bother me as much as the fact that everyone thinks Caleb and I being a couple is absurd. Everybody except for Miri and Sissel perhaps, who exchange a few knowing glances.

The meal is lovely, full of delicious food, and lively conversation. Caleb's mother told us how in the villages of Ethiopia, they knew Shabbat was starting when a man's shadow measured twelve paces under the setting sun, and how their synagogue was a grass hut with a star of David on top. Instead of rabbis, they had priests called *kessim*. And when Jack asked her for more details about her childhood, she recounted how she'd walked hundreds of miles to Sudan at the age of twelve with her baby brother on her back to escape famine and persecution from the government, and the shock she felt at seeing pale-skinned Jews after she arrived in Israel. She said it was also there that she first heard about the story of Chanukah since her tribe had been expelled before the destruction of the second Temple.

Even though Caleb and I are on opposite ends of the table, I feel his gaze on me often, and I give him a reassuring smile in response to let him know that I'm fine. At one point, merely to show how unaffected and overall cool I am, I even offer to check on his grandmother and see if she wants dessert, but so many people interject that I quickly sit back down.

After the meal, everyone gathers in the den to play cards or read, but I say goodnight and slip upstairs, claiming fatigue. There's too much on my mind and I need to be alone to sort it out. Except it turns out that I can't make sense of my feelings at all, and I end up tossing and turning for most of the night.

* * *

"Doing okay?" Jack asks me the following morning at breakfast.

"Yes." I force myself to smile, determined to stay positive. "Obviously, it's not ideal that I'm facing allegations of running a brothel, but things could be worse." I nod. "At least I didn't die in my sleep last night."

"That's some Jewish positivity right there," Sissel remarks as she pours milk into a bowl of cereal.

"Oh, Ash." Jack sighs.

"I'm doing great. Really," I say, and gesture around the room. "I'm warm and fed, and my heart is in peak condition. And hey, if it does come down to me running a brothel one day, Mrs. Schwartz has already done the PR work for me." I pour myself a cup of coffee. "It's one way to make introductions, right?" I laugh, lifting my head to gaze at Jack and Sissel. "Better profit margins, too."

"She's so far gone, it's like she doesn't even know it," Sissel remarks.

"Maybe you should see someone?" Jack says cautiously, eying me over the rim of his mug.

My eyebrows slant downwards as I take a seat. "What kind of someone?"

"A psychotherapist," Sissel answers.

I bark in laughter, but then slump in my seat and sigh. "Yeah. I probably should."

"If you haven't had therapy, have you even lived?" Jack jokes, clearly trying to make me feel better.

"I've lived my entire life without needing therapy," Sissel says, chewing with her mouth open. "And I'm doing great."

"That's a matter of opinion," Jack murmurs under his breath.

Sissel points her spoon at him, dripping milk onto the table. "I heard that."

"How's it going with Caleb?" Jack says, turning to me. "You guys seem to be getting along a lot better these days."

"Yes, we are." Why does the very mention of his name make my pulse speed up?

Jack nods. "And he's cooperating nicely about the blind dates?"

"Yes. Although I think I do need to coach him on talking to women. It's a skill that he doesn't have in his toolbox. Yet," I add. "It's something I plan to work on him with before I release him back into the wild."

"Like the injured beast he is," Sissel says.

"Er," I scratch my head, "I guess."

"I actually feel bad for him," Sissel says. "He obviously hates dating."

"Everyone hates dating." I shake my head. "It's the most miserable, soul-eating, time-sucking, nausea-inducing thing you can do. It's worse than being operated on without anesthesia or getting a root canal or being bodychecked on ice or stubbing your baby toe. It's Dante's ninth circle of hell. It's being chased by the undead."

There's a moment of silence, and then Jack says, "I'd work on that elevator pitch if I were you."

"How would you even know?" Sissel says to me. "It's not like you date."

"I went on some, back when my mother was still alive, to make her happy. I just mean that it's rough *until* you find your special someone, of course," I add, seeing their faces. "And then you live happily ever after."

"Actually," Sissel says, peeling a banana, "roughly forty-five percent of marriages end in divorce. And sometimes the couples who don't divorce only stay together for money or convenience. Statistics show that single cat ladies are the happiest people."

"Do me a favor," I tell Sissel, "and never speak of this again."

"Which part?"

"*All of it*," I say emphatically.

Jack snaps his fingers and gazes at me with excitement. "You know what you need?"

"A hitman for Mrs. Schwartz?" I say.

"No, a *hit* show. Like Netflix's *The Jewish Matchmaker* with Aleeza Ben Shalom."

"Sadly, that already exists."

"But not one with seniors, like *The Golden Bachelor*." He claps his hands. "You could have Bernice be the bachelorette! And call it *The Golden Bashert*."

"That is kinda cute," I admit.

"And Zevi could produce it." I can't quite recall seeing Jack this excited about anything. "Don't you see how this could save your company? You'd be famous and you wouldn't need to worry about finding Caleb a match!"

"But isn't Zevi already working on a reality dating show?"

"Yes, and it's been shortening his lifespan. All these twenty-something divas with their petty demands and tantrums are driving him to the breaking point."

"Really?" I say feeling guilty that I didn't know. "I didn't realize that."

"He doesn't like to worry you. But this is the perfect solution for both of you!"

A frisson of excitement runs through me, even as I warn myself not to get too excited. Projects can take years in television and even then, still fall apart. "Thanks, Jack."

"Good morning," Miri calls out cheerily, already dressed for the day in a black and white knit sweater two-piece. "What are we eating for breakfast?"

"Muffins, babka, cereal," Jack says, taking an apple from the fruit bowl.

Sissel glances around the table. "So, who's coming to shul with me?"

"Will Rocco be there?" Jack asks, peering at us with interest over his mug.

I shake my head. "I think Caleb said he's guarding Adath Israel this week. But Casanova will be."

"Never mind." Jack shudders. "I'll stay home."

"Be the strong, confident man that I know is inside of you," Miri says.

"He treated me like I was a criminal!" Jack exclaims.

"What did he do?" I ask, taking a sip of coffee.

"He interrogated me for like twenty minutes," he says, pushing his glasses up his nose.

"Was that the time you wore the plaid suit jacket and gold lamé tie?" Sissel asks. "Because anyone would look suspicious in that."

"First of all, don't get me started on *your* fashion choices, Sissel. And second of all," he mutters, frowning into his mug, "yes it was."

We cackle with laughter.

"If it makes you feel better," Miri says, "he body-searched Mrs. Weinstein last week because she refused to take her hands out of her pockets."

"She's still alive?" Sissel says, looking surprised. "I thought I went to her funeral a few months ago."

"How do you not know whose funeral you were at?" Miri says.

Sissel shrugs. "Names are hard. Anyway," she continues, unbothered, "are either of you coming?" She looks between Miri and me.

"Nah," I say, glancing out the kitchen window as I rinse out my mug. "I think I'll stay here and cuddle up with a blanket and a good book."

"I have to go, unfortunately." Miri sighs. "My cousins are in town and I told them I'd meet them there."

"Wait—" I turn around to face her. "Do you mean the hilarious twins?" I ask, perking up.

Miri nods. "They're trying to figure out whether to relocate here or Chicago for the time being."

My eyes light up. "For dating purposes?"

"Probably. There's a definite drought of Jewish men in Oklahoma. But don't get your hopes up. The bossy one is insisting on Chicago."

"But she hasn't met Caleb yet." I grin.

Jack tilts his head at me in confusion. "Didn't you say a minute ago that you wanted to rehabilitate him before you release him back into the dating jungle?"

"Yes, but this is different because I'm not going to make an introduction. He won't have the opportunity to open his mouth. I'll just point to him from across the room, and when they see the kind of hunks I have in my database, they'll totally want to move here and become my clients!"

"Huge stretch," Sissel says.

Jack nods. "I have to agree with her."

"Don't leave without me!" I call out to Sissel over my shoulder. I dress in record timing, but when I return, Jack does a double take when he sees me. It's followed by a slow up and down perusal as I grow increasingly unsettled. Finally, he says, "You look like an Orthodox Jewish dominatrix about to get her kink on at synagogue."

I frown and gaze down at myself. He must be exaggerating. "Is it the boots?" I ask, examining the high-heeled lace-ups that reach my knees.

"Yes," he nods. "And the neck chains."

"It's called a choker," I say defensively. "It just happens to be attached to the dress."

"Yes, Ashira. That's what makes it a neck chain." He circles around me. "And it's the leather bodycon too."

"It's not a bodycon," I say, turning to examine myself in the full-length mirror in the foyer. "It's . . . it's . . ." *Oh crap. He's right.* This is what happens when you buy something without trying it on first.

"It's very Kim Kardashian," Jack finishes. "Don't worry," he says when he catches my facial expression, "you've got the perfect butt for it."

"That's not what I'm worried about," I whimper. What am I going to do? I can't wear the dress I wore last night because Miri spilled wine on it and it's not like I can raid Caleb's closet for a dress. And Sissel and Miri are about two heads shorter than I am. I'm totally screwed.

Sissel enters the foyer, takes one look at me, and says, "I like your S and M dress."

"It's not a—"

"Where's the whip?" she asks, and I glare at her.

Jack turns to me. "I have a sweater you can wear, if you want. It's long enough that it should cover your butt."

And that is how I end up going to shul in a black zip-up sweater with a rainbow heart that says:

Gay and Catholic
<small>& hella charismatic</small>

Which is also why I decide to keep my coat on.

Miri, Sissel, and I make it to shul by 10.15. Casanova stands in front of the entrance, wearing aviator sunglasses and a brown leather bomber jacket.

"Good morning, Casanova." Miri waves and grins. "I like your sunglasses."

His cool expression implies he doesn't appreciate the compliment. He tilts his head to the other bodyguard to signal the okay to punch in the security code and open the door for us.

The *musaf* prayer is coming to a close as we find empty seats toward the back of the women's sections. I spy Mrs. Schwartz in the front row, flanked by her daughters. So, that's great.

Three rows ahead and to the right of us, I catch a glimpse of the identical twins' long, shiny russet-brown hair. Three other young women are with them and I almost rub my hands in glee like an evil Disney villain. Putting Caleb aside, I'm sure I could entice Bruce or any other number of men with them.

I glance up and spot Caleb through the partition that separates the men and women. The *mechitzah* is supposed to prevent the two genders from getting distracted from each other in order to focus on praying, but trust me when I say that it has little effect on the congregants whom these guidelines were created for. Specifically, a certain Mrs. Aaronson, whose creative excuses to open the door of the men's section and arch her back provocatively while trying to summon her husband, are enough to fill up an entire Talmud. Or Mr. Gordstein who spends more time in the women's section than the men's, then circulates among the women during kiddish, offering them bites of cholent from his plate.

It raises so many questions, but mainly, did his wife know about his cholent kink before they got married?

After the gabbai makes the usual announcements, everyone heads to the back of the room where a long buffet table is filled with herring, kugel, cholent, crackers, and dessert. The room goes silent as the Rav recites Kiddush, the blessing of the wine, and then the people dig in. Or swarm in, rather, in a similar style of vultures on the discovery of a fresh corpse.

"How are you doing, Ashira?"

I turn and find Mrs. Pinto, one of Mrs. Schwartz's best friends. My guard instantly goes up, but I'm careful to keep my face neutral. "I'm fine, thank G-d. Never better. How are you?"

"Baruch Hashem." She smiles. "How's the matchmaking going?"

"*Amazing*." If she thinks she can get a rise out of me, she better think again.

She lays a skinny hand on my wrist. "I've been praying for you."

"Really? How sweet." I beam and lay my other hand over her wrist and squeeze. "And *I* have been praying for you. Unfortunately," I sigh, dropping my hands, "He said no."

"Who did?"

"G-d."

She blinks rapidly, looking unsure. "About me?"

"Yes. But don't worry," I add. "I'll keep trying."

She narrows her eyes at me, then turns to go.

"Good Shabbos, Mrs. Pinto!" I call out, and she bats her hand at me dismissively.

"Hey Ash," Miri says, approaching. "Zevi wants you to know that we're leaving in five minutes."

"But I can't leave," I reply. "I didn't get to talk to your cousins yet. I need to dangle Caleb in front of them."

"Don't worry," she says, pointing toward the area between the praying section and the kitchen. "They found him on their own."

"But—" I stare. The twins are laughing as Caleb talks, and I can tell they're blushing all the way from here. "But—"

"What?"

"Look at him." I flick my hand in his direction. "He's charming them."

She nods, glancing over her shoulder at them. "I'm starting to worry they're both going to want to date him."

"What are they even talking about?" I ask, unable to stop staring.

"I think they're asking about his time in the military."

"He's telling *them* his military stories?"

She stares at me for a long moment. "Are you okay?"

"Yes, why?"

"Because you're sending legit death stares to my cousins."

"They won't notice anyway, they're too busy flirting."

Miri smacks my arm. "Are you jealous?"

"No!" I whirl to face her. "Of course not. *No*," I say firmly. "I'm just annoyed that he can act completely normal with the wrong women."

"How are they wrong?"

"They're young and silly and . . ." I struggle for other adjectives. "Young."

"You already said that, and *you're* the one who set him up with a twenty-one-year-old. Remember Rivka?"

"She was very mature for her age," I mutter and cross my arms.

"Maybe he prefers someone who's immature. Maybe the type of woman you're setting him up with isn't what he wants."

"Do you think so?" I frown thoughtfully.

"Couldn't hurt to ask."

And the very next day, that's exactly what I do.

Chapter Twenty-Six

"I cannot believe you just asked me that," Caleb says, bringing the shopping cart to a sudden stop.

"Well, I can't believe that you dragged me to a place that smells like hamster feed and doesn't have potato chips. And no," I add, "carrot chips are not potato chips." Like, seriously. He's brought me to some awful grocery store that smells like armpits and everything costs triple the price.

"I haven't had a hot dog in ages," I say. "Do they sell kosher ones here?"

"They don't sell carcinogens here period."

Worst. Store. Ever.

"Hot dogs are terrible for you," he adds. "They're one of the worst foods you can eat."

"Aren't there cheat days?"

He stops pushing the cart to glare at me. "You want cheat days for cancer?"

"Yes. Maybe?" But damn it, his glower is intimidating, and I hear myself mutter, "I guess not. Anyway," I say, as we resume walking, "there's no shame in admitting that you like younger women."

"I have nothing to admit. Did you not hear me say that I have no interest in dating either one of them?"

"Your brain says that," I say, sidestepping a shopping cart, "but your *body* was clearly saying otherwise."

"No, that's *your* brain telling you otherwise."

I clear my throat. "Some men are attracted to younger women due to ego, admiration, and evolutionary instincts—"

"Put the phone down, Wernick."

I glance up from the screen. "You aren't curious about the AI overview of your syndrome?"

"The only *syndrome* I have is wanting someone who's too much of a wimp to risk living life to its fullest."

"What is that supposed to mean?"

"It means," he says, grabbing my phone and placing it in the back pocket of his jeans—as if I can retrieve it now— "that you're too scared to get married because you're afraid of getting hurt."

My breath stalls. The raw emotion emanating from his eyes touches a place deep within my heart. It reaches straight into the dark, bottomless pit where memories collide with feelings, and love blends with pain. It's where euphoria, despair, and fear are irreversibly bound together. Love is a greedy beast. It doesn't settle for halves. If you want it, you have to surrender yourself to it completely.

I *want* to be brave. I want to be someone who isn't scared to fall in love and have a family. I want to be the kind of woman that a man like Caleb deserves.

"I—" I swallow, struggling to get the words out. "I want . . ."

"What?" he says softly. The bustle and noise of the store fades as his eyes scan my face. It feels like we're the only two people here, and that life has led me to this one crucial moment in time. I either step up the plate and be the strong, brave person that I know is inside of me, or I retreat back into my cave. "What it is that you want?"

"I want—" I glance away, unable to look in his eyes. I feel myself withdraw, cocooning in the familiar fear that keeps me safe.

Desperate for a change in subject, my eyes gaze around the store and snag on a magazine rack. It's about a celebrity sex scandal which brings me right back to my original point.

I clear my throat. "Hey Caleb—how many women have you slept with?"

He blinks. "Excuse me?"

"I don't need an exact number." I wave my hand. "A general estimation is fine."

"Why," he pauses and shakes his head, "are you asking me this?"

"Because I'm your matchmaker," I reply, in an obvious tone.

"Is that why?"

I can feel him trying to tug me back to that dangerous place. But I can't let him. Not yet, at least.

"More than five?" I guess. "But less than ten?"

"We're not playing this game." He throws a random bag of avocados in the cart, and my eyebrows lift. Even I know you're supposed to check the color, and I never eat them.

"Do you want me to go first?" I offer. "That way you won't feel so vulnerable?"

"It's not about vulnerability, and you have nothing to say."

"No?" I wrap my fingers around a zucchini and use my thumb to fan the tip. I rub the spot back and forth, like a produce pervert, but it's working. Caleb is staring at me like I'm a car crash he can't look away from. "Are you sure about that?" I add in what I hope is a husky voice, and then pump my hand up and down the length of the vegetable.

Caleb's mouth drops. I'm just considering kissing the tip, when I hear a child's voice.

"Mommy, why is dat lady doin' that?"

I turn and make eye contact with a red-faced woman behind me, a toddler on her hip. "Oh shit," I whisper, dropping the vegetable.

"Shit, shit, shit," the kid sing-songs.

"No, sweetie, we don't say that word," the mother says, glaring at me.

"Sorry about her," Caleb says, picking up the zucchini. "She was recently discharged from a rehab facility. I'm her nurse," he adds after a pause.

I smile and wave, trying to look slightly off, but not too much. I don't want to give the kid nightmares, after all.

"*Byeeee!*" the toddler yells as his mother hurries away.

Caleb and I glance at each other, and then burst into laughter.

"You know, Wernick, you're the one person in my life who always manages to bring out the child in me."

"You're welcome," I say, which earns me another chuckle.

"And where," he glances up from the pile of mandarin boxes, "did you learn that trick?"

"I'm twenty-eight years old, Caleb. Do you honestly think a woman of my mature age, born and bred in the city, wouldn't know what to do with a zucchini?"

"Aren't you full of surprises," he murmurs, pulling the cart toward the spinach section.

"Wait," I say before he gets any bad ideas. "I'm not a fan of spinach."

"You will be," he says, grabbing two bags and throwing them into the cart. "And you still plan on being single forever?"

"Of course," I say, as breezily as I can manage. The last five minutes can go straight to the attic and stay there. "And you will be too at this rate—wait." I try to stop him. "I don't like carrots—okey dokey, then," I say as he tosses several baby packs into the cart. "You have to admit," I continue, "that I've given you amazing choices. Nayma, for one, is adorable and has a great personality. Rivka is a total bosswoman. Netanya Li is a friggin' rocket scientist. And hello? Did you see her butt?" I say, as if I'm a frat boy talking to another frat boy. "I'd totally tap that."

"Jesus," he mutters, glancing at me. "Sometimes I can't believe the things that come out of your mouth."

"And she has a really beautiful voice too," I continue. "Just imagine how she'd sound moaning your name as she cam—*arrmphh*." Caleb stuffs an orange into my mouth, effectively shutting me up. "Anyway," I say, after

I spit it out. "That's all in the past. The good news is that I've found you a new woman."

Ever since Netanya Li, I've been working like a matchmaker possessed trying to find a woman to match Caleb intellectually, physically, spiritually, and emotionally. By the time I found her, I'd broken out in a bad case of hives and developed a nervous eye twitch, but nonetheless, totally *worth it*.

"Not another one," he groans.

"Don't worry, this one is definitely going to work out," I say.

Tamar is a Bukharan Jew who speaks three languages and is a graduate of Harvard Law. She's tall and athletic, with long, glossy hair that some would sell their firstborn for. And the best part is that she's a total sweetheart.

The only concerning part is that she's every bit as picky as he is, but it's a good sign that she readily agreed to the date once I mentioned who it was with. And if these two aren't soulmates, then I'm starting a change.org to send to G-d.

"I need a break."

"What?" I say, feeling blindsided. "Are you serious?"

"Dead serious."

I shake my head. "I already told her and she's super excited."

"Tell her you're sorry that you didn't bother to check with me first."

"That'll hurt her feelings. Rejection is traumatic." Despite his big, bodyguard exterior, Caleb is very sensitive to people's feelings.

"Fine," he mutters after a long pause. "I'll do it."

"Oh thank G-d," I breathe, clasping a hand over my chest. "I was so worried—"

"But you're coming with me."

I stop short and tilt my head. "What?"

"It'll be less painful that way. And you're going to eat these." He deposits two bags of frozen peas into the cart, and the timing doesn't escape me. Peas are my nemesis food. They taste gross, the texture is gross, and I shudder just by glancing at them.

He's exacting a cruel and unusual punishment, and for a moment I'm caught between my desire to argue about the peas and his bizarre request that I third-wheel his date.

"You can't be serious," I say, focusing on the latter.

"Oh, but I am." He looks much too pleased with himself, and I throw myself in front of the cart, like a tree-hugger in front of a crane.

"I can't. That's *insane*."

"Unlike the last date I went on?" he says, studying the contents inside a freezer display case. "Although I'd skip the mustache this time if I were you."

"That was completely *different*." I scratch my neck, feeling a case of hives coming on. "That was intel gathering, and neither of you were supposed to figure out I was there. Besides what exactly would I tell her? That I'm your babysitter?"

"Sure, that'll work." He opens the freezer door and selects some gross-looking liquid, then tosses it into the cart.

I bury my face in my hands. He's winning me at my own game again. Not only do I have to eat my nemesis food, but now I have to go out on dates too.

"And you need to make a few other lifestyle changes."

I stare at him like he's gone mad. "*More changes?*"

"You have the palate of a first grader—"

"Is this about the hot dogs?" I interject.

"It's more than just the hot dogs. You don't get enough sleep—"

"How would you know how much sleep I get?" I interject.

"Because you send me cat videos in the middle of the night."

"Only the best ones." Really. He should thank me for filtering out the mediocre videos. The lack of gratitude on his part is staggering.

"You don't drink enough water," Caleb continues.

"I don't need water. I have caffeinated energy drinks," I say. "Besides, my body is a lean, mean, well-oiled machine. Did I or did I not just run five-and-a-half miles this morning?"

He grins. "You were amazing."

"I was, wasn't I?" I beam.

"I'm proud of you."

"Likewise, buttercup."

He tilts his head. "Did you just call me 'buttercup'?"

A flush crawls up my neck. "I was caught up in the moment."

"Whatever you say." He flashes me a crooked grin. "*Sweetkins.*"

"No," I laugh and shake my head. "There is no right moment for that word."

He chuckles and puts a bag of chia seeds in the cart. I'm praying it's for his house and not mine, although spring is coming and I could buy a bird feeder.

"Are you still eating frosted sugar crap for breakfast?"

"Bernice starts every day with Eggo waffles, whipped cream, butter, and syrup," I say. "And she gets sad and lonely if I don't eat with her."

"I ought to leave the two of you to your own devices," he says, shaking his head. "But I'm not that evil. You know what?" he says suddenly. "I'm going to create a daily schedule and diet for you to follow."

I stop walking. "You can't be serious."

"I'm not going to force you." He shrugs. "But otherwise, I will insist on taking a three-month dating break."

"You . . . You—" I point my finger at him. "You're like the product of a one-night stand between Hitler, Stalin, and Mussolini."

"Thank you," he says, selecting something that claims to be pasta made from chick peas. "But flattery will get you nowhere."

"I'm very unhappy." I stare ahead gloomily. "The Torah says you should be kind to sad orphan girls."

"Honestly," he says, with a wink, "you're more of a cute orphan girl than a sad one."

"Thank you?"

"You're welcome. And I'm here, Tinsel." He gestures around the gross food store. "Not because the Torah says to be kind to orphans, but because your health is important to me. I want you around for a long time, I—" He stops. Takes a deep breath.

"I want you to prioritize your health as much as you prioritize keeping your family's business going. And I know if your mom were here, she'd agree with me."

Then he resumes pushing the cart, leaving me standing there feeling a bit dazed. And guilty, if I'm honest. Because he's right. That's exactly what my mom would want.

"Okay," I say, catching up to him. "I'm sorry. I'll take the whole health thing more seriously." Here I've been selfishly using his high-profile status to save my career without considering his feelings and how awful dating can be, and the whole time he's stressed out about my health.

He doesn't reply, and we silently stare at the granola options which looks identical to bird feed. I glance at the sign hanging above the aisle just to make sure we're still in the human section of the store.

"Why am I always messing up when it comes to you?" I say sadly.

I feel his gaze on me. "You're not."

"I am." I shake my head. "I keep putting my needs ahead of yours. And the worst part is that I don't even realize I'm doing it."

"But you're honest about it," he says. "Don't discount that. And," he sighs, "I can understand why you want to save Blue Moon Basherts."

I nod, not trusting myself to speak. Maybe the smell of healthy food is making me emotional.

He takes a granola package and reads the ingredients out loud, but all I catch is the word "Tocopherols."

I clear my throat, take it out of his hand, and return it to the shelf. "If I can't pronounce it, I don't eat it," I say.

"So, if I teach you how to pronounce it, you'll eat it?"

"No," I say, taking the shopping cart and moving down the aisle as fast as I can. "But," I sigh, "I agree to make some more lifestyle changes—as long as you keep up your end of the bargain. Do we have a deal?"

"Absolutely," he says, and I note how his grin reaches his eyes.

A bag of sweet potato chips catches my attention. *Finally.* Something good.

"Absolutely not," he says, snatching the bag of chips out of my hand. "I'm in charge, remember?"

"Correction—you *were* in charge, but you've been demoted."

"What for exactly?" Amused, he watches me as I toss the bag of chips into the cart.

"For not being more balanced. You need to have a certain amount of junk food to properly function."

"I'm sure you believe that."

"Damn straight I do," I reply, to which he laughs. Now that Caleb is back to his normal self, I feel better, although now my stomach is filled with dread now that I have to go on the date. What an absolute mess I've made.

"Don't you dare," I warn Caleb as he picks up a package of quinoa.

"It's packed with protein and fiber, not to mention thiamin and riboflavin."

"If that gets within two feet of me, I'll pack you with so much thiamin and riboflavin that you won't be able to walk for a week."

He deposits the quinoa into the front of the cart, as near to me as possible and then murmurs, "Now *that* is the kind of date I'd get excited about."

Chapter Twenty-Seven

It takes some time to get Caleb's and Tamar's schedules lined up, but here I am a week later, lying in wait for the couple to arrive.

Although the date isn't taking place in a dojo or battlefield, I spent a good thirty minutes over the phone with Caleb, coaching him on what *not* to say. Then he spent the next ten minutes trying to convince me not to worry. But Caleb is like one of those psychological whodunnit thrillers where you're constantly wondering what you're missing and whose narrative you can trust.

Luckily, we reached a compromise regarding me third-wheeling the date and Caleb agreed to allow me to wear a disguise of my choice.

I check the time on my phone. They should be coming into the coffee shop any minute now. I texted him to sit in the back corner near the restrooms by the sweet, little old lady in the corner—gray wig, red glasses, and a cane for me today. I'm slightly concerned about the false nose because I've already had to reshape it twice, and the second time, I'm pretty sure some of it melted into my coffee.

The café door opens and almost immediately, the energy changes. Heads turn. Three sinfully beautiful people stride inside with the confidence that only sinfully beautiful people seem to possess. I take out my phone and send a storm of angry emojis to Caleb followed by a text.

> WHAT THE HELL???!!! WHAT ARE YOU THINKING, ACTUALLY I DON'T CARE, JUST GET RID OF CASANOVA ASAP!!!!!!!!

Tamar and Casanova sit down at the table directly in front of mine and I drum my fingers impatiently as Caleb takes their orders. He then has the audacity to throw me a wink before turning and heading toward the counter. I glare holes into his back as he takes his place in line. Finally, he glances at his phone.

> Calm down

> DON'T YOU DARE TELL ME TO CALM DOWN MOTHERFUCKER

He turns around and gives me A Look. I pretend to adjust my glasses with my middle finger.

> We had a meeting right before this and he said he was getting coffee anyway. And in case Tamar and I don't hit it off, maybe she and Casanova will.

> ARE YOU KIDDING ME???!!!!!!!! WHAT, YOU'RE PLAYING MATCHMAKER NOW??????

> You never know

> WHAT DOES THAT EVEN MEAN??!!!

The barista calls his name and I put my phone down. Casanova is sitting back in his chair looking bored and a little pissed off—although I'm pretty sure that's his resting face—and Tamar keeps stealing nervous glances at him, like he's a dangerous animal that could strike at any moment. This whole thing is absolutely ridiculous. How are Caleb and Tamar supposed to have a normal date with Casanova hovering between them like a stormy thundercloud?

Caleb returns to the table with three drinks, studiously avoiding looking my way. I try to think of a clever way to get rid of Casanova that doesn't involve dragging him out by his shirt collar.

"Everyone good?" Caleb asks, arranging his chair so his back is to me.

Tamar nods and blushes. I've never seen a man possess the ability to make women blush just by looking at them. There's a business to be made somewhere in that.

"Mine taste like penicillin," Casanova grunts. Caleb laughs, Tamar looks uncertain, and I tilt my head back and groan.

"He's going through withdrawal," Caleb explains to Tamar. "I cut him off sugar for his own good."

I try not to smirk and fail. At least I'm not the only one that's getting health lessons.

"Ooh that's rough," Tamar says sympathetically as she glances at Casanova. "How long has it been?"

"An hour," he replies, and I accidentally bark in laughter. The three of them turn to me and I quickly pretend to be absorbed in my phone.

"I try cutting sugar before, but I keep cheating," Casanova adds.

"Don't worry, I'm watching you," Caleb says, then turns to Tamar. "It helps to have someone keep you accountable. Although, I've got this one friend who is really difficult about it," he adds. "I have to keep constant tabs on her otherwise she'd eat nothing but hot dogs and potato chips."

I take a slow sip of my sugary latte. Why do I get the feeling he's talking about me?

"You're friends with a woman?" Tamar is surprised and I guess I can't blame her. Not many people in our community are friends with the opposite gender.

"Yeah. We've been friends since we were kids. We grew up together."

"Oh. That's interesting."

"It's our matchmaker actually," he says.

I facepalm because *why?!*

"She's very pretty," Tamar says after a slight pause.

"I never noticed," Caleb says, and Casanova chuckles. I scowl at both of them.

"Did you guys ever . . ." She makes a hand motion and trails off.

I blush, glad he's not facing me.

"No." Caleb shakes his head. "She wanted to, of course. Begged me several times in fact, but I've always let her down gently."

My drink goes down the wrong way and I start coughing and pounding my chest. Casanova gives me a bored, slightly annoyed gaze. He'd make a great ER doctor, this one.

"Poor Ashira," Tamar sighs. "It must be painful for her to set you up with other women."

"I'm sure it is," Caleb agrees.

Still coughing, I type out a message to Caleb just to let him know what I think of that.

> Not funny

I hear his small chuckle, and then he clears his throat. "So, Tamar, how are you liking New York? You're from Chicago, right?"

"Yes. Skokie," she replies. "It's okay. I'm a little homesick, though. And my rent just went up, so I started looking for an even worse place to live. Somewhere with even more cockroaches and rats."

I try not to laugh. Poor thing.

"I'm sorry to hear that," Caleb says.

"I know French girl who wants roommate," Casanova says in his thick accent. "Is basement apartment, but a little better than sewer," he adds, as if that's a selling point.

But Tamar must be desperate because her pretty face lights up. "Really?" She brightens. "That sounds perfect, thank you!"

I take a long slurp of my drink as they exchange phone numbers and try to comfort myself with the fact that finding Tamar a place to live is still a mitzvah, just not the kind I had intended.

Casanova then rattles off something in Arabic to Caleb and then Caleb responds in Hebrew, and soon they're both talking in rapid-fire speed in two foreign languages and cracking each other up. Based on the Hebrew part, I make out that they were on a vacation together and something happened with a rat and women's underwear. I shake my head, frustrated.

> STOP TALKING TO CASANOVA!!!! Give Tamar attention. Ask her about her family.

"Do you have siblings?" Caleb asks a moment later.

"Yes. Three brothers. What about you?"

"Just me, I'm afraid."

"Oh, that's unusual," she replies, wiping her mouth with a napkin. Which is true, at least within the Orthodox world. The commandment to be fruitful and multiply is only considered complete if you have a girl and a boy.

"My parents wanted more, but it never worked," he says.

"Probably wrong hole," Casanova remarks, causing Caleb to choke on his drink.

I lay my face down on the table. This is just too painful for words.

"Here are some napkins," Tamar says.

"Thanks," Caleb coughs.

Silence settles between them and I shoot another quick text.

> Ask about her hobbies

"What do you do for fun when you're not working?" he says.

"Sadly," she laughs, "I'm always working."

Casanova lets out a loud yawn and I shake my head. This date is starting to feel worse than a dental cleaning.

> Tell her about your hobbies

> I have hobbies?

I grind my teeth as I type.

> YOU WORK OUT, YOU BOX, YOU LIKE TO COOK, GO TO CONCERTS, AND YOU PLAY FOOTBALL, TENNIS, AND SOCCER. AND PING-PONG.

> I don't think she cares

> Of course she cares, she's here to get to know you.

"So, Tamar," he says. "What's your favorite kind of music?"

"I love classical. And operas."

I don't think I can do this

I glance at Tamar, wishing she'd turn the question back to him, but she's staring into the distance looking bored. My temples start to pound. This is what a lack of chemistry looks like.

Still. It ain't over till the matchmaker sings. Or until one of them walks out.

> Give it a little longer. Tell her a funny story

> Like?

> I don't know. Something from childhood maybe?

"Do you want to hear one of my favorite childhood memories?" he asks, leaning toward her. She nods and smiles, and he continues, "My best friend is Ashira's brother. His name is Zevi. He's gay." He pauses to take a sip of his drink. "He had a hard time in school. He was good at sports, but he had to work twice as hard as everyone else when it came to academics. And kids would bully him."

I rub my temples. What part of 'funny story' did he not understand? I'm not sure where he's going with this, but I certainly don't feel like laughing.

"The boys suspected he was gay and you know how kids can be . . ." He trails off. "There was even a rumor going around that I was his boyfriend." Caleb and Casanova both chuckle, and Tamar gives a belated laugh that sounds forced.

"Then one day, we were all in the locker room getting ready for a football game and I overheard one guy call Zevi a slur."

I shake my head and type,

> When do we get to the funny part???

"I wanted to kill him, or at least beat him unconscious," he continues.

Great. Now she thinks he has a temper. One of my fake nostrils, fashioned from Mordy's Play-Doh, falls into my coffee and I can't even find it within me to care.

"I grabbed the guy by his throat, but instead of choking him, I told him that Zevi is more a man than he'd ever be and that if I was gay, I'd marry him."

Casanova nods in approval and gives him some sort of fist bump.

"And then I punched him. Just a small one," Caleb adds. "A friendly one. He hardly bled at all."

> You can go now,

I type.

> Really?

> Yes. You are past the point of no return.

"Did you know that my friend here loves to ski?" Caleb says, then turns to Casanova. "Entertain her for me while I use the restroom? Thanks, buddy."

"Hey! Wrong way," Casanova calls to Caleb who heads to the door. Caleb lifts a hand and gives a small wave. And then he's gone.

Casanova turns and glowers at me. So, I guess he knows who I am, after all.

Chapter Twenty-Eight

I turn the corner of my street, nearly finished with my evening run. With the marathon approaching in six weeks, I began doubling down on my workouts. Not that Caleb knows—I doubt he'd approve of me running after the sun sets.

The last few weeks have flown by as I've bounced between going to events at new synagogues where Mrs. Schwartz is less known. I've even managed to sign two new clients—although one of whom is so shy that she has trouble talking on dates, but I've been role-playing with her, so that's helped. It's been thrilling to sit in on meetings with Zevi and Jack as they meet with potential investors to discuss the documentary series that Jack thought of, *The Golden Bashert*. It ended up working out perfectly since Zevi's other show fell through after a drug scandal on set that landed some cast members in prison, some in rehab, and one unlucky soul in the hospital morgue.

But the best part? Watching Bernice get her sparkle back.

When I first explained my plan to Zevi, he said hell no, that my ethics were becoming shadier than Anna Delvey's, and that I should take a trip back to Hebrew school, but by the sixth attempt, he reluctantly agreed.

I knew Bernice would want to look her best if she were to "accidentally" bump into Lenny, but it was going to take something *big* to get her out of the house and glamorize her.

Bernice, as the bachelorette, has fifteen men vying for her hand who I helped select. The camera crew followed me around as I talked with Bernice and interviewed the bachelors about their life stories and what kind of partner they're hoping to find to share their golden years. They also captured my colorful commentary as I watched Bernice's dates through a hidden camera. And she's always dressed to the nines in her leather mini skirts, tiny sequin dresses, and platform wedges. Luckily, she's also forgiven me for Lenny's surprise appearance on the show—which to be honest, was *not* an easy thing to arrange in the first place. But as it turns out, a little harassment can go a long way.

I wipe a trail of sweat off my forehead as my house comes into view. I still have a million things on my mind, one of them being the wedding this Tuesday night that Caleb and I are driving to together. The bride—Esty—is not only Caleb's cousin, but my overnight camp bunkmate and longtime friend. It's an hour-and-a-half drive to Long Island, so we should have lots of time to discuss his dating life.

I jog up the front steps and let myself in, then turn on the front lights. And promptly let out a blood-curdling scream.

"What happened to knocking?" Bernice yelps, jumping back from Lenny and fumbling with the buttons of her shirt.

"*I live here*," I wail, covering my eyes. I can't believe Lenny and Bernice were making out on my couch. Who knows what else they were going to do? Now I'll have to get a new couch, even if it means going without food for the next two months.

"I'm sorry, Ashira," Lenny says, and I wince as I hear the zipping of his pants. "We didn't mean for this to happen. We only wanted to surprise you."

"Oh, I was surprised all right."

Bernice giggles. "You know what he meant. We wanted to show you that we're together."

"And you only have yourself to blame," Lenny adds. "This is what you wanted, after all."

"Was it?" I grimace at the image in my head.

"She's always been a bit of a prude," Bernice says, to which I sigh.

Lenny chuckles. "Kids nowadays."

"You can look now," Bernice says.

I lower my hands and smile at their flushed, glowing faces. "I'm really happy for you guys. When did you go from sworn enemies to . . ." I gesture in the direction of my couch.

"Once I kissed him," Bernice says, with a smug smile.

Lenny nods. "I didn't know what hit me. One minute I was telling her how much I hate her and in the next, she was kissing me."

"It was a social experiment," Bernice says. "I was curious to see what he would do in that moment. When he started kissing me back, I figured I might as well keep going."

"When did it happen? Was it on camera?" I ask, because I totally missed it if it was.

"A few nights ago. He showed up after the crew left so we could fight in private." Bernice gazes up at Lenny adoringly. "Isn't that romantic?"

"Very," I say, biting on the inside of my cheek so as not to laugh. "Does Zevi know about this new development?"

They glance at each other guiltily. "Not yet," Lenny admits. "I don't want them to try to separate us or anything."

"And either way, I have to make it look like I'm falling in love with two other men," Bernice says, leaning her head on Lenny's shoulder.

"Why two other men?"

Bernice shrugs. "Your brother said it creates more of a buzz that way with viewers. Keeps people's interest."

I nod. The investors had insisted on making this project into a reality TV series rather than a documentary. They thought it would be more entertaining and bring in a bigger viewership.

"This is pretty," Bernice says, picking up my new clutch as I walk them to the door.

"Thanks," I say, taking it back before she gets any ideas. "I bought it for the wedding I'm going to on Tuesday."

"Who's getting married?"

"Esty Kahn. She's an old friend of mine. And Caleb's cousin."

"Caleb is the man that Ashira is using to save her business," Bernice says to Lenny as she puts on her coat.

"I don't know if using is the right word," I say weakly. "I mean, he wants to get married—"

"To *you*."

My mouth drops open. How did she know?

"That man looks at you the way someone on a diet looks at an all-you-can-eat dessert buffet. Like he wants to lick every part of you and then eat you up."

I blink. "Okay, then," I say and open the front door. "Thanks for stopping by."

Bernice wags her finger at me. "Life is too short to be a virgin."

"I'll try to remember that."

"Goodnight, Ashira." Lenny grins. "Don't be strange."

I laugh. "You mean don't be a stranger."

He chuckles and as they walk away, I hear Bernice say, "Honestly, I think you're both a little strange."

* * *

Tuesday arrives, and Caleb picks me up at one o'clock in the afternoon so we'll have plenty of time to drive to Long Island, *and* practice having normal dating conversations. Unfortunately, his new cologne or shampoo or whatever scent it is that he's wearing is making me want to climb onto his lap and plant my face in the crook of his neck. And in other places too.

Focus.

I can do this. I can be a professional and stay in my own lane. I'm Caleb's matchmaker. *His matchmaker*, I remind myself, as my eyes drift to his lips.

It's just a small, annoying attraction. Nothing more.

"Okay, so here's what we'll do," I say, shaking my head and clearing my thoughts. "I'll be the man, and you'll be the woman, and we're going to pretend we're on a date."

"Got it."

"Ready?" He nods. "Hi," I say, deepening my voice, "you look lovely."

"Thank you. You look very handsome yourself."

I give him a silent thumbs-up to show my approval. "The matchmaker mentioned you were a gardener, is that right?"

"No," he says in a high girly voice, sounding slightly miffed. "I'm the CEO and president of a medical device company."

"Ah, sorry. I must've confused you with someone else."

"I see." He frowns. "Do you often date more than one woman at a time?"

"No. *No, no.*" I shake my head. "I'm just . . . confused."

"How often do you get '*confused*'?" he says, arranging his fingers into quotations marks. "Because I don't want a husband that gets confused about things."

I try not to laugh, but fail horribly.

"Are you laughing at me?" he says, picking up a British accent.

I shake my head and clutch my stomach, unable to stop giggling. So much for being a professional.

"Okay," I say, recovering my voice. "Let's end this round."

"That went well," he says, slipping back into his normal voice and adjusting the rearview mirror. "How about this time you pretend to be the man and I'll be the woman?"

"I think we can handle pretending that." He gives me a small wink and just like that, my face grows hot. *Get a grip, girl. Remember you have a job to do.*

The traffic light turns red and he brings the car to a stop. "Hi there," he says, turning to gaze at me.

"Hi."

"I love your outfit."

"This old thing?" I bat my hand. "Thank you. I appreciate the compliment."

"It really brings out the blue of your eyes."

I pause. "That's great, except your date might not have blue—" I start to say, but he cuts me off.

"They're the same color as blue jays and when I look at you, I think of them." His gaze penetrates into mine, and I'm suddenly confused on so many levels.

"Blue jays?"

He nods, and presses on the gas as the light turns green. "A lot of people don't like them because they're noisy and aggressive and eat a lot. Some people even think they're evil."

What started off as promising is quickly going downhill. "Okay, how about we take it from the top—" I start to suggest, but he cuts me off.

"But I see their intelligence, their gumption, their scrappiness," he continues. "They're not selfish for hiding seeds to eat later, and they're not aggressive just because smaller birds scatter when one approaches. And though they are noisy, their calls save other birds' lives by warning them about predators." He flicks the wrist that's resting casually on the steering wheel. "Sure, they sometimes eat other birds' babies, but no one is perfect."

"I'm sorry," I say gently, not wanting to hurt his pride, "but this is a really terrible conversation."

His voice deepens, turns more serious. "You're the same way. I see how you stand tall and strong in shul despite the gossip, and the lies and the vilification. But you don't cower. You don't hide or back down. And rightfully so." He spares me a quick glance and smiles. "You're a badass blue jay, Tinsel."

My breath gets trapped in my throat. I shake my head. "How do you do that?"

"Do what?"

"Go from not being able to talk to women on dates to *this*," I say, gesturing in the space between us. "Because that was . . ." I trail off and swallow. "It was really nice."

"Maybe it has nothing to do with them," he says in a quiet voice, "and everything to do with you."

I feel a pinch in my heart. And I find myself wondering whether it would really be so bad to fall in love. To share my life with someone who sees me the way Caleb does. Could Caleb be an exception to my rule?

I don't know. But one thing is for sure. The more I'm around Caleb, the harder it gets to resist this pull toward him. And now more than ever, I'm growing less convinced that I should be.

Chapter Twenty-Nine

An hour and a half later, we've arrived at the venue which resembles a European castle. It's made entirely of brick and has everything from gate houses, to corner towers to parapets. It even has a drawbridge.

I'm willing to bet that this place doesn't host too many Orthodox Jewish weddings.

"This is so Esty," I say, laughing as we cross over the drawbridge.

"It is, isn't it?" He chuckles. "She's always been a character."

"Where does she get it from?"

"Not my side," he says, with a sly grin.

Two men in medieval costumes greet us and open the heavy wooden door. I stand in stupefied awe, gazing at the impossibly high curved ceilings and large mullioned windows, and wrought-iron chandeliers with pillar candles on top.

Even the servers are dressed in medieval costumes, and I'm not going to lie—it's a strange sight to see someone dressed as a knight offer champagne to a guest wearing head-to-toe Hasidic garb.

"Do you think Esty's wedding dress will be from a Renaissance shop?" I say to Caleb, unbuttoning my coat.

His eyes follow the movement of my fingers and he replies, "I wouldn't be surprised if it is, knowing . . ." He trails off as I hand him my coat.

"Knowing what?" I say, fluffing my hair out.

But he doesn't respond. His eyes do a slow appraisal and I feel myself blushing under his watchfulness. "You look . . . Wow."

"You don't think it's too . . ." I trail off, not wanting to call attention to my body while at the same time trying to determine if he thinks it's *too* form-fitting. There's a slit that shows off the bottom part of my left leg, but look—my body happens to be having a good day and I can only wear this particular dress on good-body days. Therefore, this was the obvious choice to get my money's worth, you understand, and had *nothing* to do with hoping Caleb would notice my body. Because why would I want that?

"Too sexy?" he says, arching an eyebrow. "Definitely."

My heart skips a beat. "Oops," I say weakly.

"Don't worry." He throws me a sly grin. "I'm sure no one will mind."

There aren't too many people here yet, since Caleb was told to come early for the family pictures. He motions for me to follow him and I stand in the back of the room, not wanting to get in the way. At one point, Esty rushes over to me and gives me a big hug, looking stunning herself in a shimmering gown with organza and lace. She's also wearing a huge crown and carrying a scepter instead of a bouquet, which is so perfectly *her*.

Also in typical Esty fashion, she orders me to stand beside Caleb, and I turn bright pink because everyone is standing next to their spouses. And to make things worse, the photographer keeps singling me out by shouting at me and telling me to move closer to Caleb.

"Move toward your husband. He won't bite," the photographer calls out and the family laughs, either at the joke or more likely because they know Caleb isn't married and so I'm definitely not his wife.

"Mmm, I might," Caleb whispers to me under his breath.

"Get me out of here," I say through my cheery smile.

"More! Give me more!" The photographer gestures at me wildly, clearly growing impatient with me.

"I think he wants you directly on top of me," Caleb murmurs, and I try as I might, I can't control the burst of laughter that erupts from me. Caleb makes a snorting, choking sound, failing to hold back his own laughter.

"Save your lovey-dovey eyes for the camera, you two," the photographer shouts at us, eliciting another wave of laughter from the thirty or so family members watching us.

"More!" the photographer shouts.

"This is the most mortifying moment of my life," I murmur, moving my right hip and breast until it presses against the left side of Caleb's body. Although *crushing* might be a more apt description at this point.

"Really?" he murmurs back. "I'm quite enjoying it."

I snort.

"*More*, sweetheart, *more!*" The photographer waves frantically to the right and his assistant copies the motion.

"Did you pay him to do this?" I mutter, and Caleb throws his head back and laughs.

"Yes, love that! Everyone laugh like that," he commands, and the assistant mimes laughing.

The moment the photographer is done, Caleb's extended family swarm around him, like bees clustering around their queen. I stand and observe it all with a smile. I'm so proud of the man that Caleb's become. Somehow, he went from being a shy immigrant boy, who constantly felt *other*, to this strong, confident man with an intangible quality that's hard to define, but draws people in, like a moth to a flame.

I watch him lean forward to better hear them. That's another special thing about Caleb. Most people love to talk and be heard, but very few listen. Especially the way Caleb does. When he listens, his eyes never leave your face, and every muscle of his body is poised on the words coming out of your mouth. You never doubt that his attention is focused elsewhere.

"Ashira. Look at you." Dr. Sheva Kahn smiles and pulls me into a hug. "You're glowing."

"Glowing?" My cheeks stain pink. Does she believe what her mother-in-law said about me, that I'm pregnant with her grandchild? Or am I just being paranoid?

Please, let it just be my paranoia.

"You had a sparkle in your eye," she says. "Like you were thinking about someone special." Her gaze drifts to Caleb and lingers for a beat. "But," she adds, turning back to me, "it's gone now."

"Ah." I nod, unsure how to respond. Every now and then I've gotten the feeling that Dr. Kahn wouldn't mind having me as a daughter-in-law, although she's never come out and said as much.

A woman in a long floral gown steals Dr. Kahn's attention. I head to the drinks table when something tumbles over my feet.

"Oh—hi there," I coo when a small toddler trips over my feet. "Are you okay?"

The little boy is in an adorable baby tuxedo, made all the more adorable by the pigtails on his head. He stares at me as if trying to figure out if he should laugh or cry, so I do a quick round of peek-a-boo before he has time to think it over.

"Can I ask you a question about your son?" an older woman says to me sotto voce, as if afraid of being overheard. She's in a pale blue suit, matching the rest of the bride's family's color palette.

"My son?" I say confused, standing up. She gestures to the boy at my feet and I realize the mistake. "Oh, he isn't mine."

"Sorry, I just assumed—could I ask you the question anyway?"

"Sure."

"I don't understand why Orthodox Jewish boys don't get their hair cut until they're, what, four?"

"Three," I say. "It's called an *upsherin* for Ashkenazi Jews and *chalaka* for Sephardi Jews, but not all Orthodox people do it. It's a custom," I add. "Not a Jewish law."

"But what's the point of it?"

"I think there's more than one reason behind it, but one of them is education. At three, children begin to understand the reasons behind why we do things, and males are not allowed to cut off their sideburns. Trim them, but not cut them off completely."

She frowns. "Why not? And what about girls? Why are they treated differently?"

"Great questions." *Where the hell is Caleb when you need him?* Or anybody else. "I think the prohibition of cutting sideburns is related to the whole idol worshipping thing, like the idol worshippers used to cut off their sideburns, so this was a way to distinguish themselves from them."

"But what about girls?"

"The girls?" I repeat, distracted by the sight of Caleb across the room, surrounded by a gaggle of young women. His eyes find mine as if he somehow knew I was looking at him and his bottom lip quirks into a secret smile.

"Why are girls treated differently? Why aren't they given the same commandments? Sorry, is it okay that I'm asking you this?" she adds with an apologetic smile. "I've just always been curious."

"Yeah, of course. I can tell you what I was taught, although ask two Jews a question and you'll get ten different answers," I laugh. "But girls light Shabbat candles starting at the age of three because that's also the age of understanding. As to why girls aren't given the same commandments, well," I pause. "As a disclaimer, this isn't to bash men, but as a whole, they tend to be less spiritual than women. They're more removed from G-d, you know? Women are compared to angels, and men are compared to animals." The woman's eyes widen and I rush to add, "I love men, though. And I love animals. They're both great, really. It's just that women are naturally more spiritual, so we don't need to do all these commandments to remind us of G-d because we're already on that level." I chew my bottom lip and add, "See, men's commandments are all external and done in public, whereas a woman's are done internally and in private, because she can be trusted."

A long silence follows and then she murmurs, "Interesting."

"But we all have male and female characteristics," I say, "and that's why certain words in Hebrew are either female or male—"

The little boy tumbles over me again, except this time he lands on his face. I bend down and pick him up as he starts to cry and I croon in his ear, "Shhh, I've got you. Should we find Mommy? Or Tatty?" I glance around trying to figure out who the mom or dad could be and when I spot a table with desserts. "Cookies!" I say enthusiastically to the boy and point.

"Ooo-kies!" He kicks his legs excitedly against my dress.

"Do you want the pink cookie or the white cookie or the—" I catch him with my other arm as he dives towards the table, swiping at as many cookies as he can hold in his small hands. "All of the above, huh?" I laugh.

"Ooo-kies!" He grins and drools on my shoulder.

"Don't you worry about the dress, slugger. It's non-refundable and dry-clean only, and—" The boy lets out a huge sneeze. I reach for a napkin and gently wipe his face. "Ah, well. What's a little snot between friends, right?"

"Hey," Caleb says, and I turn around in surprise. "Who's this little guy?"

"Ooo-kie!" he squeals.

"Never met an Oookie before." Caleb grins at the little boy, his eyes dancing with humor. "Who is he?" he asks.

"No idea." I smooth down a lock of hair that's come loose from one of his pigtails. "He tripped over my feet and we've been best buds ever since."

Caleb offers a fist bump to him. "Smooth, Oookie. Very smooth."

I laugh. The boy lays his head on my shoulder, and warmth spreads through me. "Do you think I can keep him?" I whisper to Caleb, caressing Oookie's soft hair. But when Caleb doesn't respond, I lift my gaze only to discover that he's watching me intently. A kaleidoscope of emotions flickers across his eyes.

He clears his throat. "You're a natural."

Something unspoken crackles in the air—something that feels like yearning and hope, and smells distinctly of rainbow sprinkles. Of course, that last part is probably due to the cookie hitting my nose.

"Do you want to hold him?" I offer.

"Do you think he'd let me?"

I shrug. "I haven't known him long, but I think Oookie is happy as long as he's eating ooo-kies." I transfer him into Caleb's arms and smile as I watch the two of them make faces at each other. "You're such a natural with kids," I say.

"Thanks." He lifts his eyes to meet mine. "So are you."

An unexpected swell of emotion rises in my chest. I'd give anything to have a little family like this. A sweet, devoted man like Caleb, and a messy, yet adorable child.

The thought is jarring.

I want to have children, I realize with a startling rush of clarity. I want to have babies and a husband and a family of my own. I've spent years telling myself that being an aunt to Leah's kids was enough, but now I know that I've been lying to myself, and that this whispered longing to be a mother is no longer whispering.

"You look deep in thought."

I startle at the sound of Caleb's voice. His deep charcoal eyes dance with amusement and he looks almost painfully handsome in his navy suit and paisley pink tie. My cavewoman instincts are screaming *prime mating material*.

"Are you okay?" he asks, tilting his head. "You look a little pale."

I feel pale. Confused and terrified, too.

"I should return Oookie to his parents," I say, taking the toddler back. Let's face it—Caleb in a suit is dangerous in and of itself, but Caleb in a suit *and* holding a child?

Cata-friggin-clysmic.

"Anyone lose a kid?" I ask, approaching a group of guests. They shake their heads in bewilderment and I move on. I know I've found the mom when Oookie lunges at a woman with the enthusiasm of a dog greeting its owner. She thanks me in broken English and I respond in similarly broken Hebrew.

I stand off to the side, my arms feeling strangely bereft. I watch the kids running around, playing tag, and squealing in delight. A father walks by, cradling a small baby and looking down at it with such obvious pride that my heart tugs. An older woman, probably a grandmother, is laughing and talking with a child who looks to be about ten.

Why am I suddenly noticing children everywhere I look? This is more than annoying. It is *excruciating*.

"I brought you some water."

I accept the glass, but instead of taking a drink, I blurt, "I want a baby."

Caleb looks shocked and rightfully so. I just vomited out this big life decision as if I had just decided what to eat for dinner.

"What?" he says.

"I want a baby," I repeat. "Maybe even two or three."

"That's . . . great," he says slowly, like he's not yet sure where this is going.

"It could be a temporary thing. Maybe I'm coming down with a virus?" I say, with hope.

"Does this mean that you've changed your mind about marriage?"

"No— I mean, I don't need to get married to have children," I say, then glance at him, noting his tight jaw and the tension in the way he's holding himself.

"Ashira," he sighs. "When are you going to stop allowing your past to control your future?"

"That isn't why . . . I mean, it's not—" I break off and glance away. "I don't know," I finally say. But what I do know is that the closer I get to Caleb, the more I start to want the things I swore I'd never allow myself to have.

And that alone, terrifies me.

Chapter Thirty

There's something about weddings that spreads romance in the air. Everywhere I look, couples are laughing and talking, and a few teenagers are off to the side flirting. Even the old people in wheelchairs are holding hands and gazing into each other's eyes.

I accept a champagne flute from a waiter dressed as a horse, and order myself not to glance at Caleb even as my eyes keep finding him. His hip is pressed into a wall, hands tucked in his pant pockets, as he nods to whatever it is a woman and her twenty-something daughter are saying.

I take a sip of the bubbly drink and notice a handsome man watching me from across the room. He lifts his flute and grins at me in acknowledgement, and I smile a little back. He's older, probably in his early forties, but he's got a full head of hair and a strong build. Biceps like that were made to hold onto baby carriers. *Come to Mama.*

Bruce is right—maybe I do need chemical castration. I'm about to take out my phone and do a Google search about it, when a completely outrageous idea pops into my head. It's absurd but also has some merit—what if I marry a heterosexual man who I have sexual chemistry with, but don't love? The idea feels safe to me, much less risky in terms of possible heartbreak. Perhaps a man who would be an average dad, someone present, but not overly amazing. That way the kids wouldn't miss him too much either.

Caleb is too much like my own dad, too nice, too kind. Too good to be true. I *know* that he's going to be the type of dad who's going to play catch and read bedtime stories and kiss scrapes and boo-boos and check for monsters under the bed, exactly the way my dad did. And when something is too good to be true, it usually is.

The man starts making his way toward me and I swallow. This is the first time in my life that I actually might be interested in a future with someone—I just have to make sure that he isn't too nice, but not a jerk either.

"Hi there." The handsome man gazes down at me with a friendly grin. I swallow back. He's even more dazzling close up with big blue eyes and jet-black hair. "You looked hungry, so I got you this."

"I looked hungry?" I laugh, shaking my head in wonder at the plate in his outstretched hand, filled with steak and mini meat-filled pastries and chicken salad.

"Definitely. You were giving off starving vibes from all the way across the room. I'll bring you dessert after you're done."

I shake my head and laugh. "You're lucky I'm not a vegetarian."

He chuckles. "You're funny. I like that."

"I'm Ashira Wernick, by the way," I say, accepting the plate of food. No ring on his finger, mentally checking that off. "I'm a friend of Esty's."

"Nice to meet you, Ashira. I'm Alex Rabinowitz, friend of the groom's father."

Okay. Definitely older. "Nice to meet you."

"Trust me," he smiles, tilting his head, "the pleasure is all mine."

The flirtatiousness in his voice is so over the top that it makes me laugh, and I choke a little as the food goes down the wrong way.

"I have that effect on women," he says, after I get my coughing under control. "My mother likes to say I should come with a warning label."

"Your mother is right." I laugh. I put down my fork because I don't think I can eat and not choke while talking to this man. "So, where are you from, Alex?"

"Originally Denver, but I recently moved to Brooklyn."

I nod. "Any particular reason?"

"I got a job offer from Mount Sinai," he replies, putting his hands in his pant pockets. "I'm a general surgeon."

"So you're good with your hands," I say, then immediately feel my face heat up when I realize how that sounds.

"That's what they keep telling me." He winks.

I shake my head and giggle. This man. He's hot, but also hard to imagine having a serious conversation with. I could see us having chemistry in bed, but not falling for each other out of it. We could be roommates with benefits. And have kids together.

"Are you here with someone?" Alex asks.

"Not . . . exactly?"

"There you are," Caleb says, suddenly at my side. He reaches for my flute. "Do you mind if I try some?" He tastes it before I even have a chance to protest and then nods, like he's decided it isn't poisonous and hands it back to me. "Hi, I'm Caleb Kahn," he says, putting his hand out to Alex.

"Alex Rabinowitz."

Neither one smiles. The two of them shake hands like two MMA fighters silently sizing the other one up.

"Alex was just telling me that he's recently moved to Brooklyn," I say, jumping to fill the silence.

"Is that so," Caleb drawls.

Alex smiles. "And what do you do, Caleb?"

"I own a personal protection company."

"Sounds nice."

"Nice?" Caleb shrugs. "I wouldn't call it nice. It's hard and dirty work. Occasionally, backhanded, and borderline illegal—"

"He's kidding," I cut in, but Caleb talks over me.

"I've got contractors operating both here and abroad, and several trained dogs from the military."

"The bomb-sniffing type?" Alex asks.

"Nope." Caleb rocks back on his heels. "The killing-on-command type."

"He means bite, not kill," I say to Alex, feeling sweat form in my armpits.

"That's true." Caleb nods. "The killing is the contractor's job. So," Caleb says, "What do you do, Alan?"

"Alex," I say, but neither one seems to hear me.

"I guess you could say that I cut people for a living."

"How about that." Caleb smiles the way he does when he realizes his opponent is a lot better than he first thought, whether it's a game of Black Jack or in the boxing ring. "Well, you just got a lot more interesting, Alan."

"*Alex* is a surgeon," I say, feeling a headache coming on. "Not an assassin."

"Definitely not," Alex agrees with a chuckle. "Although, I do know exactly where and how to cut someone to create ultimate impact and suffering. In fact, you'd be amazed at the type of damage that could be done with a ballpoint pen."

"Some men don't need anything but their bare hands," Caleb counters.

On second thought, I think being a single mom is the way to go.

"True." Alex flexes his. "Large and steady hands are best."

I toss down the rest of my champagne.

"Careful now, Alan," Caleb says with a small chuckle. "You're starting to sound a little bloodthirsty."

"Look the wedding is about to start," I say. But neither of them seem to hear me, and frankly, I'm done watching this ridiculous game. They can go ahead and kill each other for all I care.

I head into the women's room, the *kabbalat panim* where the female guests will wish Esty mazel tov and try to give her words of encouragement in case she's having second thoughts. No one there will be discussing the things one could do with ballpoint pens or large, steady hands.

The band plays joyful music and Esty is seated on her makeshift throne, surrounded by loved ones. A long line of women has already formed to wish her mazel tov, and she's smiling and laughing. She doesn't seem at all freaked out by the fact that in an hour from now, she'll be a married woman.

I carry my plate to a standing table. There's something so terrifying yet romantic about making a lifetime commitment that *this* is your forever person; the one you'll have children with and wake up beside every day. The one you'll share your body with and your bathroom too. What if this person ends up clogging the toilet on a regular basis? What if their aim is poor? What if they not only squeeze the toothpaste from the wrong part of the tube, but they don't even put the cap back on afterwards? Why isn't it written in the *ketubah* that a husband must provide a wife with her own separate bathroom if he can't follow the rules she lays out for him?

Soon enough, a parade of men file into the women's room, loudly singing and clapping. The groom's face lights up like a menorah as he sees his beautiful bride for the first time in all her bridal splendor. The groom approaches her, both of them blushing and grinning, following the Jewish tradition of ensuring that this is in fact, the correct woman before putting the veil over her head—a direct result of our forefather Jacob's PTSD after accidentally marrying the wrong sister. This is the stuff of deep generational trauma.

I catch Caleb's eye. No matter how crowded a room is, my body always seems to find him, and he seems just as trained to find me. I don't see Alex anywhere, but I'm sure he's fine.

Hopefully.

The men file back out, singing and cheering on the groom as everyone except the bridal procession heads toward the large open room for the ceremony. I take a seat toward the back, figuring the family and closer friends deserve a better view than me. Even though it appears to be mixed seating, I'm surprised when Alex takes the empty seat next to mine. I'm starting to realize he's quite the bold type.

"Hello again," he says. "Are you enjoying yourself?"

"I am. What about you?"

"Eh. I give it a seven out of ten," he says.

I laugh. "Do you rate every wedding you go to?"

"Not usually, no." He sticks a shoe onto the rung of the chair in front of him and cross his arms over his chest. "Can I ask you something?"

I nod.

"Are you single?"

"Uh, yes . . . ?"

"You don't sound too sure about that."

"No, it's . . ." I laugh. "I'm just surprised by the question."

"I'm surprised by your answer." He leans a little closer and says, "How is it possible that someone hasn't snapped you up yet?"

"To be honest, I've never been interested in marriage," I say lightly.

"So you're a player, then?" He wiggles his eyebrows suggestively. "Living the life of a bachelorette with no strings?"

"Hardly." I laugh. "More like the life of a boring old maid who watches too much YouTube."

He laughs and puts his arm around the back of my chair.

"Hey," rumbles a familiar masculine voice.

"Uh, hi." I glance up at Caleb. I steel myself in case they're about to have a second round of a testosterone tournament.

"I saved a seat for you up front," Caleb says, nodding his head.

"Really?" I say surprised. "Isn't that just for family?"

"You are family," he says firmly.

Funny how three little words have such a strong effect on my heart, how something so small can unfurl such warmth and fill every inch of my body. "Sorry," I say to Alex as I stand up. "I'm family."

"No problem," he replies easily. "We'll talk later."

Caleb mutters under his breath, "Don't count on it."

"He's kidding," I tell Alex. But Alex doesn't look convinced and neither am I. It's just as well that I've decided to become a single mom because Caleb will undoubtedly scare off any guy I'd be interested in.

I follow Caleb to the second row where the canopy is a tallis held in place by four men holding poles.

"That's the same tallis that my great-grandparents married under," Caleb murmurs, pointing to the chuppah. "It's used for every wedding in the family and has the couples named embroidered on it."

"That's so beautiful," I sigh. Again, I get that tug in my heart, that feeling of wanting. How incredible to marry under a canopy that connects you to your ancestors; to stand under the exact same tallis and perform the exact same rituals that they did on their wedding days.

I wish I knew more about my mother's side of the family. As with most Orthodox couples, the wife takes on the husband's *minhagim*—traditions—so everything from the prayer book we use, to the foods we eat on Shabbos and holidays, to the shul we attend, have always reflected my father's family. Nothing to sneeze at since the Wernicks descend from a long line of impressive rabbis. Until my father came along, that is.

"It is," he says softly, but he's looking at me. His face is close and my eyes drop to the shape of his lips, the cupid's bow so perfectly well formed it might have been created by Michelangelo himself.

I swallow and look down at my hands. It will be okay. I'm sure one day I'll be able to look at Caleb and not want to climb him like a tree.

A few minutes later, Esty enters the room, flanked by her parents, and all the guests rise from their seats. The singer's voice rings clear as he begins the opening notes of 'Boi Kallah', a song that celebrates the bride as the crown of her husband.

I don't know if it's the music or all the built-up emotion of the last few days, but my eyes prickle with tears. It feels like just yesterday that Esty and I were kids, screaming with terror and jumping out of canoes after seeing a big spider, or sneaking into the kitchen at midnight and spraying whipped cream into our mouths, or waking up at sunrise to be able to take showers before the hot water ran out.

And now, here she is dressed like an Orthodox Jewish medieval princess, and moving on to the next stage in her life.

"What's wrong?" Caleb whispers to me, concern in his face.

"Nothing," I say, dabbing the corners of my eyes. "It's just making me emotional to see her as a bride."

"I know what you mean." Caleb's lips quirk. "A part of me will forever see her as the little cousin that ruined all our games."

I snort. "That's very on brand for you," I whisper, and he chuckles in response. I watch Esty hand her scepter to her sister before joining her groom under the wedding canopy. "But also," I hear myself add, "I think it makes me feel like I'm being left behind."

"Because you're single?"

I nod, then shake my head. "Because of why I'm single."

"*Shh*," someone says from behind us.

We watch the ceremony begin. I stare straight ahead and swallow against the lump in my throat.

"Let's talk after the ceremony," he whispers.

I glance at him alarmed. I didn't mean to spark a discussion about why I'm single. "What for?"

"You'll see."

"*Shh!*" the person behind us hisses. Caleb smiles and puts a finger against his lips. I blow out an exaggerated breath. The ceremony is bound to take twice as long now that I'm anxious for it to end.

Chapter Thirty-One

The groom steps on the glass, commemorating the destruction of the Temple in Jerusalem some 2,000 years ago, and the band starts to play. Guests clap and cheer as Esty and her new husband head down the aisle together, off to the *yichud* room where they will touch each other for the first time.

"This way," Caleb says, gesturing for me to follow him.

"Where are we going?" I say, trying to keep up with his long strides. My heels echo along the tile floor as I rush after him.

"Here." He opens a restroom door labeled for family usage and ushers me inside. The light clicks on and the first thing I see are dried droplets of urine on the floor surrounding the toilet.

"Here?" I say, gazing at a tampon wrapper lying beside the garbage. "Really?"

"Tell me why you're single." He crosses his arms and gazes at me. "Tell me what you're so scared of."

I instantly think of my mother. How she woke up one day to realize that her husband checked out without so much as a goodbye or an explanation. How she didn't even have time to grieve because she had three young children relying on her to put food on the table. How she went from being a stay-at-home mom in a happy relationship, to losing the love of her life and becoming impoverished in the blink of an eye. How she relied on the older kids to raise the younger ones so she could go back to school, while working as many jobs as possible in between.

"Caleb," I sigh. "My mother died of a broken heart."

He looks confused. "What?"

"You think she died because of her lifestyle, but it's not true."

"What?" He blinks, looking confused by my response. "No, I never said that."

"You implied it."

"Well then, this is me *un*-implying it," he says, shaking his head. "All I meant is that it couldn't hurt for you to adapt healthier habits."

"They call it Broken Heart Syndrome," I continue as if he hadn't spoken. I fold my arms against my chest, suddenly cold. "Genetically, there was nothing wrong with her. And yeah, she ate chemicals and didn't exercise as much as she should've, but she was far from being overweight or unhealthy. The truth is," I say, speaking the words out loud for the first time, "my mother started dying years before her death. She started dying the day my father walked out on us. And I think what eventually killed her is the fact that he never came back. I think she held out hope for the longest time, but every day that passed without him walking through that door was another stab to her heart. Ironic, isn't it?" I glance up and see Caleb's stricken face. "She was the ultimate romantic and believer of happily-ever-afters. Yet it was her own unrequited love that killed her."

"Tinsel—" He breaks off. Shakes his head. "There's no way to know what caused it."

"One of the doctors agreed with me," I say defensively.

"Doctors don't know everything."

"*It was your dad.*"

Caleb pauses, then shrugs. "He also told me that babies come from storks."

"You were probably like, five when he said it."

"I was fifteen."

"Well . . ." I lift my palms. "Reproduction is an uncomfortable topic." His lips twist with a small smirk and I find myself entranced by them. They're the most perfect lips I've ever seen. I glance down and add, "It's safer to be single. I know that makes me a coward, but . . ." I shrug.

"Do you remember when you showed up at Johnnie's and asked me about the frog tattoo?"

It takes me a moment to recall our conversation, but then I nod. "I didn't think you heard me."

"I pretended not to. It's not an easy thing for me to talk about." He pauses for a long moment, and I don't try to rush him. "It's called a Bone Frog. It commemorates all the fallen soldiers." He glances down. "I got it after a friend was killed."

"I'm sorry," I murmur. He nods in acknowledgement.

"The truth is that I've had more than one friend return to their family in a casket."

My stomach drops. I'm so naïve—of course, he's had his share of grief. Zevi used to say that twenty-five percent of SEALs won't see their thirtieth birthday which was why he never stopped trying to convince Caleb to leave.

"Garcia's death, though—" He breaks off and stares into space. "That's the one that keeps me up at night. The one I relive when I close my eyes." His voice is controlled and casual, but the tic in his jaw gives away how tense he is.

"I'm so sorry," I say uselessly. I wish I had words to bring him comfort, but I know such words don't exist. "I had no idea. You always seem so . . . so . . ." I make circling motions with my hands as I search for the right word. "Strong. Like you've got everything under control."

"I'm not. I don't." He swallows. "I'm a lot better now thanks to the support group. And my therapist."

My jaw drops to the floor and I might have let out a gasp. For some reason, Caleb in a shrink's office seems as likely as my rabbi at a biker convention. "You went to therapy?"

He nods. "I did a twelve-week CPT. My therapist was also a veteran so she got what's it's like—the combat related-PTSD."

Mind. Blown.

"Wow," is the only word that comes to mind.

"It started about nine years ago, but it got really bad the year after that. The nightmares and flashbacks. If a car so much as backfired, I'd hit the ground without thinking twice. Certain smells still take me back. Cigarettes or burning plastic. Gasoline. Wet soil."

"I never knew," I say quietly.

He nods. "My therapist is the only one I've talked to about it. And the people in support groups. But no one in my regular life." He turns his head and adds, "Until you."

My heart skips a beat and I swallow. "You're telling me that your parents don't know? Or Zevi?"

"I never said anything." He gazes back up at the ceiling. "I felt as if admitting it aloud made me less of a man. The only reason I went to therapy at all was because the military forced me to."

"Why?"

"I started making mistakes. Small ones, but even the smallest mistakes can endanger your teammates' lives. And I had gotten paranoid." He swallows. "So, I took time off, got the help I needed, and then went back for a couple more years."

"And you're okay now?"

"I'm better," he allows. "But everything I've experienced is still, and always will be here," he says, tapping the side of his head. "We all carry our experiences. It explains the why of who we are."

"Thank you for sharing that. I know that isn't easy." He nods in silent acknowledgement. "Can I ask you something else?" I say, since we seem to be laying it all out there.

"As if I could stop you," he murmurs fondly.

"Good point." I smile, then take a deep breath and go for it. "Why did you decide to return to Orthodoxy?"

"A few reasons." He smiles, a bit ruefully. "I missed a lot of it—the community, the connection, following the traditions of my people. Being in shul and keeping Shabbos and the holidays reminds me that there's a bigger purpose in this world than whatever is going on in my life. And even if I don't fit the mold of the average Jew, looks or otherwise, I'm not going to let that stop me from being the best Jew I can be. Which is," he adds, after a beat, his eyes glinting with humor, "in and of itself, very Jewish."

"Yeah?" I find myself grinning. "How so?"

"After 3,350 years of slavery, forced conversions, persecutions, exiles, pogroms, and genocide, we're still here. Still keeping our traditions alive, still proud of our heritage. It's the chutzpah in us."

I laugh. "Definitely."

"And then there was you."

"Me?" I glance up at him, startled.

He nods. "Seeing you at that restaurant and then my parents' anniversary party after all those years was unlike anything I'd ever experienced. I felt this pull toward you unlike anything I'd experienced before. But at the same time," he sighs, "I could tell it wasn't right. I didn't think you were interested, and besides, I wasn't in the right place mentally with everything that was going on. In a weird way," he adds, "part of me hoped you'd get married so I wouldn't be tempted to pursue you. I didn't think I could ever be the type of husband you deserved."

"But you didn't even know me," I protest. "At least not the adult version of me. I could've been a terrible person."

He shakes his head. "You've always worn your heart and your soul on your sleeve. That's another reason why you'd make a terrible spy." He smiles. "You're too easy to read."

I huff a laugh.

"About three years after retiring from the teams, I started thinking more and more about returning to the fold. I found myself wanting a wife and starting a family. And," he adds, holding my gaze, "I kept wondering why you hadn't gotten married."

"Because I'm messed up," I say, providing the answer for him.

"Nah." He shakes his head and chuckles. "You're just scared."

Why could Caleb overcome his challenges while I'm still stuck in the past? I'm still allowing the pain of being rejected by my father and the grief of losing my mother to stop me from living the kind of future I deserve. Caleb has come full circle, whereas I'm on permanent pause.

"What's going on in that head of yours?"

I shrug. "Just comparing us."

"How so?"

"You've fought your demons and won, whereas I'm . . ." I frown, staring into the distance. As much as I tell myself that I'm happy being single, deep inside, I know I want *more*. I want to fall in love and have children. I want to have passionate nights with my husband, legs entangled and our skin slick with sweat. I want to feel a human life grow inside of me, knowing it was the product of two *basherts* coming together as one. And I also want the hard stuff too—the sleepless nights, the occasional fighting followed by hot make-up sex, the baby vomit and diaper leakage—

I blink, surprised to realize that my cheeks are wet.

"Hey," Caleb says softly, and hesitantly wraps me in a gentle hug. "What's wrong?"

"I'm sorry, I—"

"Hey." He releases my hand to wipe the tears off my cheeks. "Don't apologize."

"It's just that . . . A part of me wants the diaper leakage," I whisper, lifting my eyes to meet Caleb's. "You know?"

Caleb nods, then seems to register my words and shakes his head. "Sorry— What?"

"You're right about what you said, how our past shapes our present, and how my dad leaving is why I am the way I am—" I break off. "And the fear of getting hurt again—it's *paralyzing*, Caleb."

He squeezes my shoulder. "I know."

"And I'm so j-jealous of you," I sniff.

"Me?" he laughs. "Why?"

"Because of your strength. You're not letting your past d-dictate your future. And I *ammmm*," I sob. I lay my head against his suit.

"Tinsel, baby," he whispers, rubbing my back in soothing circular motions, "life isn't a race."

"Th-that's r-rich coming f-from you," I cry. "You're the m-most compet-t-ive person I know."

His laughter vibrates through his body. "Okay, point taken. But it's not like the demons went away. It wasn't some epic battle that I won and took them all down. I think our experiences always stay with us, but they don't need to control us."

"You're actually . . . really," I sniff, "amazing."

"Me?" His earnest eyes are hypnotizing. "Do you have any idea how fucking incredible you are? How intelligent and insightful and strong you are? And so resilient. You kept your mom's legacy alive even though it came at a huge cost. You've been through so much, and you've done it with humor and grace, and you haven't given up, you haven't lost hope. And when you walk into a room," he adds, "everything becomes somehow brighter and warmer, simply because you're there. You have so much love to give, if you'd only let yourself."

My chest heaves with emotion. I see it all so clearly—the husband, the kids, the white picket fence. Except when I envision it, it isn't with someone like Alex. It's not with someone who might be an okay father and an average husband.

It's with Caleb. Only Caleb.

"And you're so incredibly sexy that I feel like exploding just by looking at you," he whispers, threading his fingers through my hair.

My eyes widen. "Wow."

"Yeah." He gazes at my lips hungrily, and I, in turn, gaze at his.

"I'm thinking about kissing you, to be honest."

His Adam's apple visibly jumps as he swallows. "Oh?"

"Yeah."

"Anything I can do to help you decide?" he says huskily.

"Well," I say, "I was just going through your list."

His eyes scan my face. "My list?"

"Of all the things you said you wanted in a woman. And I realized that I'm the exact opposite."

"No." He brings his hand to my jaw and cradles it gently. "That was me acting out like a child."

"But why . . ." I shiver as his thumb brushes over my bottom lip.

"Because," he says, pulling back, his eyes stormy, "it felt like a cruel joke. To be in love with a woman whose biggest goal in life was to marry me to someone else. When all I've ever wanted, the only person I've *ever* wanted, was right in front of me all along."

And then he kisses me. Softly, reverently, and when I open my mouth and welcome his tongue, he releases a sigh as if to say, *finally, I've come home.*

Chapter Thirty-Two

My entire body melts. Melts and turns to a piddly, liquid mess and if Caleb weren't holding onto me, I'd fall. He kisses the same way he banters, a little teasing here, a little nip there. A gentle sparring of our lips and tongues, a back and forth that causes electricity to race up and down my body.

I didn't know that kissing could be so all-consuming. That it could ignite a fire deep within you and drive you crazy with a need. A need to be closer, a need for more, a need that's much too intense for an amateur like me because no way in hell am I ever stopping.

I drag my nails across his scalp and he slides his hand behind my head, angling my face to deepen the kiss. I didn't think it was possible, but the kiss turns even hotter. Hungrier. As if he hasn't eaten in days and I'm an all-you-can-eat buffet.

But my body still demands more, even though I don't know what more is. All I know is that this feels like so much more than a kiss. It's a trading of secrets, an exchange of souls.

This can't be normal. How do people function and go to work and concentrate on anything at all when *this* exists? Are they doing it wrong? They must be.

When we finally pull back, we grin at each other for a long moment. Then he cradles my neck and looks at me so tenderly that it steals my breath away. How insane is this? The boy who once taught the girl how to build a campfire and ride a bike is now the man giving the woman a lesson in love.

In a public restroom, no less.

"Is it always this amazing?" I pant, searching his eyes.

"No," he says, breathes heavily. "Never like this. Never this good. If you only knew the things I've thought about doing to you . . ." he says huskily, then rains kisses down my neck. I pull my hair back to grant him easier access because I'm helpful like that. His hands glide deliciously lower, gently pressing the space between by tailbone and butt.

"You've thought about doing things to me?" I grin.

"Only every day for the last ten years," he says, and I can't help but laugh. "I'm pretty sure your body was designed to drive me crazy."

"Really?" I'm not sure why this makes me feel so giddy, but it does.

"Why do you think I work out so much?" His lips press against the skin below my collar bone. "I need an outlet for all my frustration."

"I could always, um, help you with that," I gasp as he kisses the valley of my cleavage.

"Thank fuck," he murmurs.

It feels so incredibly good that I barely notice when the door opens and an older woman in an electric wheelchair starts making her way inside. She makes a startled

"Oh!" and then I shriek, and then we both stare at each with a combination of horror and embarrassment while she switches into the reverse gear, and the automatic door slowly, *slowly,* swishes shut.

"You didn't lock it?" I say to Caleb, mortified.

"I thought I did, but I might've been distracted." He gives me a wolfish grin. "Maybe we should find a more comfortable place to continue this conversation. Or not," he adds a moment later, when he sees my face. He drops his hands and steps away. "Sorry. I shouldn't have assumed—"

"No no," I say quickly. "It's not that I don't want to, Caleb, because I do. I really, *really* do. It's just that—" Everything is moving so fast. Too fast. The fear that's been my constant companion for the last twenty-five years is rearing its ugly head again.

"What?"

"I think you would agree that, you know . . . this was fun—"

"*Fun.*"

Why is he looking at me like I just murdered a puppy? "Pleasurable?" I venture. "Hot? Titillating?"

"Is there a thesaurus stuck in your throat?"

I blink. "Huh?"

"You mean more to me than just a good time, Ashira." He exhales a long breath and drags his hand down his face. "I guess I should've figured you'd freak out."

My hackles instantly rise. "I'm not freaking out. I just want to unalive our kiss, okay?"

He gazes up at the ceiling. "Your turn of phrase is Freudianly poetic."

"I." I swallow and feel a surge of helplessness as I see the pain on his face. "Caleb, I'm sorry, I never meant to . . ." I shake my head. "Caleb—I couldn't survive losing you."

His eyes soften. "You wouldn't have to. I'm not going anywhere."

"You might." I rub my chest, trying to steady my breaths as they grow uneven. "Something could happen. It always does. You'll get run over by a car or fall in love with a waitress, or get struck by lightning—"

"Hey, hey. Shhh." He reaches for me again, and tucks my head under his chin.

"Half of Americans get divorced and those are *normal people*," I continue. "You could get sick. What if you already are?" I put a hand over my stomach to try to tamp down the queasiness. What if cancer cells are multiplying out of control somewhere in his body at this very moment? "We can't touch each other ever again," I say, pulling out of his embrace. "It comes at too high a price. I can't lose you," I repeat.

"But I'll die if I *can't* touch you again," he says, snaking an arm around my waist. "I guess I'm screwed either way."

"I'll find you someone else." I dance out of his arms, eliciting a loud groan of protest from him.

"Will she smell like you? Because she has to have your exact scent."

I have to turn away because his smile is my weak spot. "Maybe we shouldn't look at each other either."

"You know this thing between us isn't going to disappear," he says.

I pull on my bottom lip with my teeth. I have a terrible suspicion that he's right. How am I supposed to get over him now that I know that these feelings between us are mutual? Not to mention what an amazing kisser he is.

This is a disaster. No, it worse—it's a *catastrophe*.

"Ashira." He sighs. "You need to understand that the crap from your past happened *to* you, not *because* of you. I know you're scared shitless about getting hurt. I know your heart has taken a lot of hits. I know that you don't want to make yourself vulnerable because it feels safer to avoid risk than to take a huge leap of faith."

There's this feeling in my gut that I'm not meant to have the kind of happiness other people have. I can have bits and pieces of it, like slices of pie. But the moment I start getting greedy and wanting the whole pie, that's when bad things start to happen.

Maybe I can have kids and be a mom, but there's no way I could have all that *and* be married to the man I love.

The man I love.

I inhale sharply and lay a hand over my stomach. *I love Caleb*. I think I always have. Being with him is like being with your best friend who also happens to be wildly attractive and an amazing kisser.

It's all too much.

"Maybe it's best if we take some time off," I say, backing away until I hit the bathroom wall. My pulse is beating unnaturally fast and it's possible I'm dying of a heart attack. Or having a panic attack. "Date other people. Maybe even marry them." Clearly, I've shocked Caleb because his jaw drops. He stares at me for a long moment.

"Is that really what you want?"

I nod. "I'm sorry," I whisper. The pain in his eyes is too much to bear and I glance away.

"Me too," he says.

And then like the coward, I open the door and escape, all the way back to Brooklyn.

Chapter Thirty-Three

"You're a terrible businesswoman," Sissel says to me, the following night at her apartment over Chinese takeout. "The number one rule of a matchmaker is to never make out with a client."

"I know," I sigh.

"And you literally only had one client."

I actually have several, but I'm too depressed to correct her.

"And now you have zero."

I frown and pick at the rice in my cardboard box. "Whatever."

"No, that's how math works, Ashira. You have one client," she says, holding up a finger, "and then you kiss one, and then you end up with zero. That's basic math."

I told Miri what happened that very night, but Sissel isn't exactly the most sensitive when it comes to matters of the heart. At the same time, she knew something had been bothering me, and I was too tired to lie.

Sissel pops another dumpling into her mouth. "You want to know what Mrs. Schwartz has been saying about you?"

"Not really."

But Sissel being Sissel, tells me anyway. "You seduced your oncologist. Your *married* oncologist."

A small whimper escapes me.

"Hey, hey!" Miri calls out as she returns to the living room. "Did I not just tell you to watch what you say to Ashira? She's vulnerable right now."

"I was giving her business advice. I think she found it very helpful," Sissel says, wiping her mouth with a napkin, then turning to me. "Right?"

"You told me I need to disguise myself with plastic surgery and get a new identity," I say, putting down the rice. Not only have I lost my best shot at saving my mother's legacy, but I'm also too much of a coward to take a chance with the man I love. "I feel sick to my stomach."

Sissel trips over herself in her hurry to get off the couch. "Are you going to vomit?"

"Maybe." I swallow. "I don't know."

"Can you go to the bathroom then while you figure that out?" Sissel says, looking panicked.

"No, vomit on the couch," Miri says to me. "That'll teach Sissel to watch her mouth."

"*Miri!*" Sissel cries.

"You did this," Miri tells her, gesturing at me. "So fix it."

Sissel rubs her forehead and cringes, and I can practically see the wheels turning frantically in her brain. "Um—so, Ashira, you've been a matchmaker for eight years and you never kissed a client before. So that's good of you. And besides," she adds with a shrug, "Caleb was never a real client anyway."

I frown. "Why not?"

Sissel and Miri exchange a look, as if this is a discussion they've had between themselves many times.

"I've never seen him look at anyone the way he looks at you," Miri says simply.

Sissel nods. "It's true."

"So this whole time I was being his matchmaker..." I trail off, and shake my head. "Were you guys laughing at me behind my back?"

"It was more like scoffing," Sissel says, reaching for her Coke.

"It was not scoffing or laughing," Miri says firmly. "We hardly ever talked about it, anyway."

I gaze between her and Miri. "You could've said something."

"It's not like you would've believed us anyway," Sissel says. "You've been in denial about your feelings for him for *years*."

I frown because, well, she isn't wrong.

"What am I going to do?" I start to sweat. "About the matchmaking, about Caleb—"

"Don't make any decisions right now," Miri says. "There's no emergency."

"What's there to think about?" Sissel says, waving her chopstick. "Marry the poor man and put both yourselves out of misery."

"But what if I'm cursed?"

"Yeah," Sissel nods. "I could see that."

"*Sissel!*" Miri hisses.

"Everyone that gets too close to me eventually leaves, one way or another." I wave my finger at them. "You two could be next."

Sissel recoils and gazes at me in what is either shock or fear.

"That's the most absurd thing I've ever heard," Miri says firmly.

"But if you had to guess," Sissel says, glancing between Miri and me, "which one of us would go first?"

"*Sissel.*" Miri scowls at her.

"What? I'm not allowed to ask?"

"I'm not getting married," I say, shaking my head. "I'm not doing it." Saying the words out loud gives me a rush of relief, like I'm back on safe territory after visiting a beautiful island that was also fraught with danger. "Caleb can find someone else."

"And you'd be okay with that?" Miri asks, her voice laced with doubt.

"Yes," I reply, my voice also laced with doubt.

Miri shakes her head and reaches for her water. "Well, I don't think he would be."

The air feels tight, like there's not enough oxygen in the room to go around. I claw at my neck, feeling like I'm stuck on a slow-moving conveyor belt that's going to plunge off a deep cliff.

"For the record," Sissel says, "I think you'd have the cutest kids."

"I know what you're doing," I say, turning to her. "And that's not how a curse works. You can't try to flatter me out of it because I don't control it in the first place."

"I wasn't trying to flatter you," Sissel says, looking offended. "It's the truth."

"It really is." Miri smiles. "Can you imagine? They'd be too adorable."

I'm suddenly transported back to my childhood, to being seven-years-old again and having people I'd never met before pat me on the head and call me adorable. Strangers would give me secondhand toys and books, even though it wasn't my birthday or Chanukah. It was only when I was older that I realized the community had rallied together to try to help our family once my father left. But no amount of rugelach and babka, or dolls or Percy Jackson books, could remove the pain of losing the man I hero-worshipped.

Maybe I'd feel differently if my dad had been a jerk or just an average father. But he wasn't, he was awesome. He was the one who regularly took me to the park and then afterwards, go out for ice cream. He was the one who comforted me if Leah made me cry, and he was the one who told me bedtime stories and tucked me in every night.

One minute, I was his special princess, and the next, I wasn't even worthy of a goodbye.

In books and movies, people get closure. They eventually either reunite and talk, or they uncover the truth about someone after their death that can provide some sense of peace. But that's not how it works in real life, or at least, not in *my real life*.

I imagine little children with light brown skin and dark eyes, Caleb's lips and my dimples, and trying to comfort them if he were also to one day—

I stand up. "I have to go."

"Now?" Miri asks, looking alarmed. "Where?"

"I'm not sure," I say, grabbing my coat off the couch and thrusting my arms into it. "But I need air."

"Do you want me to come?" Miri offers.

"Or me?" Sissel adds.

I shake my head and zip my coat. "No, thanks. I need to think. But thanks." I give each of them and hug. "Love you, guys," I say, stepping into the hallway.

"Say no to drugs," Sissel says as her departing message, then shuts the door.

But it isn't drugs that I have to say no to.

It's Caleb.

Which is why I decide to do something that's entirely out of character, and that I'll very possibly end up regretting.

* * *

I slap my hand down on the counter and say, "Bruce, my man."

Bruce startles and knocks his head against a display shelf. "What," he says, whirling around, "are you doing here at," he glances at the clock, "six in the evening?" He rubs his head and mutters, "I thought evenings were safe."

"I've had an epiphany," I say. "And it involves you."

"I'm not going on any blind dates, Ashira, and that's final. Please don't make me have to get a restraining order on you. It's too time consuming."

I nod and put up my hands. "I'm glad to hear you say that because I don't have time for that either. And I won't bring up the blind date thing again. Besides, I'm not a matchmaker anymore."

"Why?" Bruce lifts a large metal bowl and sifts flour into it. "What happened?"

I shrug. "Eh. A lot of stuff. But that's where you come in."

"Oh yeah?" he says, glancing at me over his shoulder as he runs the faucet.

"I've got two options for you."

"I already hate both of them."

"The first option is that I work for you," I continue, undeterred. "And the second option is that we get married."

He turns off the faucet and tilts his head. "Can you repeat the second option? Because I don't think I heard you right."

"The second option is that we get married."

Bruce clasps the ends of his hair. He inhales and then lets out a breath that sounds more like a growl. "That's never going to happen."

I nod. "It won't be a love match, I know, but at least it will one based off mutual understanding and respect."

"We don't have that either."

"That's not true. I respect you plenty."

"That's where it ends."

I sigh. "Be reasonable, Bruce."

"You're telling *me* to be reasonable?" He points his finger at me. "Ha!"

"What exactly is the problem here?" I ask, spreading my hands wide. "Let's get married, have kids—"

"I'm not attracted to you."

My hands drop. "Okay. Wow." I pause. "I feel like that could've been said a thousand times more gently."

"It's not personal, really—"

"I get it—no sex. It would be more of a business relationship." I pick up the broom and start sweeping to show him how very capable I am. "I could help you run the bodega. I'm a fantastic cleaner. You'll cook, I'll clean." How would we have kids?

"*I'm gay, Ashira.*"

I stop my vigorous sweeping and blink. "Huh?"

Bruce steps around the counter and takes the broom from me. "I'm gay. It isn't exactly a secret, but with me running a kosher bodega . . ." He shrugs. "I don't see the need to advertise it, that's all."

"Oh."

"It isn't personal," he repeats, softer this time. I nod and sink onto a chair. How is it possible to be this clueless? "Are you hungry?" he asks.

I shake my head.

"You seem . . . not okay," he says, taking a seat opposite from me.

"I'm not."

He nods. "Is there anything I can do for you?"

"No." I stare at my hands.

We sit in silence for a bit. It's surprisingly soothing to just be near someone.

"It's my turn to play matchmaker," Bruce says, breaking the silence. He takes out his phone and starts to type.

I glance up at him, confused. "You want to set *me* up?"

"Yes. I've got someone you need to meet."

Chapter Thirty-Four

"Tell me why you're here."

Bruce sent me, that's why. I gaze at the fresh-faced woman who barely looks old enough to be out of high school. When I first made an appointment to see a therapist a few weeks ago, I assumed she'd be a dowdy, older grandmother type person who knitted sweaters for children in underdeveloped communities, or a man in a tweed jacket with leather pouches, with an unlit pipe dangling between his lips. I did not expect to find a young woman who introduced herself as a number—*Seven*—to call me back into her office.

Plus, where is the couch? There's always a couch in the movies. I wore these easy to remove boots specifically for this purpose.

"Ashira?" she prompts.

Crap. What was it she asked? Oh yeah. Why I'm here. "I'm a matchmaker with commitment issues. Romantically speaking. There's this man that I'm in love with, and I literally told him to date and marry someone else. How crazy is that?" I giggle because it sounds so ridiculous even to my own ears. Seven however, doesn't even crack a smile. I think I might be nervous.

"Why do you think you did that?"

I inhale deeply, then release it. "Because I'm a coward. I'm scared of what might happen if I allow myself to get close to him."

"Why do you assume something might happen?"

"It's the pattern of my life. My father abandoned our family when I was seven, and my mother died five years ago."

"I'm so sorry. That's rough."

"Yeah." I gaze down at my hands. "I guess I have this fear that people leave. Especially the ones I'm closest to."

"That's understandable given everything you've gone through."

I reach for the cup of water she gave me and take a sip. Her quiet watchfulness makes me slightly nervous and before long, I'm babbling to fill the silence. "I don't know why my dad left." I focus on the plant sitting on the windowsill. For some reason, it's easier than looking into the therapist's eyes. "But the thing is, he was a great father. And a loving husband. And then he just left." I shake my head and frown. "It's bizarre. Unsettling. No one saw it coming. I think that's what also made it so traumatic. It was like a train hitting you out of nowhere."

"How do you feel towards him now?"

"My dad?" I ask, and she nods. "Angry. Sad. But you know," I add suddenly, "I kind of pity him too because he missed out on being part of our family. And we were an awesome family."

"You used the past tense." She tilts her head. "Aren't you still an awesome family?"

"Yeah, we are. Definitely. It's just different now than before, I guess." I shrug. "My mom isn't around, and my siblings have their own families, so sometimes it feels like it's just me third-wheeling."

"Sounds lonely."

"It can be, yeah." I'm embarrassed to realize that my eyes are wet, and I mumble "sorry" as I accept the box of tissues she holds out to me.

"No, it's good to cry. It's the body's way of releasing stress in order to heal. I'm guessing you probably didn't do enough of it as a child."

I nod, dabbing the corners of my eyes. "I tried not to think about my father. It hurt too much."

"You know," Seven says, crossing her legs, "they say children are resilient, but that's only because they instinctively turn off their emotions in order to survive. And it sounds like that's what you did."

I nod. Looking back, that's exactly what I did.

"Do you know much about neural pathways and neuroplasticity?" she asks and I shake my head. "Well, it's amazing how the brain is capable of healing itself."

I listen as she explains the physiology behind anxiety and find myself fascinated by it. According to Seven, just because my brain feeds me information doesn't necessarily mean I should believe it. She talks about cognitive behavioral therapy which is the process of challenging your thoughts instead of automatically assuming they're true.

"Except for the good thoughts," she adds with a smile. "Those we don't challenge."

I schedule more appointments at the front desk before I leave. I hope Seven is right and that with enough practice, I can retrain my brain so I don't panic at the thought of being with Caleb. But at the same time, I don't know if I truly believe her either. She looks like the type who smokes a lot of weed and reads dark poetry by candlelight, and who knows what kind of neuropathways that creates?

* * *

A month later, and the day of the marathon is finally here. The city is buzzing with excitement. Live music is playing and people are dancing, holding signs, and cheering. Runners perform last-minute stretches. I scan the crowd, searching for the man who tricked me into being a health nut. Not that I'm complaining. Only someone like Caleb could take a carcinogen-loving, sloth-like creature such as myself and transform me into a running queen with the body of a goddess.

Overkill, I know.

The announcer gives us a five-minute warning. I stretch my leg and glance around. There are thousands of people with numbers taped to their backs. If Caleb and I weren't in a cold war, we'd have driven here together. Maybe even had breakfast first, and made a gameplan. But it's been weeks since The Kiss as everyone in my inner circle has come to refer to it. The good news is that I've become an expert in the art of cognitive behavioral therapy. I'm like an objective journalist when it comes to my thought patterns. Instead of automatically believing them, I question them, and search for evidence to both corroborate the theory and challenge it.

The airhorn blows and the race officially begins. I pace myself as my thoughts continue to churn.

The bad news is that Zevi told me something earlier this week that makes me want to kill myself. Okay, not actually. But it's my worst nightmare come to life, and sadly, I only have myself to blame.

Just as I was getting up the courage to call Caleb and tell him that I've been going to therapy and feel ready to date, Zevi told me he started seeing someone. Her name is Bailey Smilevitch, and she happens to be the great-great-granddaughter of a renowned rabbi from Lithuania. As far as good *yichus* goes, it doesn't get much better than that. And interestingly enough, her mother is a *Desi* Jew, a small minority of Jews whose communities are some of the oldest in world, with more than 2000 years of continuity in the Indian subcontinent.

According to her Wikipedia page, Bailey felt a calling to help other Jews of Color connect which is why she created the JOCIE organization, which stands for Jews of Color Inclusivity, and Equity. She also models for a Jewish modest clothing line as well as being the face for a Shabbos makeup brand. The woman is literally everything Caleb could ever ask for and then some.

But I was still stunned when Zevi told me that Caleb started looking at rings. Although many Orthodox Jews get engaged after a two- or three-week time frame, I always assumed Caleb wouldn't rush into anything. After all, he waited *ten years* for me.

I'm glad that Zevi gave me the heads up to prepare myself. And I have, by crying myself to sleep every night. Then waking up in the middle of the night and reading our old phone messages, the memes we sent, and the funny cat videos he kept begging me to stop sending. After that, I go through old pictures and videos that my iPhone curated into its own memory album designed to cause ultimate emotional damage.

But as I settled in bed the other night and pulled up my Spotify heartbreak playlist, I got a text from Dr. Kahn, inviting me to spend Shabbos at their house in two weeks. She wants Caleb's closest friends there to celebrate his thirty-fourth birthday.

I immediately did an emergency FaceTime conference call with Miri, Sissel, Zevi, and Jack. All four of them insisted I should go, that I couldn't avoid him for the rest of my life. I replied that it was possible. I even looked up the cost of a one-way ticket to Timbuktu but Zevi said I'd never be able to withstand the heat.

I take a break to drink water and use the porta-potty. Eight miles done.

And so, I have no choice but to go. Even if Bailey might be in attendance, and even if they are going to announce their engagement.

I run and run and run. My mind and body take turns torturing me. My shins throb, my head aches, and I think about quitting for the next seventeen miles.

But five hours, twenty-nine minutes, and three seconds later, I've done it. I ran my first marathon.

I sink to the ground as tears stream down my cheeks. I gaze up at the sky and whisper, *I did it, Mom. I did it.*

Overhead, a little blue jay lands on a nearby tree. And as it tilts its head and stares into my eyes, I'm filled with a sense of peace.

Chapter Thirty-Five

I'm the first guest to arrive which makes me feel slightly overeager, but Dr. Kahn is so thrilled to see me that my embarrassment soon fades. She puts me in the bedroom next to Caleb's old room, which I find a little odd since she normally puts the women on one side of the hall and the men on the other. But maybe Bailey is coming and has insisted on sleeping in Caleb's bed, so all the men will be moving. Not going to lie—the thought of another woman in Caleb's bed makes me feel slightly violent.

I ask Dr. Kahn if there is anything I can do to help her get ready for Shabbos and she asks if I could go through Caleb's closet and make a donation pile. Which has nothing at all to do with Shabbos and makes me feel slightly suspicious. But Dr. Kahn hands me a few trash bags and shoos me away.

Stepping inside Caleb's bedroom feels a bit like entering a time warp. It's exactly the same as it has been for the last thirty years—the same furniture, plaid blue bedding, shiny football and boxing trophies. I inhale the slightly musty scent and close my eyes, remembering all the Shabbos afternoons we snuck up candy and played boardgames in here. I glance at the window over his desk and smile, remembering the time Caleb instructed Zevi and me to stand on one side of the house while he threw a baseball over the roof for us to catch. Unfortunately, the football knocked against the chimney and then smashed this very bedroom window.

I miss those sweet, innocent days. Funny how I was in such a hurry to grow up, and now I finally have, I miss being a kid. Where did all the years go? And how did I end up back in this bedroom with trash bags to sort through his closet?

I shake my head and start the project. Twenty minutes later, I'm knee-deep in memorabilia and photographs that I can't believe Caleb kept. It's like a treasure chest of our entire childhood. Snapshots of all the food we cooked, the adventures we went on, the impromptu parties we had. I find some hilarious pencil sketches that I had totally forgotten I'd drawn of him and grin.

Then I come across an apology letter I'd written probably when I was around seven or eight.

Dear Caleb,

I'm sorry I threw pees at youre eyes and put water over youre head. It was funny for me, but maybe not for you.

Love,
Ashira

Ps I don't like pees

I'm still laughing when I glance up in surprise. Caleb stands in the doorframe, blinking at me as if I'm an apparition and he can't decide if I'm real. He looks even more handsome than I remember him, and for the life of me, I can't figure out how I could have ever turned this man down.

"Hi." I swallow, gazing back up at him. I grin and pretend this is not a weird situation at all. "Happy Birthday!" I trill, waving my hands.

He tosses his overnight bag on his bed. "Are you my present?"

It's surprisingly flirtatious for someone who's on the brink of engagement. Although he's also scowling at me which is even more confusing.

"Uh, no." I stand up and clear my throat. "But I did get you a present."

"What are you doing here?"

He looks pissed and he sounds it too. This does not bode well for the weekend vibes. "Your mom invited me."

"Great." He sits down on his bed and glances at the mess on the floor. "And you're raiding my closet, why?"

"Also, your mom."

"Of course," he mutters, rubbing his eyelids. "I'm going to kill that woman."

"Sorry. I can leave," I say, and start to head to the door, but his next words stop me.

"Why did you really come?"

I pause, hovering at the doorframe. "Because I missed you," I say bluntly, and his eyes widen in response.

"Anyway, I should go, I shouldn't be in your room, especially now that . . ."

"Now that we've kissed?" he says, standing up.

Heat crawls up my neck and face. "No! *No.*" That was the last thing I expected him to say, and I glance around furtively, as if Bailey herself might've overheard. "Because you're dating someone," I whisper. "Is she . . . coming?"

He stares at me for a beat. "No."

"Oh?" I wait for him to expound, but to my shock, he shuts the door in my face.

Okay then. I definitely shouldn't have come. I go to my room and start packing my things when I hear a ping from my phone.

> I'm sorry. Forgive me?

I stare at Caleb's text and wonder how to respond. Finally, I type back,

> Nothing to forgive. But do you want me to leave? Because I understand if you do.

His answer is immediate.

> I want you to stay.

Ridiculous how one text can spread such joy through my heart. *In that case*, I type, unsure what kind of devil is prodding me on, *meet me in the library at the stroke of midnight.*

For some reason, I want it to be just the two of us when I give him his birthday present.

> I can't decide if I should be excited or scared.

I smile and type,

> why would you be scared?

> Colonel Mustard. Library. Knife.

I snort.

> Actually, I was planning on using the candlestick. Shabbos and all.

And when I hear his peal of laughter from the other side of the wall, I feel a surge of pure happiness. We'll be okay, I realize. Somehow or other, we'll get through this.

* * *

Of all the rooms in Caleb's parents' house—and there are quite a few of them—the two-story library with its floor to ceiling windows is definitely my favorite. I smile as I enter the room and breathe in the intoxicating combination of leather and old books. There's a huge L-shaped couch in the center of the room with a loveseat and two chairs. The colorful Persian rug, houndstooth print pillows, and contemporary lighting give off an old-world, eclectic mix of style. It's got a classic, timeless elegance while still being homey.

Strangely, Bailey's name wasn't brought up the entire night. Wait, no, that's not true. At one point, Sissel asked why she wasn't here, but Caleb gave her a look of such utter contempt that she immediately bit her tongue.

The whole thing is entirely confusing. But based on Caleb's mood, it appears as though there might be trouble in paradise.

I hold on to the railing and climb the spiral staircase that leads to the second level. The bookcase in the center aisle is filled with classics like *The Great Gatsby* and *To Kill a Mockingbird*, *Pale Fire* by Vladimir Nabokov which is more Caleb's speed if he were to read fiction. It amuses me that he's this big warrior dude and also a literary snob. But he's a bit sensitive about it and says I shouldn't judge people based on their appearance, just like I wouldn't like it if someone assumed I'm flighty since I'm a blonde.

"You're early."

I shriek and place a hand over my racing heart. Caleb steps out of the shadows, dressed in his black suit pants and collared white shirt, but his tie hangs loosely around his neck and his sleeves are rolled up to his elbows.

I swallow and glance away.

Damn, but the man is hot. As in, *Bridgerton*'s Duke of Hastings-level hot. But this isn't new information, I remind myself.

"Hey, is that—" He stops and peers closer at my white shirt with a trident symbol that hits mid-thigh, then says in a strange voice, "Is that mine?"

Oh, dear. I've worn this shirt so often since I borrowed it without permission at the Chanukah party after someone spilled on me that I guess I forgot it wasn't mine.

"I can explain," I start to say, but he cuts me off with a glance.

"Do you know how long I've been looking for that?"

"Probably as long as I've had it?" I guess.

"*Months.*"

I shrug. "You could've just asked me."

"And why exactly," he says slowly, "would that have ever crossed my mind?"

"Do you want your present now?" I say in an enthusiastic tone, drumming my fingers on the frame.

"Only if it's my shirt."

"You're rich, Caleb," I say, trying to reason with him. "You can order a new one."

"But that's my *lucky* shirt."

"Really?" I glance down at it. "It's done shit good for me."

He gazes at me with renewed panic. "You didn't wash it, did you?"

"Of course, I washed it." I wrinkle my nose. "What kind of weirdo would I be if I hadn't?"

He groans and covers his eyes.

"Look on the bright side," I say. "At least you don't have to share a room with Sissel."

"No," he grumbles. "Just clothes with you. But," he adds after a moment, doing a slow perusal of my body that gives me butterflies in my stomach, "you do look a lot better in it than I ever did."

I feel myself blush. "It's the heels," I mumble offhandedly. "Everything looks better with heels." My legs are on display more than normal given that his shirt lands a few inches above the knee and coupled with the stilettos, I probably look like the owner of a brothel. Which Bubby Kahn brought up again tonight, along with the belief that I'm still pregnant with her great-grandchild. You'd think the second time around wouldn't land as awkwardly, but nope. Still thought I'd combust from embarrassment.

"No, it's your lean, muscular legs. Runner's legs," he adds.

I grin proudly. "Did Zevi tell you that I ran the marathon?"

"He didn't have to tell me. I was there."

I blink. "You were there? At the marathon?"

He nods. "Someone had to keep an eye on you in case you needed help."

Knowing that he showed up for me even though we weren't exactly on speaking terms fills me with happiness.

"Wasn't I great?" I beam.

"Yes." He grins. "I'm proud of you, Tinsel."

"Thanks." I smile mischievously. "I guess that means I won our bet."

"You did."

"I guess that means you lost," I tease.

"I like to think that we both won."

I open my mouth, a teasing reply on my tongue, when I stop and consider his words. "Yeah," I say softly. "I think we both did." I clear my throat. "Anyway. Here's your present," I say, about to hand it over, but stop and press it against my chest instead, suddenly unsure. What if he thinks it's dumb? Or what if he takes it the wrong way? What if he gets embarrassed? If he gets embarrassed, then I'll get embarrassed, and then—

"Am I allowed to see it?" he says when I make no move to give it to him.

Instead, I tighten my grip on it. "You might hate it."

"I might," he agrees, holding out his hand. "Especially knowing who it's from."

His soft, teasing eyes manage to relax me, and I take a deep breath, then shove the frame at him before I chicken out and make a run for it.

Making a genealogy tree for Caleb wasn't easy. It involved playing referee over the many heated debates between family members. No one on his father's side could agree whether Great-Great-Great Uncle Avrum Spitkovskaya was from Belarus or Kiev. His mother's siblings weren't much better, arguing over how old Tadesse Yacob had been during the famine in Northern Ethiopia that wiped out two-thirds of the Beta Israel community and how many husbands Hadas had had. After every phone call and Zoom meeting I had with his family, I had to go for a run just to clear my head.

I used a calligraphy stencil to write down names, places of birth, marriage, and timeline, starting at the deepest roots of the tree and then moving closer to the bark with every generation. In the wide bark of the tree, I wrote adjectives that I thought best described his family, words such as *strength, conviction, endurance, and valor.*

"And there you are," I say, pointing. I had left the marriage line blank, of course, and staring at it now feels . . . odd. The idea of a woman that I've never met before in that coveted spot beside Caleb's seems wrong. The only name that belongs next to his is, well, mine. Although, Bailey would probably disagree.

"I hope it's okay that I did this, I just wanted you to see what I see when I see your family," I babble as he continues to gaze at it. "You can totally throw it away if you want. Or you know, burn it. I could help you collect the firewood. Unless you prefer to use explosives because it would be more symbolic of how much you hate it which I completely unders—"

"Tinsel."

I glance up. "Yes?"

"This is the best gift I've ever gotten. Thank you."

I exhale a breath that I hadn't even known I'd been holding in. "You don't have to go that far—"

"I mean it," he says, holding my gaze.

"Are you sure you're not just saying that because you feel bad that your grandmother called me a pimp again?"

He hoots with laughter and covers his face. "No."

"Or because she said I look like a Prom Queen reject?"

"I don't even know what that means," he says, holding up his hands and laughing.

"And because she's not happy about Junior?" I add, cradling my stomach.

The laughter fades from his eyes and he holds out his arms. "C'mere."

I shouldn't. I know I shouldn't. And yet, it seems inconceivable to *not* go to him. It isn't even a conscious choice. All I know is that I need to touch him as much as I need air to breathe.

And so help me, I do.

Chapter Thirty-Six

I close my eyes and release a small sigh. I don't know if it's the weight of his arms or the fresh spring breeze scent of his clothes, but something about this—about *him*—feels right. It's like clicking the correct jigsaw piece into the correct hole after shoving thousands of others at it first. Or when you meet a new person and instantly know that this is someone who will become a forever friend.

Because it's effortless. Easy. Inevitable.

I'm suddenly hit with the realization that while some people spend a lifetime traveling the world in search of life's meaning, I, at twenty-eight-years-old, have found it in the arms of this man.

"And for the record," he whispers against my hair, tickling me, "I'd love the hell out of our baby."

I smile at that and lean back to look at him. "Would you be one of those overly protective dads?"

He smirks. "Maybe."

I arch an eyebrow and try not to laugh. "Only maybe?"

"I could be talked into letting it leave the house," he says, his hands pressing gently on my back, "if my wife insisted on it."

"I think Child Protective Services would."
"You think so?"
"I do."
"Caleb . . ." I say sternly, as his hands drifts lower.
"Hmm?"
"Your hands."
"What about them?"
"They're on my butt."

He grins and pulls me tighter against him. "I know."
"Are you dating Bailey or not?"
"No." The mention of her name snaps him out of his libido-induced haze and he instantly releases me. He collapses onto one of the wingback chairs and lets out a small groan. "It was horrible. You can't even imagine how awful it was." He closes his eyes. "I don't want to talk about it," he adds.

"Okay," I say, even though I'm dying to know the details. Who dumped who, for example? Is he heartbroken right now? He didn't seem heartbroken a minute ago when he had his hands on my butt, but he looks pretty miserable now.

I sit on the other chair and wait. And wait some more. Finally, he says, "She thought I was going to propose."

I blink. "And you didn't . . . ?"

"I was going to. I tried. I really, really tried." His eyes wince, and I can tell he's reliving the memory. "I had the ring in my pocket and everything. But the words kept getting stuck. Right here," he says, pointing halfway up his throat. "I couldn't do it," he repeats.

"I just kept thinking that this isn't the woman I want to marry."

My mouth goes dry and I swallow. "Who is?" I breathe, my heart hammering.

Instead of answering, he says, "She didn't smell right."

I turn that over in my mind. "Did she not shower?"

"No, she did."

"Was she one of those anti-deodorant hippies?"

"No, that wasn't it." He drums his fingers on the arms of the chair. "She never got excited, either," he adds.

"About what?"

He shrugs. "About anything. She didn't jump or shriek or clap her hands with enthusiasm or laugh so hard that things came out of her nostrils."

"I am so confused by the words coming out of your mouth."

"She didn't tease me or make jokes. Well," he pauses, "I suppose she laughed at mine. But she never snorted."

"You require a woman who snorts?"

"I do." He nods, turning to face me. "It's in the top five requirements, for sure."

"I think maybe you've had a stroke? Like, one of those mini ones?"

"She didn't like cats either."

"Lots of people don't like cats."

"But she didn't like cat videos."

"*You* don't like cat videos," I remind him.

"I know." He nods. "We had that in common. And she could cook," he adds. "Like, even better than me."

Huh. "How did she feel about football?" I ask.

He lifts his hands. "She loved it."

I feel suddenly annoyed that I wasn't who discovered her. "Where did you find this needle in the haystack?"

"Casanova."

I tilt my head. "What?"

"He cross-examined her outside a shul in Queens."

"That figures." I cross my arms and add, "She sounds pretty perfect."

"She is," he agrees. "But not perfect for me."

"I'm really sorry to hear that."

"I can tell by the huge grin you're trying to hide."

"I'm sorry," I say, covering my face. "I'm a really bad liar."

"Really bad," he agrees. "The worst. But I was thinking about it," he continues, "and I think the biggest problem with Bailey boiled down to one thing."

"What's that?"

"She wasn't you."

His eyes are like two black sapphires rimmed with gold and I've never seen a more beautiful color. Their intensity steals my breath away and I have to remind myself to exhale. The passion, the longing, the *goodness*—it's all there in his eyes.

"You're the one I dream about when I close my eyes. You're the one that challenges me and pushes me to be a better man. You're my North Star, Tinsel. You always have been."

I'm too afraid to move or speak. I'm terrified that I'll wake up and realize this was all just a dream.

"I know you're not interested in marriage," he says, "but I need you in my life. In any capacity, if you'll just let me."

I swallow against the sudden lump in my throat, frozen, and paralyzed with delight. Finally, I whisper, "I let."

He tilts his head. "Yeah?"

"Yeah." I swallow.

He nods. "We can be friends. Platonic, non-touching, non-sexual friends," he says as his eyes peruse up and down my legs.

"We could. Or, we could get married and have kids," I blurt. "If you want to. And I could write my name there," I say, pointing to the line in the drawing beside his name. In fact, if it wasn't Shabbos, I'd fill it in right this minute.

His face is a combination of astonishment and suspicion. "Is this a joke?"

"No." I shake my head and swallow against the sudden lump in my throat. "I love you, Caleb Hersch Kahn. I've never not loved you—not even when I really hated your guts."

He gazes at me like he still can't quite believe me. "I've been going to therapy," I explain, twisting the hem of the shirt because I need to fidget with something. "I probably should've gone a long time ago, but I realized after we, you know . . ."

"Kissed?"

I blush. "Yeah, that. And it made me realize that if I wanted a future, I needed to let go of my past first."

He's quiet for a long moment, just grinning at me. "This is surreal."

"It is." My cheeks start to ache from grinning so much. "But I have a question."

"What's that?"

"Can you take off your shirt and explain what all the tattoos mean?"

He arches an eyebrow. "You want me to get naked, right here in my parents' library?"

"*No.*" I roll my eyes. "I asked you to take off your top to discuss your tattoos. Very different."

"I don't know." He brushes his thumb against his bottom lip. "It still feels pervy."

I nod, considering. "I'm okay with that," I decide.

He tilts his chin toward me. "You want to go first?"

I laugh. "What for? I don't have tattoos."

He shrugs. "As a gesture of solidarity."

"Your flirting has just entered next-level," I inform him.

"I know." He grins.

And some devil inside me whispers for me to do it. To whip my shirt off just to see the shock on his face because I know, I just *know*, he doesn't think I actually will.

Besides, he's already seen me in leggings, which isn't that different to seeing someone topless—besides, I am wearing a bra.

So, I do it.

Caleb's mouth drops. It simply hangs open, and he seems to have trouble closing it and forming a coherent sentence. I glance down at myself just to make sure that I'm not suddenly covered in leprosy marks, but all I see is my boring cotton bra and my not particularly impressive amount of cleavage. It really doesn't warrant this amount of shock.

And then I realize that my nipples are hard.

"All righty then," I say, clutching my shirt to my chest. My face is burning so hot it feels like it's on fire. "Your turn."

He swallows and his Adam's apple jumps from the movement. His eyes seem slightly dazed as they reach mine. "What?"

"I showed my solidarity, and now it's time for you to show me your tattoos."

He unbuttons his shirt like a total tease, keeping his eyes on mine and taking his time, slowly revealing his skin inch-by-inch. It's making certain parts of my anatomy squirm. I stand up to get a closer look, and his chest rumbles with laughter.

"Do you need a magnifying glass?" he asks.

"Quiet. I'm busy."

I ignore his laughter and try to figure out where to start. I'm a kid in a candy shop, overwhelmed by the options.

In the center of his torso is an American flag wrapped around a trident that spreads across most of his chest and abdomen. Above his right nipple there's a passage of words in black:

My Trident is a symbol of honor and heritage. Bestowed upon me by the heroes that have gone before, it embodies the trust of those I have sworn to protect. By wearing the Trident I accept the responsibility of my chosen profession and way of life. It is a privilege that I must earn every day.

Something colorful catches my eye on his upper right arm, and I walk around him to get a closer look. It's an eagle flying, its claws holding onto an anchor and pistol. The sentence beneath it reads:

The only easy day was yesterday.

I so badly want to run my fingers over the defined muscles and hard ridges. "How did you get so . . . taut?"

"The usual way." He sounds amused. "Exercise."

"*Amazing*," I breathe, sounding like a crazed fangirl.

I point to the line beneath the bone frog that says:

Failure is not an option.

"I don't know why, but the combination of tattoos and a yarmulke are so . . . *hot*."

An electrical charge buzzes in the air, pulling us toward each other in a current too strong to fight. This time our kiss isn't gentle or playful—it's pure fire, burning and hot.

I feel myself being lifted in the air and hook my legs around his waist. Our lips and tongues clash in a frenzy of feasting, and my nails dig into Caleb's back. I don't recognize this version of me—this unrelenting force of pure animal instinct, demanding and insistent.

We bang into a wall and Caleb curses under his breath. I giggle, and he squeezes my bottom as he resumes the kiss. I press myself flush against him, surrendering to the waves of dizzying pleasure that are building inside of me.

"Wait! My shirt isn't on," I scream-whisper as I realize he's carrying me up the main staircase.

"Don't worry," he says, "everyone's sleeping. Besides, I'm covering all the good stuff."

I duck my head under his chin and whisper up a prayer that everyone stays asleep. Caleb finds that hilarious and laughs even as he lowers me onto his bed. He shuts the door and locks it which isn't very *yichud*, and then he swivels the Shabbos lamp, so he can see me better.

He joins me on the bed and my legs tighten their hold around him. Then, like the boss woman I am, I flip us over, so I'm on top. But based on his wide grin, he's happy to let me take the lead.

My breath hitches as his hands slide down my back and settle either side of my waist. His thumbs fan across my skin, sending shivers of pleasure up and down my body. I swallow as I see the hunger in his eyes, raw, pure. Carnivorous even. He looks like he's seconds away from losing control and turning into a werewolf because the attraction is too fierce.

Then he flips me back over, the alpha reseizing control. His fingers touch the lower swells of my breasts, and my breathing turns erratic. I accidentally-on-purpose thrust my chest out like a prize that I want him to claim. No, that I *need* him to claim.

"Tinsel," he says, drawing a ragged breath. "Tell me to stop."

"I will." I lick my lips and run my fingers down his chest. "In a minute."

"We shouldn't . . ." He shudders and closes his eyes as my fingers brush against the zipper of his pants.

"Double jeopardy," I remind him and he laughs. "Besides, weren't you the one who carried me up an entire flight of stairs to bring me to your bed?"

He visibly swallows. "I was in caveman mode. I wasn't really thinking."

I laugh and run my hands down his chest. "I like you in caveman mode."

"Tinsel." He closes his eyes and groans. "You need to be the strong one here."

"All right. I will."

I might be wrong, but he looks slightly disappointed as I get off the bed. It's clear that Caleb is out of his element, and that when faced with a woman who is attracted to him, he seizes up and goes into self-destruct mode, just like on his dates. And I'm all too happy to help a friend.

And then in an incredibly smooth move, I unhook the clasp of my bra.

"There." I nod and smile. "Now where were we?"

Caleb takes a deep, shuddering breath. His eyes don't seem to know where to land. His hand trembles as he reaches forward to remove the cup that got caught on my erect nipple, and my bra falls to the floor. His eyes turn fevered as he rubs the tips. I gasp, the pleasure bordering on pain, so exquisite that it makes the area between my legs pool with desire.

He simply stares at me. And stares. I start to feel self-conscious and try to cover myself with my arms, but he grabs them and pins them over my head.

"You're beautiful, Tinsel," he murmurs, his eyes running up and down. He stares at my breasts as if I'm the sexiest thing he's ever seen. My breath hitches as his eyes swallow up every inch of me. "Even more beautiful than I imagined."

His words embolden me and I smile. "Caleb Kahn, are you telling me you've imagined me naked?" This piece of news should probably not cause me so much unbridled happiness, but I'll worry about that later. I can barely focus because his hands are working their way up from my stomach and my nipples tingle in anticipation. I want his hands on my breasts more than I've ever wanted anything in my entire life. *Ever.*

"Every day, several times a day," he laughs. "But you've exceeded even my wildest dreams," he says, then cups my breasts with his hands again. I gasp as his thumbs stroke the sensitive tips, hardening them into peaks. When he closes his mouth over one, I throw my head back and close my eyes. The pleasure radiates throughout my body with a mind-numbing intensity.

"Finally," he murmurs against my mouth, catching his breath. "I've been wanting to do this for so long."

I bite back a smile. "Poor baby."

"You have no idea." He tugs me back to him, clearly a man on a mission. Or an addict with crack. I deepen our kiss, exploring his mouth. *I'll be your crack*, I silently communicate.

"Your perfume," he moans. "It drives me insane."

"It's probably my scented moisturizer—" I begin to say, but he cuts me off with a kiss so passionate that I feel it in the pit of my belly.

I throw my head back and moan as his thumbs brush my nipples. And when his mouth kisses my other nipple and I grab the back of his head to crush it closer. The pressure of his lips on my breast increases and his other hand finds the sweet spot between my legs, and all too soon, I cry out from intensity of the orgasm, riding out wave after wave of ecstasy.

"I-I might have come," I blush, embarrassed.

"Good," he whispers, kissing the tip of my nose. "I wanted you to."

"But . . ." I trail off, gazing at the tent bulging from his underwear. "What about you?"

"I don't have anything for protection," he says.

"As long as you're clean, it's not a problem," I say, barely able to believe my brazenness. *Who is this woman?* "I have an IUD. It gives me lighter periods."

His eyes light up like he's just won the lottery. "Seriously?" he says, and I nod. "I'm clean," he assures me. "But—" He closes his eyes as though he's in physical pain. "Wouldn't you rather wait for marriage—"

"No," I say, putting a finger to his lips. "I want this, and I want it with you. And I want it *now*."

"You're sure?"

I nod. "Very." And it's true, I've never felt more confident about anything than in this decision. With his eyes on mine and a smile on his lips, he slides off his underwear and his penis springs to life, much larger and much more *alive* than any naked sculpture I've ever seen.

"Don't worry," he says, and it's only then that I realize that I was looking at it with horror etched on my face.

"Sorry." I shake my head. "I'm just surprised—it's so . . ."

"So?"

"*Big*." I tilt my head and peer closer. "Has your doctor seen this?"

"No, Ashira. My doctor has not seen my erect penis." I can tell by the way his cheeks are sucked in that he's trying to withhold laughter.

"I've never seen one before," I say defensively. "It's intimidating."

He laughs and then flips me over so I'm on my back. "I'm not going to be able to last much longer if you keep up with this flattery," he says. "And I want to come inside you," he whispers, nipping my earlobe.

"There is no way in hell that that—" I point my finger at his penis, "will fit inside me."

"It will."

"It won't."

"How do you know?" I say, a bit panicked.

"Because that's how vaginas work, sweetheart. They stretch to accommodate the penis."

"Fine. I'll let you try," I say, a little peevishly. "But I know I'm not going to like it." He buries his face in the crook of my neck and laughs.

"Then tell me and I'll stop, okay?"

I nod and then he starts kissing me all over again, teasing me, and I gasp with surprise as he inserts a finger within my folds. I squirm and feel my muscles contract, my hips bucking as if my body knows exactly what to do.

"Fuck, you're so wet. Do you like this?" he says huskily and I clench the bedspread and gasp a yes. "What about this?" he says, adding a second finger.

"Yes, yes," I pant. Then feeling a little crazed, I realize that I *want* the monstrous part of him inside me, that in fact, my body craves it. That it was meant for this. "Please, Caleb. Come inside me."

"Are you sure?"

"Yes!" I shriek, and he laughs, trying to shush me.

And then, bit by bit, he enters me. My face pinches from the slight pain, but then he starts kissing me and massaging my breasts, and the pain turns to waves of pleasure.

"Oh fuck, you feel so good," he groans. "So wet and tight."

"Don't stop," I moan and he doesn't. Soon, I'm overwhelmed by an orgasm so powerful that it rips a scream from me. His pumping turns harder and faster, and his own climax comes on the heels of my own. Afterwards, we lie together, still entwined.

"Wow," I say, trying to catch my breath. "That was . . . wow."

Caleb laughs and shakes his head. "I . . . I . . . can't even talk."

"When can we do it again?"

He laughs, glistening with sweat as he pulls out. "Give me five minutes."

"I love you," I say impulsively, cradling his face.

"I love you too." He grins. "Thanks for finding me my perfect match."

"I saved the best for last," I tease.

Later that night, as I lie against his warm naked body, I think about love. It's not always rainbows and butterflies and fireworks. Sometimes it's slow and confusing, frustrating and maddening. It can linger just beneath the surface, and you barely realize what's been happening under your nose until it's too late, and you're a goner.

Even though life is messy and predictable, there's one thing I know for sure: love *is* always the answer. And it starts within you.

Epilogue

Three years later

I glance down at the crib and smile. My heart so full it might burst. Two-year-old Ariel Kfir is curled up, finally asleep, with his thumb in his mouth. Miri and Sissel were right when they said Caleb and I would have the cutest kids. But I'm probably a little biased.

Life has been crazy and chaotic, but only in the best of ways. Netflix ended up buying the rights to Zevi and Jack's reality show, *The Golden Bashert*, and it became a major hit. And thanks to Zevi insisting on putting me in the show, *I* became a major hit too. In fact, my website crashed within twenty-four hours of the show airing because of all the people wanting to sign up as a client. And with all the profit pouring in, I was able to convert my mother's house into Blue Moon Basherts' official headquarters.

Bernice and Lenny got married as soon as the show wrapped up. She sold her house and is now happily living in the funeral home with him, and I'm no longer frightened to walk into my own house.

Life has been less kind to Mrs. Schwartz. As it turns out, her husband had been cheating on her for quite some time, and news of the scandal traveled around the community at breakneck speed. Their divorce was nasty and highly publicized.

Now, at fifty-five, she's single and looking for her next husband. Just the other week, she showed up on my doorstep, cool as a cucumber, requesting that I set her up. Acting as if she hadn't destroyed my business three years earlier, for which she never apologized.

So, we made a deal. I'd take her on as a client if she could look me in the eye and tell me she was sorry. And I'm happy to report that after several false attempts, lots of tears and excuses, she finally managed to get the word out. Afterwards, we hugged.

What can I say? I'm a sucker for a happy ending.

"Is he finally asleep?" Caleb whispers, tip-toeing into the room.

I nod. "Isn't he so cute? Have you ever seen such a perfect child?" My eyes well up with tears because I'm so happy. And also, pregnancy hormones.

"He is, and I haven't," Caleb answers solemnly. He wipes the tears from my cheeks and puts his hands over my swollen belly, and adds, "Except maybe for this one."

"I-I'm so happy," I sniff, cuddling into his arms. "I can't s-stop crying."

He laughs and kisses the top of my head. "Come on," he says, putting his hands on my hips and guiding me out of the room. "I've got a surprise for you."

"Again?" I say. "We just did it a few hours ago."

"Not *that*," he laughs. "Is that the only thing you ever think about, Mrs. Kahn?"

I snort. I don't know what it is about these pregnancy hormones, but I've been a bit demanding lately in the bedroom.

"Guess what?" I grin, turning around.

"What?"

"I thought of the *best* match today."

"Oh yeah?" he says, kissing the side of my neck. "Tell me more."

"Are you ready for your mind to be blown?"

"So ready."

"Ariel Kfir and Chaiky."

He stops moving and tilts his head. "Okay. I wasn't ready for that."

"I know he's only two," I say, "so there's no rush—"

"I'm sure he'll be relieved to hear that."

"But I spoke to Penina today about it—"

"She's the woman that Zevi was once engaged to?"

"Exactly. But then she married her boss and they adopted two kids. The youngest is called Chaiky, and she's the most adorable little redhead."

He chuckles. "And Penina is also okay with the match?"

I nod. "Chaiky is the worst sleeper, so she's said that the marriage can take place any day now as long as we take turns with the night shifts."

He shakes his head as he turns on our bedroom light. "Hard to believe that there's two of you in the world."

I sigh. "I can't wait to be a grandmother."

"Can we let them grow up a little bit first?" he says, pulling back the covers and handing me my pregnancy pillow.

"I suppose." I let out a sound of pure ecstasy as he reaches for my feet and starts massaging.

"Ready for the surprise?" he says, reaching for the remote.

"Mmm hmm."

The screen fills with a cat jumping off a kitchen cabinet, and he turns to me and says, "This is the compilation of the *best* cat videos of all time."

I laugh so hard that I snort and nearly pee my pants. "You really are the perfect husband."

"And you really are the sexiest woman."

I grin. The man is well trained. "Even though my feet are swollen?"

"Especially because your feet are swollen."

We laugh and cuddle together, watching cats do what they do best—knock into furniture and scare the living crap out of dogs.

I sigh in contentment. Life doesn't get any better than this.

Acknowledgements

This book wouldn't exist without the help and encouragement of so many people that I barely know where to begin. I suppose I'll start with G-d. G-d, thank You for providing me with Netflix, where I first laid eyes on Regé-Jean Page. Without the Duke of Hastings as inspiration, would I even have a hero to write about?

Second to G-d are my agents, Hannah Schofield and Claire Friedman. Hannah, thank you for reading countless versions of this book and for gently pointing out which jokes were "a bit too edgy." C, your swift email responses are the stuff of legends, as is your sharp business acumen.

To my publisher, Embla—thank you for your patience as I healed from breast cancer, and for publishing an interracial love story between two Orthodox Jews. It is my fervent hope that it builds bridges across communities.

Behind every great author stands an even greater editor—and I was lucky enough to have three of them! I couldn't have asked for a more talented team. Hannah Smith, you are a legend. Melanie Hayes and Jon Appleton, we had SO MUCH fun together. Bea Grabowska, thank you for helping me cross the finish line—I'm very grateful to you. To my copy editor, Siân Heap—you're going places, kid. Lisa Horton, you've bewitched me with this book cover design. Thank you, Charlotte Brown, for doing an amazing job with the audio. Much gratitude to the fabulous marketing team, Katie Williams and Vishani Perera.

Jean Meltzer—not only are you my fun rabbi, but also a very dear friend. One day soon, we will go clubbing in matching leather outfits and dance *allll* night long.

To my Jewish Joy LLC family—Tracey Kumer, Jev Maskuli, and Jannete—you're the best co-workers ever, and I cannot wait to celebrate together at the Jewish Joy Con!!!

Sara Goodman Confino and Annie Cathryn—I would be lost without our hilarious chats. I forgive you, Sara, for getting the first "LOL" from my copy line editor. The kugel line was pretty epic. Annie, you get credit for Ashira's sage-burning joke. I love you guys.

Jean Meltzer, Meredith Schorr, Felicia Grossman, Stacey Agdern, and Sara Goodman Confino—I've never felt so cool as working alongside you on our Facebook group, Jewish Women Who Read Romance Books. May our coolness continue to go from strength to strength.

To my author friends and personal heroes—Lisa Barr, Ali Brady, Alison Hammer, Zibby Owens, Rochelle Weinstein, Dahlia Adler, Lynne Golodner, Jennifer Wilck, Michelle Mars, Jessica Calepe, Amanda Elliot, Dara Levon, Eliana West, Arden Joy, Michelle Cruz, Christy Schillig, M.A. Wardell, Rochelle Weinstein, Andrea Stein, Cary Gitter, Lisa Williamson Rosenberg—I so admire each and every one of you.

Thank you to my beta readers—Kristi Oman, Judo, Na'ama Rosenberg, Elisheva Wrotslovsky, and Rae Ann Wexler. Each of you helped shape this book into what it is today.

Huge gratitude to my overworked volunteer publicists, Jennifer Ebner and Julie Carpenter. Maybe one day I'll pay you.

To the Instagrammers who tirelessly championed my debut *Unorthodox Love*—your social media posts never fail to bring a smile to my face: Kayla // Book Blogger, rachels.booknook, amy.bookstacks, Jamie // beautyandthebook, courts.book.nook, Jocasta Vilela, reading.with.jen. I appreciate you!

Thank you to Julia Bendis for answering all my matchmaking questions. Not only is Julia a phenomenal matchmaker, but she and her husband do amazing numerology charts. For more about Julia Bendis, visit linktree.com/juliabendis.

Thank you to Barri Leiner Grant for taking the time to answer my questions about grieving. Talking with you felt like medicine for my soul. For those seeking support with grief and loss, contact Barri at www.thememorycircle.com

Thank you, Gisele Strauch, for answering my random New York questions. If anyone wants to collaborate on a Holocaust book, please contact her on Facebook Messenger.

To my besties, Kim and Sarah—thank you for still answering the phone when I call. Writing deadlines are a test of any true friendship, but you've both passed with flying colors.

Huge gratitude to my parents for providing meals, cleaning help, child entertainment, doggie daycare, and everything in between. Ditto for my sister, Elisheva, who humored my request to be pushed in a wheelchair at the oncologist. To my father-in-law, Joel—thank you for playing with Ari and for helping me with my edits. To Yossi, Chaya, Dov, Stacey, Mike, Mike Tyson, my nieces, nephews, and cousins – I love you, guys!

Asher, editing this book wouldn't have been possible without you following me around the house while strumming your guitar. I appreciate the times you woke me up by screeching "cock-a-doodle-doo" in Elmo's voice this past summer. #GoodTimes

Ari, I love that your first question upon returning home from school each day is, "How much have you written?" One day, you and I will co-write a toilet humor book, and it will be an instant bestseller.

Esty, thank you for being "the mom" of the house for most of your high school career. You cooked, cleaned, walked the dog, got Ari ready for school each day, took me to appointments, and still managed to graduate. Much of Ashira's backstory is based on you.

To my husband and best friend, Daniel—you're right. You do deserve to have every book dedicated to you. Thank you for sharing the emotional trauma of writing deadlines.

Lastly, special thanks to those who trusted me with their stories—Chaim Levin, Netanya Paxton, Judo, and my friends who wish to remain anonymous. I hope this book makes you feel seen.

About the Author

Heidi Shertok is an Orthodox Jewish woman, wife, and mom of three. When she isn't making up stories in her head, she can be found walking her seventy-pound psychopathic bernedoodle, admiring other people's gardens, or hiking in heels.

About Embla Books

Embla Books is a digital-first publisher of standout commercial adult fiction. Passionate about storytelling, the team at Embla believe our lives are built on stories – and publish books that will make you 'laugh, love, look over your shoulder and lose sleep'. Launched by Bonnier Books UK in 2021, the imprint is named after the first woman from the creation myth in Norse mythology. Embla was carved by the gods from a tree trunk found on the seashore; an image of the kind of creative work and crafting that writers do, and a symbol of how stories shape our lives.

Find out about some of our other books and stay in touch:

X, Facebook, Instagram: @emblabooks
Newsletter: https://bit.ly/emblanewsletter